NEBULA AWARDS
SHOWCASE
2009

THE YEAR'S BEST SF AND FANTASY

Selected by the Science Fiction and
Fantasy Writers of America©

EDITED BY

Ellen Datlow

A ROC BOOK

ROC
Published by New American Library,
a division of Penguin Group (USA) Inc.,
375 Hudson Street, New York, New York 10014, USA
Penguin Group (Canada), 90 Eglinton Avenue East, Suite 700, Toronto,
Ontario M4P 2Y3, Canada (a division of Pearson Penguin Canada Inc.)
Penguin Books Ltd., 80 Strand, London WC2R 0RL, England
Penguin Ireland, 25 St. Stephen's Green, Dublin 2,
Ireland (a division of Penguin Books Ltd.)
Penguin Group (Australia), 250 Camberwell Road, Camberwell,
Victoria 3124, Australia (a division of Pearson Australia Group Pty. Ltd.)
Penguin Books India Pvt. Ltd., 11 Community Centre,
Panchsheel Park, New Delhi - 110 017, India
Penguin Group (NZ), 67 Apollo Drive, Rosedale, North Shore 0632,
New Zealand (a division of Pearson New Zealand Ltd.)
Penguin Books (South Africa) (Pty.) Ltd., 24 Sturdee Avenue,
Rosebank, Johannesburg 2196, South Africa

Penguin Books Ltd., Registered Offices:
80 Strand, London WC2R 0RL, England

Published by Roc, an imprint of New American Library,
a division of Penguin Group (USA) Inc.

First Printing, April 2009
3   5   7   9   10   8   6   4

 REGISTERED TRADEMARK—MARCA REGISTRADA

Set in Bembo • Designed by Elke Sigal

Printed in the United States of America

Praise for the Previous Volumes of
Nebula Awards Showcase

"The pulse of modern science fiction."
—*The New York Times Book Review*

"Reading all of *Nebula Awards Showcase 2002* is a way of reading a bunch of good stories. It is also a very good way to explore the writing of tomorrow." —John Clute, scifi.com

"Conveys a sense of the vitality and excitement that have characterized the field's internal dialogues and debate over the last few years. One of the most entertaining Nebula volumes in years."
—*Locus*

"The vast majority of the stories included are simply wonderful and absolutely deserve recognition. . . . Bottom line: This year's Nebula Showcase actually succeeds in showcasing a great variety of truly good work. Read it now."
—InterGalactic Medicine Show

"There are plenty of solid, entertaining pieces in this anthology."
—*Subterranean*

"As always, a fine anthology." —Alternative Worlds

continued . . .

"Stellar. . . . This is not only a must-read for anyone with an interest in the field, but a pleasure to read. . . . That's more reassuring than surprising, of course, given that this collection has little if any agenda besides quality writing, but it is reassuring to see that so many fresh voices are so much fun. . . . Worth picking up."   —SF Revu

"While the essays offer one answer to the question of where does SF go now, the stories show that science fiction writers continue to reexamine their vision of the future. It's a continuing dialogue, and by including critical essays along with the stories, the *Nebula Awards Showcase 2002* does more to present the SF field as an on-going conversation and discussion of ideas than any of the other best of the year anthologies. It's a worthy contribution and a good volume to have on your shelf."   —SF Site

"Every fan will have their favorites; there's pretty much something for everyone. . . . Overall, *Nebula Awards Showcase 2006* gets it right. I judge it a keeper."   —Scifi Dimensions

"The variety of taste shown by the SFWA continues to be striking and heartening."   —*Publishers Weekly*

"Invaluable, not just for the splendid fiction and lively nonfiction, but as another annual snapshot, complete with grins and scowls."
—*Kirkus Reviews*

CONTENTS

ACKNOWLEDGMENTS

I'd like to thank Michael Capobianco, Mike Resnick, Gardner Dozois, Jack Dann, Pamela Sargent, George Zebrowski, Gordon Van Gelder, Jonathan Strahan, Sheila Williams, and Del Howison for their advice and help with the book.

NEBULA
AWARDS©
SHOWCASE

2009

INTRODUCTION

ELLEN DATLOW

People are still saying that science fiction is dead, but I've been editing SF/F for over twenty-five years, and I see science fiction and fantasy writers continuing to create vibrant, original, provocative fiction. Both subgroups of fantastic fiction have branched out into a variety of subgenres and readers can find *their* kind of SF/F that still gives them a kick, as there are book publishers and professional magazines and webzines catering to many different tastes.

The delivery systems for text are evolving too: from print to the Internet, on to portable electronic readers. Sony's Reader and Amazon's Kindle *may* herald an important shift that can only help our field. But that doesn't mean that print is going away.

The "mainstream" of fiction has been embracing science fiction and fantasy for a very long time—it just perhaps hasn't acknowledged it. Science fiction and fantasy stories, some from genre sources, have been chosen for the *Best American Short Stories* and the *O'Henry Award* volumes for decades, including work by Harlan Ellison, Kelly Link, Tim Pratt, James P. Blaylock, Ray Bradbury, Kevin Brockmeier, Stephen King, Cory Doctorow, A. S. Byatt, George Saunders, Dan Chaon, Bruce McAllister, and Michael Bishop. Every year the discerning reader can discover fantastic literature—stories and novels—not marketed as science fiction or fantasy but as mainstream.

Sometimes I worry that the ghetto mentality has closed us off in a little bubble, blinding us from acknowledging the fact that *sometimes* writers outside our field get it right. So I'm always delighted to be proven wrong—perhaps the fact that Michael Chabon's wonderful alternative history, *The Yiddish Policemen's Union*, won the Nebula Award for best novel this year is a positive step in breaking down our own biased walls.

New writers are still published by magazines and publishing houses, and some SF/F novels make the bestseller lists and are read by people outside the field. Magazines and webzines continue to pop up and publish noteworthy stories. What's this all mean? To me, it's that the Nebula Awards are a celebration of a field that has endured.

This is the *Nebula Awards Showcase* of 2009, reprinting the winners and several of the nominees from 2007, plus an excerpt from the award-winning novel. In addition, there is a classic story by our new Grand Master, Michael Moorcock.

The Rhysling Award–winning poems are also part of the volume, as are essays on a number of subjects. Ellen Asher looks back at her thirty-four-year tenure with the Science Fiction Book Club. Barry N. Malzberg provides an entertainingly jaundiced view of the state of the art of science fiction and its blurring with fantasy fiction and Kathleen Ann Goonan responds with a passionate counterpunch as to why she believes the writing of science fiction is not only a viable career choice for writers but important for our society. Gwenda Bond celebrates the booming market for young adult science fiction and fantasy. Howard Waldrop covers the movies: the good, the bad, the awful. And Tim Lucas, editor and publisher of *Video Watchdog*, writes about Guillermo del Toro's screenwriting award–winner, *Pan's Labyrinth*.

And so here is the Science Fiction and Fantasy Writers of America's annual snapshot of the field—I hope you enjoy what you see as much as I do.

ABOUT THE SCIENCE FICTION AND FANTASY WRITERS OF AMERICA

The Science Fiction and Fantasy Writers of America, Incorporated, includes among its members most of the active writers of science fiction and fantasy. According to the by-laws of the organization, its purpose "shall be to promote the furtherance of the writing of science fiction, fantasy, and related genres as a profession." SFWA® informs writers on professional matters, protects their interests, and helps them in dealings with agents, editors, anthologists, and producers of nonprint media. It also strives to encourage public interest in and appreciation of science fiction and fantasy. At the beginning of 2008, SFWA had more than 1,500 members.

Anyone may become an active member of SFWA after the acceptance of and payment for one professionally published novel, one professionally produced dramatic script, or three professionally published pieces of short fiction. Only science fiction, fantasy, horror, or other prose fiction of a related genre, in English, shall be considered as qualifying for active membership. Beginning writers who do not yet qualify for active membership but have published qualifying professional work may join as associate members; other classes of membership include affiliate members (editors, agents, reviewers, and anthologists), estate members (representatives of the estates of active members who have died), and institutional members (high schools, colleges, universities, libraries, broadcasters, film producers, futurist groups, and individuals associated with such an institution).

Anyone who is not a member of SFWA may subscribe to *The Bulletin of the Science Fiction and Fantasy Writers of America*. The magazine is published quarterly and contains articles by well-known writers on all aspects of their profession. Subscriptions are $21 a year or $37 for two years. For information on how to subscribe to the *Bulletin*, or for more information about SFWA, visit www.sfwa.org/bulletin/subscribe.htm or write to:

SFWA Bulletin
P.O. Box 10126
Rochester, NY 14610

Readers are also invited to visit the SFWA site on the World Wide Web at the following address:

www.sfwa.org

Throughout every calendar year, the members of the Science Fiction and Fantasy Writers of America read and recommend novels, stories, and scripts for the annual Nebula Awards. The editor of the *Nebula Awards Report* collects the recommendations and publishes them in the *SFWA Forum* and on the members' private interactive web page. At the end of the year, the *NAR* editor tallies the endorsements, draws up a preliminary ballot containing all works that have received ten or more recommendations, and sends it to all active SFWA members. Under the current rules, each novel and story enjoys a one-year eligibility period from its date of publication in the United States. A script begins its eligibility period on the day of its first release in a U.S. public theater or first airdate on U.S. television. If the work fails to receive ten recommendations during that interval, it is dropped from further Nebula consideration.

The *NAR* editor processes the results of the preliminary ballot and then compiles a final ballot listing the five most popular novels, novellas, novelettes, short stories, and scripts. For purposes of the Nebula Awards, a novel is 40,000 words or more; a novella is 17,500 to 39,999 words; a novelette is 7,500 to 17,499 words; and a short story is 7,499 words or fewer. Additionally, SFWA impanels member juries for the novel, short fiction, and script categories. These juries are empowered to supplement the five nominees with a sixth choice in cases where a worthy title was neglected by the membership at large. Thus, the appearance of extra finalists in any category bespeaks two distinct processes: jury discretion and ties. A complete set of Nebula rules can be found at www.sfwa .org/awards/rules.htm. A three-member SFWA Awards Rules Committee rules on questions pertaining to the Nebula and other SFWA awards rules in the event of a dispute.

Founded in 1965 by Damon Knight, the Science Fiction Writers of America began with a charter membership of seventy-eight authors. Today it boasts over fifteen hundred members and a name befitting the wider reach of speculative fiction. Early in his tenure, Lloyd Biggle Jr., SFWA's first secretary-treasurer, proposed that the organization periodically select and publish the year's best stories. This notion quickly evolved into the elaborate balloting process, an annual awards banquet, and a series of Nebula anthologies. Judith Ann Lawrence designed the trophy from a sketch by Kate Wilhelm. It is a block of clear Lucite containing planetlike polished rocks, crystals, and a spiral nebula made of metallic glitter. The prize is handmade, and no two are exactly alike.

NOVELS

Ragamuffin by Tobias Buckell (Tor, Jun07)

The Yiddish Policemen's Union by Michael Chabon (HarperCollins, May07)

The Accidental Time Machine by Joe Haldeman (Ace, Aug07)

The New Moon's Arms by Nalo Hopkinson (Warner Books, Feb07)

Odyssey by Jack McDevitt (Ace, Nov06)

NOVELLAS

"Awakening" by Judith Berman (*Black Gate 10*, Spr07)

"The Helper and His Hero" by Matt Hughes (*The Magazine of Fantasy & Science Fiction*, Mar07 (Feb07 & Mar07))

"Fountain of Age" by Nancy Kress (*Asimov's Science Fiction*, Jul07)

"Stars Seen Through Stone" by Lucius Shepard (*The Magazine of Fantasy & Science Fiction*, Jul07)

"Kiosk" by Bruce Sterling (*The Magazine of Fantasy & Science Fiction*, Jan07)

"Memorare" by Gene Wolfe (*The Magazine of Fantasy & Science Fiction*, Apr07)

NOVELETTES

"The Children's Crusade" by Robin Wayne Bailey (*Heroes*

in Training, Martin H. Greenberg and Jim C. Hines, Ed., DAW, Sep07)

"Child, Maiden, Woman, Crone" by Terry Bramlett (*Jim Baen's Universe* 7, June 2007)

"The Merchant and the Alchemist's Gate" by Ted Chiang (*The Magazine of Fantasy & Science Fiction*, Sep07)

"The Evolution of Trickster Stories Among the Dogs of North Park After the Change" by Kij Johnson (*Coyote Road: Trickster Tales*, Ellen Datlow and Terri Windling, Ed., Viking Juvenile, Jul07)

"Safeguard" by Nancy Kress (*Asimov's Science Fiction*, Jan07)

"Pol Pot's Beautiful Daughter (Fantasy)" by Geoff Ryman (*The Magazine of Fantasy & Science Fiction*, Nov06)

"The Fiddler of Bayou Teche" by Delia Sherman (*Coyote Road: Trickster Tales*, Ellen Datlow and Terri Windling, Ed., Viking Juvenile, Jul07)

SHORT STORIES

"Unique Chicken Goes in Reverse" by Andy Duncan (*Eclipse 1: New Science Fiction and Fantasy*, Jonathan Strahan, Ed., Night Shade Books, Oct07)

"Always" by Karen Joy Fowler (*Asimov's Science Fiction*, May07 (Apr/May07 issue))

"Titanium Mike Saves the Day" by David D. Levine (*The Magazine of Fantasy & Science Fiction*, Apr07)

"The Story of Love" by Vera Nazarian (*Salt of the Air*, Prime Books, Sep06)

"Captive Girl" by Jennifer Pelland (*Helix: A Speculative Fiction Quarterly*, WS & LWE, Ed., Oct06 (Fall06 issue—#2))

"Pride" by Mary Turzillo (*Fast Forward 1*, Pyr, Feb07)

SCRIPTS

Children of Men by Alfonso Cuaron, Timothy J. Sexton, David Arata, Mark Fergus, and Hawk Ostby (Universal Studios, Dec06)

Pan's Labyrinth by Guillermo del Toro (Time/Warner, Jan07)

Blink by Steven Moffat (*Doctor Who*, BBC/The Sci-Fi Channel, Sep07 (Aired on SciFi Channel 14 Sep07))

The Prestige by Christopher Nolan and Jonathan Nolan (Newmarket Films, Oct06 (Oct 20, 2006—based on the novel by Christopher Priest))

V for Vendetta by Larry Wachowski and Andy Wachowski (Warner Films, Mar06 (released 3/17/2006—Written by the Wachowski Brothers, based on the graphic novel illustrated by David Lloyd and published by Vertigo/DC Comics))

World Enough and Time by Marc Scott Zicree and Michael Reaves (*Star Trek: New Voyages*, http://www.startreknewvoyages.com, Aug07 (Aired 8/23/07))

ANDRE NORTON AWARD

Vintage: A Ghost Story by Steve Berman (Haworth Positronic Press, Mar07)

Into the Wild by Sarah Beth Durst (Penguin Razorbill, Jun07)

The Shadow Speaker by Nnedi Okorafor-Mbachu (Jump at the Sun, Sep07)

The True Meaning of Smek Day by Adam Rex (Hyperion, Oct07)

Harry Potter and the Deathly Hallows by J. K. Rowling (Scholastic Press, Jul07)

Flora Segunda: Being the Magickal Mishaps of a Girl of Spirit, Her Glass-Gazing Sidekick, Two Ominous Butlers (One Blue), a House with Eleven Thousand Rooms, and a Red Dog by Ysabeau S. Wilce (Harcourt, Jan07)

The Lion Hunter by Elizabeth Wein (Viking Juvenile, Jun07 (*The Mark of Solomon*, Book 1))

THE MERCHANT AND
THE ALCHEMIST'S GATE

TED CHIANG

Ted Chiang lives outside of Seattle, Washington. He holds a degree in computer science and makes his living as a technical writer.

Mighty Caliph and Commander of the Faithful, I am humbled to be in the splendor of your presence; a man can hope for no greater blessing as long as he lives. The story I have to tell is truly a strange one, and were the entirety to be tattooed at the corner of one's eye, the marvel of its presentation would not exceed that of the events recounted, for it is a warning to those who would be warned and a lesson to those who would learn.

My name is Fuwaad ibn Abbas, and I was born here in Baghdad, City of Peace. My father was a grain merchant, but for much of my life I have worked as a purveyor of fine fabrics, trading in silk from Damascus and linen from Egypt and scarves from Morocco that are embroidered with gold. I was prosperous, but my heart was troubled, and neither the purchase of luxuries nor the giving of alms was able to soothe it. Now I stand before you without a single dirham in my purse, but I am at peace.

Allah is the beginning of all things, but with Your Majesty's permission, I begin my story with the day I took a walk through the district of metalsmiths. I needed to purchase a gift for a man I had to do business with, and had been told he might appreciate a tray made of silver. After browsing for half an hour, I noticed that one of the largest shops in the market had been taken over by a new merchant. It was a prized location that must have been expensive to acquire, so I entered to peruse its wares.

Never before had I seen such a marvelous assortment of goods. Near the entrance there was an astrolabe equipped with seven plates inlaid with silver, a water-clock that chimed on the hour, and a nightingale made of brass that sang when the wind blew. Farther inside there were even more ingenious mechanisms, and I stared at them the way a child watches a juggler, when an old man stepped out from a doorway in the back.

"Welcome to my humble shop, my lord," he said. "My name is Bashaarat. How may I assist you?"

"These are remarkable items that you have for sale. I deal with traders from every corner of the world, and yet I have never seen their like. From where, may I ask, did you acquire your merchandise?"

"I am grateful to you for your kind words," he said. "Everything you see here was made in my workshop, by myself or by my assistants under my direction."

I was impressed that this man could be so well versed in so many arts. I asked him about the various instruments in his shop, and listened to him discourse learnedly about astrology, mathematics, geomancy, and medicine. We spoke for over an hour, and my fascination and respect bloomed like a flower warmed by the dawn, until he mentioned his experiments in alchemy.

"Alchemy?" I said. This surprised me, for he did not seem the type to make such a sharper's claim. "You mean you can turn base metal into gold?"

"I can, my lord, but that is not in fact what most seek from alchemy."

"What do most seek, then?"

"They seek a source of gold that is cheaper than mining ore from the ground. Alchemy does describe a means to make gold, but the procedure is so arduous that, by comparison, digging beneath a mountain is as easy as plucking peaches from a tree."

I smiled. "A clever reply. No one could dispute that you are a learned man, but I know better than to credit alchemy."

Bashaarat looked at me and considered. "I have recently built something that may change your opinion. You would be the first person I have shown it to. Would you care to see it?"

"It would be a great pleasure."

"Please follow me." He led me through the doorway in the rear of his shop. The next room was a workshop, arrayed with devices whose functions I could not guess—bars of metal wrapped with enough copper thread to reach the horizon, mirrors mounted on a circular slab of granite floating in quicksilver—but Bashaarat walked past these without a glance.

Instead he led me to a sturdy pedestal, chest high, on which a stout metal hoop was mounted upright. The hoop's opening was as wide as two outstretched hands, and its rim so thick that it would tax the strongest man to carry. The metal was black as night, but polished to such smoothness that, had it been a different color, it could have served as a mirror. Bashaarat bade me stand so that I looked upon the hoop edgewise, while he stood next to its opening.

"Please observe," he said.

Bashaarat thrust his arm through the hoop from the right side, but it did not extend out from the left. Instead, it was as if his arm were severed at the elbow, and he waved the stump up and down, and then pulled his arm out intact.

I had not expected to see such a learned man perform a conjuror's trick, but it was well done, and I applauded politely.

"Now wait a moment," he said as he took a step back.

I waited, and behold, an arm reached out of the hoop from its left side, without a body to hold it up. The sleeve it wore matched Bashaarat's robe. The arm waved up and down, and then retreated through the hoop until it was gone.

The first trick I had thought a clever mime, but this one seemed far superior, because the pedestal and hoop were clearly too slender to conceal a person. "Very clever!" I exclaimed.

"Thank you, but this is not mere sleight of hand. The right side of the hoop precedes the left by several seconds. To pass through the hoop is to cross that duration instantly."

"I do not understand," I said.

"Let me repeat the demonstration." Again he thrust his arm through the hoop, and his arm disappeared. He smiled, and pulled back and forth as if playing tug-a-rope. Then he pulled his arm out again, and presented his hand to me with the palm open. On it lay a ring I recognized.

"That is my ring!" I checked my hand, and saw that my ring still lay on my finger. "You have conjured up a duplicate."

"No, this is truly your ring. Wait."

Again, an arm reached out from the left side. Wishing to discover the mechanism of the trick, I rushed over to grab it by the hand. It was not a false hand, but one fully warm and alive as mine. I pulled on it, and it pulled back. Then, as deft as a pickpocket, the hand slipped the ring from my finger and the arm withdrew into the hoop, vanishing completely.

"My ring is gone!" I exclaimed.

"No, my lord," he said. "Your ring is here." And he gave me the ring he held. "Forgive me for my game."

I replaced it on my finger. "You had the ring before it was taken from me."

At that moment an arm reached out, this time from the right side of the hoop. "What is this?" I exclaimed. Again I recognized it as his by the sleeve before it withdrew, but I had not seen him reach in.

"Recall," he said, "the right side of the hoop precedes the left." And he walked over to the left side of the hoop, and thrust his arm through from that side, and again it disappeared.

Your Majesty has undoubtedly already grasped this, but it was only then that I understood: whatever happened on the right side of the hoop was complemented, a few seconds later, by an event on the left side. "Is this sorcery?" I asked.

"No, my lord, I have never met a djinni, and if I did, I would not trust it to do my bidding. This is a form of alchemy."

He offered an explanation, speaking of his search for tiny pores in the skin of reality, like the holes that worms bore into wood, and how upon finding one he was able to expand and stretch it the way a glassblower turns a dollop of molten glass into a long-necked pipe, and how he then allowed time to flow like water at one mouth while causing it to thicken like syrup at the other. I confess I did not really understand his words, and cannot testify to their truth. All I could say in response was, "You have created something truly astonishing."

"Thank you," he said, "but this is merely a prelude to what I intended to show you." He bade me follow him into another room, farther in the back. There stood a circular doorway whose massive frame was made of the same polished black metal, mounted in the middle of the room.

"What I showed you before was a Gate of Seconds," he said. "This is a Gate of Years. The two sides of the doorway are separated by a span of twenty years."

I confess I did not understand his remark immediately. I imagined him reaching his arm in from the right side and waiting twenty years before it emerged from the left side, and it seemed a very obscure magic trick. I said as much, and he laughed. "That is one use for it," he said, "but consider what would happen if you were to step through." Standing on the right side, he gestured for me to come closer, and then pointed through the doorway. "Look."

I looked, and saw that there appeared to be different rugs and pillows on the other side of the room than I had seen when I had entered. I moved my head from side to side, and realized that when I peered through the doorway, I was looking at a different room from the one I stood in.

"You are seeing the room twenty years from now," said Bashaarat.

I blinked, as one might at an illusion of water in the desert, but what I saw did not change. "And you say I could step through?" I asked.

"You could. And with that step, you would visit the Baghdad of twenty years hence. You could seek out your older self and have a conversation with him. Afterwards, you could step back through the Gate of Years and return to the present day."

Hearing Bashaarat's words, I felt as if I were reeling. "You have done this?" I asked him. "You have stepped through?"

"I have, and so have numerous customers of mine."

"Earlier you said I was the first to whom you showed this."

"This Gate, yes. But for many years I owned a shop in Cairo, and it was there that I first built a Gate of Years. There were many to whom I showed that Gate, and who made use of it."

"What did they learn when talking to their older selves?"

"Each person learns something different. If you wish, I can tell you the story of one such person." Bashaarat proceeded to tell me such a story, and if it pleases Your Majesty, I will recount it here.

THE TALE OF THE FORTUNATE ROPE-MAKER

There once was a young man named Hassan who was a maker of rope. He stepped through the Gate of Years to see the Cairo of twenty years later, and upon arriving he marveled at how the city had grown. He felt as if he had stepped into a scene embroidered on a tapestry, and even though the city was no more and no less than Cairo, he looked upon the most common sights as objects of wonder.

He was wandering by the Zuweyla Gate, where the sword dancers and snake charmers perform, when an astrologer called to him. "Young man! Do you wish to know the future?"

Hassan laughed. "I know it already," he said.

"Surely you want to know if wealth awaits you, do you not?"

"I am a rope-maker. I know that it does not."

"Can you be so sure? What about the renowned merchant Hassan al-Hubbaul, who began as a rope-maker?"

His curiosity aroused, Hassan asked around the market for others who knew of this wealthy merchant, and found that the name was well known. It was said he lived in the wealthy Habbaniya quarter of the city, so Hassan walked there and asked people to point out his house, which turned out to be the largest one on its street.

He knocked at the door, and a servant led him to a spacious and well-appointed hall with a fountain in the center. Hassan waited while the servant went to fetch his master, but as he looked at the polished ebony and marble around him, he felt that he did not belong in such surroundings, and was about to leave when his older self appeared.

"At last you are here!" the man said. "I have been expecting you!"

"You have?" said Hassan, astounded.

"Of course, because I visited my older self just as you are visiting me. It has been so long that I had forgotten the exact day. Come, dine with me."

The two went to a dining room, where servants brought chicken stuffed with pistachio nuts, fritters soaked in honey, and roast lamb with spiced pomegranates. The older Hassan gave few details of his life: he mentioned business interests of many varieties, but did not say how he had become a merchant; he mentioned a wife, but said it was not time for the younger man to meet her. Instead, he asked young Hassan to remind him of the pranks he had played as a child, and he laughed to hear stories that had faded from his own memory.

At last the younger Hassan asked the older, "How did you make such great changes in your fortune?"

"All I will tell you right now is this: when you go to buy hemp from the market, and you are walking along the Street of Black Dogs, do not walk along the south side as you usually do. Walk along the north."

"And that will enable me to raise my station?"

"Just do as I say. Go back home now; you have rope to make. You will know when to visit me again."

Young Hassan returned to his day and did as he was instructed, keeping to the north side of the street even when there was no shade there. It was a few days later that he witnessed a maddened horse run amok on the south side of the street directly opposite him, kicking several people, injuring another by knocking a heavy jug of palm oil onto him, and even trampling one person under its hooves. After the commotion had subsided, Hassan prayed to Allah for the injured to be healed and the dead to be at peace, and thanked Allah for sparing him.

The next day Hassan stepped through the Gate of Years and sought out his older self. "Were you injured by the horse when you walked by?" he asked him.

"No, because I heeded my older self's warning. Do not forget, you and I are one; every circumstance that befalls you once befell me."

And so the elder Hassan gave the younger instructions, and the younger obeyed them. He refrained from buying eggs from his usual grocer, and thus avoided the illness that struck customers who bought eggs from a spoiled basket. He bought extra hemp, and thus had material to work with when others suffered a shortage due to a delayed caravan. Following his older self's instructions spared Hassan many troubles, but he wondered why his older self would not tell him more. Who would he marry? How would he become wealthy?

Then one day, after having sold all his rope in the market and carrying an unusually full purse, Hassan bumped into a boy while walking on the street. He felt for his purse, discovered it missing, and turned around with a shout to search the crowd for the pickpocket. Hearing Hassan's cry, the boy immediately began running through the crowd. Hassan saw that the boy's tunic was torn at the elbow, but then quickly lost sight of him.

For a moment Hassan was shocked that this could happen

with no warning from his older self. But his surprise was soon replaced by anger, and he gave chase. He ran through the crowd, checking the elbows of boys' tunics, until by chance he found the pickpocket crouching beneath a fruit wagon. Hassan grabbed him and began shouting to all that he had caught a thief, asking them to find a guardsman. The boy, afraid of arrest, dropped Hassan's purse and began weeping. Hassan stared at the boy for a long moment, and then his anger faded, and he let him go.

When next he saw his older self, Hassan asked him, "Why did you not warn me about the pickpocket?"

"Did you not enjoy the experience?" asked his older self.

Hassan was about to deny it, but stopped himself. "I did enjoy it," he admitted. In pursuing the boy, with no hint of whether he'd succeed or fail, he had felt his blood surge in a way it had not for many weeks. And seeing the boy's tears had reminded him of the Prophet's teachings on the value of mercy, and Hassan had felt virtuous in choosing to let the boy go.

"Would you rather I had denied you that, then?"

Just as we grow to understand the purpose of customs that seemed pointless to us in our youth, Hassan realized that there was merit in withholding information as well as in disclosing it. "No," he said, "it was good that you did not warn me."

The older Hassan saw that he had understood. "Now I will tell you something very important. Hire a horse. I will give you directions to a spot in the foothills to the west of the city. There you will find within a grove of trees one that was struck by lightning. Around the base of the tree, look for the heaviest rock you can overturn, and then dig beneath it."

"What should I look for?"

"You will know when you find it."

The next day Hassan rode out to the foothills and searched until he found the tree. The ground around it was covered in rocks, so Hassan overturned one to dig beneath it, and then another, and then another. At last his spade struck something besides rock and soil. He cleared aside the soil and discovered a bronze chest filled with gold dinars and assorted jewelry. Hassan had never seen its like in all his life. He loaded the chest onto the horse, and rode back to Cairo.

The next time he spoke to his older self, he asked, "How did you know where the treasure was?"

"I learned it from myself," said the older Hassan, "just as you did. As to how we came to know its location, I have no explanation except that it was the will of Allah, and what other explanation is there for anything?"

"I swear I shall make good use of these riches that Allah has blessed me with," said the younger Hassan.

"And I renew that oath," said the older. "This is the last time we shall speak. You will find your own way now. Peace be upon you."

And so Hassan returned home. With the gold he was able to purchase hemp in great quantity, and hire workmen and pay them a fair wage, and sell rope profitably to all who sought it. He married a beautiful and clever woman, at whose advice he began trading in other goods, until he was a wealthy and respected merchant. All the while he gave generously to the poor and lived as an upright man. In this way Hassan lived the happiest of lives until he was overtaken by death, breaker of ties and destroyer of delights.

"That is a remarkable story," I said. "For someone who is debating whether to make use of the Gate, there could hardly be a better inducement."

"You are wise to be skeptical," said Bashaarat. "Allah rewards those he wishes to reward and chastises those he wishes to chastise. The Gate does not change how he regards you."

I nodded, thinking I understood. "So even if you succeed in avoiding the misfortunes that your older self experienced, there is no assurance you will not encounter other misfortunes."

"No, forgive an old man for being unclear. Using the Gate is not like drawing lots, where the token you select varies with each turn. Rather, using the Gate is like taking a secret passageway in a palace, one that lets you enter a room more quickly than by walking down the hallway. The room remains the same, no matter which door you use to enter."

This surprised me. "The future is fixed, then? As unchangeable as the past?"

"It is said that repentance and atonement erase the past."

"I have heard that too, but I have not found it to be true."

"I am sorry to hear that," said Bashaarat. "All I can say is that the future is no different."

I thought on this for a while. "So if you learn that you are dead twenty years from now, there is nothing you can do to avoid your death?" He nodded. This seemed to me very disheartening, but then I wondered if it could not also provide a guarantee. I said, "Suppose you learn that you are alive twenty years from now. Then nothing could kill you in the next twenty years. You could then fight in battles without a care, because your survival is assured."

"That is possible," he said. "It is also possible that a man who would make use of such a guarantee would not find his older self alive when he first used the Gate."

"Ah," I said. "Is it then the case that only the prudent meet their older selves?"

"Let me tell you the story of another person who used the Gate, and you can decide for yourself if he was prudent or not." Bashaarat proceeded to tell me the story, and if it pleases Your Majesty, I will recount it here.

THE TALE OF THE WEAVER WHO STOLE FROM HIMSELF

There was a young weaver named Ajib who made a modest living as a weaver of rugs, but yearned to taste the luxuries enjoyed by the wealthy. After hearing the story of Hassan, Ajib immediately stepped through the Gate of Years to seek out his older self, who, he was sure, would be as rich and as generous as the older Hassan.

Upon arriving in the Cairo of twenty years later, he proceeded to the wealthy Habbaniya quarter of the city and asked people for the residence of Ajib ibn Taher. He was prepared, if he met someone who knew the man and remarked on the similarity of their features, to identify himself as Ajib's son, newly arrived from Damascus. But he never had the chance to offer this story, because no one he asked recognized the name.

Eventually he decided to return to his old neighborhood, and see if anyone there knew where he had moved to. When he got to his old street, he stopped a boy and asked him if he knew where to find a man named Ajib. The boy directed him to Ajib's old house.

"That is where he used to live," Ajib said. "Where does he live now?"

"If he has moved since yesterday, I do not know where," said the boy.

Ajib was incredulous. Could his older self still live in the same house, twenty years later? That would mean he had never become wealthy, and his older self would have no advice to give him, or at least none Ajib would profit by following. How could his fate differ so much from that of the fortunate rope-maker? In hopes that the boy was mistaken, Ajib waited outside the house, and watched.

Eventually he saw a man leave the house, and with a sinking heart recognized it as his older self. The older Ajib was followed by a woman that he presumed was his wife, but he scarcely noticed her, for all he could see was his own failure to have bettered himself. He stared with dismay at the plain clothes the older couple wore until they walked out of sight.

Driven by the curiosity that impels men to look at the heads of the executed, Ajib went to the door of his house. His own key still fit the lock, so he entered. The furnishings had changed, but were simple and worn, and Ajib was mortified to see them. After twenty years, could he not even afford better pillows?

On an impulse, he went to the wooden chest where he normally kept his savings, and unlocked it. He lifted the lid, and saw the chest was filled with gold dinars.

Ajib was astonished. His older self had a chest of gold, and yet he wore such plain clothes and lived in the same small house for twenty years! What a stingy, joyless man his older self must be, thought Ajib, to have wealth and not enjoy it. Ajib had long known that one could not take one's possessions to the grave. Could that be something that he would forget as he aged?

Ajib decided that such riches should belong to someone who appreciated them, and that was himself. To take his older self's wealth would not be stealing, he reasoned, because it was he himself who would receive it. He heaved the chest onto his shoulder, and with much effort was able to bring it back through the Gate of Years to the Cairo he knew.

He deposited some of his newfound wealth with a banker, but always carried a purse heavy with gold. He dressed in a Damascene robe and Cordovan slippers and a Khurasani turban bearing a jewel. He rented a house in the wealthy quarter, furnished it with the finest rugs and couches, and hired a cook to prepare him sumptuous meals.

He then sought out the brother of a woman he had long desired from afar, a woman named Taahira. Her brother was an apothecary, and Taahira assisted him in his shop. Ajib would occasionally purchase a remedy so that he might speak to her. Once he had seen her veil slip, and her eyes were as dark and beautiful as a gazelle's. Taahira's brother would not have consented to her marrying a weaver, but now Ajib could present himself as a favorable match.

Taahira's brother approved, and Taahira herself readily consented, for she had desired Ajib, too. Ajib spared no expense for their wedding. He hired one of the pleasure barges that floated in the canal south of the city and held a feast with musicians and dancers, at which he presented her with a magnificent pearl necklace. The celebration was the subject of gossip throughout the quarter.

Ajib reveled in the joy that money brought him and Taahira, and for a week the two of them lived the most delightful of lives. Then one day Ajib came home to find the door to his house broken open and the interior ransacked of all silver and gold items. The terrified cook emerged from hiding and told him that robbers had taken Taahira.

Ajib prayed to Allah until, exhausted with worry, he fell asleep. The next morning he was awoken by a knocking at his door. There was a stranger there. "I have a message for you," the man said.

"What message?" asked Ajib.

"Your wife is safe."

Ajib felt fear and rage churn in his stomach like black bile. "What ransom would you have?" he asked.

"Ten thousand dinars."

"That is more than all I possess!" Ajib exclaimed.

"Do not haggle with me," said the robber. "I have seen you spend money like others pour water."

Ajib dropped to his knees. "I have been wasteful. I swear by the name of the Prophet that I do not have that much," he said.

The robber looked at him closely. "Gather all the money you have," he said, "and have it here tomorrow at this same hour. If I believe you are holding back, your wife will die. If I believe you to be honest, my men will return her to you."

Ajib could see no other choice. "Agreed," he said, and the robber left.

The next day he went to the banker and withdrew all the money that remained. He gave it to the robber, who gauged the desperation in Ajib's eyes and was satisfied. The robber did as he promised, and that evening Taahira was returned.

After they had embraced, Taahira said, "I didn't believe you would pay so much money for me."

"I could not take pleasure in it without you," said Ajib, and he was surprised to realize it was true. "But now I regret that I cannot buy you what you deserve."

"You need never buy me anything again," she said.

Ajib bowed his head. "I feel as if I have been punished for my misdeeds."

"What misdeeds?" asked Taahira, but Ajib said nothing. "I did not ask you this before," she said. "But I know you did not inherit all the money you gained. Tell me: did you steal it?"

"No," said Ajib, unwilling to admit the truth to her or himself. "It was given to me."

"A loan, then?"

"No, it does not need to be repaid."

"And you don't wish to pay it back?" Taahira was shocked. "So you are content that this other man paid for our wedding? That he paid my ransom?" She seemed on the verge of tears. "Am I your wife then, or this other man's?"

"You are my wife," he said.

"How can I be, when my very life is owed to another?"

"I would not have you doubt my love," said Ajib. "I swear to you that I will pay back the money, to the last dirham."

And so Ajib and Taahira moved back into Ajib's old house and began saving their money. Both of them went to work for Taahira's brother the apothecary, and when he eventually became a perfumer to the wealthy, Ajib and Taahira took over the business of selling remedies to the ill. It was a good living, but they spent as little as they could, living modestly and repairing damaged furnishings instead of buying new. For years, Ajib smiled whenever he dropped a coin into the chest, telling Taahira that it was a reminder of how much he valued her. He would say that even after the chest was full, it would be a bargain.

But it is not easy to fill a chest by adding just a few coins at a time, and so what began as thrift gradually turned into miserliness, and prudent decisions were replaced by tight-fisted ones. Worse, Ajib's and Taahira's affections for each other faded over time, and each grew to resent the other for the money they could not spend.

In this manner the years passed and Ajib grew older, waiting for the second time that his gold would be taken from him.

"What a strange and sad story," I said.

"Indeed," said Bashaarat. "Would you say that Ajib acted prudently?"

I hesitated before speaking. "It is not my place to judge him," I said. "He must live with the consequences of his actions, just as I must live with mine." I was silent for a moment, and then said, "I admire Ajib's candor, that he told you everything he had done."

"Ah, but Ajib did not tell me of this as a young man," said Bashaarat. "After he emerged from the Gate carrying the chest, I did not see him again for another twenty years. Ajib was a much older man when he came to visit me again. He had come home and found his chest gone, and the knowledge that he had paid his debt made him feel he could tell me all that had transpired."

"Indeed? Did the older Hassan from your first story come to see you as well?"

"No, I heard Hassan's story from his younger self. The older Hassan never returned to my shop, but in his place I had a different visitor, one who shared a story about Hassan that he himself could never have told me." Bashaarat proceeded to tell me that visitor's story, and if it pleases Your Majesty, I will recount it here.

THE TALE OF THE WIFE AND HER LOVER

Raniya had been married to Hassan for many years, and they lived the happiest of lives. One day she saw her husband dine with a young man, whom she recognized as the very image of Hassan when she had first married him. So great was her astonishment that she could scarcely keep herself from intruding on their conversation. After the young man left, she demanded that Hassan tell her who he was, and Hassan related to her an incredible tale.

"Have you told him about me?" she asked. "Did you know what lay ahead of us when we first met?"

"I knew I would marry you from the moment I saw you,"

Hassan said, smiling, "but not because anyone had told me. Surely, wife, you would not wish to spoil that moment for him?"

So Raniya did not speak to her husband's younger self, but only eavesdropped on his conversation, and stole glances at him. Her pulse quickened at the sight of his youthful features; sometimes our memories fool us with their sweetness, but when she beheld the two men seated opposite each other, she could see the fullness of the younger one's beauty without exaggeration. At night, she would lie awake, thinking of it.

Some days after Hassan had bid farewell to his younger self, he left Cairo to conduct business with a merchant in Damascus. In his absence Raniya found the shop that Hassan had described to her, and stepped through the Gate of Years to the Cairo of her youth.

She remembered where he had lived back then, and so was easily able to find the young Hassan and follow him. As she watched him, she felt a desire stronger than she had felt in years for the older Hassan, so vivid were her recollections of their youthful lovemaking. She had always been a loyal and faithful wife, but here was an opportunity that would never be available again. Resolving to act on this desire, Raniya rented a house, and in subsequent days bought furnishings for it.

Once the house was ready, she followed Hassan discreetly while she tried to gather enough boldness to approach him. In the jewelers' market, she watched as he went to a jeweler, showed him a necklace set with ten gemstones, and asked him how much he would pay for it. Raniya recognized it as one Hassan had given to her in the days after their wedding; she had not known he had once tried to sell it. She stood a short distance away and listened, pretending to look at some rings.

"Bring it back tomorrow, and I will pay you a thousand dinars," said the jeweler. Young Hassan agreed to the price, and left.

As she watched him leave, Raniya overheard two men talking nearby:

"Did you see that necklace? It is one of ours."

"Are you certain?" asked the other.

"I am. That is the bastard who dug up our chest."

"Let us tell our captain about him. After this fellow has sold his necklace, we will take his money, and more."

The two men left without noticing Raniya, who stood with her heart racing but her body motionless, like a deer after a tiger has passed. She realized that the treasure Hassan had dug up must have belonged to a band of thieves, and these men were two of its members. They were now observing the jewelers of Cairo to identify the person who had taken their loot.

Raniya knew that since she possessed the necklace, the young Hassan could not have sold it. She also knew that the thieves could not have killed Hassan. But it could not be Allah's will for her to do nothing. Allah must have brought her here so that he might use her as his instrument.

Raniya returned to the Gate of Years, stepped through to her own day, and at her house found the necklace in her jewelry box. Then she used the Gate of Years again, but instead of entering it from the left side, she entered it from the right, so that she visited the Cairo of twenty years later. There she sought out her older self, now an aged woman. The older Raniya greeted her warmly, and retrieved the necklace from her own jewelry box. The two women then rehearsed how they would assist the young Hassan.

The next day, the two thieves were back with a third man, whom Raniya assumed was their captain. They all watched as Hassan presented the necklace to the jeweler.

As the jeweler examined it, Raniya walked up and said, "What a coincidence! Jeweler, I wish to sell a necklace just like that." She brought out her necklace from a purse she carried.

"This is remarkable," said the jeweler. "I have never seen two necklaces more similar."

Then the aged Raniya walked up. "What do I see? Surely my eyes deceive me!" And with that she brought out a third identical necklace. "The seller sold it to me with the promise that it was unique. This proves him a liar."

"Perhaps you should return it," said Raniya.

"That depends," said the aged Raniya. She asked Hassan, "How much is he paying you for it?"

"A thousand dinars," said Hassan, bewildered.

"Really! Jeweler, would you care to buy this one too?"

"I must reconsider my offer," said the jeweler.

While Hassan and the aged Raniya bargained with the jeweler, Raniya stepped back just far enough to hear the captain berate the other thieves. "You fools," he said. "It is a common necklace. You would have us kill half the jewelers in Cairo and bring the guardsmen down upon our heads." He slapped their heads and led them off.

Raniya returned her attention to the jeweler, who had withdrawn his offer to buy Hassan's necklace. The older Raniya said, "Very well. I will try to return it to the man who sold it to me." As the older woman left, Raniya could tell that she smiled beneath her veil.

Raniya turned to Hassan. "It appears that neither of us will sell a necklace today."

"Another day, perhaps," said Hassan.

"I shall take mine back to my house for safekeeping," said Raniya. "Would you walk with me?"

Hassan agreed, and walked with Raniya to the house she had rented. Then she invited him in, and offered him wine, and after they had both drunk some, she led him to her bedroom. She covered the windows with heavy curtains and extinguished all lamps so that the room was as dark as night. Only then did she remove her veil and take him to bed.

Raniya had been flush with anticipation for this moment, and so was surprised to find that Hassan's movements were clumsy and awkward. She remembered their wedding night very clearly; he had been confident, and his touch had taken her breath away.

She knew Hassan's first meeting with the young Raniya was not far away, and for a moment did not understand how this fumbling boy could change so quickly. And then of course the answer was clear.

So every afternoon for many days, Raniya met Hassan at her rented house and instructed him in the art of love, and in doing so she demonstrated that, as is often said, women are Allah's most wondrous creation. She told him, "The pleasure you give is returned in the pleasure you receive," and inwardly she smiled as she thought of how true her words really were. Before long, he gained the expertise she remembered, and she took greater enjoyment in it than she had as a young woman.

All too soon, the day arrived when Raniya told the young Hassan that it was time for her to leave. He knew better than to press her for her reasons, but asked her if they might ever see each other again. She told him, gently, no. Then she sold the furnishings to the house's owner, and returned through the Gate of Years to the Cairo of her own day.

When the older Hassan returned from his trip to Damascus, Raniya was home waiting for him. She greeted him warmly, but kept her secrets to herself.

I was lost in my own thoughts when Bashaarat finished this story, until he said, "I see that this story has intrigued you in a way the others did not."

"You see clearly," I admitted. "I realize now that, even though the past is unchangeable, one may encounter the unexpected when visiting it."

"Indeed. Do you now understand why I say the future and the past are the same? We cannot change either, but we can know both more fully."

"I do understand; you have opened my eyes, and now I wish to use the Gate of Years. What price do you ask?"

He waved his hand. "I do not sell passage through the Gate," he said. "Allah guides whom he wishes to my shop, and I am content to be an instrument of his will."

Had it been another man, I would have taken his words to be a negotiating ploy, but after all that Bashaarat had told me, I knew that he was sincere. "Your generosity is as boundless as your learning," I said, and bowed. "If there is ever a service that a merchant of fabrics might provide for you, please call upon me."

"Thank you. Let us talk now about your trip. There are some matters we must speak of before you visit the Baghdad of twenty years hence."

"I do not wish to visit the future," I told him. "I would step through in the other direction, to revisit my youth."

"Ah, my deepest apologies. This Gate will not take you there. You see, I built this Gate only a week ago. Twenty years ago, there was no doorway here for you to step out of."

My dismay was so great that I must have sounded like a forlorn child. I said, "But where does the other side of the Gate lead?" and walked around the circular doorway to face its opposite side.

Bashaarat walked around the doorway to stand beside me. The view through the Gate appeared identical to the view outside it, but when he extended his hand to reach through, it stopped as if it met an invisible wall. I looked more closely, and noticed a brass lamp set on a table. Its flame did not flicker, but was as fixed and unmoving as if the room were trapped in clearest amber.

"What you see here is the room as it appeared last week," said Bashaarat. "In some twenty years' time, this left side of the Gate will permit entry, allowing people to enter from this direction and visit their past. Or," he said, leading me back to the side of the doorway he had first shown me, "we can enter from the right side now, and visit them ourselves. But I'm afraid this Gate will never allow visits to the days of your youth."

"What about the Gate of Years you had in Cairo?" I asked.

He nodded. "That Gate still stands. My son now runs my shop there."

"So I could travel to Cairo, and use the Gate to visit the Cairo of twenty years ago. From there I could travel back to Baghdad."

"Yes, you could make that journey, if you so desire."

"I do," I said. "Will you tell me how to find your shop in Cairo?"

"We must speak of some things first," said Bashaarat. "I will not ask your intentions, being content to wait until you are ready to tell me. But I would remind you that what is made cannot be unmade."

"I know," I said.

"And that you cannot avoid the ordeals that are assigned to you. What Allah gives you, you must accept."

"I remind myself of that every day of my life."

"Then it is my honor to assist you in whatever way I can," he said.

He brought out some paper and a pen and inkpot and began writing. "I shall write for you a letter to aid you on your journey." He folded the letter, dribbled some candle wax over the edge, and pressed his ring against it. "When you reach Cairo, give this to my son, and he will let you enter the Gate of Years there."

A merchant such as myself must be well-versed in expressions of gratitude, but I had never before been as effusive in giving thanks as I was to Bashaarat, and every word was heartfelt. He gave me directions to his shop in Cairo, and I assured him I would tell him all upon my return. As I was about to leave his shop, a thought occurred to me. "Because the Gate of Years you have here opens to the future, you are assured that the Gate and this shop will remain standing for twenty years or more."

"Yes, that is true," said Bashaarat.

I began to ask him if he had met his older self, but then I bit back my words. If the answer was no, it was surely because his older self was dead, and I would be asking him if he knew the date of his death. Who was I to make such an inquiry, when this man was granting me a boon without asking my intentions? I saw from his expression that he knew what I had meant to ask, and I bowed my head in humble apology. He indicated his acceptance with a nod, and I returned home to make arrangements.

The caravan took two months to reach Cairo. As for what occupied my mind during the journey, Your Majesty, I now tell you what I had not told Bashaarat. I was married once, twenty years before, to a woman named Najya. Her figure swayed as gracefully as a willow bough and her face was as lovely as the moon, but it was her kind and tender nature that captured my heart. I had just begun my career as a merchant when we married, and we were not wealthy, but did not feel the lack.

We had been married only a year when I was to travel to Basra to meet with a ship's captain. I had an opportunity to profit by trading in slaves, but Najya did not approve. I reminded her that the Koran does not forbid the owning of slaves as long as one treats them well, and that even the Prophet owned some. But she said there was no way I could know how my buyers would treat their slaves, and that it was better to sell goods than men.

On the morning of my departure, Najya and I argued. I spoke harshly to her, using words that it shames me to recall, and I beg Your Majesty's forgiveness if I do not repeat them here. I left in anger, and never saw her again. She was badly injured when the wall of a mosque collapsed, some days after I left. She was taken to the bimaristan, but the physicians could not save her, and she died soon after. I did not learn of her death until I returned a week later, and I felt as if I had killed her with my own hand.

Can the torments of Hell be worse than what I endured in the days that followed? It seemed likely that I would find out, so near to death did my anguish take me. And surely the experience must be similar, for like infernal fire, grief burns but does not consume; instead, it makes the heart vulnerable to further suffering.

Eventually my period of lamentation ended, and I was left a hollow man, a bag of skin with no innards. I freed the slaves I had bought and became a fabric merchant. Over the years I became wealthy, but I never remarried. Some of the men I did business with tried to match me with a sister or a daughter, telling me that the love of a woman can make you forget your pains. Perhaps they are right, but it cannot make you forget the pain you caused another. Whenever I imagined myself marrying another woman, I remembered the look of hurt in Najya's eyes when I last saw her, and my heart was closed to others.

I spoke to a mullah about what I had done, and it was he who told me that repentance and atonement erase the past. I repented and atoned as best I knew how; for twenty years I lived as an upright man, I offered prayers and fasted and gave alms to those less fortunate and made a pilgrimage to Mecca, and yet I was still haunted by guilt. Allah is all-merciful, so I knew the failing to be mine.

Had Bashaarat asked me, I could not have said what I hoped to achieve. It was clear from his stories that I could not change what I knew to have happened. No one had stopped my younger self from arguing with Najya in our final conversation. But the tale of Raniya, which lay hidden within the tale of Hassan's life without his knowing it, gave me a slim hope: perhaps I might be able to play some part in events while my younger self was away on business.

Could it not be that there had been a mistake, and my Najya had survived? Perhaps it was another woman whose body had been wrapped in a shroud and buried while I was gone. Perhaps I could rescue Najya and bring her back with me to the Baghdad of my own day. I knew it was foolhardy; men of experience say, "Four things do not come back: the spoken word, the sped arrow, the past life, and the neglected opportunity," and I understood the truth of those words better than most. And yet I dared to hope that Allah had judged my twenty years of repentance sufficient, and was now granting me a chance to regain what I had lost.

The caravan journey was uneventful, and after sixty sunrises and three hundred prayers, I reached Cairo. There I had to navigate the city's streets, which are a bewildering maze compared to the harmonious design of the City of Peace. I made my way to the Bayn al-Qasrayn, the main street that runs through the Fatimid quarter of Cairo. From there I found the street on which Bashaarat's shop was located.

I told the shopkeeper that I had spoken to his father in Baghdad, and gave him the letter Bashaarat had given me. After reading it, he led me into a back room, in whose center stood another Gate of Years, and he gestured for me to enter from its left side.

As I stood before the massive circle of metal, I felt a chill, and chided myself for my nervousness. With a deep breath I stepped through, and found myself in the same room with different furnishings. If not for those, I would not have known the Gate to be different from an ordinary doorway. Then I recognized that the chill I had felt was simply the coolness of the air in this room, for the day here was not as hot as the day I had left. I could feel its warm breeze at my back, coming through the Gate like a sigh.

The shopkeeper followed behind me and called out, "Father, you have a visitor."

A man entered the room, and who should it be but Bashaarat, twenty years younger than when I'd seen him in Baghdad. "Welcome, my lord," he said. "I am Bashaarat."

"You do not know me?" I asked.

"No, you must have met my older self. For me, this is our first meeting, but it is my honor to assist you."

Your Majesty, as befits this chronicle of my shortcomings, I must confess that, so immersed was I in my own woes during the journey from Baghdad, I had not previously realized that Bashaarat had likely recognized me the moment I stepped into his shop. Even as I was admiring his water-clock and brass songbird, he had known that I would travel to Cairo, and likely knew whether I had achieved my goal or not.

The Bashaarat I spoke to now knew none of those things. "I am doubly grateful for your kindness, sir," I said. "My name is Fuwaad ibn Abbas, newly arrived from Baghdad."

Bashaarat's son took his leave, and Bashaarat and I conferred; I asked him the day and month, confirming that there was ample time for me to travel back to the City of Peace, and promised him I would tell him everything when I returned. His younger self was as gracious as his older. "I look forward to speaking with you on your return, and to assisting you again twenty years from now," he said.

His words gave me pause. "Had you planned to open a shop in Baghdad before today?"

"Why do you ask?"

"I had been marveling at the coincidence that we met in Baghdad just in time for me to make my journey here, use the Gate, and travel back. But now I wonder if it is perhaps not a co-incidence at all. Is my arrival here today the reason that you will move to Baghdad twenty years from now?"

Bashaarat smiled. "Coincidence and intention are two sides of a tapestry, my lord. You may find one more agreeable to look at, but you cannot say one is true and the other is false."

"Now as ever, you have given me much to think about," I said.

I thanked him and bid farewell. As I was leaving his shop, I passed a woman entering with some haste. I heard Bashaarat greet her as Raniya, and stopped in surprise.

From just outside the door, I could hear the woman say, "I have the necklace. I hope my older self has not lost it."

"I am sure you will have kept it safe, in anticipation of your visit," said Bashaarat.

I realized that this was Raniya from the story Bashaarat had told me. She was on her way to collect her older self so that they might return to the days of their youth, confound some thieves with a doubled necklace, and save their husband. For a moment I was unsure if I were dreaming or awake, because I felt as if I had stepped into a tale, and the thought that I might talk to its players and partake of its events was dizzying. I was tempted to speak, and see if I might play a hidden role in that tale, but then I remembered that my goal was to play a hidden role in my own tale. So I left without a word, and went to arrange passage with a caravan.

It is said, Your Majesty, that Fate laughs at men's schemes. At first it appeared as if I were the most fortunate of men, for a caravan headed for Baghdad was departing within the month, and I was able to join it. In the weeks that followed I began to curse my luck, because the caravan's journey was plagued by delays. The wells at a town not far from Cairo were dry, and an expedition had to be sent back for water. At another village, the soldiers protecting the caravan contracted dysentery, and we had to wait for weeks for their recovery. With each delay, I revised my estimate of when we'd reach Baghdad, and grew increasingly anxious.

Then there were the sandstorms, which seemed like a warning from Allah, and truly caused me to doubt the wisdom of my actions. We had the good fortune to be resting at a caravanserai west of Kufa when the sandstorms first struck, but our stay was prolonged from days to weeks as, time and again, the skies became clear, only to darken again as soon as the camels were reloaded. The day of Najya's accident was fast approaching, and I grew desperate.

I solicited each of the camel drivers in turn, trying to hire one to take me ahead alone, but could not persuade any of them. Eventually I found one willing to sell me a camel at what would have been an exorbitant price under ordinary circumstances, but which I was all too willing to pay. I then struck out on my own.

It will come as no surprise that I made little progress in the storm, but when the winds subsided, I immediately adopted a rapid pace. Without the soldiers that accompanied the caravan, however, I was an easy target for bandits, and sure enough, I was stopped after two days' ride. They took my money and the camel I had purchased, but spared my life, whether out of pity or because they could not be bothered to kill me I do not know. I began walking back to rejoin the caravan, but now the skies tormented me with their cloudlessness, and I suffered from the heat. By the time the caravan found me, my tongue was swollen and my lips were as cracked as mud baked by the sun. After that I had no choice but to accompany the caravan at its usual pace.

Like a fading rose that drops its petals one by one, my hopes dwindled with each passing day. By the time the caravan reached the City of Peace, I knew it was too late, but the moment we rode through the city gates, I asked the guardsmen if they had heard of a mosque collapsing. The first guardsman I spoke to had not, and for a heartbeat I dared to hope that I had misremembered the date of the accident, and that I had in fact arrived in time.

Then another guardsman told me that a mosque had indeed collapsed just yesterday in the Karkh quarter. His words struck me with the force of the executioner's axe. I had traveled so far, only to receive the worst news of my life a second time.

I walked to the mosque, and saw the piles of bricks where there had once been a wall. It was a scene that had haunted my dreams for twenty years, but now the image remained even after I opened my eyes, and with a clarity sharper than I could endure. I turned away and walked without aim, blind to what was around me, until I found myself before my old house, the one where Najya and I had lived. I stood in the street in front of it, filled with memory and anguish.

I do not know how much time had passed when I became aware that a young woman had walked up to me. "My lord," she said, "I'm looking for the house of Fuwaad ibn Abbas."

"You have found it," I said.

"Are you Fuwaad ibn Abbas, my lord?"

"I am, and I ask you, please leave me be."

"My lord, I beg your forgiveness. My name is Maimuna, and I assist the physicians at the bimaristan. I tended to your wife before she died."

I turned to look at her. "You tended to Najya?"

"I did, my lord. I am sworn to deliver a message to you from her."

"What message?"

"She wished me to tell you that her last thoughts were of you.

She wished me to tell you that while her life was short, it was made happy by the time she spent with you."

She saw the tears streaming down my cheeks, and said, "Forgive me if my words cause you pain, my lord."

"There is nothing to forgive, child. Would that I had the means to pay you as much as this message is worth to me, because a lifetime of thanks would still leave me in your debt."

"Grief owes no debt," she said. "Peace be upon you, my lord."

"Peace be upon you," I said.

She left, and I wandered the streets for hours, crying tears of release. All the while I thought on the truth of Bashaarat's words: past and future are the same, and we cannot change either, only know them more fully. My journey to the past had changed nothing, but what I had learned had changed everything, and I understood that it could not have been otherwise. If our lives are tales that Allah tells, then we are the audience as well as the players, and it is by living these tales that we receive their lessons.

Night fell, and it was then that the city's guardsmen found me, wandering the streets after curfew in my dusty clothes, and asked who I was. I told them my name and where I lived, and the guardsmen brought me to my neighbors to see if they knew me, but they did not recognize me, and I was taken to jail.

I told the guard captain my story, and he found it entertaining, but did not credit it, for who would? Then I remembered some news from my time of grief twenty years before, and told him that Your Majesty's grandson would be born an albino. Some days later, word of the infant's condition reached the captain, and he brought me to the governor of the quarter. When the governor heard my story, he brought me here to the palace, and when your lord chamberlain heard my story, he in turn brought me here to the throne room, so that I might have the infinite privilege of recounting it to Your Majesty.

Now my tale has caught up to my life, coiled as they both are, and the direction they take next is for Your Majesty to decide. I know many things that will happen here in Baghdad over the next twenty years, but nothing about what awaits me now. I have no money for the journey back to Cairo and the Gate of Years there, yet I count myself fortunate beyond measure, for I was given the opportunity to revisit my past mistakes, and I have learned what remedies Allah allows. I would be honored to relate everything I know of the future, if Your Majesty sees fit to ask, but for myself, the most precious knowledge I possess is this:

Nothing erases the past. There is repentance, there is atonement, and there is forgiveness. That is all, but that is enough.

TED CHIANG

Back in the 1980s, the physicist Kip Thorne described a kind of time machine that was consistent with the principles of Einstein's general relativity. This time machine wasn't like a vehicle, but more like a road you could travel along, and the direction of travel determined whether you moved into the past or the future. You couldn't travel to a date earlier than the creation of the time machine, in the same way that you can't keep driving when there's no more road. Furthermore, Thorne's analysis indicated that you couldn't create a paradox with this time machine, and that only a single, self-consistent timeline was possible.

For a long time I thought about writing a hard SF story around this idea, but one day it occurred to me that the basic mechanism might not appear out of place in a low-tech setting. I eventually decided that an "Arabian Nights"–style story would be an interesting way to use it, because the recursive nature of time travel fit with the convention of nested stories, and the idea of a fixed timeline seemed to mesh well with Islamic notions of destiny.

ALWAYS

KAREN JOY FOWLER

Karen Joy Fowler is the author of five novels and two short-story collections. Her first novel, *Sarah Canary,* won the Commonwealth Medal for best first novel by a Californian. *Sister Noon* was a finalist for the PEN/Faulkner Award, and *The Jane Austen Book Club* was a *New York Times* best-seller. A new novel, *Wit's End,* was published in April 2008.

How I Got Here:
    I was seventeen years old when I heard the good news from Wilt Loomis, who had it straight from Brother Porter himself. Wilt was so excited he was ready to drive to the city of Always that very night. Back then I just wanted to be anywhere Wilt was. So we packed up.

Always had two openings and these were going for five thousand apiece, but Wilt had already talked to Brother Porter, who said, seeing as it was Wilt, who was good with cars, he'd take twenty-five hundred down and give us another three years to come up with the other twenty-five, and let that money cover us both. You average that five thousand, Wilt told me, over the infinite length of your life and it worked out to almost nothing a year. Not exactly nothing, but as close to nothing as you could get without getting to nothing. It was too good a deal to pass up. They were practically paying us.

My stepfather was drinking again and it looked less and less like I was going to graduate high school. Mother was just as glad to have me out of the house and harm's way. She did give me some advice. You can always tell a cult from a religion, she said, because a cult is just a set of rules that lets certain men get laid.

And then she told me not to get pregnant, which I could have taken as a shot across the bow, her new way of saying her life would have been so much better without me, but I chose not to. Already I was taking the long view.

The city of Always was a lively place then—this was back in 1938—part commune and part roadside attraction, set down in the Santa Cruz Mountains with the redwoods all around. It used to rain all winter and be damp all summer, too. Slug weather for those big yellow slugs you never saw anywhere but Santa Cruz. Out in the woods it smelled like bay leaves.

The old Santa Cruz Highway snaked through and the two blocks right on the road were the part open to the public. People would stop there for a soda—Brother Porter used to brag that he'd invented Hawaiian Punch, though the recipe had been stolen by some gang in Fresno who took the credit for it—and to look us over, whisper about us on their way to the beach. We offered penny peep shows for the adults, because Brother Porter said you ought to know what sin was before you abjured it, and a row of wooden Santa Claus statues for the kids. In our heyday we had fourteen gas pumps to take care of all the gawkers.

Brother Porter founded Always in the early twenties, and most of the other residents were already old when I arrived. That made sense, I guess, that they'd be the ones to feel the urgency, but I didn't expect it and I wasn't pleased. Wilt was twenty-five when we first went to Always. Of course, that too seemed old to me then.

The bed I got had just been vacated by a thirty-two-year-old woman named Maddie Beckinger. Maddie was real pretty. She'd just filed a suit against Brother Porter alleging that he'd promised to star her in a movie called *The Perfect Woman*, and when it opened she was supposed to fly to Rome in a replica of *The Spirit of St.*

Louis, only this plane would be called *The Spirit of Love*. She said in her suit that she'd always been more interested in being a movie star than in living forever. Who, she asked, was more immortal than Marlene Dietrich? Brother Porter hated it when we got dragged into the courts, but, as I was to learn, it did keep happening. Lawyers are forever, Brother Porter used to say.

He'd gotten as far as building a sound stage for the movie, which he hoped he might be able to rent out from time to time, and Smitty LeRoy and the Watsonville Wranglers recorded there, but mainly we used it as a dormitory.

Maddie's case went on for two whole years. During this time she came by occasionally to pick up her mail and tell us all she'd never seen such a collection of suckers as we were. Then one day we heard she'd been picked up in Nevada for passing bad checks, which turned out not to be her first offense. So off she went to San Quentin instead of to Rome. It seemed like a parable to me, but Brother Porter wasn't the sort who resorted to parables.

Lots of the residents had come in twos like Wilt and me, like animals to the ark, only to learn that there was a men's dormitory and a women's, with Brother Porter living up the hill in his own big house, all by himself and closer to the women's dorm than to the men's. Brother Porter told us right after we got there (though not a second before) that even the married couples weren't to sleep together.

There you go, Mother, was my first thought. Not a cult. Only later it was clarified to me that I *would* be having sex with Brother Porter and so, not a religion, after all.

Frankie Frye and Eleanor Pillser were the ones who told me. I'd been there just about a week and, then, one morning, while we were straightening up our cots and brushing our teeth and whatnot, they just came right out with it. At dinner the night before there'd been a card by my plate, the queen of hearts, which was Brother Porter's signal, only I didn't know that so I didn't go.

Frankie Frye, yes, that Frankie Frye, I'll get to all that, had the cot on one side of me and Eleanor the cot on the other. The dormitory was as dim in the morning as at night on account of also being a sound stage and having no windows. There was just one light dangling from the ceiling, with a chain that didn't reach down far enough so about a foot of string had been added to it. "The thing the men don't get," Frankie said to me, snapping her pillowcase smooth, "The thing the men mustn't get," Eleanor added on, "is that sleeping with Brother Porter is no hardship," said Frankie.

Frankie was thirty-five then and the postmistress. Eleanor was in her early forties and had come to Always with her husband, Rog. I can't tell you how old Brother Porter was, because he always said he wouldn't give an irrelevant number the power of being spoken out loud. He was a fine-looking man though. A man in his prime.

Wilt and I had done nothing but dry runs so far and he'd brought me to Always and paid my way into eternity with certain expectations. He was a fine-looking man, too, and I won't say I wasn't disappointed, just that I took the news better than he did. "I can't lie to you," he told me in those few days after he learned he wouldn't be having sex, but before he learned that I would be. "This is not the way I pictured it. I sort of thought with all that extra time, I'd get to be with more people, not less."

And when he did hear about me and Brother Porter, he pointed out that the rest of the world only had to be faithful until death did them part. "I don't care how good he is," Wilt said. "You won't want to be with him and no one else forever." Which I suspected he would turn out to be right about and he was. But in those early days, Brother Porter could make my pulse dance like a snake in a basket. In those early days, Brother Porter never failed to bring the goods.

We had a lot of tourists back then, especially in the summer. They would sidle up to us in their beach gear, ten-cent barbecue in one hand and skepticism in the other, to ask how we could really be sure Brother Porter had made us immortal. At first I tried to explain that it took two things to be immortal: it took Brother Porter and it took faith in Brother Porter. If I started asking the question, then I was already missing one of the two things it took.

But this in no way ended the matter. You think about hearing the same question a couple hundred times, and then add to that the knowledge that you'll be hearing it forever, because the way some people see it, you could be two hundred and five and then suddenly die when you're two hundred and six. The world is full of people who couldn't be convinced of cold in a snowstorm.

I was made the Always zookeeper. We had a petting zoo, three goats, one llama, a parrot named Parody, a dog named Chowder, and a monkey named Monkeyshines, but Monkeyshines bit and couldn't be let loose among the tourists no matter how much simple pleasure it would have given me to do so.

We immortals didn't leave Always much. We didn't have to; we grew our own food, had our own laundry, tailor, barber (though the lousy haircuts figured prominently in Maddie's suit), and someone to fix our shoes. At first, Brother Porter discouraged field trips, and then later we just found we had less and less in common with people who were going to die. When I complained about how old everyone else at Always was, Wilt pointed out that I was actually closer in age to some seventy-year-old who, like me, was going to live forever, than to some eighteen-year-old with only fifty or so years left. Wilt was as good with numbers as he was with cars and he was as right about that as everything else. Though some might go and others with five thousand to slap down might arrive, we were a tight community then, and I felt as comfortable in Always as I'd felt anywhere.

The Starkes were the first I ever saw leave. They were a married couple in their mid-forties. (Evelyn Barton and Harry Capps were in their forties, too. Rog and Eleanor, as I've said. Frankie a bit younger. The rest, and there were about thirty of us all told, were too old to guess at, in my opinion.)

The Starkes had managed our radio station, KFQU (which looks nasty, but was really just sequential) until the FRC shut us down, claiming we deviated from our frequency. No one outside Always wanted to hear Brother Porter sermonizing, because no one outside Always thought life was long enough.

The Starkes quit on eternity when Brother Porter took their silver Packard and crashed it on the fishhook turn just outside Los Gatos. Bill Starkes loved that Packard and, even though Brother Porter walked away with hardly a scratch, something about the accident made Bill lose his faith. For someone with all the time in the world, he told us while he waited for his wife to fetch her things, Brother Porter surely does drive fast. (In his defense, Brother Porter did tell the police he wasn't speeding and he stuck to that. He was just in the wrong lane, he said, for the direction in which he was driving.) (He later said that the Starkes hadn't quit over the crash, after all. They'd been planted as fifth columnists in Always and left because we were all such patriots, they saw there was no point to it. Or else they were about to be exposed. I forget which.)

The next to go were Joseph Fitton and Cleveland March. The men just woke up one morning to find Joe and Cleveland's cots stripped bare and Cleveland's cactus missing from the windowsill, without a word said, but Wilt told me they'd been caught doing something they didn't think was sex, but Brother Porter did.

I couldn't see leaving myself. The thing I'd already learned was that when you remove death from your life, you change everything that's left. Take the petting zoo. Parrots are pretty long-lived compared to dogs and goats, but even they die. I'd been there less than two years when Chowder, our little foxhound, had to be put down because his kidneys failed. He wasn't the first dog I'd ever lost; he was just the first I'd lost since I wasn't dying myself. I saw my life stretching forward, all counted out in dead dogs, and I saw I couldn't manage that.

I saw that my pets from now on would have to be turtles or

trees or nothing. Turtles and trees don't engage the way dogs do, but you can only have your heart broken so many times until it just won't mend again. I sat with Chowder and pulled him into my lap as he died and I was crying so hard for all the Chowder-less years ahead that I understood then and there that immortality was going to bring a certain coldness, a remoteness into my life. I hadn't expected that, but I didn't see a way out of it.

Here's another thing that changes: your investment strategies. As Wilt would say, we were all about T-bills now. Wilt said that often. I got real tired of Wilt saying that.

How It Went On:

Time passed and I felt pretty good about my situation. No one at Always died, and this was a powerful persuasion given how very old some of them were. Not that I needed persuading. I wasn't the youngest woman anymore, that was Kitty Strauss, and I didn't get the queen of hearts so often, but that was okay with me. Only the parrot was left from the petting zoo, so you couldn't really call it a zoo now, and I didn't see as much of the tourists and that was okay with me, too.

Three years in, Wilt had decided he'd gone for immortality prematurely. It had occurred to him that the older residents lived their full lives first, and only arrived in Always when they were tired of the flesh. Not that he wanted to wait as long as some. Winnifred spent every meal detailing the sufferings her arthritis caused her, as if we women weren't already listening to her toss and turn and hack and snore all night long.

Also, he hadn't managed to scrape up the second twenty-five hundred dollars we owed and it wasn't likely he would, since Brother Porter collected all our paychecks as a matter of course.

So Wilt told me that he wouldn't ante up again for eternity until he'd slept with at least twenty-five women, but no sooner did he move into San Jose than he was on his way to the Pacific Theater as a mechanic on the USS *Aquarius*. For a while I got postcards from the Gilberts, Marshalls, Marianas, and Carolines.

It would have been a real good time for Wilt to be immortal, but if he was thinking that too, he never said it.

In fact, the postcards didn't say much of anything. Maybe this was navy policy or maybe Wilt remembered that Brother Porter vetted all our mail first. Whichever, Brother Porter handed Wilt's postcards to me without comment, but he read Mother's letters aloud in the dining hall after dinner, especially if someone was in the hospital and not expected to recover or was cheating on her husband or her ration card. I listened just like everyone else, only mildly interested, as if these weren't mostly people I'd once known.

Brother Porter said Mother's letters were almost as good as the *Captain Midnight* radio show, which I guess meant that up in the big house, he had a radio and listened to it. Lots of Mother's friends were being neglected by their children. You might say this was a theme. No one ever needed a secret decoder ring to figure Mother out.

It didn't seem to me that the war lasted all that long, though Wilt felt otherwise. When he got back, I'd meet him from time to time in San Jose and we'd have a drink. The city of Always was dry, except for once when a bunch of reporters in the Fill Your Hole club rented out our dining space, invited us to join them, and spiked the punch so as to get a story from it. It ended in a lot of singing and Winnifred Allington fell off Brother Porter's porch, and Jeb Porter, Brother Porter's teenage son, punched out Harry Capps as a refutation of positive thinking, but the reporters had left by then so they missed it all.

Anyway Brother Porter never explicitly made abstention a condition and I never asked him about it in case he would. I still got my age checked whenever we went to a bar, so that was good. It renewed my faith every time it happened. Not that my faith needed renewing.

Now that Wilt was dying again, our interests had diverged. He was caught up in politics, local corruptions, national scandals. He read the newspapers. He belonged to the auto mechanics' union and he told me he didn't care that the war had ended so much as I might think. The dead were still dead and he'd seen way too many of them. He said that war served the purposes of corporations and politicians so exactly that there would always be another one, and then another, until the day some president or prime minister figured out how to declare a war that lasted forever. He said he hoped he'd die before that day came. I wonder sometimes if that worked out for him.

Once while he was still at Always, Wilt took me to the ocean so that we could stand on the edge and imagine eternity. Now when Wilt talked politics, I'd fill my ears with the sound of the ocean instead. Corporate puppet masters and congressional witch-hunts and union payola—they all drowned together in the pounding of the sea.

Still I went out with Wilt every time he asked. Mostly this was gratitude because he'd bought me eternity. Love had gone the way of the petting zoo for me. Sex was a good thing and there were plenty of times I couldn't sleep for wanting it. But even if sleeping with Wilt wouldn't have cost my life, I wouldn't have. *There was a match found for me at last. I fell in love with a shrub oak,* I read once in high school in a book about Thoreau, who died more than a hundred years ago and left that shrub oak a grieving widow.

When I first came to Always, there were six Erle Stanley Gardner mysteries in the women's dormitory that used to belong to Maddie. I read them all several times. But I wasn't reading anymore and certainly not murder mysteries. I'd even stopped liking music. I'd always supposed that art was about beauty and that beauty was forever. Now I saw that music was all about time. You take a photograph and it's all about moment and how that moment will never come again. You go into a library and every book on the shelves is all about death, even the ones pretending to be about birth or rebirth or resurrection or reincarnation.

Only the natural world is rendered eternal. Always was

surrounded by the Santa Cruz Mountains, which meant tree trunks across streams, ghostly bear prints deep inside the forest, wild berries, tumbles of rocks, mosses, earthquakes and storms. Out behind the post office was a glade where Brother Porter gave his sermons, had sex, and renewed our lifespans. It was one of those rings of redwoods made when the primary tree in the center dies. Brother Porter had us brick a wall in a half circle behind the trees so it would be more churchlike and the trees grew straight as candles; you could follow along their trunks all the way to the stars. The first time Brother Porter took me there and I lay smelling the loam and the bay (and also Brother Porter) and looking up, I thought to myself that no matter how long I lived, this place would always be beautiful to me.

I talked less and less. At first, my brain tried to make up the loss, dredging up random flashes from my past—advertising slogans, old songs, glimpses of shoes I'd worn, my mother's jewelry, the taste of an ant I'd once eaten. A dream I'd had in which I was surrounded by food that was bigger than me, bread slices the size of mattresses, which seems like it should have been a good dream, but it wasn't. Memories fast and scattershot. It pleased me to think my last experience of mortality would be a toothpaste commercial. Good-bye to all that.

Then I smoothed out and days would go by when it seemed I hardly thought at all. Tree time.

So it wasn't just Wilt, I was finding it harder to relate to people in general, and, no, this is not a complaint. I never minded having so little in common with those outside Always and their revved-up, streaming-by lives.

While inside Always, I already knew what everyone was going to say.

1. Winnifred was going to complain about her arthritis.
2. John was going to tell us that we were in for a cold winter.
   He'd make it sound like he was just reading the signs, like

he had all this *lore,* the fuzzy caterpillars coming early or being especially fuzzy or some such thing. He was going to
remind us that he hadn't always lived in California so he
knew what a cold winter really was. He was going to say
that Californians didn't know cold weather from their
asses.

3. Frankie was going to say that it wasn't her job to tape our
mail shut for us and she wasn't doing it anymore, we needed
to bring it already taped.

4. Anna was going to complain that her children wouldn't talk
to her just because she'd spent their inheritance on immortality. That their refusal to be happy for her was evidence
that they'd never loved her.

5. Harry was going to tell us to let a smile be our umbrella.

6. Brother Porter was going to wonder why the arcade wasn't
bringing in more money. He was going to add that he
wasn't accusing any of us of pocketing, but that it did make
you wonder how all those tourists could stop and spend so
little money.

7. Kitty was going to tell us how many boys in the arcade had
come onto her that day. Her personal best was seventeen.
She would make this sound like a problem.

8. Harry would tell us to use those lemons and make lemon-
ade.

9. Vincent was going to say that he thought his watch was fast
and make everyone else still wearing a watch tell him what
time they had. The fact that the times would vary minutely
never ceased to interest him and was good for at least another hour of conversation.

10. Frankie was going to say that no one ever listened to her.

It was a kind of conversation that required nothing in response. On and on it rolled, like the ocean.

Wilt always made me laugh and that never changed either,

only it took me so much longer to get the joke. Sometimes I'd be back at Always before I noticed how witty he'd been.

What Happened Next:

Here's the part you already know. One day one spring—one day when the Canada geese were passing overhead yet again, and we were out at the arcades, taking money from tourists, and I was thrilling for the umpteenth time to the sight of the migration, the chevron, the honking, the sense of a wild, wild spirit in the air—Brother Porter took Kitty out to the cathedral ring and he died there.

At first Kitty thought she'd killed him by making the sex so exciting, though anyone else would have been tipped off by the frothing and the screaming. The police came and they shermanned their way through Always. Eventually they found a plastic bag of rat poison stuffed inside one of the unused post office boxes and a half drunk cup of Hawaiian Punch on the mail scale that tested positive for it.

Inside Always, we all got why it wasn't murder. Frankie Frye reminded us that she had no way of suspecting it would kill him. She was so worked up and righteous, she made the rest of us feel we hadn't ever had the same faith in Brother Porter she'd had or we would have poisoned him ourselves years ago.

But no one outside of Always could see this. Frankie's lawyers refused to plead it out that way; they went with insanity and made all the inner workings of Always part of their case. They dredged up the old string of arsons as if they were relevant, as if they hadn't stopped entirely the day Brother Porter finally threw his son out on his ear. Jeb was a witness for the prosecution and a more angelic face you never saw. In retrospect, it was a great mistake to have given immortality to a fourteen-year-old boy. When he had it, he was a jerk, and I could plainly see that not having it had only made him an older jerk.

Frankie's own lawyers made such a point of her obesity that they reduced her to tears. It was a shameful performance and showed how little they understood us. If Frankie ever wished to lose weight, she had all the time in the world to do so. There was nothing relevant or even interesting in her weight.

The difficult issue for the defense was whether Frankie was insane all by herself or along with all the rest of us. Sometimes they seemed to be arguing the one and sometimes the other, so when they chose not to call me to the stand I didn't know if this was because I'd make us all look more crazy or less so. Kitty testified nicely. She charmed them all and the press dubbed her the Queen of Hearts at her own suggestion.

Wilt was able to sell his three years among the immortals to a magazine and recoup every cent of that twenty-five hundred he put up for me. There wasn't much I was happy about right then, but I was happy about that. I didn't even blame him for the way I came off in the article. I expect coquettish was the least I deserved. I'd long ago stopped noticing how I was behaving at any given moment.

I would have thought the trial would be just Mother's cup of tea, even without me on the witness stand, so I was surprised not to hear from her. It made me stop and think back, try to remember when her last letter had come. Could have been five years, could have been ten. Could have been twenty, could have been two. I figured she must be dead, which was bound to happen sooner or later, though I did think she was young to go, but that might only have been because I'd lost track of how old she was. I never heard from her again so I think I had it right. I wonder if it was the cigarettes. She always said that smoking killed germs.

Not one of the immortals left Always during the trial. Partly we were in shock and huddled up as a result. Partly there was so much to be done, so much money to be made.

The arcade crawled with tourists and reporters, too. Looking for a story, but also, as always, trying to make one. "Now that Brother Porter is dead," they would ask, exact wording to change, but point always the same, "don't you have some doubts? And if you have some doubts, well, then, isn't the game already over?"

They were tiresome, but they paid for their Hawaiian Punch just like everyone else and we all knew Brother Porter wouldn't have wanted them kept away.

Frankie was let off by reason of insanity. Exactly two days later Harry Capps walked into breakfast just when Winnifred Allington was telling us how badly she'd slept the night before on account of her arthritis. By the time he ran out of bullets, four more immortals were dead.

Harry's defense was no defense. "Not one of them ever got a good night's sleep," he said. "Someone had to show them what a good night's sleep was."

The politicians blamed the overly lenient Frankie Frye verdict for the four new deaths and swore the same mistake would not be made twice. Harry got life.

Why I'm Still Here:
Everyone else either died or left and now I'm the whole of it. The last of the immortals; City of Always, population one. I moved up to the big house and I'm the postmistress now, along with anything else I care to keep going. I get a salary from the government with benefits and a pension they'll regret if I live forever. They have a powerful faith I won't.

The arcade is closed except for the peep shows, which cost a quarter now and don't need me to do anything to run them but collect the coins after. People don't come through so much since they built the 17, but I still get customers from time to time. They buy a postcard and they want the Always postmark on it.

Wilt came to fetch me after the noise died down. "I brought you here," he said. "Seems like I should take you away." He never did understand why I wouldn't leave. He hadn't lived here long enough to understand it.

I tried the easy answer first. I got shot by Harry Capps, I said. Right through the heart. Was supposed to die. Didn't.

But then I tried again, because that wasn't the real answer and if I'd ever loved anyone, I'd loved Wilt. Who'll take care of the redwoods if I go? I asked him. Who'll take care of the mountains? He still didn't get it, though he said he did. I wouldn't have known how to leave even if I'd wanted to. What I was and what he was—they weren't the same thing at all anymore. There was no way back to what I'd been. The actual living forever part? That was always, always the least of it.

Which is the last thing I'm going to say on the subject. There is no question you can ask I haven't already answered and answered and answered again. Time without end.

KAREN JOY FOWLER

The cult in "Always" is a fusion of two real cults. I was researching one—Holy City in the Santa Cruz Mountains—and I found the other—a cult with no name which once existed in Oroville, California. What I took from Holy City was the location and an arcade Holy City ran in order to raise money. What I took from the Oroville cult was the leader's name, Brother Isaiah, and his claims of immortality. Brother Isaiah said he could confer immortality on anyone. For a fee. He gathered and fleeced his flock and then promptly died of a heart attack. The rest is made up.

"Always" was much improved by the suggestions of the Sycamore Hill workshop and I owe everyone there a great debt of gratitude. But primary thanks go to my editor Sheila Williams, who gave it its final critique and then a space in the pages of Asimov's. *I'd like to dedicate its appearance here to her as it certainly wouldn't be here without her.*

BARRY N. MALZBERG

Barry N. Malzberg's collected essays on science fiction, *Breakfast in the Ruins,* was published in 2007; the book conflates his 1982 classic *Engines of the Night* and all of the essays published since. His collection *In the Stone House* was published in 2000; several of his 1970s science fiction novels have been reissued within the past half decade.

He has been publishing science fiction and fantasy for over forty years.

Thirty years ago, Brian Stableford theorized that it was all over for science fiction. It was a literature for a transitional period, the transition between the technological and post-technological eras, which in the West could be placed roughly in the period 1900–1980, when the machines and all of the devices of mass communication went wild and society, however unwillingly, had to adjust to these enormous changes. The automobile, radio, television, mass marketing, national publications, mass advertising, the airplane, the telephone, the atom bomb, the hydrogen bomb, radar, the bombsight, the typewriter, the computer. Enormous changes all seemingly at the last minute.

Science fiction, a literature showing the integration of technology into the culture, on Earth or off, was evolved as a kind of protocol. It indicated means—multiple, often conflicting means—of adjustment. Wasn't it Gernsback the Founder (science fiction as a distinct genre is commonly dated as originating with the April 1926 issue of *Amazing Stories*) who proposed that this new litera-ture of science would encourage young boys to pursue careers in science? Sure, there were crazy extrapolations to the stars, mon-sters prowling the spacecraft, radio cabinets on rubbery legs light-ing cigarettes for their owners . . . still, that originating purpose was present in every Campbell editorial, every *Case of Conscience*, every curse of Gully Foyle . . . science fiction would enable us to imagine and then practice ways to live in a world that technology had overtaken and utterly changed.

That era of adjustment, Stableford wrote in 1978, was end-ing. We had adjusted more or less, had adjusted as best we could anyway. Science fiction had served its purpose; now in a time when technology was becoming fully integrated, it was only an appendix, a vestigial form attached only through inheritance. Decadence—form prevailing over function—would prevail and then the withering into eventual uselessness. Or as John Clute suggested early in the New Millennium, "Science fiction was a 20th century thing, the way that the symphony is essentially a 19th century thing. For a few years it seemed to be riding the saddle on the steed taking us to the future . . . but that is gone now."

Is this true? There are at least ten ways of looking at a black-bird; certainly this is one of them. These annual Nebula anthologies—of which this is the forty-third—have in their own way tracked the latter course of a genre that was approximately half its present age when the series began, and in many ways Clute and Stableford's assessment can be seen refracted through the books. Much of the fiction in the most recent volumes isn't science fiction at all, it is fantasy, and the science fiction content has become blurred in its tilt away from the rigor to which the genre had aspired in its halcyon '50s. You'll find the anthologies in the years of this vested third millennium to be suspiciously replete with zombies, voodoo, strange doings in basements, vampires, space travel accomplished through psychic means, alternate histories blurring into or around the known present. This is not your grandfather's or father's science fiction and much of it is not science fiction at all. The moving finger having writ and so on. One could well conclude that science fiction, having served its essential, originating purpose as a commercial format, was now, like Marx's idealized State, in the process of withering away.

This is of course simplistic argument. It avoids—as perhaps Clute and Stableford have also—any real complexity and also the real sociological fact of culture lag: organized society is in a perpetual state of catch-up, its mores and processes and accepted ethics significantly behind the actual pace of change. The culture is still trying to deal with the birth control pill or stem cell research within a Calvinistic frame of denial that was relevant centuries ago but is now inevitably intrusive or irrelevant.

And that might be descriptive of science fiction itself—"inevitably intrusive or irrelevant" in an era when technology and the culture have essentially interfaced, when everything has moved on except, perhaps, First Fandom and the persistent squabblers of the Science Fiction and Fantasy Writers of America. Still, here is the forty-third annual volume in an unbroken run and like its forty-two predecessors it contains some good stories as well as some stories that comprise a statement of other issues, and who knows if a consensus could be reached? These annuals are testimony, a series of friezes that are snapshots of the period, and their very inconclusiveness embraces the point.

"I want forward-looking, affirmative commentary," the editor of this anthology said to me and then after a long pause, "Except, I guess, from you." Granted this dispensation I have not looked backward any more than necessary and I refuse to look forward. The present is about all I can handle. But whether science fiction is a finished thing or not, what a glorious instrument it was! The symphony may be a finished thing but, oh, the roar of

Brahms and Mahler and even, at its effective end, Franz Schmidt.
Oh, the madder music, the wild darkness of the '50s! Our future
may have been snatched away but the past is ours always and, ah:
such sweet thunder.

New Jersey, 2008

WHY I WRITE SCIENCE FICTION

KATHLEEN ANN GOONAN

Kathleen Ann Goonan (www.goonan.com) has been writing science fiction for twenty years and gives talks about science, technology, education, and the future. Her latest novel, *In War Times,* is the American Library Association's Best Adult Genre Novel of 2007/08. She is working on a new novel, *This Shared Dream Called Earth.*

In 1959, C. P. Snow gave his famous Two Cultures lecture at Cambridge, in which he spoke of a separation between the culture of science and that of "literary intellectuals." He said that academe and society in general were separating into scientists and humanists, and that any common language or viewpoint was fast vanishing.

He was right.

Most of the great scientific discoveries of our era—those of Darwin, Einstein, Curie—were made by those who knew how to wield the pen. The great literary harbingers of the modern age, which was ushered in by these new insights into the natural world, were Virginia Woolf, James Joyce, and others who used the energy of consciousness to look directly at their own minds. They used literature in ways that reflected the social shocks and indeterminacy revealed by the theory of evolution and the theory of relativity, as well as the perceived fragmentation of time and lives brought about by industrialization.

Sometime in the early sixties, I was sorted into a group defined by "good with words." I'm not blaming anyone—I was—and yet, I was therefore not given any formal overview of science or mathematics because someone assumed it would be a waste of time. Instead, I was told to solve problems. Achieving the correct answer—learning how to think—was not the point. One was to memorize one particular process with which to achieve the correct answer. But now, I suspect that the teachers didn't really understand what they were doing and so could not evaluate alternative processes. My good-with-words track had to learn the periodic table, which I did, and dissect a frog, which I did not. Never was it breathed to me why such information might lead to future fascination or might eventually spark my imagination, as words had been doing for quite some time. I read biographies of scientific pioneers with great interest, yet never considered that I might become one, or at least eventually understand what had led to the polio vaccine, which changed my life (I could, thereafter, swim in public pools), sulfa drugs (which saved my life when I got peritonitis), or the atomic bomb (which elicited a Wednesday noon air-raid-signal test for the first fifteen years of my life, although we never, in history or science class, got around to why). I knew about "evolution" because I read the encyclopedia, but I didn't understand its paradigm-shattering implications. And, by the way, my school system, Fairfax County, Virginia, was then and is now one of the "best" in the country.

A true future scientist would not have let this slow her down for a second, of course. She would have been blowing up her garage or classifying plants with the best of them.

Still. I could have read Darwin, and would have, had it been suggested. I was a curious girl. Instead, I immersed myself, and gladly, in classical, medieval, and seventeenth-century literature. After college, a great stroke of luck, hunger, or foresight caused me to take a master's-equivalent Montessori certification course. As Maria Montessori was a scientist, and her method of teaching quintessentially scientific, I thereby learned the magic, the potency, of the simple act of dispassionate observation, which is the basis of understanding how children learn.

I caught a glimpse of the other culture.

Like most writers, I always defined myself, past, present, and future, as one. When I finally moved from poet to short story writer to novelist, a strange thing happened. The other culture, the one that sustained my very life but was as invisible and as taken for granted as air, grabbed me and took hold. Books written by scientists in plain English were suddenly available. I noticed that the magazine *Science*, to which my father subscribed, was actually fascinating. And when I began writing for publication, at age thirty-five, something strange happened. Science fiction came out.

At first, it resembled fantasy, and might feel quite at home today, in a market where science and fantasy freely mix in the same work. But there was no box of old musty pulp magazines under the bed in my grandmother's guest room lurking in my literary subconscious, ready to supply the rules, the bones, the tone. In 1961, I was reading the big fat paperbacks from Drug Fair that littered the house—*Catch-22*, *Hawaii*, *Exodus*. And though science fiction was quite fairly represented, I rarely read it. I'm not sure why. Just out of high school I worked in a book store, and read just about every Lin Carter Ballantine fantasy out at that time. I also read *Steps*, *Hopscotch*, *The Trial*; anything that brought me into the territory of strangeness; mysteries, philosophy, and history, all at a marvelous discount. Had their work been available, I would have added E. O. Wilson, Oliver Sacks, Freeman Dyson, and, probably, ever more esoteric works. I may even have become interested in pursuing in college the world they opened.

So why write science fiction? Perhaps it was just a process of waking up. Without an overview of how our technological world came about, despite my father's repeated explanations of how radar works and, for that matter, how everything works, I was previously asleep to everything except the intellectual world of one culture, that of literature. The culture of science was as irrelevant,

I thought, as it was impenetrable. And in these rather backward and quaint educational times in which we live, I don't think that many American children will be pulled toward the culture of science very soon.

But I write SF because I am trying to catch up with the world, to explore the insights that others more accomplished in using the tools of science have had, and to ponder. The fruits of science—artificial DNA, atomic energy, the ability to explore space and the human mind—cannot be ignored, as they are in most literary fiction.

Science has brought our present into being, and will create our future. It is my goal, in the time I have left, to understand. I don't. I can see only fragments. When they use words, scientists tell stories that often can only be accurately shown through mathematics, which I have not adequately studied. But from those fragments I can read, peopled stories emerge. These stories are niched, labeled, and marketed as science fiction, and they fit all the parameters. Yet, like most science fiction, which encompasses a spectrum of work, they are more than their confining labels. Marketing forces limit us, as writers. They always have. It's nothing new.

Perhaps, in the future, we will beam our stories at one another in changing patterns of color, like squid, and maybe, enhanced by a singular human grammar, they will mean more than "Let's mate." Science fiction is an art form, and to survive, it must grow. Science, and its fiction, is the fabric of the future. No matter what it may be called in the future, it will survive, if literature survives.

At its best, science fiction has the power to unite the two cultures. It has the power to show anything—love, death, war, peace—and the power to ring the great bells.

That is what I'm trying to do, however imperfectly, when I write science fiction.

TITANIUM MIKE SAVES THE DAY

DAVID D. LEVINE

David D. Levine is a lifelong SF reader whose midlife crisis was to take a sabbatical from his high-tech job to attend Clarion West in 2000. He made his first professional sale in 2001, won the Writers of the Future Contest in 2002, was nominated for the John W. Campbell Memorial Award in 2003 and 2004, and won a Hugo in 2006 (Best Short Story, for "Tk'tk'tk").

"Titanium Mike Saves the Day" was his first appearance on the Nebula ballot. A collection of his short stories, *Space Magic,* is available from Wheatland Press. He lives in Portland, Oregon, with his wife, Kate Yule, with whom he edits the fanzine *Bento*, and their website is www .BentoPress.com.

> *V. An emergency radiation shelter near the asteroid Chiron,*
> *December 2144*

"Gramma, I'm scared."

The poor girl wasn't just scared, she was terrified. Behind a faceplate fogged with rapid breaths, her skin was pale and clammy and her sapphire-blue eyes twitched like small frightened animals.

Helen wasn't exactly calm herself. "Don't fret, Sophie," she said, but her own voice trembled. She muted her helmet mike and took a deep breath before continuing. "We'll be safe here." For a while, anyway, she added silently.

In all Helen Buchanan's seventy-eight years she'd never seen a solar flare so strong come on so fast. They'd had barely enough warning to reach this abandoned mining module before a storm of protons moving at near-lightspeed began to scour this sector of the Belt. And her lightweight two-seater jump bug offered almost no shielding against the radiation, so they were trapped here until the storm passed. Which might be hours, or days, or weeks.

"Now, you just try to keep calm," she told Sophie, "while I see what we have in the way of supplies." But the module's cupboards contained only dust. Its oxy tanks were still welded to the wall, but when she put her helmet against each one and tapped it with her hand light, all she heard was the dim *tink* of metal in vacuum.

That wasn't good. Not good at all.

She took another calming breath, then checked the oxy meter on her wrist: twenty-one hours at the current rate of consumption. She tweaked the mixture a little leaner; it might give her headaches, but that beat the alternative. "All right now, sugar, let me check your tanks." Helen turned Sophie around, stopping the rotation with a practiced tap on the shoulder as she bent to peer at the girl's tank-mounted meter. And gasped.

Only six hours left.

"W-what's wrong, Gramma?"

She considered her response while thinning Sophie's mix. Panic would drive the child's oxy consumption up, but she'd know if she was being lied to. She turned Sophie to face herself and looked her straight in the eye. "Well, kiddo, we're a little light on the oxy. Now, most flares only last a few hours, but this one's a real whopper—no telling how long it'll go on." She reached behind herself and began unshipping her #3 tank. "So I'm going to give you some of mine. Hold still."

The emergency connector hose was too short, the light was giving out, and Helen hadn't done this kind of detail work with gloves on in years. But eventually she got everything connected together and bungeed the extra tank to the child's pack.

Sophie's meter now read ten hours.

Only four hours more? That tank would have kept Helen going for seven! The poor frightened child was gulping down the oxy like nobody's business.

This had to stop.

Standard practice was to use sleeping pills, but Sophie's bubblegum-pink suit lacked such grown-up supplies. She'd have to find another way.

Helen thought back to her days raising Sophie's mother, but no situation this worrisome had ever come up then. Then she thought back a little further . . .

And she had just the thing.

"Sweetie, do you know about Titanium Mike?"

Sophie didn't reply, just shook her head slowly inside her helmet.

"Well then, looks like I need to fill in a few holes in your education." She drew Sophie to herself, chestplate against chestplate, so the girl could feel her voice in her bones, not just hear it filtered through radio. "Titanium Mike is . . . well, he's more a force of nature than a man, really. They say his father was Gravity and his mother was Vacuum."

"Is he going to come and help us?"

Helen considered the question for a moment. "Well, he might—you never can tell where old Mike might show up. When Cassandra Station was coming apart, he stuck the two halves back together with spit. And he's the one who stopped Ceres from spinning."

"Ceres doesn't spin. Everyone knows that."

"Not anymore! But back in the old days she rolled like a stuck gyro and it wasn't safe to get near. Mike lassoed her with a bungee cord and straightened her out."

Sophie looked mighty dubious at that. But dubious didn't use nearly as much oxy as panicked.

"No, really, it's true. If you don't believe me, you can ask Mike yourself the next time you see him. He's done all sorts of things. Why, when he was just a kid, he put rockets in his pockets and scrubbers in his rubbers and walked all the way around the Sun just to see where he'd come from."

At that, Sophie actually managed a weak little smile.

Helen smiled back at her. As she warmed to her subject, she found her own mood changing—the stories took her back to the early days of the Aurora Mining Company, when a certain amount of privation and danger was just a part of the job.

"Mike was born on Earth, but he never fit in there. He was a big man and always kept hitting his head on things, or tripping over his own big feet. One day he said to himself, 'Why can't I just float around and avoid all this bother?' So he decided to go to space, where he could do just that.

"But he realized he'd need something to breathe when he got there, so he took an old pickle jar, stuck some seaweed on the bottom, and screwed it onto the neck of his suit, and that was the beginning of hydroponics. Then he found some old thrusters that were lying around, but he was too big for just one thruster to lift so he stacked up a few of them on top of each other, and that was the beginning of the multi-stage lifter.

"When he got to space all the people were just drifting around with nothing to do. So he took some old foil food wrappers and spun them together into a big shiny dish to concentrate the sunlight, and then he went down to Luna and started throwing rocks into the hot spot, and that was the beginning of solar smelting.

"Mike took the smelted ore and started making cans and spikes and bubbles and donkeys and all kinds of other things that no one had ever seen before, but they didn't know how to use them. So Mike started to teach them . . ."

And so it went, the end of each tale sparking the beginning of the next, and pretty soon Sophie started asking questions, and it wasn't long before she was contributing her own outlandish details.

Then Helen's voice grew tired and they both slept for a while, and when Sophie woke up she asked for another Mike story.

When the all-clear sounded, somehow it had gotten to be twelve hours later. And Sophie still had more than an hour left in her tank.

IV. A mining facility near the asteroid Vesta,
October 2088

"Don't give me that bull!"

Orchekowski brought his massive fist down on the metal table with a resounding blow that knocked a squeeze-bulb of coffee loose from its grip-pad, but nobody at the table noticed the bulb as it tumbled away—they were all busy shouting at each other.

Javon Carter, floating near the door, snagged the bulb from the air with one long brown hand. He stared at it a moment, then stuck it to the wall beside him with a sigh. The canteen was the largest space they had, and it still wasn't big enough to contain the tension between the two groups of miners—as thick and foul as the air that puffed from the helmet rings of their well-worn suits with every vehement gesture.

"Listen to me!" Orchekowski was yelling over and over. The muscular sapper had enough lung power to overtop the others. "We need to take what we can and get out!"

"No way!" Enriquez shouted back, veins standing out on his forehead. "We've all worked too hard to give up now!"

Orchekowski spread his hands. "Face it—Aurora's over."

"Aurora is *not over!*" That was Buchanan, a feisty red-headed kid who emphasized her words with a finger in Orchekowski's face. "We've pulled out of worse situations than this."

The big man ignored the intruding finger. "Maybe," he said, "but we didn't have an alternative before." He glared at Buchanan, who stared back, her sapphire-blue eyes defiant. "We'd be insane to pass up this offer."

Enriquez made a rude noise. "Pennies on the dollar."

Griswold, the gray-haired accountant, rolled his eyes at that.

"It's the best we're going to get!" Orchekowski nodded vigorously as Griswold continued. "Hardcastle is the only other company in a position to exploit our claims. No one else would even touch us!"

A half-dozen voices exploded at that, and Carter shook his head. This argument was going nowhere—running in circles and feeding on itself. If it wasn't settled soon, and decisively, it would tear the group apart.

Carter was just an engineer, but someone had to do something about this situation, and it looked like it had to be him. He thought back to his first job in space, and his favorite boss . . . how would Ray Chen have handled it?

"That's exactly why we have to stay independent!" Buchanan shouted over the others, gaining the floor for a moment. "Hardcastle has already bought out every other molybdenum miner in the Belt. If they get us too . . ."

Griswold waved his hands. "They've just proved they're the only ones who can make moly pay."

"We can—" began Buchanan, and "Exactly!" screamed Orchekowski, and "Bull!" said Enriquez, and ten other voices were all raised at once . . .

. . . and Carter pressed his thumb over the relief port on his airpack and goosed the nitro valve. The escaping gas shrilled into the tumult with a screaming whistle that brought the argument to a sudden halt.

Everyone looked at Carter. " 'Scuse me," he said, with a hand on his stomach as though he'd just burped, and a few people chuckled at that. The rest simply waited for him to speak. His forty years in the Belt had earned him a certain amount of respect.

"I know you're all kind of upset," he said at last, "but I was just reminded of a little story that might help to put this situation into perspective. It's a Titanium Mike story."

"What the . . . ?" snarled Orchekowski, but several people shushed him. Others just looked baffled.

"For those of you who don't know him," Carter said, "Titanium Mike was nothing less than the greatest Belter who ever scratched his helmet on a rock. They say his father was the Sun and his mother was the Moon. And a long time ago, when everything in the System flew about every which way and no one could ever find their way from one place to another, Mike decided he ought to do something about it."

Carter noticed Griswold nodding thoughtfully—he'd recognized the story. Bingo.

"Mike went to the Sun," Carter continued, "and said, 'Old Sol, it sure would be easier on everyone if things had some kind of predictable orbits.' And the Sun said, 'You're right, Mike, and you know there's nothing I wouldn't do for you.' So the Sun puffed and grunted and sent out flares and winds and magnetic fields and jostled all the planets and asteroids into orbit around himself. Mike thanked him kindly, and the Sun was satisfied because now he was in the center of everything.

"But now that everything was going around the Sun, things were crossing each other's orbits and crashing into each other all the time, and . . ." Carter paused and gnawed on his lower lip for a bit. ". . . and you know, I'm having a little trouble remembering what comes next. Griswold, can you help me out here?"

Griswold gave Carter a look that said *you sly old dog, I know exactly what you're doing*, but what he said was "I do believe I can."

The gray-haired accountant took a pull from his coffee bulb and said, "Now that all that stuff was going around the Sun, everything was crashing into everything else all the time. So Mike went to Jupiter and said, 'Old Jove, it sure would be easier on everyone if things didn't cross each other up like that.' And Jupiter said, 'You're right, Mike, and you know there's nothing I wouldn't do for you.' So Jupiter threw his weight around and tugged and pulled until all the planets and asteroids were orbiting clockwise in the plane of the ecliptic. Mike thanked him kindly, and Jupiter was satisfied because now he didn't have all kinds of planetesimals and things bumping into him.

"But now that everything was spread across a big plane instead of going around in a tight little knot in the middle, it took a lifetime and a half just to walk from Venus to Mars." Then he pulled a fresh bulb of coffee from the dispenser on the table and tossed it to Enriquez. "Enriquez, you know this one, don't you?"

The dark-skinned little pilot caught the bulb. "Yeah," he said as he pulled the tab. "Mike went to Ceres and said, 'Old Cere, it sure would be easier on everyone if there were a quicker way to get from one place to another.' And Ceres said, 'You're right, Mike, and you know there's nothing I wouldn't do for you.' So Ceres called all her sisters together, and they hustled and bustled and fiddled and twiddled until there were orbital paths all over the System, with Hohmann transfer ellipses and slingshot maneuvers and all the other things that make the trip go a little faster. Mike thanked her kindly, and Ceres was satisfied because now people would have to visit her and her sisters all the time if they wanted yttrium to keep their fusion drives going and carbos to eat on the trip.

"And Mike looked out on the System . . . and realized he'd made a mess of everything. Because now, even though you could be sure where your destination was and which way it was going, it took years to get there even with the best orbital path and a full tank of hydro. But he couldn't go back to his friends and ask them to undo what they'd worked so hard to do at his request." He paused and sipped his coffee, then cocked an eyebrow at Orchekowski. "You know how it ends, don't you?"

Orchekowski just glared back at him.

"C'mon," Buchanan said. "Didn't you grow up on Titanium Mike stories, just like the rest of us?"

"I know you did," said Carter. "I've heard you telling 'em to your kids over the radio."

The big sapper looked at the expectant faces all around him, then let out a sigh. "Oh, all right," he said.

"Mike went to Pluto," he said—and he said it in his best storytelling voice, a voice as big and rough and full of vinegar as Mike himself—"crotchety old Pluto, who was so cold and distant and independent that he didn't exactly orbit the Sun and didn't exactly stay in the plane of the ecliptic and wasn't exactly easy to get to even after everything else had changed, but he always was a hard-headed practical sort and full of good advice. And Mike said to Pluto, 'Old Plute, it sure would be easier on everyone if things were the way they'd been before.'

"And Pluto said, 'You're right, Mike, and you know there's nothing I wouldn't do for you . . . but I'm just a tired old planet, and this is all I have to offer.' And he handed Mike a thing that looked like a little shiny pebble. 'What's this?' said Mike. 'It's a little thing called Persistence,' said Pluto.

"So Mike thanked Pluto kindly, and dogged down his helmet and set to work. And ever since then, whenever people have wanted things to be better they've had to work them out for themselves. It's a hard job, but with Persistence all things are possible."

Several people applauded Orchekowski's performance, and he made a little bow in the air. Then he told another story, the one about how Mike climbed from LEO to L5 on a cosmic string, which reminded Enriquez of the bawdy one about how Titanium Mike and Satellite Sal made Venus spin backwards . . . and Carter just floated there in the corner, sipped his coffee, and smiled.

Quite a while later, someone remembered why they'd gathered, and called for a vote. It was nineteen to zero to reject Hardcastle's offer.

III. A rented office at Chaffee Station in Low Earth Orbit,
July 2052

"It certainly is an . . . interesting proposal."

Raymond Chen forced himself to smile broadly at that, just as though he hadn't heard the same reaction from five other venture capitalists this month, and just as though all five of them hadn't eventually said no. "Glad you like it," he said, and busied himself shutting down the projector. Orbital diagrams and financial projections faded from the air like unfunded dreams.

Valerie Itsui, principal of Itsui Investments, sat with fingers steepled and a stiff unreadable expression on her face.

"Well . . ." said Jan, at the same time Kellie said, "Well then . . ." The twins shared a momentary glance, then Kellie continued, ". . . why don't we adjourn to the outer office? I believe lunch is ready." Ray swallowed; the Griffin sisters almost never stepped on each other's lines. That they would do so now showed just how nervous they were.

As the twins and Ms. Itsui moved toward the door, the fourth and newest member of the fledgling Asteroid Metals Extraction Corporation touched Raymond's hand. "Might as well start packing up now," Javon muttered low. "I was watching her the whole time you were talking and I swear her face never moved once."

"You just leave her to me," Ray replied, and clapped Javon on the shoulder. But after Javon turned and followed the other three, Ray pursed his lips and sighed.

Money was getting tight, for the industry as a whole as much as for AMEC. The nearby Moon and the resource-rich satellites of Saturn and Jupiter had been snapped up years ago, and after the recent series of space development bankruptcies some people were saying the scattered rocks of the Asteroid Belt could never be successfully exploited. But Ray was convinced that the twins' novel refinery technology could make mining the asteroids for molybdenum possible, young Javon's engineering talents could make it practical, and his own money skills could make it profitable. First, though, he had to sell that concept to the people with the money, and so far he'd failed.

What was he doing wrong? The technology would work, he was sure of it. The financials were rock-solid. He'd put every bit of supporting data he could into his presentation. So why weren't the big fish biting?

Ray drummed his fingers on the table. Maybe . . . maybe he was using the wrong bait.

Venture capitalists like Valerie Itsui spent their days in meetings like this one, looking at charts full of optimistic projections. What made the difference between the one that caught her attention and the many that didn't?

Not data. Dreams.

He had to make her *believe in the dream*. He had to make her feel the same excitement he felt for AMEC's plan.

The same excitement that had driven him into space development in the first place.

Ray nodded to himself, tucked the folded projector into a pocket, and stepped into the outer office.

He made his selections from the tray of sushi laid out on the reception desk, then sat next to Ms. Itsui. "So," he said, "what made you decide to invest in space development in the first place?"

She wiped her lips with a precisely folded napkin before replying. "Profit, Mr. Chen. There's more upside potential in space than anywhere on Earth, even now."

"It wasn't the money for me," Ray said. The twins looked at each other in surprise. "Oh, sure, I got my MBA, because I didn't have the head for science or the guts for zero-gee construction. But ever since I was a teenager I wanted to go to space." He leaned forward in his chair. "Because of the stories."

They were all looking at him now, giving him their complete attention in a way he'd never managed with any number of rosy financial projections. Ms. Itsui cocked her head in consideration of his words; the others were flat astonished. This was a side of himself he'd never revealed before.

"What stories, Mr. Chen?"

"Tales of exploration and adventure and derring-do, Ms. Itsui. Do you know the name Titanium Mike?"

"I can't say that I do."

Ray settled back in his chair. "Well, most folks say Mike is just a myth. But the fact is that he's been kicking around the System since Branson Station was just a loose mess of bolts and girders. His father was a thruster and his mother was an asteroid, and he's the one who figured out how to spin a station for gravity without making everyone inside dizzy."

"I hadn't been aware of that being a problem." It wasn't, of course, but a twinkle of interest had appeared in her eyes.

"Mike's responsible for a lot of things that people take for granted today. For instance, he's the one who cleared the Cassini Gap."

Ms. Itsui set down her chopsticks. "And how did he manage that?"

"Well, it all started one day when Mike got a call from a friend of his on Titan. 'We're in a bad way,' he said. Now Mike wasn't the kind of guy to just sit around when a friend was in trouble, so he grabbed a pony-can and threw it in the direction of Saturn, then he climbed in real quick before it got away, and it carried him off to Titan as neat as you please."

Javon was gaping like a trout now, and Kellie was giving Ray an I-hope-you-know-what-you're-doing look. But Jan got it.

"When he got there," Ray continued, "his friend said, 'Thank goodness you're here, Mike; we've got plenty of atmosphere here, but there's nothing to eat and we're plumb miserable.' Well, there's nothing that matters more to an old space-hog like Mike than a good hot meal. He snagged a nickel-iron asteroid that happened to be drifting by, and he took his trusty ore hammer and he pounded it into a skillet—eighteen meters across and with a handle twenty-two meters long. Then he pulled out his hand thruster, which was ten meters wide and pushed a million and three centigees, and headed off to look for something to put in that skillet.

"He looked at Iapetus, but there wasn't anything there but ice. And he looked at Dione, but there wasn't anything there but rocks. He looked at every one of Saturn's moons and moonlets, but there wasn't anything there to eat at all. So he dug in his heels to kill his orbital velocity, dropped right down to Saturn himself, and took a big bite out of the old man's atmosphere. But it was cold and smelly, and none too filling besides, so he just spat it out."

At that Ms. Itsui actually smiled. Ray kept going.

"But there was one more place he hadn't tried, and that was the rings. Now, in those days people thought Saturn's rings were nothing but ice and rocks, but Mike had an idea that might not be the case. So he grabbed the rescue handle on the back of his suit and lifted himself up to the rings. The first ring was nothing but ice; the second one was nothing but rocks. But the third one wasn't ice, or rocks . . . it was all made up of carbo-nubs and jerkie-bits and other tasty things. He pulled out his skillet and filled it up, then took it back to Titan and cooked it up over one of the volcanoes there, and the people ate it all up and asked for seconds. So he went back and got another skillet-full, and then another and another. Pretty soon that tasty ring was all gone, and the place it used to be is what we call the Cassini Gap. But Mike was always a little sloppy, and while he was scooping all that stuff out he scattered bits and pieces all over the place. So people have been extracting carbohydrates from Saturn's rings ever since."

There was a long pause then, with Ray and Javon and the twins all waiting for Ms. Itsui to speak. "I can see that this means a lot to you, Mr. Chen," she said at last.

"It means a lot to all of us, Ms. Itsui."

She set her plate aside and pulled out her datapad. "I'd like to take a closer look at some of your numbers."

"Of course."

There was still a lot of work to do. But that was the moment that Ray knew she was hooked.

II. A corporate cubicle in Cocoa, Florida,
April 2041

"Delete. Delete. Delete. Delete."

Tony Ramirez was pruning ideas. His desk was crowded with icons, each one representing an idea he'd invested five minutes or a day or a week on.

None of them were any good. He needed a fresh start.

He paused with his finger on the icon labeled "Embrace Space!"

He was still fond of that slogan—the rhythm and rhyme were compelling, and the text treatment the graphic artists had come up with had a lot of snap. But the client thought it was "too pedestrian."

"Delete." The icon dissolved beneath his fingertip in a puff of pixels.

Damn the client, anyway. Damn all clients everywhere.

Tony stood and stretched. The clock in one corner of his desk read four o'clock . . . one more hour and it would be the weekend. Maybe he should knock off early, get in a little surfing.

He touched a control on his desk and the window blinds rotated, letting in the sun and the view. Just a few miles away, across the Indian River, one of the client's boosters stood idle—a slim white cigar crammed with construction supplies for Virgin LLC's growing Branson Station, pinned to the launchpad by lawsuits over noise.

There was the problem in a nutshell: the thunder of rocket engines had changed from a triumph to an annoyance. Noise lawsuits, problems hiring and retaining qualified people, stagnant stock price—all of these were symptoms of the public image problem that Virgin had hired Tony's firm to solve. If this launch hiatus went on much longer they might pull out of Florida. They might even give up on space altogether.

Tony paced behind his desk, the surf momentarily forgotten. How the heck was he supposed to make space exciting? He'd interviewed dozens of people—space workers as well as the general public—and not one of them thought of it as much more than just another place to work. Sure, there was some danger to it. But driving to work was dangerous right here on Earth.

He scrolled through the interview folder on his desk, looking for inspiration, and paused at the image of an eighty-year-old Anglo who still remembered the California redwoods and the space race with the Russians. "When I was a kid," he'd said, "astronauts were heroes, not people. You only ever saw them in black and white, on teevee or in the papers. These days they're everywhere, in living color. But they're just like all the rest of my neighbors—boring!" And he'd laughed, showing perfect white reconstructed teeth.

Tony had written off that guy at the time as just another disaffected boomer. But now he wondered if people like him might find it easier to get excited about space if it was smaller and further away again—squished down to fit into a tiny black and white teevee screen.

No, that wasn't quite it. But there was something there he could use.

Black and white, yes. Plain. Simplistic. A plain and simple hero. Something people could believe in. Something *real*.

Tony was starting to get excited about this one. "New file." A window opened on his desk, the blinking cursor awaiting his words.

An astronaut, like in the space race? No . . . too old-fashioned, too militaristic for today's audience. It had to be some kind of space worker.

He scrolled back through the interview folder until he found an orbital welder named Sara he'd cornered for an hour in a bar on Merritt Island, and touched Play. "There was this guy called Mike," the welder's image said. "I'll never forget him. We called him Titanium-Belly Mike—he'd drink *anything*."

Tony's lip quirked. That wasn't the right image at all. But the name . . .

And then the whole thing snapped together in his head.

"This is the story of Titanium Mike," he said, and the words appeared silently on the screen. "His father was a shuttle pilot and his mother was a welder. He was born wearing a space suit, and when he was nine days old he built himself a rocket and took off for orbit. Then, when his rocket ran low on fuel, he lassoed a satellite with a length of high-tensile cable and pulled himself up the rest of the way on that. He was so tough that radiation just bounced off him . . ."

It was crazy and nonsensical and childish, and it desperately needed editing, but something about it really resonated. Tony stayed at his desk until well after midnight, the tale growing and embellishing itself as though it were passing through him from somewhere else rather than him making it up.

He mocked it up over the weekend and showed it to his boss first thing Monday morning. They presented it to the client on Thursday and it went national the following month.

Twelve-year-old Ray Chen and millions of other kids took Titanium Mike into their hearts.

Later, they took him with them into space.

I. A bar in Port Canaveral, Florida,
January 2023

Sara Perez rolled her beer bottle around and around in the little sticky puddle on the bar, resting her chin on her fist. She really ought to go back to her room and pack up. Tomorrow was going to be a very long day.

"Well, if it isn't my best girl Sara! Why so glum?"

Sara didn't even have to look up. She'd know that rough, alcohol-soaked voice anywhere. Especially here. "I'm through with space, Mike." The words caught in her throat—it was the first time she'd spoken the truth out loud. "I'm heading home tomorrow."

Mike plopped his gray-stubbled chin down on the bar next to hers. His breath was flammable. "And why would Polara want to get rid of a fine young welder like you?"

"They don't." And then the whole story came pouring out in a rush—how she'd run away from home at fifteen, made her way to Florida, worked her way up from waitress to welder, and now, when she was just about to launch on her first orbital gig, her family had finally tracked her down. "They'll be here tomorrow morning to drag me back to that same safe suburban deep-freeze I escaped from two years ago."

"So don't be here."

Sara raised her head and met Mike's bloodshot eyes with her

own. "No point running again—they've already made sure every cop in Florida knows who I am."

"Hmm." Mike scratched his wiry chin with work-hardened fingers. "I guess you'll just have to go somewhere else, then. Somewhere without cops." He jerked a thumb skyward.

"Yeah, right." She put her forehead on the edge of the bar, stared down into her lap. "Like I can afford that." If she could have held on until next Monday, when her contract started, Polara would have paid her boost fees.

A tapping sound caught her attention. She rolled her head to one side to see what it was.

Mike was tapping a gold-edged transparent card on the bar. When he saw she'd seen it, he let it fall into the beer puddle. "Now you can."

Sara jerked herself upright, snatched up the card. "Where did you get *this*?"

"Let me tell you a little something about myself," Mike said, and suddenly he didn't seem drunk at all. "My father was a bank teller, and my mother was a CPA. Nothing special, but they were good people and they taught me the value of a dollar. I might enjoy a good stiff drink, but I know my limits and I know to pay myself first, and I know that the real value of a dollar is in what you can do with it when a friend's in trouble." He pointed to the card with one grimy finger. "There's enough there to get you on tonight's LEO booster and pay for your air until your contract starts. Now get going."

The card was cold and stiff between her fingers. "I can't possibly pay you back."

"Live well, fly high, and kick ass. That's all the payment I need." He waved her away. "Now shoo."

She shoo'd. But she gave him a big hug first.

DAVID D. LEVINE

"Titanium Mike Saves the Day" is a story about stories—about the power that stories have to change people's lives. It's also a story about how "the street finds its own uses for things," how even a stupid little advertisement can grow into something with real meaning once the common people get ahold of it. It's based on the true story of Paul Bunyan, who may or may not have been invented as an advertisement but was definitely popularized through ads. Thanks to Gordon Van Gelder for insisting on the fifth scene, in which the original Titanium-Belly Mike actually appears onstage.

POL POT'S BEAUTIFUL DAUGHTER
(FANTASY)

GEOFF RYMAN

Geoff Ryman's first novel was a gender-bending sword-and-sorcery novel called *The Warrior Who Carried Life.* His books, short fiction, and an anthology of original SF by Canadians have won fourteen awards. *The Child Garden* won the Arthur C. Clarke Award and the John W. Campbell Memorial Award. *Air* won the Arthur C. Clarke Award, the James Tiptree, Jr. Award, the Sunburst Award, and the British Science Fiction Association Award. His first story about Cambodia, "The Unconquered Country" (1985), won the World Fantasy Award and the BSFA Award. The book version was a finalist for a Nebula. The country continues to feature in his fiction, including his latest novel, *The King's Last Song,* which intertwines a historical fiction about the Angkor Wat era's greatest king with recent Cambodian history.

In Cambodia people are used to ghosts. Ghosts buy newspapers. They own property.

A few years ago, spirits owned a house in Phnom Penh, at the Tra Bek end of Monivong Boulevard. Khmer Rouge had murdered the whole family and there was no one left alive to inherit it. People cycled past the building, leaving it boarded up. Sounds of weeping came from inside.

Then a professional inheritor arrived from America. She'd

done her research and could claim to be the last surviving relative of no fewer than three families. She immediately sold the house to a Chinese businessman, who turned the ground floor into a photocopying shop.

The copiers began to print pictures of the original owners.

At first, single black-and-white photos turned up in the copied dossiers of aid workers or government officials. The father of the murdered family had been a lawyer. He stared fiercely out of the photos as if demanding something. In other photocopies, his beautiful daughters forlornly hugged each other. The background was hazy like fog.

One night the owner heard a noise and trundled downstairs to find all five photocopiers printing one picture after another of faces: young college men, old women, parents with a string of babies, or government soldiers in uniform. He pushed the big green off-buttons. Nothing happened.

He pulled out all the plugs, but the machines kept grinding out face after face. Women in beehive hairdos or clever children with glasses looked wistfully out of the photocopies. They seemed to be dreaming of home in the 1960s, when Phnom Penh was the most beautiful city in Southeast Asia.

News spread. People began to visit the shop to identify lost relatives. Women would cry, "That's my mother! I didn't have a photograph!" They would weep and press the flimsy A4 sheets to their breasts. The paper went limp from tears and humidity as if it too were crying.

Soon, a throng began to gather outside the shop every morning to view the latest batch of faces. In desperation, the owner announced that each morning's harvest would be delivered direct to *The Truth,* a magazine of remembrance.

Then one morning he tried to open the house-door to the shop and found it blocked. He went 'round to the front of the building and rolled open the metal shutters.

The shop was packed from floor to ceiling with photocopies. The ground floor had no windows—the room had been filled from the inside. The owner pulled out a sheet of paper and saw himself on the ground, his head beaten in by a hoe. The same image was on every single page.

He buried the photocopiers and sold the house at once. The new owner liked its haunted reputation; it kept people away. The FOR SALE sign was left hanging from the second floor.

In a sense, the house had been bought by another ghost.

This is a completely untrue story about someone who must exist.

Pol Pot's only child, a daughter, was born in 1986. Her name was Sith, and in 2004, she was eighteen years old.

Sith liked air conditioning and luxury automobiles. Her hair was dressed in cornrows and she had a spiky piercing above one eye. Her jeans were elaborately slashed and embroidered. Her pink T-shirts bore slogans in English: CARE KOOKY. PINK MOLL.

Sith lived like a woman on Thai television, doing as she pleased in lip-gloss and Sunsilked hair. Nine simple rules helped her avoid all unpleasantness.

1. Never think about the past or politics.

2. Ignore ghosts. They cannot hurt you.

3. Do not go to school. Hire tutors. Don't do homework. It is disturbing.

4. Always be driven everywhere in either the Mercedes or the BMW.

5. Avoid all well-dressed Cambodian boys. They are the sons of the estimated 250,000 new generals created by the regime. Their sons can behave with impunity.

6. Avoid all men with potbellies. They eat too well and therefore must be corrupt.

7. Avoid anyone who drives a Toyota Viva or Honda Dream motorcycle.

8. Don't answer letters or phone calls.

9. Never make any friends.

There was also a tenth rule, but that went without saying.

Rotten fruit rinds and black mud never stained Sith's designer sports shoes. Disabled beggars never asked her for alms. Her life began yesterday, which was effectively the same as today.

Every day, her driver took her to the new Soriya Market. It was almost the only place that Sith went. The color of silver, Soriya rose up in many floors to a round glass dome.

Sith preferred the 142nd Street entrance. Its green awning made everyone look as if they were made of jade. The doorway went directly into the ice-cold jewelry rotunda with its floor of polished black and white stone. The individual stalls were hung with glittering necklaces and earrings.

Sith liked tiny shiny things that had no memory. She hated politics. She refused to listen to the news. Pol Pot's beautiful daughter wished the current leadership would behave decently, like her dad always did. To her.

She remembered the sound of her father's gentle voice. She remembered sitting on his lap in a forest enclosure, being bitten by mosquitoes. Memories of malaria had sunk into her very bones. She now associated forests with nausea, fevers, and pain. A flicker of tree-shade on her skin made her want to throw up and the odor of soil or fallen leaves made her gag. She had never been to Angkor Wat. She read nothing.

Sith shopped. Her driver was paid by the government and always carried an AK-47, but his wife, the housekeeper, had no idea who Sith was. The house was full of swept marble, polished teak furniture, iPods, Xboxes, and plasma screens.

Please remember that every word of this story is a lie. Pol Pot was no doubt a dedicated communist who made no money from ruling Cambodia. Nevertheless, a hefty allowance arrived for Sith every month from an account in Switzerland.

Nothing touched Sith, until she fell in love with the salesman at Hello Phones.

Cambodian readers may know that in 2004 there was no mobile phone shop in Soriya Market. However, there was a branch of Hello Phone Cards that had a round blue sales counter with orange trim. This shop looked like that.

Every day Sith bought or exchanged a mobile phone there. She would sit and flick her hair at the salesman.

His name was Dara, which means Star. Dara knew about deals on call prices, sim cards, and the new phones that showed videos. He could get her any call tone she liked.

Talking to Dara broke none of Sith's rules. He wasn't fat, nor was he well dressed, and far from being a teenager, he was a comfortably mature twenty-four years old.

One day, Dara chuckled and said, "As a friend I advise you, you don't need another mobile phone."

Sith wrinkled her nose. "I don't like this one anymore. It's blue. I want something more feminine. But not frilly. And it should have better sound quality."

"Okay, but you could save your money and buy some more nice clothes."

Pol Pot's beautiful daughter lowered her chin, which she knew made her neck look long and graceful. "Do you like my clothes?"

"Why ask me?"

She shrugged. "I don't know. It's good to check out your look."

Dara nodded. "You look cool. What does your sister say?"

Sith let him know she had no family. "Ah," he said and quickly changed the subject. That was terrific. Secrecy and sympathy in one easy movement.

Sith came back the next day and said that she'd decided that the rose-colored phone was too feminine. Dara laughed aloud and his eyes sparkled. Sith had come late in the morning just so that he could ask this question. "Are you hungry? Do you want to meet for lunch?"

Would he think she was cheap if she said yes? Would he say she was snobby if she said no?

"Just so long as we eat in Soriya Market," she said.

She was torn between BBWorld Burgers and Lucky7. BBWorld was big, round, and just two floors down from the dome. Lucky7 Burgers was part of the Lucky Supermarket, such a good store that a tiny jar of Maxwell House cost US$2.40.

They decided on BBWorld. It was full of light and they could see the town spread out through the wide clean windows. Sith sat in silence.

Pol Pot's daughter had nothing to say unless she was buying something.

Or rather she had only one thing to say, but she must never say it.

Dara did all the talking. He talked about how the guys on the third floor could get him a deal on original copies of *Grand Theft Auto*. He hinted that he could get Sith discounts from Bsfashion, the spotlit modern shop one floor down.

Suddenly he stopped. "You don't need to be afraid of me, you know." He said it in a kindly, grown-up voice. "I can see, you're a properly brought-up girl. I like that. It's nice."

Sith still couldn't find anything to say. She could only nod. She wanted to run away.

"Would you like to go to K-Four?"

K-Four, the big electronics shop, stocked all the reliable brand names: Hitachi, Sony, Panasonic, Philips, or Denon. It was so expensive that almost nobody shopped there, which is why Sith liked it. A crowd of people stood outside and stared through the window at a huge home entertainment center showing a DVD of *Ice Age*. On the screen, a little animal was being chased by a glacier. It was so beautiful!

Sith finally found something to say. "If I had one of those, I would never need to leave the house."

Dara looked at her sideways and decided to laugh.

The next day Sith told him that all the phones she had were too big. Did he have one that she could wear around her neck like jewelry?

This time they went to Lucky7 Burgers, and sat across from

the Revlon counter. They watched boys having their hair layered by Revlon's natural beauty specialists.

Dara told her more about himself. His father had died in the wars. His family now lived in the country. Sith's Coca-Cola suddenly tasted of antimalarial drugs.

"But . . . you don't want to *live* in the country," she said.

"No. I have to live in Phnom Penh to make money. But my folks are good country people. Modest." He smiled, embarrassed.

They'll have hens and a cousin who shimmies up coconut trees. There will be trees all around but no shops anywhere. The earth will smell.

Sith couldn't finish her drink. She sighed and smiled and said abruptly, "I'm sorry. It's been cool. But I have to go." She slunk sideways out of her seat as slowly as molasses.

Walking back into the jewelry rotunda with nothing to do, she realized that Dara would think she didn't like him.

And that made the lower part of her eyes sting.

She went back the next day and didn't even pretend to buy a mobile phone. She told Dara that she'd left so suddenly the day before because she'd remembered a hair appointment.

He said that he could see she took a lot of trouble with her hair. Then he asked her out for a movie that night.

Sith spent all day shopping in K-Four.

They met at six. Dara was so considerate that he didn't even suggest the horror movie. He said he wanted to see *Buffalo Girl Hiding,* a movie about a country girl who lives on a farm. Sith said with great feeling that she would prefer the horror movie.

The cinema on the top floor opened out directly onto the roof of Soriya. Graffiti had been scratched into the green railings. Why would people want to ruin something new and beautiful? Sith put her arm through Dara's and knew that they were now boyfriend and girlfriend.

"Finally," he said.

"Finally what?"

"You've done something."

They leaned on the railings and looked out over other people's apartments. West toward the river was a building with one huge roof terrace. Women met there to gossip. Children were playing toss-the-sandal. From this distance, Sith was enchanted.

"I just love watching the children."

The movie, from Thailand, was about a woman whose face turns blue and spotty and who eats men. The blue woman was yucky, but not as scary as all the badly dubbed voices. The characters sounded possessed. It was as though Thai people had been taken over by the spirits of dead Cambodians.

Whenever Sith got scared, she chuckled.

So she sat chuckling with terror. Dara thought she was laughing at a dumb movie and found such intelligence charming. He started to chuckle too. Sith thought he was as frightened as she was. Together in the dark, they took each other's hands.

Outside afterward, the air hung hot even in the dark and 142nd Street smelled of drains. Sith stood on tiptoe to avoid the oily deposits and cast-off fishbones.

Dara said, "I will drive you home."

"My driver can take us," said Sith, flipping open her Kermit-the-Frog mobile.

Her black Mercedes Benz edged to a halt, crunching old plastic bottles in the gutter. The seats were upholstered with tan leather and the driver was armed.

Dara's jaw dropped. "Who . . . *who* is your father?"

"He's dead."

Dara shook his head. "Who was he?"

Normally Sith used her mother's family name, but that would not answer this question. Flustered, she tried to think of someone who could be her father. She knew of nobody the right age. She remembered something about a politician who had died. His name came to her and she said it in panic. "My father was Kol Vireakboth." Had she got the name right? "Please don't tell anyone."

Dara covered his eyes. "We—my family, my father—we fought for the KPLA."

Sith had to stop herself asking what the KPLA was.

Kol Vireakboth had led a faction in the civil wars. It fought against the Khmer Rouge, the Vietnamese, the King, and corruption. It wanted a new way for Cambodia. Kol Vireakboth was a Cambodian leader who had never told a lie or accepted a bribe.

Remember that this is an untrue story.

Dara started to back away from the car. "I don't think we should be doing this. I'm just a villager, really."

"That doesn't matter."

His eyes closed. "I would expect nothing less from the daughter of Kol Vireakboth."

Oh for gosh sake, she just picked the man's name out of the air, she didn't need more problems. "Please!" she said.

Dara sighed. "Okay. I said I would see you home safely. I will." Inside the Mercedes, he stroked the tan leather.

When they arrived, he craned his neck to look up at the building. "Which floor are you on?"

"All of them."

Color drained from his face.

"My driver will take you back," she said to Dara. As the car pulled away, she stood outside the closed garage shutters, waving forlornly.

Then Sith panicked. Who was Kol Vireakboth? She went online and Googled. She had to read about the wars. Her skin started to creep. All those different factions swam in her head: ANS, NADK, KPR, and KPNLF. The very names seemed to come at her spoken by forgotten voices.

Soon she had all she could stand. She printed out Vireakboth's picture and decided to have it framed. In case Dara visited.

Kol Vireakboth had a round face and a fatherly smile. His eyes seemed to slant upward toward his nose, looking full of kindly insight. He'd been killed by a car bomb.

All that night, Sith heard whispering.

In the morning, there was another picture of someone else in the tray of her printer.

A long-faced, buck-toothed woman stared out at her in black and white. Sith noted the victim's fashion lapses. The woman's hair was a mess, all frizzy. She should have had it straightened and put in some nice highlights. The woman's eyes drilled into her.

"Can't touch me," said Sith. She left the photo in the tray. She went to see Dara, right away, no breakfast.

His eyes were circled with dark flesh and his blue Hello trousers and shirt were not properly ironed.

"Buy the whole shop," Dara said, looking deranged. "The guys in K-Four just told me some girl in blue jeans walked in yesterday and bought two home theatres. One for the salon, she said, and one for the roof terrace. She paid for both of them in full and had them delivered to the far end of Monivong."

Sith sighed. "I'm sending one back." She hoped that sounded abstemious. "It looked too metallic against my curtains."

Pause.

"She also bought an Aido robot dog for fifteen hundred dollars."

Sith would have preferred that Dara did not know about the dog. It was just a silly toy; it hadn't occurred to her that it might cost that much until she saw the bill. "They should not tell everyone about their customers' business or soon they will have no customers."

Dara was looking at her as if thinking: *This is not just a nice sweet girl.*

"I had fun last night," Sith said in a voice as thin as high clouds.

"So did I."

"We don't have to tell anyone about my family. Do we?" Sith was seriously scared of losing him.

"No. But Sith, it's stupid. Your family, my family, we are not equals."

"It doesn't make any difference."

"You lied to me. Your family is not dead. You have famous uncles."

She did indeed—Uncle Ieng Sary, Uncle Khieu Samphan, Uncle Ta Mok. All the Pol Pot clique had been called her uncles.

"I didn't know them that well," she said. That was true, too.

What would she do if she couldn't shop in Soriya Market anymore? What would she do without Dara?

She begged. "I am not a strong person. Sometimes I think I am not a person at all. I'm just a space."

Dara looked suddenly mean. "You're just a credit card." Then his face fell. "I'm sorry. That was an unkind thing to say. You are very young for your age and I'm older than you and I should have treated you with more care."

Sith was desperate. "All my money would be very nice."

"I'm not for sale."

He worked in a shop and would be sending money home to a fatherless family; of course he was for sale!

Sith had a small heart, but a big head for thinking. She knew that she had to do this delicately, like picking a flower, or she would spoil the bloom. "Let's . . . let's just go see a movie?"

After all, she was beautiful and well brought up and she knew her eyes were big and round. Her tiny heart was aching.

This time they saw *Tum Teav*, a remake of an old movie from the 1960s. If movies were not nightmares about ghosts, then they tried to preserve the past. *When*, thought Sith, *will they make a movie about Cambodia's future? Tum Teav* was based on a classic tale of a young monk who falls in love with a properly brought-up girl but her mother opposes the match. They commit suicide at the end, bringing a curse on their village. Sith sat through it stony-faced. *I am not going to be a dead heroine in a romance.*

Dara offered to drive her home again and that's when Sith found out that he drove a Honda Dream. He proudly presented to her the gleaming motorcycle of fast young men. Sith felt backed into a corner. She'd already offered to buy him. Showing off her car again might humiliate him.

So she broke rule number seven.

Dara hid her bag in the back and they went soaring down Monivong Boulevard at night, past homeless people, prostitutes, and chefs staggering home after work. It was late in the year, but it started to rain.

Sith loved it, the cool air brushing against her face, the cooler rain clinging to her eyelashes.

She remembered being five years old in the forest and dancing in the monsoon. She encircled Dara's waist to stay on the bike and suddenly found her cheek was pressed up against his back. She giggled in fear, not of the rain, but of what she felt.

He dropped her off at home. Inside, everything was dark except for the flickering green light on her printer. In the tray were two new photographs. One was of a child, a little boy, holding up a school prize certificate. The other was a tough, wise-looking old man, with a string of muscle down either side of his ironic, bitter smile. They looked directly at her.

They know who I am.

As she climbed the stairs to her bedroom, she heard someone sobbing, far away, as if the sound came from next door. She touched the walls of the staircase. They shivered slightly, constricting in time to the cries.

In her bedroom she extracted one of her many iPods from the tangle of wires and listened to *System of a Down,* as loud as she could. It helped her sleep. The sound of nu-metal guitars seemed to come roaring out of her own heart.

She was woken up in the sun-drenched morning by the sound of her doorbell many floors down. She heard the housekeeper Jorani call and the door open. Sith hesitated over choice of jeans and top. By the time she got downstairs she found the driver and the housemaid joking with Dara, giving him tea.

Like the sunshine, Dara seemed to disperse ghosts.

"Hi," he said. "It's my day off. I thought we could go on a motorcycle ride to the country."

But not to the country. Couldn't they just spend the day in

Soriya? No, said Dara, there's lots of other places to see in Phnom Penh.

He drove her, twisting through back streets. How did the city get so poor? How did it get so dirty?

They went to a new and modern shop for CDs that was run by a record label. Dara knew all the cool new music, most of it influenced by Khmer-Americans returning from Long Beach and Compton: Sdey, Phnom Penh Bad Boys, Khmer Kid.

Sith bought twenty CDs.

They went to the National Museum and saw the beautiful Buddha-like head of King Jayavarman VII. Dara without thinking ducked and held up his hands in prayer. They had dinner in a French restaurant with candles and wine, and it was just like in a karaoke video, a boy, a girl, and her money all going out together. They saw the show at Sovanna Phum, and there was a wonderful dance piece with sampled 1940s music from an old French movie, with traditional Khmer choreography.

Sith went home, her heart singing, *Dara, Dara, Dara.*

In the bedroom, a mobile phone began to ring, over and over. *Call 1* said the screen, but gave no name or number, so the person was not on Sith's list of contacts.

She turned off the phone. It kept ringing. That's when she knew for certain.

She hid the phone in a pillow in the spare bedroom and put another pillow on top of it and then closed the door.

All forty-two of her mobile phones started to ring. They rang from inside closets, or from the bathroom where she had forgotten them. They rang from the roof terrace and even from inside a shoe under her bed.

"I am a very stubborn girl!" she shouted at the spirits. "You do not scare me."

She turned up her iPod and finally slept.

As soon as the sun was up, she roused her driver, slumped deep in his hammock.

"Come on, we're going to Soriya Market," she said.

The driver looked up at her dazed, then remembered to smile and lower his head in respect.

His face fell when she showed up in the garage with all forty-two of her mobile phones in one black bag.

It was too early for Soriya Market to open. They drove in circles with sunrise blazing directly into their eyes. On the streets, men pushed carts like beasts of burden, or carried cascades of belts into the old Central Market. The old market was domed, art deco, the color of vomit, French. Sith never shopped there.

"Maybe you should go visit your mom," said the driver. "You know, she loves you. Families are there for when you are in trouble."

Sith's mother lived in Thailand and they never spoke. Her mother's family kept asking for favors: money, introductions, or help with getting a job. Sith didn't speak to them any longer.

"My family is only trouble."

The driver shut up and drove.

Finally Soriya opened. Sith went straight to Dara's shop and dumped all the phones on the blue countertop. "Can you take these back?"

"We only do exchanges. I can give a new phone for an old one." Dara looked thoughtful. "Don't worry. Leave them here with me, I'll go sell them to a guy in the old market, and give you your money tomorrow." He smiled in approval. "This is very sensible."

He passed one phone back, the one with video and e-mail. "This is the best one, keep this."

Dara was so competent. Sith wanted to sink down onto him like a pillow and stay there. She sat in the shop all day, watching him work. One of the guys from the games shop upstairs asked, "Who is this beautiful girl?"

Dara answered proudly, "My girlfriend."

Dara drove her back on the Dream and at the door to her house, he chuckled. "I don't want to go." She pressed a finger against his naughty lips, and smiled and spun back inside from happiness.

She was in the ground-floor garage. She heard something like a rat scuttle. In her bag, the telephone rang. Who were these people to importune her, even if they were dead? She wrenched the mobile phone out of her bag and pushed the green button and put the phone to her ear. She waited. There was a sound like wind.

A child spoke to her, his voice clogged as if he was crying. "They tied my thumbs together."

Sith demanded. "How did you get my number?"

"I'm all alone!"

"Then ring somebody else. Someone in your family."

"All my family are dead. I don't know where I am. My name is . . ."

Sith clicked the phone off. She opened the trunk of the car and tossed the phone inside it. Being telephoned by ghosts was so . . . *unmodern*. How could Cambodia become a number one country if its cell phone network was haunted?

She stormed up into the salon. On top of a table, the $1,500, no-mess dog stared at her from out of his packaging. Sith clumped up the stairs onto the roof terrace to sleep as far away as she could from everything in the house.

She woke up in the dark, to hear thumping from downstairs.

The sound was metallic and hollow, as if someone were locked in the car. Sith turned on her iPod. Something was making the sound of the music skip. She fought the tangle of wires, and wrenched out another player, a Xen, but it too skipped, burping the sound of speaking voices into the middle of the music.

Had she heard a ripping sound? She pulled out the earphones, and heard something climbing the stairs.

A sound of light, uneven lolloping. She thought of crippled children. Frost settled over her like a heavy blanket and she could not move.

The robot dog came whirring up onto the terrace. It paused at the top of the stairs, its camera nose pointing at her to see, its useless eyes glowing cherry red.

The robot dog said in a warm, friendly voice, "My name is Phalla. I tried to buy my sister medicine and they killed me for it."

Sith tried to say, "Go away," but her throat wouldn't open.

The dog tilted its head. "No one even knows I'm dead. What will you do for all the people who are not mourned?"

Laughter blurted out of her, and Sith saw it rise up as cold vapor into the air.

"We have no one to invite us to the feast," said the dog.

Sith giggled in terror. "Nothing. I can do nothing!" she said, shaking her head.

"You laugh?" The dog gathered itself and jumped up into the hammock with her. It turned and lifted up its clear plastic tail and laid a genuine turd alongside Sith. Short brown hair was wound up in it, a scalp actually, and a single flat white human tooth smiled out of it.

Sith squawked and overturned both herself and the dog out of the hammock and onto the floor. The dog pushed its nose up against hers and began to sing an old-fashioned children's song about birds.

Something heavy huffed its way up the stairwell toward her. Sith shivered with cold on the floor and could not move. The dog went on singing in a high, sweet voice. A large shadow loomed out over the top of the staircase, and Sith gargled, swallowing laughter, trying to speak.

"There was thumping in the car and no one in it," said the driver.

Sith sagged toward the floor with relief. "The ghosts," she said. "They're back." She thrust herself to her feet. "We're getting out now. Ring the Hilton. Find out if they have rooms."

She kicked the toy dog down the stairs ahead of her. "We're moving now!"

Together they all loaded the car, shaking. Once again, the house was left to ghosts. As they drove, the mobile phone rang over and over inside the trunk.

The new Hilton (which does not exist) rose up by the river across from the Department for Cults and Religious Affairs. Tall and marbled and pristine, it had crystal chandeliers and fountains, and wood and brass handles in the elevators.

In the middle of the night only the Bridal Suite was still available, but it had an extra parental chamber where the driver and his wife could sleep. High on the twenty-first floor, the night sparkled with lights and everything was hushed, as far away from Cambodia as it was possible to get.

Things were quiet after that, for a while.

Every day she and Dara went to movies, or went to a restaurant. They went shopping. She slipped him money and he bought himself a beautiful suit. He said, over a hamburger at Lucky7, "I've told my mother that I've met a girl."

Sith smiled and thought: and I bet you told her that I'm rich.

"I've decided to live in the Hilton," she told him.

Maybe we could live in the Hilton. A pretty smile could hint at that.

The rainy season ended. The last of the monsoons rose up dark gray with a froth of white cloud on top, looking exactly like a giant wave about to break.

Dry cooler air arrived.

After work was over Dara convinced her to go for a walk along the river in front of the Royal Palace. He went to the men's room to change into a new luxury suit and Sith thought: he's beginning to imagine life with all that money.

As they walked along the river, exposed to all those people, Sith shook inside. There were teenage boys everywhere. Some of them were in rags, which was reassuring, but some of them were very well dressed indeed, the sons of Impunity who could do anything. Sith swerved suddenly to avoid even seeing them. But Dara in his new beige suit looked like one of them, and the generals' sons nodded to him with quizzical eyebrows, perhaps wondering who he was.

In front of the palace, a pavilion reached out over the water. Next to it a traditional orchestra bashed and wailed out something old-fashioned. Hundreds of people crowded around a tiny wat. Dara shook Sith's wrist and they stood up to see.

People held up bundles of lotus flowers and incense in prayer. They threw the bundles into the wat. Monks immediately shoveled the joss sticks and flowers out of the back.

Behind the wat, children wearing T-shirts and shorts black with filth rooted through the dead flowers, the smoldering incense, and old coconut shells.

Sith asked, "Why do they do that?"

"You are so innocent!" chuckled Dara and shook his head. The evening was blue and gold. Sith had time to think that she did not want to go back to a hotel and that the only place she really felt happy was next to Dara. All around that thought was something dark and tangled.

Dara suggested with affection that they should get married.

It was as if Sith had her answer ready. "No, absolutely not," she said at once. "How can you ask that? There is not even anyone for you to ask! Have you spoken to your family about me? Has your family made any checks about my background?"

Which was what she really wanted to know.

Dara shook his head. "I have explained that you are an orphan, but they are not concerned with that. We are modest people. They will be happy if I am happy."

"Of course they won't be! Of course they will need to do checks."

Sith scowled. She saw her way to sudden advantage. "At least they must consult fortunetellers. They are not fools. I can help them. Ask them the names of the fortunetellers they trust."

Dara smiled shyly. "We have no money."

"I will give them money and you can tell them that you pay."
Dara's eyes searched her face. "I don't want that."

"How will we know if it is a good marriage? And your poor mother, how can you ask her to make a decision like this without information? So. You ask your family for the names of good professionals they trust, and I will pay them, and I will go to Prime Minister Hun Sen's own personal fortuneteller, and we can compare results."

Thus she established again both her propriety and her status.

In an old romance, the parents would not approve of the match and the fortuneteller would say that the marriage was ill-omened. Sith left nothing to romance.

She offered the family's fortunetellers whatever they wanted—a car, a farm—and in return demanded a written copy of their judgment. All of them agreed that the portents for the marriage were especially auspicious.

Then she secured an appointment with the Prime Minister's fortuneteller.

Hun Sen's *Kru Taey* was a lady in a black business suit. She had long fingernails like talons, but they were perfectly manicured and frosted white.

She was the kind of fortuneteller who is possessed by someone else's spirit. She sat at a desk and looked at Sith as unblinking as a fish, both her hands steepled together. After the most basic of hellos, she said, "Dollars only. Twenty-five thousand. I need to buy my son an apartment."

"That's a very high fee," said Sith.

"It's not a fee. It is a consideration for giving you the answer you want. My fee is another twenty-five thousand dollars."

They negotiated. Sith liked the Kru Taey's manner. It confirmed everything Sith believed about life.

The fee was reduced somewhat but not the consideration.

"Payment upfront now," the Kru Taey said. She wouldn't take a check. Like only the very best restaurants she accepted foreign credit cards. Sith's Swiss card worked immediately. It had unlimited credit in case she had to leave the country in a hurry.

The Kru Taey said, "I will tell the boy's family that the marriage will be particularly fortunate."

Sith realized that she had not yet said anything about a boy, his family, or a marriage.

The Kru Taey smiled. "I know you are not interested in your real fortune. But to be kind, I will tell you unpaid that this marriage really is particularly well favored. All the other fortunetellers would have said the same thing without being bribed."

The Kru Taey's eyes glinted in the most unpleasant way. "So you needn't have bought them farms or paid me an extra twenty-five thousand dollars."

She looked down at her perfect fingernails. "You will be very happy indeed. But not before your entire life is overturned."

The back of Sith's arms prickled as if from cold. She should have been angry but she could feel herself smiling. Why?

And why waste politeness on the old witch? Sith turned to go without saying good-bye.

"Oh, and about your other problem," said the woman.

Sith turned back and waited.

"Enemies," said the Kru Taey, "can turn out to be friends."

Sith sighed. "What are you talking about?"

The Kru Taey's smile was as wide as a tiger-trap. "The million people your father killed."

Sith went hard. "Not a million," she said. "Somewhere between two hundred and fifty and five hundred thousand."

"Enough," smiled the Kru Taey. "My father was one of them." She smiled for a moment longer. "I will be sure to tell the Prime Minister that you visited me."

Sith snorted as if in scorn. "I will tell him myself."

But she ran back to her car.

That night, Sith looked down on all the lights like diamonds. She settled onto the giant mattress and turned on her iPod.

Someone started to yell at her. She pulled out the earpieces and jumped to the window. It wouldn't open. She shook it and wrenched its frame until it reluctantly slid an inch and she threw the iPod out of the twenty-first-floor window.

She woke up late the next morning, to hear the sound of the TV. She opened up the double doors into the salon and saw Jorani, pressed against the wall.

"The TV . . . ," Jorani said, her eyes wide with terror.

The driver waited by his packed bags. He stood up, looking as mournful as a bloodhound.

On the widescreen TV there was what looked like a pop music karaoke video. Except that the music was very old-fashioned. Why would a pop video show a starving man eating raw maize in a field? He glanced over his shoulder in terror as he ate. The glowing singalong words were the song that the dog had sung at the top of the stairs. The starving man looked up at Sith and corn mash rolled out of his mouth.

"It's all like that," said the driver. "I unplugged the set, but it kept playing on every channel." He sompiahed but looked miserable. "My wife wants to leave."

Sith felt shame. It was miserable and dirty, being infested with ghosts. Of course they would want to go.

"It's okay. I can take taxis," she said.

The driver nodded, and went into the next room and whispered to his wife. With little scurrying sounds, they gathered up their things. They sompiahed, and apologized.

The door clicked almost silently behind them.

It will always be like this, thought Sith. Wherever I go. It would be like this with Dara.

The hotel telephone started to ring. Sith left it ringing. She covered the TV with a blanket, but the terrible, tinny old music kept wheedling and rattling its way out at her, and she sat on the edge of her bed, staring into space.

I'll have to leave Cambodia.

At the market, Dara looked even more cheerful than usual. The fortunetellers had pronounced the marriage as very favorable. His mother had invited Sith home for the Pchum Ben festival.

"We can take the bus tomorrow," he said.

"Does it smell? All those people in one place?"

"It smells of air freshener. Then we take a taxi, and then you will have to walk up the track." Dara suddenly doubled up in laughter. "Oh, it will be good for you."

"Will there be dirt?"

"Everywhere! Oh, your dirty Nikes will earn you much merit!"

But at least, thought Sith, there will be no TV or phones.

Two days later, Sith was walking down a dirt track, ducking tree branches. Dust billowed all over her shoes. Dara walked behind her, chuckling, which meant she thought he was scared too.

She heard a strange rattling sound. "What's that noise?"

"It's a goat," he said. "My mother bought it for me in April as a present."

A goat. How could they be any more rural? Sith had never seen a goat. She never even imagined that she would.

Dara explained. "I sell them to the Muslims. It is Agricultural Diversification."

There were trees everywhere, shadows crawling across the ground like snakes. Sith felt sick. *One mosquito,* she promised herself, *just one and I will squeal and run away.*

The house was tiny, on thin twisting stilts. She had pictured a big fine country house standing high over the ground on concrete pillars with a sunburst carving in the gable. The kitchen was a hut that sat directly on the ground, no stilts, and it was made of palm-leaf panels and there was no electricity. The strip light in the ceiling was attached to a car battery and they kept a live fire on top of the concrete table to cook. Everything smelled of burnt fish.

Sith loved it.

Inside the hut, the smoke from the fires kept the mosquitoes away. Dara's mother, Mrs. Non Kunthea, greeted her with a smile. That triggered a respectful sompiah from Sith, the prayer-like gesture leaping out of her unbidden. On the platform table was a plastic sack full of dried prawns.

Without thinking, Sith sat on the table and began to pull the salty prawns out of their shells.

Why am I doing this!

Because it's what I did at home.

Sith suddenly remembered the enclosure in the forest, a circular fenced area. Daddy had slept in one house, and the women in another. Sith would talk to the cooks. For something to do, she would chop vegetables or shell prawns. Then Daddy would come to eat and he'd sit on the platform table and she, little Sith, would sit between his knees.

Dara's older brother Yuth came back for lunch. He was pot-bellied and drove a taxi for a living, and he moved in hard jabs like an angry old man. He reached too far for the rice and Sith could smell his armpits.

"You see how we live," Yuth said to Sith. "This is what we get for having the wrong patron. Sihanouk thought we were anti-monarchist. To Hun Sen, we were the enemy. Remember the Work for Money program?"

No.

"They didn't give any of those jobs to us. We might as well have been the Khmer Rouge!"

The past, thought Sith, *why don't they just let it go? Why do they keep boasting about their old wars?*

Mrs. Non Kunthea chuckled with affection. "My eldest son was born angry," she said. "His slogan is 'ten years is not too late for revenge.'"

Yuth started up again. "They treat that old monster Pol Pot better than they treat us. But then, he was an important person. If you go to his stupa in Anlong Veng, you will see that people leave offerings! They ask him for lottery numbers!"

He crumpled his green, soft, old-fashioned hat back onto his head and said, "Nice to meet you, Sith. Dara, she's too high class for the likes of you." But he grinned as he said it. He left, swirling disruption in his wake.

The dishes were gathered. Again without thinking, Sith swept up the plastic tub and carried it to the blackened branches. They rested over puddles where the washing-up water drained.

"You shouldn't work," said Dara's mother. "You are a guest."

"I grew up in a refugee camp," said Sith. After all, it was true.

Dara looked at her with a mix of love, pride, and gratitude for the good fortune of a rich wife who works.

And that was the best Sith could hope for. This family would be fine for her.

In the late afternoon, all four brothers came with their wives for the end of Pchum Ben, when the ghosts of the dead can wander the Earth. People scatter rice on the temple floors to feed their families. Some ghosts have small mouths so special rice is used.

Sith never took part in Pchum Ben. How could she go to the temple and scatter rice for Pol Pot?

The family settled in the kitchen chatting and joking, and it all passed in a blur for Sith. Everyone else had family they could honor. To Sith's surprise one of the uncles suggested that people should write names of the deceased and burn them, to transfer merit. It was nothing to do with Pchum Ben, but a lovely idea, so all the family wrote down names.

Sith sat with her hands jammed under her arms.

Dara's mother asked, "Isn't there a name you want to write, Sith?"

"No," said Sith in a tiny voice. How could she write the name Pol Pot? He was surely roaming the world let loose from hell. "There is no one."

Dara rubbed her hand. "Yes, there is, Sith. A very special name."

"No, there's not."

Dara thought she didn't want them to know her father was Kol Vireakboth. He leant forward and whispered. "I promise. No one will see it."

Sith's breath shook. She took the paper and started to cry.

"Oh," said Dara's mother, stricken with sympathy. "Everyone in this country has a tragedy."

Sith wrote the name Kol Vireakboth.

Dara kept the paper folded and caught Sith's eyes. *You see?* he seemed to say. *I have kept your secret safe.* The paper burned.

Thunder slapped a clear sky about the face. It had been sunny, but now as suddenly as a curtain dropped down over a doorway, rain fell. A wind came from nowhere, tearing away a flap of palm-leaf wall, as if forcing entrance in a fury.

The family whooped and laughed and let the rain drench their shoulders as they stood up to push the wall back down, to keep out the rain.

But Sith knew. Her father's enemy was in the kitchen.

The rain passed; the sun came out. The family chuckled and sat back down around or on the table. They lowered dishes of food and ate, making parcels of rice and fish with their fingers. Sith sat rigidly erect, waiting for misfortune.

What would the spirit of Kol Vireakboth do to Pol Pot's daughter? Would he overturn the table, soiling her with food? Would he send mosquitoes to bite and make her sick? Would he suck away all her good fortune, leaving the marriage blighted, her new family estranged?

Or would a kindly spirit simply wish that the children of all Cambodians could escape, escape the past?

Suddenly, Sith felt at peace. The sunlight and shadows looked new to her and her senses started to work in magic ways.

She smelled a perfume of emotion, sweet and bracing at the same time. The music from a neighbor's cassette player touched her arm gently. Words took the form of sunlight on her skin.

No one is evil, the sunlight said. *But they can be false.*

False, how? Sith asked without speaking, genuinely baffled.

The sunlight smiled with an old man's stained teeth. *You know very well how.*

All the air swelled with the scent of the food, savoring it. The trees sighed with satisfaction.

Life is true. Sith saw steam from the rice curl up into the branches. *Death is false.*

The sunlight stood up to go. It whispered. *Tell him.*

The world faded back to its old self.

That night in a hammock in a room with the other women, Sith suddenly sat bolt upright. Clarity would not let her sleep. She saw that there was no way ahead. She couldn't marry Dara. How could she ask him to marry someone who was harassed by one million dead? How could she explain I am haunted because I am Pol Pot's daughter and I have lied about everything?

The dead would not let her marry; the dead would not let her have joy. So who could Pol Pot's daughter pray to? Where could she go for wisdom?

Loak kru Kol Vireakboth, she said under her breath. *Please show me a way ahead.*

The darkness was sterner than the sunlight.

To be as false as you are, it said, *you first have to lie to yourself.*

What lies had Sith told? She knew the facts. Her father had been the head of a government that tortured and killed hundreds of thousands of people and starved the nation through mismanagement. I know the truth.

I just never think about it.

I've never faced it.

Well, the truth is as dark as I am, and you live in me, the darkness.

She had read books—well, the first chapter of books—and then dropped them as if her fingers were scalded. There was no truth for her in books. The truth ahead of her would be loneliness, dreary adulthood, and penance.

Grow up.

The palm-leaf panels stirred like waiting ghosts.

All through the long bus ride back, she said nothing. Dara went silent too, and hung his head.

In the huge and empty hotel suite, darkness awaited her. She'd had the phone and the TV removed; her footsteps sounded hollow. Jorani and the driver had been her only friends.

The next day she did not go to Soriya Market. She went instead to the torture museum of Tuol Sleng.

A cadre of young motoboys waited outside the hotel in baseball caps and bling. Instead, Sith hailed a sweet-faced older motoboy with a battered, rusty bike.

As they drove she asked him about his family. He lived alone and had no one except for his mother in Kompong Thom.

Outside the gates of Tuol Sleng he said, "This was my old school."

In one wing there were rows of rooms with one iron bed in each with handcuffs and stains on the floor. Photos on the wall showed twisted bodies chained to those same beds as they were found on the day of liberation. In one photograph, a chair was overturned as if in a hurry.

Sith stepped outside and looked instead at a beautiful house over the wall across the street. It was a high white house like her own, with pillars and a roof terrace and bougainvillaea, a modern daughter's house. What do they think when they look out from that roof terrace? How can they live here?

The grass was tended and full of hopping birds. People were painting the shutters of the prison a fresh blue-gray.

In the middle wing, the rooms were galleries of photographed faces. They stared out at her like the faces from her printer. Were some of them the same?

"Who are they?" she found herself asking a Cambodian visitor.

"Their own," the woman replied. "This is where they sent Khmer Rouge cadres who had fallen out of favor. They would not waste such torture on ordinary Cambodians."

Some of the faces were young and beautiful men. Some were children or dignified old women.

The Cambodian lady kept pace with her. Company? Did she guess who Sith was? "They couldn't simply beat party cadres to death. They sent them and their entire families here. The children too, the grandmothers. They had different days of the week for killing children and wives."

An innocent-looking man smiled out at the camera as sweetly as her aged motoboy, directly into the camera of his torturers. He seemed to expect kindness from them, and decency. *Comrades,* he seemed to say.

The face in the photograph moved. It smiled more broadly and was about to speak.

Sith's eyes darted away. The next face sucked all her breath away.

It was not a stranger. It was Dara, her Dara, in black shirt and black cap. She gasped and looked back at the lady. Her pinched and solemn face nodded up and down. Was she a ghost too?

Sith reeled outside and hid her face and didn't know if she could go on standing. Tears slid down her face and she wanted to be sick and she turned her back so no one could see.

Then she walked to the motoboy, sitting in a shelter. In complete silence, she got on his bike feeling angry at the place, angry at the government for preserving it, angry at the foreigners who visited it like a tourist attraction, angry at everything.

That is not who we are! That is not what I am!

The motoboy slipped onto his bike, and Sith asked him: What happened to your family? It was a cruel question. He had to smile and look cheerful. His father had run a small shop; they went out into the country and never came back. He lived with his brother in a jeum-room, a refugee camp in Thailand. They came back to fight the Vietnamese and his brother was killed.

She was going to tell the motoboy, drive me back to the Hilton, but she felt ashamed. Of what? Just how far was she going to run?

She asked him to take her to the old house on Monivong Boulevard.

As the motorcycle wove through back streets, dodging red-earth ruts and pedestrians, she felt rage at her father. How dare he involve her in something like that! Sith had lived a small life and had no measure of things so she thought: *it's as if someone tinted my hair and it all fell out. It's as if someone pierced my ears and they got infected and my whole ear rotted away.*

She remembered that she had never felt any compassion for her father. She had been twelve years old when he stood trial, old and sick and making such a show of leaning on his stick. Everything he did was a show. She remembered rolling her eyes in constant embarrassment. Oh, he was fine in front of rooms full of adoring students. He could play the *bong thom* with them. They thought he was enlightened. He sounded good, using his false, soft and kindly little voice, as if he was dubbed. He had made Sith recite Verlaine, Rimbaud, and Rilke. He killed thousands for having foreign influences.

I don't know what I did in a previous life to deserve you for a father. But you were not my father in a previous life and you won't be my father in the next. I reject you utterly. I will never burn your name. You can wander hungry out of hell every year for all eternity. I will pray to keep you in hell.

I am not your daughter!

If you were false, I have to be true.

Her old house looked abandoned in the stark afternoon light, closed and innocent. At the doorstep she turned and thrust a fistful of dollars into the motoboy's hand. She couldn't think straight; she couldn't even see straight, her vision blurred.

Back inside, she calmly put down her teddy-bear rucksack and walked upstairs to her office. Aido the robot dog whirred his way toward her. She had broken his back leg kicking him downstairs. He limped, whimpering like a dog, and lowered his head to have it stroked.

To her relief, there was only one picture waiting for her in the tray of the printer.

Kol Vireakboth looked out at her, middle-aged, handsome, worn, wise. Pity and kindness glowed in his eyes.

The land line began to ring.

"Youl prom," she told the ghosts. Agreed.

She picked up the receiver and waited.

A man spoke. "My name was Yin Bora." His voice bubbled up brokenly as if from underwater.

A light blinked in the printer. A photograph slid out quickly. A young student stared out at her looking happy at a family feast. He had a Beatle haircut and a striped shirt.

"That's me," said the voice on the phone. "I played football."

Sith coughed. "What do you want me to do?"

"Write my name," said the ghost.

"Please hold the line," said Sith, in a hypnotized voice. She fumbled for a pen, and then wrote on the photograph *Yin Bora, footballer.* He looked so sweet and happy. "You have no one to mourn you," she realized.

"None of us have anyone left alive to mourn us," said the ghost.

Then there was a terrible sound down the telephone, as if a thousand voices moaned at once.

Sith involuntarily dropped the receiver into place. She listened to her heart thump and thought about what was needed. She fed the printer with the last of her paper. Immediately it began to roll out more photos, and the land line rang again.

She went outside and found the motoboy, waiting patiently for her. She asked him to go and buy two reams of copying paper. At the last moment she added pens and writing paper and matches. He bowed and smiled and bowed again, pleased to have found a patron.

She went back inside, and with just a tremor in her hand picked up the phone.

For the next half hour, she talked to the dead, and found photographs and wrote down names. A woman mourned her children. Sith found photos of them all, and united them, father, mother, three children, uncles, aunts, cousins and grandparents, taping their pictures to her wall. The idea of uniting families appealed. She began to stick the other photos onto her wall.

Someone called from outside and there on her doorstep was the motoboy, balancing paper and pens. "I bought you some soup." The broth came in neatly tied bags and was full of rice and prawns. She thanked him and paid him well and he beamed at her and bowed again and again.

All afternoon, the pictures kept coming. Darkness fell, the phone rang, the names were written, until Sith's hand, which was unused to writing anything, ached.

The doorbell rang, and on the doorstep, the motoboy sompiahed. "Excuse me, Lady, it is very late. I am worried for you. Can I get you dinner?"

Sith had to smile. He sounded motherly in his concern. They are so good at building a relationship with you, until you cannot do without them. In the old days she would have sent him away with a few rude words. Now she sent him away with an order.

And wrote.

And when he came back, the aged motoboy looked so happy. "I bought you fruit as well, Lady," he said, and added, shyly, "You do not need to pay me for that."

Something seemed to bump under Sith, as if she was on a motorcycle, and she heard herself say, "Come inside. Have some food too."

The motoboy sompiahed in gratitude and as soon as he entered, the phone stopped ringing.

They sat on the floor. He arched his neck and looked around at the walls.

"Are all these people your family?" he asked.

She whispered. "No. They're ghosts who no one mourns."

"Why do they come to you?" His mouth fell open in wonder.

"Because my father was Pol Pot," said Sith, without thinking.

The motoboy sompiahed. "Ah." He chewed and swallowed

and arched his head back again. "That must be a terrible thing. Everybody hates you."

Sith had noticed that wherever she sat in the room, the eyes in the photographs were directly on her. "I haven't done anything," said Sith.

"You're doing something now," said the motoboy. He nodded and stood up, sighing with satisfaction. Life was good with a full stomach and a patron. "If you need me, Lady, I will be outside."

Photo after photo, name after name.

> *Youk Achariya: touring dancer*
> *Proeung Chhay: school superintendent*
> *Sar Kothida, child, aged 7, died of "swelling disease"*
> *Sar Makara, her mother, nurse*
> *Nath Mittapheap, civil servant, from family of farmers*
> *Chor Monirath: wife of award-winning engineer*
> *Yin Sokunthea: Khmer Rouge commune leader*

She looked at the faces and realized. *Dara, I'm doing this for Dara.*

The city around her went quiet and she became aware that it was now very late indeed. Perhaps she should just make sure the motoboy had gone home.

He was still waiting outside.

"It's okay. You can go home. Where do you live?"

He waved cheerfully north. "Oh, on Monivong, like you." He grinned at the absurdity of the comparison.

A new idea took sudden form. Sith said, "Tomorrow, can you come early, with a big feast? Fish and rice and greens and pork: curries and stir-fries and kebabs." She paid him handsomely, and finally asked him his name. His name meant Golden.

"Good night, Sovann."

For the rest of the night she worked quickly like an answering service. This is like a cleaning of the house before a festival, she thought. The voices of the dead became ordinary, familiar. Why are people afraid of the dead? The dead can't hurt you. The dead want what you want: justice.

The wall of faces became a staircase and a garage and a kitchen of faces, all named. She had found Jorani's colored yarn, and linked family members into trees.

She wrote until the electric lights looked discolored, like a headache. She asked the ghosts, "Please can I sleep now?" The phones fell silent and Sith slumped with relief onto the polished marble floor.

She woke up dazed, still on the marble floor. Sunlight flooded the room. The faces in the photographs no longer looked swollen and bruised. Their faces were not accusing or mournful. They smiled down on her. She was among friends.

With a whine, the printer started to print; the phone started to ring. Her doorbell chimed, and there was Sovann, white cardboard boxes piled up on the back of his motorcycle. He wore the same shirt as yesterday, a cheap blue copy of a Lacoste. A seam had parted under the arm. He only has one shirt, Sith realized. She imagined him washing it in a basin every night.

Sith and Sovann moved the big tables to the front windows. Sith took out her expensive tablecloths for the first time, and the bronze platters. The feast was laid out as if at New Year. Sovann had bought more paper and pens. He knew what they were for. "I can help, Lady."

He was old enough to have lived in a country with schools, and he could write in a beautiful, old-fashioned hand. Together he and Sith spelled out the names of the dead and burned them.

"I want to write the names of my family too," he said. He burnt them weeping.

The delicious vapors rose. The air was full of the sound of breathing in. Loose papers stirred with the breeze. The ash filled the basins, but even after working all day, Sith and the motoboy had only honored half the names.

"Good night, Sovann," she told him.

"You have transferred a lot of merit," said Sovann, but only to be polite.

If I have any merit to transfer, thought Sith.

He left and the printers started, and the phone. She worked all night, and only stopped because the second ream of paper ran out.

The last picture printed was of Kol Vireakboth.

Dara, she promised herself. *Dara next.*

In the morning, she called him. "Can we meet at lunchtime for another walk by the river?"

Sith waited on top of the marble wall and watched an old man fish in the Tonlé Sap river and found that she loved her country. She loved its tough, smiling, uncomplaining people, who had never offered her harm, after all the harm her family had done them. Do you know you have the daughter of the monster sitting here among you?

Suddenly all Sith wanted was to be one of them. The monks in the pavilion, the white-shirted functionaries scurrying somewhere, the lazy bones dangling their legs, the young men who dress like American rappers and sold something dubious, drugs, or sex.

She saw Dara sauntering toward her. He wore his new shirt, and smiled at her but he didn't look relaxed. It had been two days since they'd met. He knew something was wrong, that she had something to tell him. He had bought them lunch in a little cardboard box. Maybe for the last time, thought Sith.

They exchanged greetings, almost like cousins. He sat next to her and smiled and Sith giggled in terror at what she was about to do.

Dara asked, "What's funny?"

She couldn't stop giggling. "Nothing is funny. Nothing." She sighed in order to stop and terror tickled her and she spurted out laughter again. "I lied to you. Kol Vireakboth is not my father. Another politician was my father. Someone you've heard of . . . ."

The whole thing was so terrifying and absurd that the laughter squeezed her like a fist and she couldn't talk. She laughed and wept at the same time. Dara stared.

"My father was Saloth Sar. That was his real name." She couldn't make herself say it. She could tell a motoboy, but not Dara? She forced herself onward. "My father was Pol Pot."

Nothing happened.

Sitting next to her, Dara went completely still. People strolled past; boats bobbed on their moorings.

After a time Dara said, "I know what you are doing."

That didn't make sense. "Doing? What do you mean?"

Dara looked sour and angry. "Yeah, yeah, yeah, yeah." He sat, looking away from her. Sith's laughter had finally shuddered to a halt. She sat peering at him, waiting. "I told you my family were modest," he said quietly.

"Your family are lovely!" Sith exclaimed.

His jaw thrust out. "They had questions about you too, you know."

"I don't understand."

He rolled his eyes. He looked back 'round at her. "There are easier ways to break up with someone."

He jerked himself to his feet and strode away with swift determination, leaving her sitting on the wall.

Here on the riverfront, everyone was equal. The teenage boys lounged on the wall; poor mothers herded children; the foreigners walked briskly, trying to look as if they didn't carry moneybelts. Three fat teenage girls nearly swerved into a cripple in a pedal chair and collapsed against each other with raucous laughter.

Sith did not know what to do. She could not move. Despair humbled her, made her hang her head.

I've lost him.

The sunlight seemed to settle next to her, washing up from its reflection on the wake of some passing boat.

No you haven't.

The river water smelled of kindly concern. The sounds of traffic throbbed with forbearance.

Not yet.

There is no forgiveness in Cambodia. But there are continual miracles of compassion and acceptance.

Sith appreciated for just a moment the miracles. The motoboy buying her soup. She decided to trust herself to the miracles.

Sith talked to the sunlight without making a sound. *Grandfather Vireakboth. Thank you. You have told me all I need to know.*

Sith stood up and from nowhere, the motoboy was there. He drove her to the Hello Phone shop.

Dara would not look at her. He bustled back and forth behind the counter, though there was nothing for him to do. Sith talked to him like a customer. "I want to buy a mobile phone," she said, but he would not answer. "There is someone I need to talk to."

Another customer came in. She was a beautiful daughter too, and he served her, making a great show of being polite. He complimented her on her appearance. "Really, you look cool." The girl looked pleased. Dara's eyes darted in Sith's direction.

Sith waited in the chair. This was home for her now. Dara ignored her. She picked up her phone and dialed his number. He put it to his ear and said, "Go home."

"You are my home," she said.

His thumb jabbed the C button.

She waited. Shadows lengthened.

"We're closing," he said, standing by the door without looking at her.

Shamefaced, Sith ducked away from him, through the door.

Outside Soriya, the motoboy played dice with his fellows. He stood up. "They say I am very lucky to have Pol Pot's daughter as a client."

There was no discretion in Cambodia, either. Everyone will know now, Sith realized.

At home, the piles of printed paper still waited for her. Sith ate the old, cold food. It tasted flat, all its savor sucked away. The phones began to ring. She fell asleep with the receiver propped against her ear.

The next day, Sith went back to Soriya with a box of the printed papers.

She dropped the box onto the blue plastic counter of Hello Phones.

"Because I am Pol Pot's daughter," she told Dara, holding out a sheaf of pictures toward him, "all the unmourned victims of my father are printing their pictures on my printer. Here. Look. These are the pictures of people who lost so many loved ones there is no one to remember them."

She found her cheeks were shaking and that she could not hold the sheaf of paper. It tumbled from her hands, but she stood back, arms folded.

Dara, quiet and solemn, knelt and picked up the papers. He looked at some of the faces. Sith pushed a softly crumpled green card at him. Her family ID card.

He read it. Carefully, with the greatest respect, he put the photographs on the countertop along with the ID card.

"Go home, Sith," he said, but not unkindly.

"I said," she had begun to speak with vehemence but could not continue. "I told you. My home is where you are."

"I believe you," he said, looking at his feet.

"Then . . ." Sith had no words.

"It can never be, Sith," he said. He gathered up the sheaf of photocopying paper. "What will you do with these?"

Something made her say, "What will *you* do with them?"

His face was crossed with puzzlement.

"It's your country too. What will you do with them? Oh, I know, you're such a poor boy from a poor family, who could expect anything from you? Well, you have your whole family and many people have no one. And you can buy new shirts and some people only have one."

Dara held out both hands and laughed. "Sith?" *You, Sith, are accusing me of being selfish?*

"You own them too." Sith pointed to the papers, to the faces. "You think the dead don't try to talk to you, too?"

Their eyes latched. She told him what he could do. "I think you should make an exhibition. I think Hello Phones should sponsor it. You tell them that. You tell them Pol Pot's daughter wishes to make amends and has chosen them. Tell them the dead speak to me on their mobile phones."

She spun on her heel and walked out. She left the photographs with him.

That night she and the motoboy had another feast and burned the last of the unmourned names. There were many thousands.

The next day she went back to Hello Phones.

"I lied about something else," she told Dara. She took out all the reports from the fortunetellers. She told him what Hun Sen's fortuneteller had told her. "The marriage is particularly well favored."

"Is that true?" He looked wistful.

"You should not believe anything I say. Not until I have earned your trust. Go consult the fortunetellers for yourself. This time you pay."

His face went still and his eyes focused somewhere far beneath the floor. Then he looked up, directly into her eyes. "I will do that."

For the first time in her life Sith wanted to laugh for something other than fear. She wanted to laugh for joy.

"Can we go to lunch at Lucky7?" she asked.

"Sure," he said.

All the telephones in the shop, all of them, hundreds all at once began to sing.

A waterfall of trills and warbles and buzzes, snatches of old songs or latest chart hits. Dara stood dumbfounded. Finally he picked one up and held it to his ear.

"It's for you," he said and held out the phone for her.

There was no name or number on the screen.

Congratulations, dear daughter, said a warm kind voice.

"Who is this?" Sith asked. The options were severely limited.

Your new father, said Kol Vireakboth. The sound of wind. *I adopt you.*

A thousand thousand voices said at once, *We adopt you.*

In Cambodia, you share your house with ghosts in the way you share it with dust. You hear the dead shuffling alongside your own footsteps. You can sweep, but the sound does not go away.

On the Tra Bek end of Monivong there is a house whose owner has given it over to ghosts. You can try to close the front door. But the next day you will find it hanging open. Indeed you can try, as the neighbors did, to nail the door shut. It opens again.

By day, there is always a queue of five or six people wanting to go in, or hanging back, out of fear. Outside are offerings of lotus or coconuts with embedded joss sticks.

The walls and floors and ceilings are covered with photographs. The salon, the kitchen, the stairs, the office, the empty bedrooms, are covered with photographs of Chinese-Khmers at weddings, Khmer civil servants on picnics, Chams outside their mosques, Vietnamese holding up prize catches of fish; little boys going to school in shorts; cyclopousse drivers in front of their odd, old-fashioned pedaled vehicles; wives in stalls stirring soup. All of them are happy and joyful, and the background is Phnom Penh when it was the most beautiful city in Southeast Asia.

All the photographs have names written on them in old-fashioned handwriting.

On the table is a printout of thousands of names on slips of paper. Next to the table are matches and basins of ash and water. The implication is plain. Burn the names and transfer merit to the unmourned dead.

Next to that is a small printed sign that says in English HELLO.

Every Pchum Ben, those names are delivered to temples throughout the city. Gold foil is pressed onto each slip of paper, and attached to it is a parcel of sticky rice. At 8 A.M. food is delivered for the monks, steaming rice and fish, along with bolts of new cloth. At 10 A.M. more food is delivered, for the disabled and the poor.

And most mornings a beautiful daughter of Cambodia is seen walking beside the confluence of the Tonlé Sap and Mekong rivers. Like Cambodia, she plainly loves all things modern. She dresses in the latest fashion. Cambodian R&B whispers in her ear. She pauses in front of each new waterfront construction whether built by improvised scaffolding or erected with cranes. She buys noodles from the grumpy vendors with their tiny stoves. She carries a book or sits on the low marble wall to write letters and look at the boats, the monsoon clouds, and the dop-dops. She talks to the reflected sunlight on the river and calls it Father.

GEOFF RYMAN

"Pol Pot's Beautiful Daughter (Fantasy)" came upon me when I was in Cambodia doing writer workshops. I had just been to Surya market on the day after high school exams, which was packed, exciting, and completely different from the rural Cambodia I had seen. The "(Fantasy)" is there because I also wrote a version of the story with no magic in it and because I wanted to remind people frequently that this is indeed a fiction. Saloth Sith is a real person, totally unlike my heroine, and I wanted people to be clear this was a fantasy. This beautiful daughter shaped by Pol Pot is Cambodia itself—wanting to be modern, free from the past, with a style and culture all its own.

THE YIDDISH POLICEMEN'S UNION

MICHAEL CHABON

Michael Chabon is the bestselling author of *The Amazing Adventures of Kavalier & Clay,* which won the 2001 Pulitzer Prize for fiction. That novel and *The Yiddish Policemen's Union* are both infused with his genre influences, as are the two original anthologies he edited for McSweeney's: *McSweeney's Mammoth Treasury of Thrilling Tales* in 2003 and *McSweeney's Enchanted Chamber of Astonishing Stories* in 2004.

He lives in Berkeley, California, with his wife, the novelist Ayelet Waldman, and their children.

1

Nine months Landsman's been flopping at the Hotel Zamenhof without any of his fellow residents managing to get themselves murdered. Now somebody has put a bullet in the brain of the occupant of 208, a yid who was calling himself Emanuel Lasker.

"He didn't answer the phone, he wouldn't open his door," says Tenenboym the night manager when he comes to roust Landsman. Landsman lives in 505, with a view of the neon sign on the hotel across Max Nordau Street. That one is called the Blackpool, a word that figures in Landsman's nightmares. "I had to let myself into his room."

The night manager is a former U.S. Marine who kicked a

heroin habit of his own back in the sixties, after coming home from the shambles of the Cuban war. He takes a motherly interest in the user population of the Zamenhof. He extends credit to them and sees that they are left alone when that is what they need.

"Did you touch anything in the room?" Landsman says.

Tenenboym says, "Only the cash and jewelry."

Landsman puts on his trousers and shoes and hitches up his suspenders. Then he and Tenenboym turn to look at the door-knob, where a necktie hangs, red with a fat maroon stripe, already knotted to save time. Landsman has eight hours to go until his next shift. Eight rat hours, sucking at his bottle, in his glass tank lined with wood shavings. Landsman sighs and goes for the tie. He slides it over his head and pushes up the knot to his collar. He puts on his jacket, feels for the wallet and shield in the breast pocket, pats the sholem he wears in a holster under his arm, a chopped Smith & Wesson Model 39.

"I hate to wake you, Detective," Tenenboym says. "Only I noticed that you don't really sleep."

"I sleep," Landsman says. He picks up the shot glass that he is currently dating, a souvenir of the World's Fair of 1977. "It's just I do it in my underpants and shirt." He lifts the glass and toasts the thirty years gone since the Sitka World's Fair. A pinnacle of Jewish civilization in the north, people say, and who is he to argue? Meyer Landsman was fourteen that summer, and just discovering the glories of Jewish women, for whom 1977 must have been some kind of a pinnacle. "Sitting up in a chair." He drains the glass. "Wearing a sholem."

According to doctors, therapists, and his ex-wife, Landsman drinks to medicate himself, tuning the tubes and crystals of his moods with a crude hammer of hundred-proof plum brandy. But the truth is that Landsman has only two moods: working and dead. Meyer Landsman is the most decorated shammes in the District of Sitka, the man who solved the murder of the beautiful Froma Lefkowitz by her furrier husband, and caught Podolsky the Hospital Killer. His testimony sent Hyman Tsharny to federal prison for life, the first and last time that criminal charges against a Verbover wiseguy have ever been made to stick. He has the memory of a convict, the balls of a fireman, and the eyesight of a housebreaker. When there is crime to fight, Landsman tears around Sitka like a man with his pant leg caught on a rocket. It's like there's a film score playing behind him, heavy on the castanets. The problem comes in the hours when he isn't working, when his thoughts start blowing out the open window of his brain like pages from a blotter. Sometimes it takes a heavy paperweight to pin them down.

"I hate to make more work for you," Tenenboym says.

During his days working Narcotics, Landsman arrested Tenenboym five times. That is all the basis for what passes for friendship between them. It is almost enough.

"It's not work, Tenenboym," Landsman says. "I do it for love."

"It's the same for me," the night manager says. "With being a night manager of a crap-ass hotel."

Landsman puts his hand on Tenenboym's shoulder, and they go down to take stock of the deceased, squeezing into the Zamenhof's lone elevator, or ELEVATORO, as a small brass plate over the door would have it. When the hotel was built fifty years ago, all of its directional signs, labels, notices, and warnings were printed on brass plates in Esperanto. Most of them are long gone, victims of neglect, vandalism, or the fire code.

The door and door frame of 208 do not exhibit signs of forced entry. Landsman covers the knob with his handkerchief and nudges the door open with the toe of his loafer.

"I got this funny feeling," Tenenboym says as he follows Landsman into the room. "First time I ever saw the guy. You know the expression 'a broken man'?"

Landsman allows that the phrase rings a bell.

"Most of the people it gets applied to don't really deserve it," Tenenboym says. "Most men, in my opinion, they have nothing there to break in the first place. But this Lasker. He was like one of those sticks you snap, it lights up. You know? For a few hours. And you can hear broken glass rattling inside of it. I don't know, forget it. It was just a funny feeling."

"Everybody has a funny feeling these days," Landsman says, making a few notes in his little black pad about the situation of the room, even though such notes are superfluous, because he rarely forgets a detail of physical description. Landsman has been told, by the same loose confederacy of physicians, psychologists, and his former spouse, that alcohol will kill his gift for recollection, but so far, to his regret, this claim has proved false. His vision of the past remains unimpaired. "We had to open a separate phone line just to handle the calls."

"These are strange times to be a Jew," Tenenboym agrees. "No doubt about it."

A small pile of paperback books sits atop the laminate dresser. On the bedside table Lasker kept a chessboard. It looks like he had a game going, a messy-looking middle game with Black's king under attack at the center of the board and White having the advantage of a couple of pieces. It's a cheap set, the board a square of card that folds down the middle, the pieces hollow, with plastic nubs where they were extruded.

One light burns in a three-shade floor lamp by the television. Every other bulb in the room apart from the bathroom tube has been removed or allowed to burn out. On the windowsill sits a package of a popular brand of over-the-counter laxative. The window is cranked open its possible inch, and every few seconds the metal blinds bang in the stiff wind blowing in off the Gulf of Alaska. The wind carries a sour tang of pulped lumber, the smell of boat diesel and the slaughter and canning of salmon. According to "Nokh Amol," a song that Landsman and every other Alaskan Jew of his generation learned in grade school, the smell of the wind from the Gulf fills a Jewish nose with a sense of promise, opportunity, the chance to start again. "Nokh Amol" dates from the Polar Bear days, the early forties, and it's supposed to be an expression of gratitude for another miraculous deliverance: Once Again. Nowadays the Jews of the Sitka District tend to hear the ironic edge that was there all along.

"Seems like I've known a lot of chess-playing yids who used smack," Tenenboym says.

"Same here," Landsman says, looking down at the deceased, realizing he has seen the yid around the Zamenhof. Little bird of a man. Bright eye, snub beak. Bit of a flush in the cheeks and throat that might have been rosacea. Not a hard case, not a scumbag, not quite a lost soul. A yid not too different from Landsman, maybe, apart from his choice of drug. Clean fingernails. Always a tie and hat. Read a book with footnotes once. Now Lasker lies on his belly, on the pull-down bed, face to the wall, wearing only a pair of regulation white underpants. Ginger hair and ginger freckles and three days of golden stubble on his cheek. A trace of a double chin that Landsman puts down to a vanished life as a fat boy. Eyes swollen in their blood-dark orbits. At the back of his head is a small, burnt hole, a bead of blood. No sign of a struggle. Nothing to indicate that Lasker saw it coming or even knew the instant when it came. The pillow, Landsman notices, is missing from the bed. "If I'd known, maybe I would have proposed a game or two."

"I didn't know you play."

"I'm weak," Landsman says. By the closet, on plush carpet the medicated yellow-green of a throat lozenge, he spots a tiny white feather. Landsman jerks open the closet door, and there on the floor is the pillow, shot through the heart to silence the concussion of bursting gases in a shell. "I have no feel for the middle game."

"In my experience, Detective," Tenenboym says, "it's all middle game."

"Don't I know it," Landsman says.

He calls to wake his partner, Berko Shemets.

"Detective Shemets," Landsman says into his mobile phone, a department-issue Shoyfer AT. "This is your partner."

"I begged you not to do this anymore, Meyer," Berko says.

Needless to say, he also has eight hours to go until his next shift.

"You have a right to be angry," Landsman says. "Only I thought maybe you might still be awake."

"I *was* awake."

Unlike Landsman, Berko Shemets has not made a mess of his marriage or his personal life. Every night he sleeps in the arms of his excellent wife, whose love for him is merited, requited, and appreciated by her husband, a steadfast man who never gives her any cause for sorrow or alarm.

"A curse on your head, Meyer," Berko says, and then, in American, "God damn it."

"I have an apparent homicide here at my hotel," Landsman says. "A resident. A single shot to the back of the head. Silenced with a pillow. Very tidy."

"A hit."

"That's the only reason I'm bothering you. The unusual nature of the killing."

Sitka, with a population in the long jagged strip of the metro area of three point two million, averages about seventy-five homicides a year. Some of these are gang-related: Russian shtarkers whacking one another freestyle. The rest of Sitka's homicides are so-called crimes of passion, which is a shorthand way of expressing the mathematical product of alcohol and firearms. Cold-blooded executions are as rare as they are tough to clear from the big whiteboard in the squad room, where the tally of open cases is kept.

"You're off duty, Meyer. Call it in. Give it to Tabatchnik and Karpas."

Tabatchnik and Karpas, the other two detectives who make up B Squad in the Homicide Section of the District Police, Sitka Headquarters, are holding down the night shift this month. Landsman has to acknowledge a certain appeal in the idea of letting this pigeon shit on their fedoras.

"Well, I would," Landsman says. "Except for this is my place of residence."

"You knew him?" Berko says, his tone softening.

"No," Landsman says. "I did not know the yid."

He looks away from the pale freckled expanse of the dead man stretched out on the pull-down bed. Sometimes he can't help feeling sorry for them, but it's better not to get into the habit.

"Look," Landsman says, "you go back to bed. We can talk about it tomorrow. I'm sorry I bothered you. Good night. Tell Ester-Malke I'm sorry."

"You sound a little off, Meyer," Berko says. "You okay?"

In recent months Landsman has placed a number of calls to his partner at questionable hours of the night, ranting and rambling in an alcoholic dialect of grief. Landsman bailed out on his marriage two years ago, and last April his younger sister crashed her Piper Super Cub into the side of Mount Dunkelblum, up in the bush. But Landsman is not thinking of Naomi's death now, nor of the shame of his divorce. He has been sandbagged by a vision of sitting in the grimy lounge of the Hotel Zamenhof, on a couch that was once white, playing chess with Emanuel Lasker, or whatever his real name was. Shedding the last of their fading glow on each other and listening to the sweet chiming of broken glass inside. That Landsman loathes the game of chess does not make the picture any less touching.

"The guy played chess, Berko. I never knew. That's all."

"Please," Berko says, "please, Meyer, I beg you, don't start with the crying."

"I'm fine," Landsman says. "Good night."

Landsman calls the dispatcher to make himself the primary detective on the Lasker case. Another piece-of-shit homicide is not going to put any special hurt on his clearance rate as primary. Not that it really matters. On the first of January, sovereignty over the whole Federal District of Sitka, a crooked parenthesis of rocky shoreline running along the western edges of Baranof and

Chichagof islands, will revert to the state of Alaska. The District Police, to which Landsman has devoted his hide, head, and soul for twenty years, will be dissolved. It is far from clear that Landsman or Berko Shemets or anybody else will be keeping his job. Nothing is clear about the upcoming Reversion, and that is why these are strange times to be a Jew.

While he waits for the beat latke to show, Landsman knocks on doors. Most of the occupants of the Zamenhof are out for the night, in body or mind, and for all that he gets out of the rest of them, he might as well be knocking on doors at the Hirshkovits School for the Deaf. They are a twitchy, half-addled, rank, and cranky bunch of yids, the residents of the Hotel Zamenhof, but none of them seems any more disturbed than usual tonight. And none of them strikes Landsman as the type to jam a large-caliber handgun against the base of a man's skull and kill him in stone-cold blood.

"I'm wasting my time with these buffaloes," Landsman tells Tenenboym. "And you, you're sure you didn't see anybody or anything out of the ordinary?"

"I'm sorry, Detective."

"You're a buffalo, too, Tenenboym."

"I don't dispute the charge."

"The service door?"

"Dealers were using it," Tenenboym says. "We had to put in an alarm. I would have heard."

Landsman gets Tenenboym to telephone the day manager and the weekend man, snug at home in their beds. These gentlemen agree with Tenenboym that, as far as they know, no one has called for the dead man or asked after him. Ever. Not during the entire course of his stay at the Zamenhof. No visitors, no friends, not even the delivery boy from Pearl of Manila. So, Landsman thinks, there's a difference between him and Lasker: Landsman has occasional visits from Romel, bearing a brown paper bag of *lumpia*.

"I'm going to go check out the roof," Landsman says. "Don't let anybody leave, and call me when the latke decides to show up."

Landsman rides the elevatoro to the eighth floor and then bangs his way up a flight of steel-edged concrete steps to the roof of the Zamenhof. He walks the perimeter, looking across Max Nordau Street to the roof of the Blackpool. He peers over the north, east, and south cornices to the surrounding low structures six or seven stories down. Night is an orange smear over Sitka, a compound of fog and the light of sodium-vapor streetlamps. It has the translucence of onions cooked in chicken fat. The lamps of the Jews stretch from the slope of Mount Edgecumbe in the west, over the seventy-two infilled islands of the Sound, across the Shvartsn-Yam, Halibut Point, South Sitka, and the Nachtasyl, across Harkavy and the Untershtat, before they are snuffed in the east by the Baranof range. On Oysshtelung Island, the beacon at the tip of the Safety Pin—sole remnant of the World's Fair—blinks out its warning to airplanes or yids. Landsman can smell fish offal from the canneries, grease from the fry pits at Pearl of Manila, the spew of taxis, an intoxicating bouquet of fresh hat from Grin-spoon's Felting two blocks away.

"It's nice up there," Landsman says when he gets back down to the lobby, with its ashtray charm, the yellowing sofas, the scarred chairs and tables at which you sometimes see a couple of hotel residents killing an hour with a game of pinochle. "I should go up more often."

"What about the basement?" Tenenboym says. "You going to look down there?"

"The basement," Landsman says, and his heart describes a sudden knight move in his chest. "I guess I'd better."

Landsman is a tough guy, in his way, given to the taking of wild chances. He has been called hard-boiled and foolhardy, a momzer, a crazy son of a bitch. He has faced down shtarkers and psychopaths, has been shot at, beaten, frozen, burned. He has pursued suspects between the flashing walls of urban firefights and deep into bear country. Heights, crowds, snakes, burning houses, dogs schooled to hate the smell of a policeman, he has shrugged them all off or functioned in spite of them. But when he finds himself in lightless or confined spaces, something in the animal core of Meyer Landsman convulses. No one but his ex-wife knows it, but Detective Meyer Landsman is afraid of the dark.

"Want me to go with you?" Tenenboym says, sounding off-hand, but you never know with a sensitive old fishwife like Tenenboym.

Landsman affects to scorn the offer. "Just give me a damn flashlight," he says.

The basement exhales its breath of camphor, heating oil, and cold dust. Landsman jerks a string that lights a naked bulb, holds his breath, and goes under.

At the bottom of the steps, he passes through the lost-articles room, lined with pegboard, furnished with shelves and cubby-holes that hold the thousand objects abandoned or forgotten in the hotel. Unmated shoes, fur hats, a trumpet, a windup zeppelin. A collection of wax gramophone cylinders featuring the entire recorded output of the Orchestra Orfeon of Istanbul. A logger's ax, two bicycles, a partial bridge in a hotel glass. Wigs, canes, a glass eye, display hands left behind by a mannequin salesman. Prayer books, prayer shawls in their velvet zipper pouches, an outlandish idol with the body of a fat baby and the head of an elephant. There is a wooden soft-drink crate filled with keys, another with the entire range and breadth of hairstyling tools, from irons to eyelash crimpers. Framed photographs of families in better days. A cryptic twist of rubber that might be a sex toy, or a contraceptive device, or the patented secret of a foundation garment. Some yid even left behind a taxidermy marten, sleek and leering, its glass eye a hard bead of ink.

Landsman probes the box of keys with a pencil. He looks in-

THE YIDDISH POLICEMEN'S UNION

side each hat, gropes along the shelves behind the abandoned paperback books. He can hear his own heart and smell his own aldehyde breath, and after a few minutes in the silence, the sound of blood in his ears begins to remind him of somebody talking. He checks behind the hot-water tanks, lashed to one another with straps of steel like comrades in a doomed adventure.

The laundry is next. When he pulls the string for the light, nothing happens. It's ten degrees darker in here, and there's nothing to see but blank walls, severed hookups, drain holes in the floor. The Zamenhof has not done its own wash in years. Landsman looks into the drain holes, and the darkness in them is oily and thick. Landsman feels a flutter, a worm, in his belly. He flexes his fingers and cracks the bones of his neck. At the far end of the laundry room, a door that is three planks nailed together by a diagonal fourth seals a low doorway. The wooden door has a loop of rope for a latch and a peg to hook it on.

A crawl space. Landsman half dreads the phrase alone.

He calculates the chance that a certain style of killer, not a professional, not a true amateur, not even a normal maniac, might be hiding in that crawl space. Possible; but it would be pretty tough for the freak to have hooked the loop over the peg from inside. That logic alone is almost enough to persuade him not to bother with the crawl space. In the end Landsman switches on the flash and notches it between his teeth. He hikes up his pants legs and gets down on his knees. Just to spite himself, because spiting himself, spiting others, spiting the world is the pastime and only patrimony of Landsman and his people. With one hand he unholsters his big little S&W, and with the other he fingers the loop of rope. He yanks open the door of the crawl space.

"Come out," he says, lips dry, rasping like a scared old fart.

The elation he experienced on the roof has cooled like blown filament. His nights are wasted, his life and career a series of mistakes, his city itself a bulb that is about to go black.

He thrusts his upper body into the crawl space. The air is cold, with a bitter smell of mouse shit. The beam of the pocket flash dribbles over everything, shadowing as much as it reveals. Walls of cinder block, an earthen floor, the ceiling a loathsome tangle of wires and foam insulation. In the middle of the dirt floor, at the back, a disk of raw plywood lies set in a circular metal frame, flush with the floor. Landsman holds his breath and swims through his panic to the hole in the floor, determined to stay under for as long as he can. The dirt around the frame is undisturbed. An even layer of dust lies over wood and metal alike, no marks, no streaks. There is no reason to think anyone has been fooling with it. Landsman fits his fingernails between the plywood and the frame and pries off the crude hatch. The flashlight reveals a threaded tube of aluminum screwed into the earth, laddered with steel cleats. The frame turns out to be the edge of the tube itself. Just wide enough to admit a full-grown psychopath. Or a Jewish policeman with fewer phobias than Landsman. He clings to the sholem as to a handle, wrestling with a crazy need to fire it into the throat of the darkness. He drops the plywood disk back into its frame with a clatter. No way is he going down there.

The darkness follows him all the way back up the stairs to the lobby, reaching for his collar, tugging at his sleeve.

"Nothing," he tells Tenenboym, pulling himself together. He gives the word a cheery ring. It might be a prediction of what his investigation into the murder of Emanuel Lasker is bound to reveal, a statement of what he believes Lasker lived for and died for, a realization of what will remain, after the Reversion, of Landsman's hometown. "Nothing."

"You know what Kohn says," says Tenenboym. "Kohn says we got a ghost in the house." Kohn is the day manager. "Taking shit, moving shit around. Kohn figures it for the ghost of Professor Zamenhof."

"If they named a dump like this after me," Landsman says, "I'd haunt it, too."

"You never know," Tenenboym observes. "Especially nowadays."

Nowadays one never knows. Out at Povorotny, a cat mated

with a rabbit and produced adorable freaks whose photos graced the front page of the *Sitka Tog*. Last February five hundred witnesses all up and down the District swore that in the shimmer of the aurora borealis, for two nights running, they observed the outlines of a human face, with beard and sidelocks. Violent arguments broke out over the identity of the bearded sage in the sky, whether or not the face was smiling (or merely suffering from a mild attack of gas), and the meaning of the weird manifestation. And just last week, amid the panic and feathers of a kosher slaughterhouse on Zhitlovsky Avenue, a chicken turned on the shochet as he raised his ritual knife and announced, in Aramaic, the imminent advent of Messiah. According to the *Tog*, the miraculous chicken offered a number of startling predictions, though it neglected to mention the soup in which, having once more fallen silent as God Himself, it afterward featured. Even the most casual study of the record, Landsman thinks, would show that strange times to be a Jew have almost always been, as well, strange times to be a chicken.

MICHAEL CHABON

I was inspired to write The Yiddish Policemen's Union *by the haunting example of another book:* Say It in Yiddish, *a pocket-sized, sobersided "phrasebook for travelers" to a land where every level of human interaction, from the everyday to the governmental, is conducted in Yiddish. It was the nonexistence of such a land that haunted me, and as time went on I found myself increasingly hungering for a visit. So I wrote this book.*

ince 1978, when Suzette Haden Elgin founded the Science Fiction Poetry Association, its members have recognized achievement in the field of speculative poetry by presenting the Rhysling Awards, named after the blind bard protagonist of Robert A. Heinlein's "The Green Hills of Earth."

Every year, each SFPA member is allowed to nominate two poems from the previous year for the Rhysling Awards: one in the "long" category and one in the "short" category. Because it's practically impossible for each member to have read every nominated poem in the various publications where they originally appeared, the nominees are all collected into one volume, called *The Rhysling Anthology*. Copies of this anthology are mailed to all the members, who read it and vote for their favorites. The top vote-getters in each of the two categories become the Rhysling winners. Past winners have included Michael Bishop, Bruce Boston, Tom Disch, Joe Haldeman, Alan P. Lightman, Ursula K. Le Guin, Susan Palwick, Lucius Shepard, Jeff VanderMeer and Gene Wolfe.

In 2006, the SFPA created a new award, the Dwarf Stars Award, to honor poems of ten lines or less.

For more information on the SFPA, see its website at www. sfpoetry.com.

Jane Yolen, often called "the Hans Christian Andersen of America," admits to actually being the Hans Jewish Andersen of America. She is the author of more than three hundred books, ranging from picture books and baby board books to middle-grade fiction, poetry collections, nonfiction, novels, graphic novels, and story collections. Her books and stories have won many awards, including two Nebulas, a World Fantasy Award, a Caldecott, the Golden Kite, three Mythopoeic Awards, two Christopher Medals, the Jewish Book Award, and nomination for the National Book Award. She has also won the Kerlan Award and the Catholic Library's Regina Medal. Six colleges and universities have given her honorary doctorates.

LAST UNICORN

JANE YOLEN

Others, like foxes, go to ground,
But the last unicorn, whitened,
Faded the color of old sheets hung
On a trailer park line,
Goes to the edge of the ocean.
The tops of waves are as white as he.
Brothers, he thinks, sisters,
And plunges in, not so much a death
As a transfiguration.

Rich Ristow was born in Bitburg, Germany. He's also lived in England, Bermuda, Belgium, and the Netherlands. He holds a master of fine arts in poetry from UNC–Wilmington. Currently, he lives in New Jersey with his wife. In 2008, Skullvines Press published his novelette "Into the Cruel Sea," which is available only at www.skullvines.com.

THE GRAVEN IDOL'S GODHEART

RICH RISTOW

The Baghdad Battery, thought to be about two thousand years old,
is the oldest known generator of electricity. Some historians believe
it was used to give a small electric charge to statues.

The godheart of your graven idol is a clay pot
of grape juice, a copper sheet, and an iron rod
that creates a weak volt, like an electric shot

to the finger, if you touched your golden god.
The stern high priest hid it, but he surely knew
of grape juice, a copper sheet, and an iron rod.

His authority your fear and faith would renew.
As you fell to the floor and sobbed into the sand
the stern high priest hid it, but he surely knew

you'd give more gold and do as he'd demand,
like let your baby boy die on the bloody altar.
You fell to the floor and sobbed into the sand

before you watched it all and would not falter.
Fearing a greater smiting or even failed crops,
you let your baby boy die on a bloody altar.

You never knew the high priest used props:
the godheart of your graven idol is a clay pot
that gives other metal a static sizzle and a pop
created by one weak volt, like an electric shot.

Mike Allen lives in Roanoke, Virginia, with his wife, Anita, and a demonic cat and comical dog. By day he covers court cases for the city's daily newspaper; in his spare time the hats he wears include editor of the poetry journal *Mythic Delirium* and the anthology series *Clockwork Phoenix*. He's a semiregular performer in the local improv theater and a three-time winner of the Rhysling Award for poetry. The *Philadelphia Inquirer* called his work "poetry for goths of all ages." His newest books are *The Journey to Kailash,* a poetry collection published by Norilana Books, and *Follow the Wounded One,* a dark fantasy novelette from the publishers of *Not One of Us* magazine.

THE JOURNEY TO KAILASH

MIKE ALLEN

When Ganesh marries my mother,
I am 18, my own man
in the eyes of the law; but barely a zygote
in his eyes. He calls me *spermling*
the first time we speak in private;
I tell him I know a doctor
who can do something about that nose.
Trunk curls up, perhaps to strike?
—a smile beneath
that touched the ancient folds around his eyes.
Kid, he says, *we'll get along fine.*

In my neighborhood, unseen trains
shake the ground every day at 5.
Streets without sidewalks slide between houses
tiny as boxcars, or old and rambling
as the stories the fogeys at the gas station tell,
like them eaten from inside and about to fall,
unlike them divided into 4 apartments each.
Ganesh and I play Xbox
before my afternoon shifts (of course he's great,
with all those hands he's at least two players
at once) and I steal glances
at his impossible profile, framed
by the dusty window: lumpy wrinkled nose

like a seasoned draft guard, curled
in inverse question mark of concentration;
on this day, clad in coveralls
with the bib undone: *How is it*, I wonder,
that you feel like you belong?
As if he heard, he mumbles,
Wherever someone loves me, I'm in like Flynn.

No, no, Mom, I don't want to know
(but as always, she tells me—
I know, he could use a few weeks at the Y,
and yeah, he's a lot older than your father
but turn off the lights
and you wouldn't know it. Sure,
sometimes the beginning is way better
than the end, but who cares
when he gets the party rolling . . .
Oh, when he gets rolling . . . and that trunk!)
No, no, Mom, I don't want to know . . .

I still don't have a clue how they met.
Mom can't remember, and my stepdad
always changes the subject, spins me
yet another harrowing first-person account
of leading his father's troops against demonkind.
For me there was no warning: after a long
afternoon behind the Burger King counter
I come home, to find him on the couch,
Mom asleep against his pillowy chest,
a bowl of popcorn in his lap, quietly munching;
his huge ears fanned out, cupped forward
as he watches *Temple of Doom* on cable
and giggles under his breath. In retrospect
I was far less surprised than
what the moment warranted.

As we wait in matching tuxes
for the justice of the peace to call us in
I feel new respect, even affection—
he didn't have to do this, we all know it,
but he agreed without a gripe when Mom asked.
See, kid, he whispers around a tusk,
your mother, she has this vivaciousness, *this* pluck,
this drive to defy all odds and plow on
that's like a bath of rakta chandan
for pranapratishhtha—*she makes me feel*
alive, you understand? This aatma
I want to catch with all my hands, and when
it flutters, let it go, watch its flight in awe,
then catch it again. An essence such as that
pumps new blood through an old heart.
Do you comprehend?
                              I nod "I do." *I knew*
you would, he says. *You have it too.* An arm
around my shoulders; three more hands
pinch my cheeks. *Too bad you're not a woman.*
A grin, a wink. The moment nearly ruined,
but some part of me still flattered.
After the vows and the happy tears, he lifts
his trunk to kiss me wetly on one ear.

My son, he says.
At the reception, for the first time, I see him dance.
No wonder Mom can't get enough.

You would think,
with a household god,
(of great luck and strong starts, yet!)

that I wouldn't still be slaving behind
the grease-smeared Burger King counter
(to be honest, I'm in dual-job hell;
come night, *yo no quiero Taco Bell*).
I finally ask him about this lack of riches,
and he sighs and blinks those dewy eyes.
Spermling—he wags his trunk—*it don't work
like that. Luck, okay, luck is when
you're driving in downtown Manhattan, fighting
for every gap that opens in all that hurtling metal,
and your car, it's been threatening to stall
since the last tollbooth on the Jersey Turnpike,
and you made it, but your tank's on Empty,
and you beg that car,* Please don't die—
and it's like it hears you, like it's packed with prana,
*and goes twenty miles further than possible,
and just when you feel rigor mortis
in the gas pedal, there is a pump station
at this corner, that you didn't see seconds ago—
and the $20 you thought you dropped
at the rest stop is in your pocket after all.*
All four hands spread wide.
That's what luck is all about.

You would think, given all the above,
that I'd have never come home
in the early a.m. to find Mom
in the kitchen dark, crouched
over the cooking sherry, her silent tears
revealed when the lights come on.
What's wrong with me, she asks.
*Is there some little demon inside me
that refuses to believe I deserve this?
Why don't I want to be happy?*

I ask, *is it the other wives?*
She shakes her head.

How distracted he seems when he's present;
how lost she seems when he's gone.

Mothers, he grumps one morning
and pauses *Halo* to rest his chin on his hands.
No, not yours.
          Some mothers sure do hate
to give up their sons.
               Did I ever tell you
what my mother did to me?
                    A dirty trick.
It was, you know, long before time
really got rolling, and I was playing with
my kitten, and I played with her a little
too rough (but I didn't mean to, see,
it had only been a few years since
Shiva first fused my head on).

I came home and my mom was bleeding
from her bindi, and when I asked what's wrong
she says to me, what ever I do to any ladki
I do to her. How cruel a thing
to do to a son! But I was still young,
didn't see it that way then. So I vowed
to never ever marry.
               Well.
A few millenniums of celibacy

will make you decide there's some consequences
you can live with. So I took three wives—
take that, Mom!—but you'd think by now
she'd forgive me. Her unhappiness,
well, sometimes it still comes through.

He offered me the remains of his beer
(I refused) then polished it off with a chug,
and lamented:
Is it so hard for a mother to want
eternal happiness for her Dumbo-headed boy?

I haven't shared a word of this with Mom,
and won't.
I look at these checks I drag home,
compute how they add up with hers,
and know
we need every bit of luck we can hold on to.

But one late sleepless night
I Googled my stepfather and gawked
at hundreds of prettified statues and
read about Ganesh Chaturthi;
days of hymns and feasting,
red silk and red ointment,
the eleventh day my stepdad's image
submerged in the sea, symbolizing
his journey home to Kailash
bad luck drawn away like pilot fish
following his wake.
And I love him so
that I can't bring myself to ask him yet:
is it when he *leaves*
that misfortune truly goes away?

STARS SEEN THROUGH STONE

LUCIUS SHEPARD

Lucius Shepard was born in Lynchburg, Virginia; grew up in Daytona Beach, Florida; and lives in Vancouver, Washington. His short fiction has won the Nebula Award, the Hugo Award, the International Horror Writers Award, the National Magazine Award, the Locus Award, the Theodore Sturgeon Award, and the World Fantasy Award.

His latest books are a nonfiction book about Honduras, *Christmas in Honduras;* a short novel, *Softspoken;* and a short fiction collection, *The Iron Shore.* Forthcoming are two novels, tentatively titled *The Piercefields* and *The End of Life as We Know It,* and two short novels, *Beautiful Blood, Unknown Admirer,* and *The House of Everything and Nothing.*

I was smoking a joint on the steps of the public library when a cold wind blew in from no cardinal point, but from the top of the night sky, a force of pure perpendicularity that bent the sparsely leaved boughs of the old alder shadowing the steps straight down toward the Earth, as if a gigantic someone directly above were pursing his lips and aiming a long breath directly at the ground. For the duration of that gust, fifteen or twenty seconds, my hair did not flutter but was pressed flat to the crown of my head and the leaves and grass and weeds on the lawn also lay flat. The phenomenon had a distinct border—leaves drifted along the sidewalk, testifying that a less forceful, more fitful wind presided beyond the perimeter of the lawn. No one else appeared to notice. The library, a blunt nineteenth-century relic of undressed stone, was not a popular point of assembly at any time of day, and the sole potential witness apart from myself was an elderly gentleman who was hurrying toward McGuigan's Tavern at a pace that implied a severe alcohol dependency. This happened seven months prior to the events central to this story, but I offer it to suggest that a good deal of strangeness goes unmarked by the world (at least by the populace of Black William, Pennsylvania), and, when taken in sum, such occurrences may be evidence that strangeness is visited upon us with some regularity and we only notice its extremes.

Ten years ago, following my wife's graduation from Yale Law, we set forth in our decrepit Volvo, heading for northern California, where we hoped to establish a community of sorts with friends who had moved to that region the previous year. We chose to drive on blue highways for their scenic value and decided on a route that ran through Pennsylvania's Bittersmith Hills, knuckled chunks of coal and granite, forested with leafless oaks and butternut, ash and elder, that—under heavy snow and threatening skies—composed an ominous prelude to the smoking redbrick town nestled in their heart. As we approached Black William, the Volvo began to rattle, the engine died, and we coasted to a stop on a curve overlooking a forbidding vista: row houses the color of dried blood huddled together along the wend of a sluggish, dark river (the Polozny), visible through a pall of gray smoke that settled from the chimneys of a sprawling prisonlike edifice—also of brick—on the opposite shore. The Volvo proved to be a total loss. Since our funds were limited, we had no recourse other than to find temporary housing and take jobs so as to pay for a new car in which to continue our trip. Andrea, whose specialty was labor law, caught on with a firm involved in fighting for the rights of embattled steelworkers. I hired on at the mill, where I encountered three part-time musicians lacking a singer. This led to that, that to this, Andrea and I grew apart in our obsessions, had affairs, divorced, and, before we realized it, the better part of a decade had rolled past. Though initially I felt trapped in an ugly, dying town, over the years I had developed an honest affection for Black William and its citizens, among whom I came to number myself.

After a brief and perhaps illusory flirtation with fame and fortune, my band broke up, but I managed to build a home recording studio during its existence and this became the foundation of a career. I landed a small business grant and began to record local bands on my own label, Soul Kiss Records. Most of the CDs I released did poorly, but in my third year of operation, one of my projects, a metal group calling themselves Meanderthal, achieved a regional celebrity and I sold management rights and the masters for their first two albums to a major label. This success gave me a degree of visibility and my post office box was flooded with demos from bands all over the country. Over the next six years I released a string of minor successes and acquired an industry-wide reputation of having an eye for talent. It had been my immersion in the music business that triggered the events leading to my divorce and, while Andrea was happy for me, I think it galled her that I had exceeded her low expectations. After a cooling-off period, we had become contentious friends and whenever we met for drinks or lunch, she would offer deprecating comments about the social value of my enterprise, and about my girlfriend, Mia, who was nine years younger than I, heavily tattooed, and—in Andrea's words—dressed "like a color-blind dominatrix."

"You've got some work to do, Vernon," she said once. "You know, on the taste thing? It's like you traded me in for a Pinto with flames painted on the hood."

I stopped myself from replying that it wasn't I who had done the trading in. I understood her comments arose from the fact that she had regrets and that she was angry at herself: Andrea was an altruist and the notion that her renewed interest in me might be partially inspired by envy or venality caused her to doubt her moral legitimacy. She was attractive, witty, slender, with auburn hair and patrician features and a forthright poise that caused men in bars, watching her pass, to describe her as "classy." Older and

wiser, able by virtue of the self-confidence I had gained to cope
with her sharp tongue, I had my own regrets; but I thought we
had moved past the point at which a reconciliation was possible
and refrained from giving them voice.

In late summer of the year when the wind blew straight
down, I listened to a demo sent me by one Joseph Stanky of Mc-
Keesport, Pennsylvania. Stanky billed himself as Local Profitt, Jr.,
and his music, postmodern deconstructed blues sung in a gravelly,
powerful baritone, struck me as having cult potential. I called his
house that afternoon and was told by his mother that "Joey's
sleeping." That night, around three A.M., Stanky returned my
call. Being accustomed to the tactless ways of musicians, I set
aside my annoyance and said I was interested in recording him.
In the course of our conversation, Stanky told me he was twenty-
six, virtually penniless, and lived in his mother's basement, main-
taining throughout a churlish tone that dimmed my enthusiasm.
Nevertheless, I offered to pay his bus fare to Black William and to
put him up during the recording process. Two days later, when
he stepped off a bus at the Trailways station, my enthusiasm
dimmed further. A more unprepossessing human would be difficult to imagine. He was short, pudgy, with skin the color of a
new potato and so slump-shouldered that for a moment I thought
he might be deformed. Stringy brown hair provided an unsightly
frame for a doughy face with a bulging forehead and a wispy soul
patch. His white T-shirt was spattered with food stains, a Jackson
Pollock work-in-progress; the collar of his windbreaker was stiff
with grime. Baggy chinos and a trucker wallet completed his en-
semble. I knew this gnomish figure must be Stanky, but didn't
approach until I saw him claim two guitar cases from the luggage
compartment. When I introduced myself, instead of expressing
gratitude or pleasure, he put on a pitiful expression and said in a
wheedling manner, "Can you spot me some bucks for cigarettes,
man? I ran out during the ride."

I advanced him another hundred, with which he purchased
two cartons of Camel Lights and a twelve-pack of Coca-Cola

Classic (these, I learned, were basic components of his nutrition and, along with Quaker Instant Grits, formed the bulk of his diet), and took a roundabout way home, thinking I'd give him a tour of the town where he would spend the next few weeks. Stanky displayed no interest whatsoever in the mill, the Revolutionary War–era Lutheran Church, or Garnant House (home of the town's founding father), but reacted more positively to the ziggurat at the rear of Garnant House, a corkscrew of black marble erected in eccentric tribute to the founding father's wife, Ethelyn Garnant, who had died in childbirth; and when we reached the small central park where stands the statue of her son, Stanky said, "Hey, that's decent, man!" and asked me to stop the car.

The statue of William Garnant had been labeled an eyesore by the Heritage Committee, a group of women devoted to preserving our trivial past, yet they were forced to include it in their purview because it was the town's most recognizable symbol—gift shops sold replica statuettes and the image was emblazoned on coffee mugs, postcards, paperweights, on every conceivable type of souvenir. Created in the early 1800s by Gunter Hahn, the statue presented Black William in age-darkened bronze astride a rearing stallion, wearing a loose-fitting shirt and tight trousers, gripping the reins with one hand, pointing toward the library with the other, his body twisted and head turned in the opposite direction, his mouth open in—judging by his corded neck—a cry of alarm, as if he were warning the populace against the dangers of literacy. Hahn did not take his cues from the rather sedentary monuments of his day, but (impossibly) appeared to have been influenced by the work of heroic comic book artists such as Jim Steranko and Neal Adams, and thus the statue had a more fluid dynamic than was customary . . . or perhaps he was influenced by Black William himself, for it was he who had commissioned the sculpture and oversaw its construction. This might explain the figure's most controversial feature, that which had inspired generations of high school students to highlight it when they painted the statue after significant football victories: Thanks to an elevated position in the saddle, Black William's crotch was visible, and—whether intended or an inadvertency, an error in the casting process that produced an unwanted rumple in the bronze—it seems that he possessed quite a substantial package. It always gladdened my heart to see the ladies of the Heritage Committee, embarked upon their annual spring clean-up, scrubbing away with soap and rags at Black William's genital pride.

I filled Stanky in on Black William's biography, telling him that he had fought with great valor in the Revolutionary War, but had not been accorded the status of hero, this due to his penchant for executing prisoners summarily, even those who had surrendered under a white flag. Following the war, he returned home in time to watch his father, Alan Garnant, die slowly and in agony. It was widely held that William had poisoned the old man. Alan resented the son for his part in Ethelyn's death and had left him to be raised by his slaves, in particular by an immense African man to whom he had given the name Nero. Little is known of Nero; if more were known, we might have a fuller understanding of young William, who—from the war's end until his death in 1808—established a reputation for savagery, his specialities being murder and rape (both heterosexual and homosexual). By all accounts, he ruled the town and its environs with the brutal excess of a feudal duke. He had a coterie of friends who served as his loyal protectors, a group of men whose natures he had perverted, several of whom failed to survive his friendship. Accompanied by Nero, they rode roughshod through the countryside, terrorizing and defiling, killing anyone who sought to impede their progress. Other than that, his legacy consisted of the statue, the ziggurat, and a stubby tower of granite block on the bluff overlooking the town, long since crumbled into ruin.

Stanky's interest dwindled as I related these facts, his responses limited to the occasional "Cool," a word he pronounced as if it had two syllables; but before we went on our way he asked, "If the guy was such a bastard, how come they named the town after him?"

"It was a P.R. move," I explained. "The town was incorporated as Garnantsburgh. They changed it after World War Two. The city council wanted to attract business to the area and they hoped the name Black William would be more memorable. Church groups and the old lady vote, pretty much all the good Christians, they disapproved of the change, but the millworkers got behind it. The association with a bad guy appealed to their self-image."

"Looks like the business thing didn't work out. This place is deader than McKeesport." Stanky raised up in the seat to scratch his ass. "Let's go, okay? I couldn't sleep on the bus. I need to catch up on my Zs."

My house was one of the row houses facing the mill, the same Andrea and I had rented when we first arrived. I had since bought the place. The ground floor I used for office space, the second floor for the studio, and I lived on the third. I had fixed up the basement, formerly Andrea's office, into a musician-friendly apartment— refrigerator, stove, TV, etc.—and that is where I installed Stanky. The bus ride must have taken a severe toll. He slept for twenty hours.

After three weeks I recognized that Stanky was uncommonly gifted and it was going to take longer to record him than I had presumed—he kept revealing new facets of his talent and I wanted to make sure I understood its full dimension before getting too deep into the process. I also concluded that although musicians do not, in general, adhere to an exacting moral standard, he was, talent aside, the most worthless human being I had ever met. Like many of his profession, he was lazy, irresponsible, untrustworthy, arrogant, slovenly, and his intellectual life consisted of comic books and TV. To this traditional menu of character flaws, I would add "deviant." The first inkling I had of his deviancy was when Sabela, the Dominican woman who cleaned for me twice a week, complained about the state of the basement apartment. Since Sabela never complained, I had a look downstairs. In less than a week, he had trashed the place. The garbage was overflowing and the sink piled high with scummy dishes and pots half-full of congealed grits; the floors covered in places by a slurry of cigarette ash and grease, littered with candy wrappers and crumpled Coke cans. A smell compounded of spoilage, bad hygiene, and sex seemed to rise from every surface. The plastic tip of a vibrator peeked out from beneath his grungy sheets. I assured Sabela I'd manage the situation, whereupon she burst into tears. I asked what else was troubling her and she said, "Mister Vernon, I no want him."

My Spanish was poor, Sabela's English almost nonexistent, but after a few minutes I divined that Stanky had been hitting on her, going so far as to grab at her breasts. This surprised me—Sabela was in her forties and on the portly side. I told her to finish with the upstairs and then she could go home. Stanky returned from a run to the 7-Eleven and scuttled down to the basement, roachlike in his avoidance of scrutiny. I found him watching *Star Trek* in the dark, remote in one hand, *TV Guide* (he called it "the *Guide*") resting on his lap, gnawing on a Butterfinger. Seeing him so at home in his filthy nest turned up the flame under my anger.

"Sabela refuses to clean down here," I said. "I don't blame her."

"I don't care if she cleans," he said with a truculent air.

"Well, I do. You've turned this place into a shithole. I had a metal band down here for a month, it never got this bad. I want you to keep it presentable. No stacks of dirty dishes. No crud on the floor. And put your damn sex toys in a drawer. Understand?"

He glowered at me.

"And don't mess with Sabela," I went on. "When she wants to clean down here, you clear out. Go up to the studio. I hear about you groping her again, you can hump your way back to McKeesport. I need her one hell of a lot more than I need you."

He muttered something about "another producer."

"You want another producer? Go for it! No doubt major labels are beating down my door this very minute, lusting after your sorry ass."

Stanky fiddled with the remote and lowered his eyes, offering me a look at his infant bald spot. Authority having been established, I thought I'd tell him what I had in mind for the next weeks, knowing that his objections—given the temper of the moment—would be minimal; yet there was something so repellent about him, I still wanted to give him the boot. I had the idea that one of Hell's lesser creatures, a grotesque, impotent toad, banished by the Powers of Darkness, had landed with a foul stink on my sofa. But I've always been a sucker for talent and I felt sorry for him. His past was plain. Branded as a nerd early on and bullied throughout high school, he had retreated into a life of flipping burgers and getting off on a four-track in his mother's basement. Now he had gravitated to another basement, albeit one with a more hopeful prospect and a better recording system.

"Why did you get into music?" I asked, sitting beside him. "Women, right? It's always women. Hell, I was married to a good-looking woman, smart, sexy, and that was my reason."

He allowed that this had been his reason as well.

"So how's that working out? They're not exactly crawling all over you, huh?"

He cut his eyes toward me and it was as if his furnace door had slid open a crack, a blast of heat and resentment shooting out. "Not great," he said.

"Here's what I'm going to do." I tapped out a cigarette from his pack, rolled it between my fingers. "Next week, I'm bringing in a drummer and a bass player to work with you. I own a part-interest in the Crucible, the alternative club in town. As soon as you get it together, we'll put you in there for a set and showcase you for some people."

Stanky started to speak, but I beat him to the punch. "You follow my lead, you do what I know you can . . . ," I said, leaving a significant pause. "I guarantee you won't be going home alone."

He waited to hear more, he wanted to bask in my vision of his future, but I knew I had to use rat psychology; now that I had supplied a hit of his favorite drug, I needed to buzz him with a jolt of electricity.

"First off," I said, "we're going to have to get you into shape. Work off some of those man-tits."

"I'm not much for exercise."

"That doesn't come as a shock," I said. "Don't worry. I'm not going to make a new man out of you, I just want to make you a better act. Eat what I eat for a month or so, do a little cardio. You'll drop ten or fifteen pounds." Falsely convivial, I clapped him on the shoulder and felt a twinge of disgust, as if I had touched a hypoallergenic cat. "The other thing," I said. "That Local Profitt Junior name won't fly. It sounds too much like a country band."

"I like it," he said defiantly.

"If you want the name back later, that's up to you. For now, I'm billing you as Joe Stanky."

I laid the unlit cigarette on the coffee table and asked what he was watching, thinking that, for the sake of harmony, I'd bond with him a while.

"*Trek* marathon," he said.

We sat silently, staring at the flickering black-and-white picture. My mind sang a song of commitments, duties, other places I could be. Stanky laughed, a cross between a wheeze and a hiccup.

"What's up?" I asked.

"John Colicos sucks, man!"

He pointed to the screen, where a swarthy man with Groucho Marx eyebrows, pointy sideburns, and a holstered ray gun seemed to be undergoing an agonizing inner crisis. "Michael Ansara's the only real Vulcan." Stanky looked at me as if seeking validation. "At least," he said, anxious lest he offend, "on the original *Trek*."

Absently, I agreed with him. My mind rejoined its song. "Okay," I said, and stood. "I got things to do. We straight about Sabela? About keeping the place . . . you know? Keeping the damage down to normal levels?"

He nodded.

"Okay. Catch you later."

I started for the door, but he called to me, employing that wheedling tone with which I had become all too familiar. "Hey, Vernon?" he said. "Can you get me a trumpet?" This asked with an imploring expression, screwing up his face like a child, as if he were begging me to grant a wish.

"You play the trumpet?"

"Uh-huh."

"If you promise to take care of it. Yeah, I can get hold of one."

Stanky rocked forward on the couch and gave a tight little fist-pump. "Decent!"

I don't know when Stanky and I got married, but it must have been sometime between the incident with Sabela and the night Mia went home to her mother. Certainly my reaction to the latter was more restrained than was my reaction to the former, and I attribute this in part to our union having been joined. It was a typical rock-and-roll marriage: talent and money making beautiful music together and doomed from the start, on occasion producing episodes in which the relationship seemed to be crystallized, allowing you to see (if you wanted to) the messy bed you had made for yourself.

Late one evening, or maybe it wasn't so late—it was starting to get dark early—Mia came downstairs and stepped into my office and set a smallish suitcase on my desk. She had on a jacket with a fake fur collar and hood, tight jeans, and her nice boots. She'd put a fresh raspberry streak in her black hair and her makeup did a sort of Nefertiti-meets-Liza thing. All I said was, "What did I do this time?"

Mia's lips pursed in a moue—it was her favorite expression and she used it at every opportunity, whether appropriate or not. She became infuriated whenever I caught her practicing it in the bathroom mirror.

"It's not what you did," she said. "It's that clammy little troll in the basement."

"Stanky?"

"Do you have another troll? Stanky! God, that's the perfect name for him." Another moue. "I'm sick of him rubbing up against me."

Mia had, as she was fond of saying, "been through some stuff," and, if Stanky had done anything truly objectionable, she would have dealt with him. I figured she needed a break or else there was someone in town with whom she wanted to sleep.

"I take it this wasn't consensual rubbing," I said.

"You think you're so funny! He comes up behind me in tight places. Like in the kitchen. And he pretends he has to squeeze past."

"He's in our kitchen?"

"You send him up to use the treadmill, don't you?"

"Oh . . . right."

"And he has to get water from the fridge, doesn't he?"

I leaned back in the chair and clasped my hands behind my head. "You want me to flog him? Cut off a hand?"

"Would that stop it? Give me a call when he's gone, okay?"

"You know I will. Say hi to Mom."

A final moue, a moue that conveyed a *soupçon* of regret, but—more pertinently—made plain how much I would miss her spoonful of sugar in my coffee.

After she had gone, I sat thinking nonspecific thoughts, vague appreciations of her many virtues, then I handicapped the odds that her intricate makeup signaled an affair and decided just how pissed off to be at Stanky. I shouted downstairs for him to come join me and dragged him out for a walk into town.

A mile and a quarter along the Polozny, then up a steep hill, would bring you to the park, a triangular section of greenery (orange-and-brownery at that time of year) bordered on the east by the library, on the west by a row of brick buildings containing gentrified shops, and, facing the point of the triangle, by McGuigan's. For me alone, it was a brisk half-hour walk; with Stanky in tow, it took an extra twenty minutes. He was not one to hide his discomfort or displeasure. He panted, he sagged, he limped, he sighed. His breathing grew labored. The next step would be his last. Wasn't it enough I forced him to walk three blocks to the 7-Eleven? If his heart failed, drop his bones in a bucket of molten steel and ship his guitars home to McKeesport, where his mother would display them, necks crossed, behind the urn on the mantel.

These comments went unvoiced, but they were eloquently stated by his body language. He acted out every nuance of emotion, like a child showing off a new skill. Send him on an errand he considered important and he would give you his best White Rabbit, head down, hustling along on a matter of urgency to the Queen. Chastise him and he would play the penitent altar boy. When ill, he went with a hand clutching his stomach or cheek or lower back, grimacing and listless. His posturing was so pitifully false, it was disturbing to look at him. I had learned to ignore these symptoms, but I recognized the pathology that bred them—I had seen him, thinking himself unwatched, slumped on the couch, clicking the remote, the *Guide* spread across his lap, mired in the quicksand of depression, yet more arrogant than depressed, a crummy king forsaken by his court, desperate for admirers.

On reaching the library, I sat on a middle step and fingered out a fatty from my jacket pocket. Stanky collapsed beside me, exhausted by the Polozny Death March he had somehow survived. He flapped a hand toward McGuigan's and said, hopefully, "You want to get a beer?"

"Maybe later."

I fired up the joint.

"Hey!" Stanky said. "We passed a cop car on the hill, man."

"I smoke here all the time. As long as you don't flaunt it, nobody cares."

I handed him the joint. He cupped the fire in his palm, smoking furtively. It occurred to me that I wouldn't drink from the same glass as him—his gums were rotting, his teeth horribly decayed—but sharing a joint? What the hell. The air was nippy and the moon was hidden behind the alder's thick leaves, which had turned but not yet fallen. Under an arc lamp, the statue of Black William gleamed as if fashioned of obsidian.

"Looks like he's pointing right at us, huh?" said Stanky.

When I was good and stoned, once the park had crystallized

into a Victorian fantasy of dark green lawns amid crisp shadows and fountaining shrubs, the storefronts beyond hiding their secrets behind black glass, and McGuigan's ornate sign with its ruby coat of arms appearing to occupy an unreal corner in the dimension next door, I said, "Mia went back to her mom's tonight. She's going to be there for a while."

"Bummer." He had squirreled away a can of Coke in his coat pocket, which he now opened.

"It's normal for us. Chances are she'll screw around on me a little and spend most of the time curled up on her mom's sofa, eating Cocoa Puffs out of the box and watching soaps. She'll be back eventually."

He had a swig of Coke and nodded.

"What bothers me," I said, "is the reason she left. Not the real reason, but the excuse she gave. She claims you've been touching her. Rubbing against her and making like it was an accident."

This elicited a flurry of protests and I-swear-to-Gods. I let him run down before I said, "It's not a big deal."

"She's lying, man! I . . ."

"Whatever. Mia can handle herself. You cross the line with her, you'll be picking your balls up off the floor."

I could almost hear the gears grinding as he wondered how close he had come to being deballed.

"I want you to listen," I went on. "No interruptions. Even if you think I'm wrong about something. Deal?"

"Sure. . . . Yeah."

"Most of what I put out is garbage music. Meanderthal, Big Sissy, the Swimming Holes, Junk Brothers . . ."

"I love the Junk Brothers, man! They're why I sent you my demo."

I gazed at him sternly—he ducked his head and winced by way of apology.

"So rock-and-roll is garbage," I said. "It's disposable music. But once in a great while, somebody does something perfect. Something that makes the music seem indispensable. I think you can make something perfect. You may not ever get rock star money. I doubt you can be mainstreamed. The best you can hope for, probably, is Tom Waits money. That's plenty, believe me. I think you'll be huge in Europe. You'll be celebrated there. You've got a false bass that reminds me of Blind Willie Johnson. You write tremendous lyrics. That fractured guitar style of yours is unique. It's out there, but it's funky and people are going to love it. You have a natural appeal to punks and art rockers. To rock geeks like me. But there's one thing can stop you—that's your problem with women."

Not even this reference to his difficulties with Sabela and Mia could disrupt his rapt attentiveness.

"You can screw this up very easily," I told him. "You let that inappropriate touching thing of yours get out of hand, you *will* screw it up. You have to learn to let things come. To do that, you have to believe in yourself. I know you've had a shitty life so far, and your self-esteem is low. But you have to break the habit of thinking that you're getting over on people. You don't need to get over on them. You've got something they want. You've got talent. People will cut you a ton of slack because of that talent, but you keep messing up with women, their patience is going to run out. Now I don't know where all that music comes from, but it doesn't sound like it came from a basement. It's a gift. You have to start treating it like one."

I asked him for a cigarette and lit up. Though I'd given variations of the speech dozens of times, I bought into it this time and I was excited.

"Ten days from now you'll be playing for a live audience," I said. "If you put in the work, if you can believe in yourself, you'll get all you want of everything. And that's how you do it, man. By putting in the work and playing a kick-ass set. I'll help any way I can. I'm going to do publicity, T-shirts . . . and I'm going to give them away if I have to. I'm going to get the word out that Joe Stanky is something special. And you know what? Industry people will listen, because I have a track record." I blew a smoke ring and watched it disperse. "These are things I won't usually do for a band until they're farther along, but I believe in you. I believe in your music. But you have to believe in yourself and you have to put in the work."

I'm not sure how much of my speech, which lasted several minutes more, stuck to him. He acted inspired, but I couldn't tell how much of the act was real; I knew on some level he was still running a con. We cut across the park, detouring so he could inspect the statue again. I glanced back at the library and saw two white lights shaped like fuzzy asterisks. At first I thought they were moving across the face of the building, that some people were playing with flashlights; but their brightness was too sharp and erratic, and they appeared to be coming from behind the library, shining through the stone, heading toward us. After ten or fifteen seconds, they faded from sight. Spooked, I noticed that Stanky was staring at the building and I asked if he had seen the lights.

"That was weird, man!" he said. "What was it?"

"Swamp gas. UFOs. Who knows?"

I started walking toward McGuigan's and Stanky fell in alongside me. His limp had returned.

"After we have those beers, you know?" he said.

"Yeah?"

"Can we catch a cab home?" His limp became exaggerated. "I think I really hurt my leg."

Part of the speech must have taken, because I didn't have to roust Stanky out of bed the next morning. He woke before me, ate his grits (I allowed him a single bowl each day), knocked back a couple of Diet Cokes (my idea), and sequestered himself in the studio, playing adagio trumpet runs and writing on the Casio. Later, I heard the band thumping away. After practice, I caught Geno, the drummer, on his way out the door, brought him into the office and asked how the music was sounding.

"It doesn't blow," he said.

I asked to him to clarify.

"The guy writes some hard drum parts, but they're tasty, you know. Tight."

Geno appeared to want to tell me more, but spaced and ran a beringed hand through his shoulder-length black hair. He was a handsome kid, if you could look past the ink, the brands, and the multiple piercings. An excellent drummer and reliable. I had learned to be patient with him.

"Overall," I said, "how do you think the band's shaping up?"

He looked puzzled. "You heard us."

"Yes. I know what I think. I'm interested in what you think."

"Oh . . . okay." He scratched the side of his neck, the habitat of a red and black Chinese tiger. "It's very cool. Strong. I never heard nothing like it. I mean, it's got jazz elements, but not enough to where it doesn't rock. The guy sings great. We might go somewhere if he can control his weirdness."

I didn't want to ask how Stanky was being weird, but I did.

"He and Jerry got a conflict," Geno said. "Jerry can't get this one part down, and Stanky's on him about it. I keep telling Stanky to quit ragging him. Leave Jerry alone and he'll stay on it until he can play it backward. But Stanky, he's relentless and Jerry's getting pissed. He don't love the guy, anyway. Like today, Stanky cracks about we should call the band Stanky and Our Gang."

"No," I said.

"Yeah, right. But it was cute, you know. Kind of funny. Jerry took it personal, though. He like to got into it with Stanky."

"I'll talk to them. Anything else?"

"Naw. Stanky's a geek, but you know me. The music's right and I'm there."

The following day I had lunch scheduled with Andrea. It was also the day that my secretary, Kiwanda, a petite Afro-American woman in her late twenties, came back to work after a leave during which she had been taking care of her grandmother. I needed an afternoon off—I thought I'd visit friends, have a few drinks—so I gave over Stanky into her charge, warning her that he was prone to getting handsy with the ladies.

"I'll keep that in mind," she said, sorting through some new orders. "You go have fun."

Andrea had staked out one of the high-backed booths at the rear of McGuigan's and was drinking a martini. She usually ran late, liked sitting at the front, and drank red wine. She had hung her jacket on the hook at the side of the booth and looked fetching in a cream-colored blouse. I nudged the martini glass and asked what was up with the booze.

"Bad day in court. I had to ask for a continuance. So . . ." She hoisted the martini. "I'm boozing it up."

"Is this that pollution thing?"

"No, it's a pro bono case."

"Thought you weren't going to do any pro bono work for a while."

She shrugged, drank. "What can I say?"

"All that class guilt. It must be tough." I signaled a waitress, pointed to Andrea's martini and held up two fingers. "I suppose I should be grateful. If you weren't carrying around that guilt, you would have married Snuffy Huffington the Third or somebody."

"Let's not banter," Andrea said. "We always banter. Let's just talk. Tell me what's going on with you."

I was good at reading Andrea, but it was strange how well I read her at that moment. Stress showed in her face. Nervousness. Both predictable components. But mainly I saw a profound loneliness and that startled me. I'd never thought of her as being lonely. I told her about Stanky, the good parts, his writing, his musicianship.

"The guy plays everything," I said. "Guitar, flute, sax, trumpet. Little piano, little drums. He's like some kind of mutant they produced in a secret high school band lab. And his voice. It's the Jim Nabors effect. You know, the guy who played Gomer Pyle? Nobody expected a guy who looked that goofy could sing, so when he did, they thought he was great, even though he sounded like he had sinus trouble. It's the same with Stanky, except his voice really is great."

"You're always picking up these curious strays," she said. "Remember the high school kid who played bass, the one who fainted every time he was under pressure? Brian Something. You'd come upstairs and say, 'You should see what Brian did,' and tell me he laid a bass on its side and played Mozart riffs on it. And I'd go . . ."

"Bach," I said.

"And I'd go, 'Yeah, but he faints!'" She laughed. "You always think you can fix them."

"You're coming dangerously close to banter," I said.

"You owe me one." She wiggled her forefinger and grinned. "I'm right, aren't I? There's a downside to this guy."

I told her about Stanky's downside and, when I reached the part about Mia leaving, Andrea said, "The circus must be in town."

"Now you owe me one."

"You can't expect me to be reasonable about Mia." She half-sang the name, did a little shimmy, made a moue.

"That's two you owe me," I said.

"Sorry." She straightened her smile. "You know she'll come back. She always does."

I liked that she was acting flirty and, though I had no resolution in mind, I didn't want her to stop.

"You don't have to worry about me," she said. "Honest."

"Huh?"

"So how talented is this Stanky? Give me an example."

"What do you mean, I don't have to worry about you?"

"Never mind. Now come on! Give me some Stanky."

"You want me to sing?"

"You were a singer, weren't you? A pretty good one, as I recall."

"Yeah, but I can't do what he does."

She sat expectantly, hands folded on the tabletop.

"All right," I said. I did a verse of "Devil's Blues," beginning with the lines:

> "*There's a grapevine in heaven,*
> *There's a peavine in hell,*

One don't grow grapes,
The other don't grow peas as well. . . ."

I sailed on through to the chorus, getting into the vocal:

"Devil's Blues!
God owes him. . . ."

A bald guy popped his head over the top of an adjacent booth and looked at me, then ducked back down. I heard laughter.

"That's enough," I said to Andrea.

"Interesting," she said. "Not my cup of tea, but I wouldn't mind hearing him."

"He's playing the Crucible next weekend."

"Is that an invitation?"

"Sure. If you'll come."

"I have to see how things develop at the office. Is a tentative yes okay?"

"Way better than a firm no," I said.

We ordered from the grill and, after we had eaten, Andrea called her office and told them she was taking the rest of the day. We switched from martinis to red wine, and we talked, we laughed, we got silly, we got drunk. The sounds of the bar folded around us and I started to remember how it felt to be in love with her. We wobbled out of McGuigan's around four o'clock. The sun was lowering behind the Bittersmiths, but shed a rich golden light; it was still warm enough for people to be sitting in sweaters and shirts on park benches under the orange leaves.

Andrea lived around the corner from the bar, so I walked her home. She was weaving a little and kept bumping into me. "You better take a cab home," she said, and I said, "I'm not the one who's walking funny," which earned me a punch in the arm. When we came to her door, she turned to me, gripping her briefcase with both hands, and said, "I'll see you next weekend, maybe."

"That'd be great."

She hovered there a second longer and then she kissed me. Flung her arms about my neck, clocking me with the briefcase, and gave me a one-hundred-percent all-Andrea kiss that, if I were a cartoon character, would have rolled my socks up and down and levitated my hat. She buried her face in my neck and said, "Sorry. I'm sorry." I was going to say, For what?, but she pulled away in a hurry, appearing panicked, and fled up the stairs.

I nearly hit a parked car on the drive home, not because I was drunk, but because thinking about the kiss and her reaction afterward impaired my concentration. What was she sorry about? The kiss? Flirting? The divorce? I couldn't work it out, and I couldn't work out, either, what I was feeling. Lust, certainly. Having her body pressed against mine had fully engaged my senses. But there was more. Considerably more. I decided it stood a chance of becoming a mental health issue and did my best to put it from mind.

Kiwanda was busy in the office. She had the computers networking and was going through prehistoric paper files on the floor. I asked what was up and she told me she had devised a more efficient filing system. She had never been much of an innovator, so this unnerved me, but I let it pass and asked if she'd had any problems with my boy Stanky.

"Not so you'd notice," she said tersely.

From this, I deduced that there *had* been a problem, but I let that pass as well and went upstairs to the apartment. Walls papered with flyers and band photographs; a grouping of newish, ultra-functional Swedish furniture—I realized I had liked the apartment better when Andrea did the decorating, this despite the fact that interior design had been one of our bones of contention. The walls, in particular, annoyed me. I was being stared at by young men with shaved heads and flowing locks in arrogant poses, stupid with tattoos, by five or six bands that had tried to stiff me, by a few hundred bad-to-indifferent memories and a dozen good ones. Maybe a dozen. I sat on a leather and chrome couch (it was a showy piece, but uncomfortable) and watched the early news. George Bush, Iraq, the price of gasoline . . . Fuck! Restless, I went down to the basement.

Stanky was watching Comedy Central. *Mad TV.* Another of his passions. He was slumped on the couch, remote in hand, and had a Coke and a cigarette working, an ice pack clamped to his cheek. I had the idea the ice pack was for my benefit, so I didn't ask about it, but knew it must be connected to Kiwanda's attitude. He barely acknowledged my presence, just sat there and pouted. I took a chair and watched with him. At last he said, "I need a rhythm guitar player."

"I'm not going to hire another musician this late in the game."

He set down the ice pack. His cheek was red, but that might have been from the ice pack itself . . . although I thought I detected a slight puffiness. "I seriously need him," he said.

"Don't push me on this."

"It's important, man! For this one song, anyway."

"What song?"

"A new one."

I waited and then said, "That's all you're going to tell me?"

"It needs a rhythm guitar."

This tubby little madman recumbent on my couch was making demands—it felt good to reject him, but he persisted.

"It's just one song, man," he said in full-on wheedle. "Please! It's a surprise."

"I don't like surprises."

"Come on! You'll like this one, I promise."

I told him I'd see what I could do, had a talk with him about Jerry, and the atmosphere lightened. He sat up straight, chortling at *Mad TV,* now and then saying, "Decent!" his ultimate accolade. The skits were funny and I laughed, too.

"I did my horoscope today," he said as the show went to commercial.

"Let me guess," I said. "You're a Cancer."

He didn't like that, but maintained an upbeat air. "I don't mean astrology, man. I use the *Guide.*" He slid the *TV Guide* across the coffee table, pointing out an entry with a grimy finger, a black-rimmed nail. I snatched it up and read:

> "*King Creole*: ★★★ Based on a Harold Robbins novel. A young man (Elvis Presley) with a gang background rises from the streets to become a rock-and-roll star. Vic Morrow. 1:30."

"Decent, huh!" said Stanky. "You try it. Close your eyes and stick your finger in on a random page and see what you get. I use the movie section in back, but some people use the whole programming section."

"Other people do this? Not just you?"

"Go ahead."

I did as instructed and landed on another movie:

> "*A Man and a Woman*: ★★★★ A widow and a widower meet on holiday and are attracted to one another, but the woman backs off because memories of her dead husband are still too strong. Jean-Louis Trintignant, Anouk Aimée. 1:40."

Half-believing, I tried to understand what the entry portended for me and Andrea.

"What did you get?" asked Stanky.

I tossed the *Guide* back to him and said, "It didn't work for me."

I thought about calling Andrea, but business got in the way—I suppose I allowed it to get in the way, due to certain anxieties relating to our divorce. There was publicity to do, Kiwanda's new filing system to master (she kept on tweaking it), recording (we laid down two tracks for Stanky's first EP), and a variety of other duties. And so the days went quickly. Stanky began going to the library after every practice, walking without a limp; he said he was doing research. He didn't have enough money to get into trouble and I had too much else on my plate to stress over it. The night before he played the Crucible, I was in the office, going over everything in my mind, wondering what I had overlooked, thinking I had accomplished an impossible amount of work that week, when the doorbell rang. I opened the door and there on the stoop was Andrea, dressed in jeans and a bulky sweater, cheeks rosy from the night air. An overnight bag rested at her feet. "Hi," she said, and gave a chipper smile, like a tired Girl Scout determined to keep pimping her cookies.

Taken aback, I said, "Hi," and ushered her in.

She went into the office and sat in the wooden chair beside my desk. I followed her in, hesitated, and took a seat in my swivel chair.

"You look . . . rattled," she said.

"That about covers it. Good rattled. But rattled, nonetheless."

"I am, too. Sorta." She glanced around the office, as if noticing the changes. I could hear every ticking clock, every digital hum, all the discrete noises of the house.

She drew in breath, exhaled, clasped her hands in her lap. "I thought we could try," she said quietly. "We could do a trial period or something. Some days, a week. See how that goes." She paused. "The last few times I've seen you, I've wanted to be with you. And I think you've wanted to be with me. So . . ." She made a flippy gesture, as if she were trying to shade things toward the casual. "This seemed like an opportunity."

You would have thought, even given the passage of time, after all the recriminations and ugliness of divorce, some measure of negativity would have cropped up in my thoughts; but it did not and I said, "I think you're right."

"Whew!" Andrea pretended to wipe sweat from her brow and grinned.

An awkward silence; the grin flickered and died.

"Could I maybe go upstairs," she asked.

"Oh! Sure. I'm sorry." I had the urge to run up before her and rip down the crapfest on the wall, chuck all the furniture out the window, except for a mattress and candles.

"You're still rattled," she said. "Maybe we should have a drink before anything." She stretched out a hand to me. "Let's get good and drunk."

As it happened, we barely got the drinks poured before we found our groove and got busy. It was like old times, cozy and familiar, and yet it was like we were doing it for the first time, too. Every touch, every sensation, carried that odd *frisson*. We woke late, with the frost almost melted from the panes, golden light chuting through the high east windows, leaving the bed in a bluish shadow. We lay there, too sleepy to make love, playing a little, talking, her telling me how she had plotted her approach, me telling her how I was oblivious until that day at lunch when I noticed her loneliness, and what an idiot I had been not to see what was happening. . . . Trivial matters, but they stained a few brain cells, committing those moments to memory and marking them as Important, a red pin on life's map. And then we did make love, as gently as that violence can be made. Afterward, we showered and fixed breakfast. Watching her move about the kitchen in sweats and a T-shirt, I couldn't stop thinking how great this was, and I wanted to stop, to quit footnoting every second. I mentioned this as we ate and she said, "I guess that means you're happy."

"Yeah! Of course."

"Me, too." She stabbed a piece of egg with her fork, tipped her head to the side as if to get a better angle on me. "I don't know when it was I started to be able to read you so well. Not that you were that hard to read to begin with. It just seems there's nothing hidden in your face anymore."

"Maybe it's a case of heightened senses."

"No, really. At times it's like I know what you're about to say."

"You mean I don't have to speak?"

She adopted the manner of a legal professional. "Unfortunately, no. You have to speak. Otherwise, it would be difficult to catch you in a lie."

"Maybe we should test this," I said. "You ask my name, and I'll say Helmut or Torin."

She shook her head. "I'm an organic machine, not a lie detector. We have different ways. Different needs."

"Organic. So that would make you . . . softer than your basic machine? Possibly more compliant?"

"Very much so," she said.

"You know, I think I may be reading you pretty well myself." I leaned across the table, grabbed a sloppy kiss, and, as I sat back down, I remembered something. "Damn!" I said, and rapped my forehead with my knuckles.

"What is it?"

"I forgot to take Stanky for his haircut."

"Can't he take care of it himself?"

"Probably not. You want to go with us? You might as well meet him. Get it over with."

She popped egg into her mouth and chewed. "Do we have to do it now?"

"No, he won't even be up for a couple of hours."

"Good," she said.

The Crucible, a concrete block structure on the edge of Black William, off beyond the row houses, had once been a dress outlet store. We had put a cafeteria in the front, where we served breakfast and lunch—we did a brisk business because of the mill. Separate from the cafeteria, the back half of the building was given over to a bar with a few ratty booths, rickety chairs, and tables. We had turned a high-school artist loose on the walls and she had painted murals that resembled scenes from J. R. R. Tolkien's lost labor-union novel. An immense crucible adorned the wall behind the stage; it appeared, thanks to the artist's inept use of perspective, to be spilling a flood of molten steel down upon an army of orclike workers.

There was a full house that night, attracted by local legends the Swimming Holes, a girl band who had migrated to Pittsburgh, achieving a degree of national renown, and I had packed the audience with Friends of Vernon whom I had enjoined to applaud and shout wildly for Stanky. A haze of smoke fogged the stage lights and milling about were fake punks, the odd goth, hippies from Garnant College in Waterford, fifteen miles away: the desperate wannabe counterculture of the western Pennsylvania barrens. I went into the dressing rooms, gave each Swimming Hole a welcome-home hug, and checked in on Stanky. Jerry, a skinny guy with buzzcut red hair, was plunking on his bass, and Geno was playing fills on the back of a chair; Ian, the rhythm guitarist, was making a cell call in the head. Stanky was on the couch, smoking a Camel, drinking a Coke, and watching the SciFi Channel. I asked if he felt all right. He said he could use a beer. He seemed calm, supremely confident, which I would not have predicted and did not trust. But it was too late for concern and I left him to God.

I joined Andrea at the bar. She had on an old long-sleeved Ramones shirt, the same that she had worn to gigs back when my band was happening. Despite the shirt, she looked out of place in the Crucible, a swan floating on a cesspool. I ordered a beer to be carried to Stanky, a shot of tequila for myself. Andrea put her mouth to my ear and shouted over the recorded music, "Don't get drunk!" and then something else that was lost in the din. I threw down the shot and led her into the cafeteria, which was serving coffee and soda to a handful of kids, some of whom appeared to be trying to straighten out. I closed the door to the bar, cutting the volume by half.

"What were you saying?" I asked.

"I said not to get drunk, I might have use for you later." She sat at the counter, patted the stool beside her, encouraging me to sit.

"They're about to start," I said, joining her. "I've only got a minute."

"How do you think it'll go?"

"With Stanky? I'm praying it won't be a disaster."

"You know, he didn't seem so bad this afternoon. Not like you described, anyway."

"You just like him because he said you were a babe."

I took a loose cigarette from my shirt pocket, rolled it between my thumb and forefinger, and she asked if I was smoking again.

"Once in a while. Mainly I do this," I said, demonstrating my rolling technique. "Anyway . . . Stanky. You caught him on his best behavior."

"He seemed sad to me." She lifted a pepper shaker as she might a chess piece and set it closer to the salt. "Stunted. He has some adult mannerisms, adult information, but it's like he's still fourteen or fifteen."

"There you go," I said. "Now ask yourself how it would be, being around a twenty-six-year-old fourteen-year-old on a daily basis."

One of the kids, boys, men—there should be, I think, a specific word for someone old enough to die for his country, yet who can't grow a proper mustache and is having difficulty focusing because he recently ate some cheap acid cut with crank—one of the *guys* at the end of the counter, then, came trippingly toward us, wearing an army field jacket decorated with a braid of puke on the breast pocket, like a soggy service ribbon. He stopped to leer at Andrea, gave me the high sign, said something unintelligible, possibly profane, and staggered on into the club.

It had been Andrea's stance, when we were married, that episodes such as this were indicative of the sewer in which she claimed I was deliquescing, a.k.a. the music business. Though I had no grounds to argue the point, I argued nonetheless, angry because I hated the idea that she was smarter than I was—I compensated by telling myself I had more soul. There had been other, less defined reasons for anger, and the basic argument between us had gotten vicious. In this instance, however, she ignored the kid and returned to our conversation, which forced me to consider anew the question of my milieu and the degradation thereof, and to wonder if she had, by ignoring the kid, manipulated me into thinking that she had changed, whereas I had not, and it might be that the music business was to blame, that it had delimited me, warped and stunted my soul. I knew she was still the smart one.

The music cut off midsong and I heard Rudy Bowen, my friend and partner in the Crucible, on the mike, welcoming people and making announcements. On our way back into the club, Andrea stopped me at the door and said, "I love you, Vernon." She laid a finger on my lips and told me to think about it before responding, leaving me mightily perplexed.

Stanky walked out onto the stage of the Crucible in a baggy white T-shirt, baggy chinos and his trucker wallet. He would have been semipresentable had he not also been wearing a battered top hat. Somebody hooted derisively, and that did not surprise me. The hat made him look clownish. I wanted to throw a bottle and knock it off his head. He began whispering into the mike. Another hoot, a piercing whistle. Not good. But the whisper evolved into a chant, bits of Latin, Spanish, rock-and-roll clichés, and nonsense syllables. Half-spoken, half-sung, with an incantatory vibe, scatted in a jump-blues rhythm that the band, coming in underneath the vocal, built into a sold groove, and then Stanky, hitting his mark like a ski jumper getting a lift off a big hill, began to sing:

> "I heard the Holy Ghost moan . . .
> Stars seen through stone . . ."

Basically, the song consisted of those two lines repeated, but sung differently—made into a gospel plaint, a rock-and-roll howl, a smooth Motown styling, a jazzy lilt, and so on. There was a break with more lyrics, but the two lines were what mattered. The first time he sang them, in that heavy false bass, a shock ripped through the audience. People looked up, they turned toward the stage, they stopped drinking, their heads twitched, their legs did impromptu dance steps. Stanky held the word "moan" out for three bars, working it like a soul singer, then he picked up the trumpet and broke into a solo that was angry like Miles, but kept a spooky edge. When he set the trumpet down, he went to singing the lyric double time, beating the top hat against his thigh, mangling it. The crowd surged forward, everyone wanting to get next to the stage, dancing in place, this strange, shuffling dance, voodoo zombies from hell, and Stanky strapped on his guitar. I missed much of what happened next, because Andrea dragged me onto the dance floor and started making slinky moves, and I lost my distance from the event. But Stanky's guitar work sent the zombies into a convulsive fever. We bumped into a punk who was jerking like his strings were being yanked; we did a three-some with a college girl whose feet were planted, yet was shaking it like a tribal dancer in a *National Geographic Special*; we were cor-ralled briefly by two millworkers who were dancing with a goth girl, watching her spasm, her breasts flipping every which way. At the end of the song, Jerry and Geno started speaking the lyric into their mikes, adding a counterpoint to Stanky's vocal, cooling things off, bringing it down to the creepy chant again; then the band dropped out of the music and Stanky went a capella for a final repetition of his two lines.

Applause erupted, and it was as idiosyncratic as the dancing had been. This one guy was baying like a hound; a blond girl bounced up and down, clapping gleefully like a six-year-old. I didn't catch much of the set, other than to note the audience's positive response, in particular to the songs "Average Joe" and "Can I Get a Waitress?" and "The Sunset Side of You"—I was working the room, gathering opinions, trying to learn if any of the industry people I'd invited had come, and it wasn't until twenty minutes after the encore that I saw Stanky at the bar, talk-ing to a girl, surrounded by a group of drunken admirers. I heard another girl say how cute he was and that gave me pause to won-der at the terrible power of music. The hooker I had hired to guarantee my guarantee, a long-legged brunette named Carol, dish-faced but with a spectacular body, was biding her time, waiting for the crowd around Stanky to disperse. He was in competent hands. I felt relief, mental fatigue, the desire to be alone with Andrea. There was no pressing reason to stay. I said a couple of good-byes, accepted congratulations, and we drove home, Andrea and I, along the Polozny.

"He's amazing," she said. "I have to admit, you may be right about him."

"Yep," I said proudly.

"Watch yourself, Sparky. You know how you get when these things start to go south."

"What are you talking about?"

"When one of your problem children runs off the tracks, you take it hard. That's all I'm saying." Andrea rubbed my shoulder. "You may want to think about speeding things up with Stanky. Walk him a shorter distance and let someone else deal with him. It might save you some wear and tear."

We drove in silence; the river widened, slowed its race, flowing in under the concrete lees of the mill; the first row house came up on the right. I was tempted to respond as usually I did to her advice, to say it's all good, I've got it under control, but for some reason I listened that night and thought about everything that could go wrong.

Carol was waiting for me in the office when I came downstairs at eight o'clock the following morning. She was sitting in my swivel chair, going through my Rolodex. She looked weary, her hair mussed, and displeased. "That guy's a freak," she said flatly. "I want two hundred more. And in the future, I want to meet the guys you set me up with before I commit."

"What'd he do?" I asked.

"Do you really want to know?"

"I'm kind of curious. . . . Yeah."

She began to recite a list of Stanky-esque perversion—I cut her off.

"Okay," I said, and reached for my checkbook. "He didn't get rough, did he?"

"*Au contraire.*" She crossed her legs. "He wanted me to. . . ."

"Please," I said. "Enough."

"I don't do that sort of work," she said primly.

I told her I'd written the check for three hundred and she was somewhat mollified. I apologized for Stanky and told her I hadn't realized he was so twisted.

"We're okay," she said. "I've had . . . Hi, sweetie!"

She directed this greeting to a point above my shoulder as Andrea, sleepily scratching her head, wearing her sweats, entered the office. "Hi, Carol," she said, bewildered.

Carol hugged her, then turned to me and waved good-bye with my check. "Call me."

"Pretty early for hookers," Andrea said, perching on the edge of the desk.

"Let me guess. You defended her."

"Nope. One of her clients died and left her a little money. I helped her invest. But that begs the question, what was she doing here?"

"I got her for Stanky."

"A reward?"

"Something like that."

She nodded and idly kicked the back of her heel against the side of the desk. "How come you were never interested in the men I dated after we broke up?"

I was used to her sudden conversational U-turns, but I had expected her to interrogate me about Carol and this caught me off-guard. "I don't know. I suppose I didn't want to think about who you were sleeping with."

"Must be a guy thing. I always checked out your girlfriends. Even the ones you had when I was mad at you." She slipped off the desk and padded toward the door. "See you upstairs."

I spent the next two days between the phone and the studio, recording a good take of "The Sunset Side of You"—it was the closest thing Stanky had to a ballad, and I thought, with its easy, Dr. John-ish feel, it might get some play on college radio:

> *"I'm gonna crack open my venetian blind*
> *and let that last bit of old orange glory shine,*
> *so I can catch an eyeful*
> *of my favorite trifle,*
> *my absoutely perfect point of view. . . .*
> *That's an eastbound look,*
> *six inches from the crook*
> *of my little finger,*
> *at the sunset side of you. . . ."*

Stanky wasn't happy with me—he was writing a song a day, sometimes two songs, and didn't want to disrupt his creative process by doing something that might actually make money, but I gamed him into cutting the track.

Wednesday morning, I visited Rudy Bowen in his office. Rudy was an architect who yearned to be a cartoonist, but who had never met with much success in the latter pursuit, and the resonance of our creative failures, I believe, helped to cement our friendship. He was also the only person I knew who had caught a fish in the Polozny downstream from the mill. It occupied a place of honor in his office, a hideous thing mounted on a plaque, some sort of mutant trout nourished upon pollution. Whenever I saw it, I would speculate on what else might lurk beneath the surface of the cold, deep pools east of town, imagining telepathic monstrosities plated with armor like fish of the Mesozoic and frail tentacled creatures, their skins having the rainbow sheen of an oil slick, to whom mankind were sacred figures in their dream of life.

Rudy's secretary, a matronly woman named Gwen, told me he had gone out for a latte and let me wait in his private office. I stepped over to his drafting table, curious about what he was working on. Held in place on the table was a clean sheet of paper, but in a folder beside the table was a batch of new cartoons, a series featuring shadowy figures in a mineshaft who conversed about current events, celebrities, etc., while excavating a vein of pork that twisted through a mountain. . . . This gave rise to the title of the strip: *Meat Mountain Stories*. They were silhouettes, really. Given identity by their shapes, eccentric hairstyles, and speech signatures. The strip was contemporary and hilarious—everything Rudy's usual work was not. In some frames, a cluster of tiny white objects appeared to be floating. Moths, I thought. Lights of some kind. They, too, carried on conversations, but in pictographs. I was still going through them when Rudy came in, a big, blond man with the beginnings of a gut and thick glasses that lent him a baffled look. Every time I saw him, he looked more depressed, more middle-aged.

"These are great, man!" I said. "They're new, right?"

He crossed the room and stood beside me.

"I been working on them all week. You like 'em, huh?"

"I love them. You did all this this week? You must not be sleeping." I pointed to the white things. "What're these?"

"Stars. I got the idea from that song Stanky did. 'Stars Seen Through Stone.' "

"So they're seeing them, the people in the mine?"

"Yeah. They don't pay much attention to them, but they're going to start interacting soon."

"It must be going around." I told him about Stanky's burst of writing, Kiwanda's adventures in office management.

"That's odd, you know." He sipped his latte. "It seems like there's been a real rash of creativity in town. Last week, some grunt at the mill came up with an improvement in the cold forming process that everybody says is a huge deal. Jimmy Galvin, that guy who does handyman work? He invented a new gardening tool. Bucky Bucklin's paying his patent fees. He says they're going to make millions. Beth started writing a novel. She never said anything to me about wanting to write, but she's hardly had time for the kids, she's been so busy ripping off the pages. It's not bad."

"Well, I wish I'd catch it," I said. "With me, it's same old same old. Drudgeree, drudgeroo. Except for Andrea's back."

"Andrea? You mean you guys are dating?"

"I mean back as in back in my house. Living with me."

"Damn!" he said. "That's incredible!"

We sat in two chairs like two inverted tents on steel frames, as uncomfortable as my upstairs couch, and I told him about it.

"So it's going okay?" he asked.

"Terrific, I think. But what do I know? She said it was a trial period, so I could get home tonight and she might be gone. I've never been able to figure her out."

"Andrea. Damn! I saw her at the club, but I didn't realize she was with you. I just had time to wave." He leaned across the space between us and high-fived me. "Now maybe you'll stop going around like someone stole your puppy."

"It wasn't like that," I said.

He chuckled. "Naw. Which is why the people of Black William, when asked the date, often reply, 'Six years, two months, and twelve days since the advent of Vernon's Gloom.'"

We moved on to other topics, among them the club, business, and, as I made to leave, I gestured at Rudy's grotesque trophy and said, "While those creative juices are flowing, you ought to design a fishing lure, so I can watch you hook into the Loch Polozny Monster."

Rudy laughed and said, "Maybe if I have a couple of minutes. I'm going to keep working on the comic. Whatever this shit is, it's bound to go away."

I was fooling around in the studio one evening, ostensibly cleaning up the tape we'd rolled the previous weekend at the Crucible, hoping to get a live rendition of "Stars Seen Through Stone" clean enough for the EP, but I was, instead, going over a tape I'd made, trying to find some ounce of true inspiration in it, finding none, wondering why this wave of creativity—if it, indeed, existed—had blessed Rudy's house and not mine. It was after seven; Stanky was likely on his way home from the library, and I was thinking about seeing if Andrea wanted to go out, when she leaned in the doorway and asked if she was interrupting. I told her, no, not at all, and she came into the booth and sat next to me at the board, looking out at the drum kit, the instruments, the serpents' nest of power cords.

"When we were married, I didn't get what you saw in this," she said. "All I saw was the damage, the depravity, the greed. Now I've been practicing, I realize there's more or less the same degree of damage and greed and depravity in every enterprise. You can't see it as clearly as you do in the music business, but it's there."

"Tell me what I see that's good."

"The music, the people."

"None of that lasts," I said. "All I am's a yo-yo tester. I test a thousand busted yo-yos, and occasionally I run across one that lights up and squeals when it spins."

"What I do is too depressing to talk about. It's rare when anyone I represent has a good outcome, even if they win. Corporations delay and delay."

"So it's disillusionment that's brought us together again."

"No." She looked at me steadily. "Do you love me?"

"Yeah, I love you. You know I do. I never stopped. There was a gap. . . ."

"A big gap!"

"The gap made it more painful, but that's all it did."

She played with dials on the sound board, frowning as if they were refusing to obey her fingers.

"You're messing up my settings," I said.

"Oh . . . sorry."

"What's wrong?"

"Nothing. It's just you don't lie to me anymore. You used to lie all the time, even about trivial things. I'm having trouble adjusting."

I started to deny it, but recognized that I couldn't. "I was angry at you. I can't remember why, exactly. Lying was probably part of it."

"I was angry at you, too." She put her hands back on the board, but twisted no dials. "But I didn't lie to you."

"You stopped telling me the truth," I said.

"Same difference."

The phone rang; in reflex, I picked up and said, "Soul Kiss."

It was Stanky. He started babbling, telling me to come downtown quick.

"Whoa!" I said. "If this is about me giving you a ride . . ."

"No, I swear! You gotta see this, man! The stars are back!"

"The stars."

"Like the ones we saw at the library. The lights. You better come quick. I'm not sure how long it'll last."

"I'm kind of busy," I said.

"Dude, you have got to see this! I'm not kidding!"

I covered the phone and spoke to Andrea. "Want to ride uptown? Stanky says there's something we should see."

"Maybe afterward we could stop by my place and I could pick up a few things?"

I got back on the phone. "Where are you?"

Five minutes later we were cutting across the park toward the statue of Black William, beside which Stanky and several people were standing in an island of yellow light—I had no time to check them out, other than to observe that one was a woman, because Stanky caught my arm and directed me to look at the library and what I saw made me unmindful of any other sight. The building had been rendered insubstantial, a ghost of itself, and I was staring across a dark plain ranged by a dozen fuzzy white lights, some large, some small, moving toward us at a slow rate of speed, and yet perhaps it was not slow—the perspective seemed infinite, as if I were gazing into a depth that, by comparison to which, all previously glimpsed perspectives were so limited as to be irrelevant. As the lights approached, they appeared to vanish, passing out of frame, as if the viewing angle we had been afforded was too narrow to encompass the scope of the phenomenon. Within seconds, it began to fade, the library to regain its ordinary solidity, and I thought I heard a distant gabbling, the sound of many voices speaking at once, an army of voices (though I might have manufactured this impression from the wind gusting through the boughs); and then, as that ghostly image winked out of existence, a groaning noise that, in my opinion, issued from no fleshly throat, but may have been produced by some cosmic stress, a rip in the continuum sealing itself or something akin.

Andrea had at some point latched onto my arm, and we stood gaping at the library; Stanky and the rest began talking excitedly. There were three boys, teenagers, two of them carrying skateboards. The third was a pale, skinny, haughty kid, bespotted with acne, wearing a black turtleneck sweater, black jeans, black overcoat. They displayed a worshipful attitude toward Stanky, hanging on his every word. The woman might have been the one with whom Stanky had been speaking at the Crucible before Carol made her move. She was tiny, barely five feet tall, Italian-looking, with black hair and olive skin, in her twenties, and betrayed a compete lack of animation until Stanky slipped an arm around her; then she smiled, an expression that revealed her to be moderately attractive.

The skateboarders sped off to, they said, "tell everybody," and this spurred me to take out my cell phone, but I could not think who to call. Rudy, maybe. But no one in authority. The cops would laugh at the report. Stanky introduced us to Liz (the woman lowered her eyes) and Pin (the goth kid looked away and nodded). I asked how long the phenomenon had been going on before we arrived and Stanky said, "Maybe fifteen minutes."

"Have you seen it before?"

"Just that time with you."

I glanced up at Black William and thought that maybe he *had* intended the statue as a warning . . . though it struck me now that he was turning his head back toward the town and laughing.

Andrea hugged herself. "I could use something hot to drink."

McGuigan's was handy, but that would have disincluded Pin, who obviously was underage. I loaded him, Stanky, and Liz into the back of the van and drove to Szechuan Palace, a restaurant on the edge of the business district, which sported a five-foot-tall gilt fiberglass Buddha in the foyer that over the years had come to resemble an ogre with a skin condition, the fiberglass weave showing through in patches, and whose dining room (empty but for a bored waitstaff) was lit like a Macao brothel in lurid shades of red, green, and purple. On the way to the restaurant, I replayed the incident in my head, attempting to understand what I had witnessed not in rational terms, but in terms that would make sense to an ordinary American fool raised on science fiction and horror movies. Nothing seemed to fit. At the restaurant, Andrea and Pin ordered tea, Liz and Stanky gobbled moo shu pork and lemon chicken, and I picked at an egg roll. Pin started talking to Andrea in an adenoidal voice, lecturing her on some matter regarding Black William, and, annoyed because he was treating her like an idiot, I said, "What does Black William have to do with this?"

"Not a thing," Pin said, turning on me a look of disdain that aspired to be the kind of look Truman Capote once fixed upon a reporter from the *Lincoln Journal-Star* who had asked if he was a homosexual. "Not unless you count the fact that he saw something similar two hundred years ago and it probably killed him."

"Pin's an expert on Black William," Stanky said, wiping a shred of pork from his chin.

"What little there is to know," said Pin grandly, "I know."

It figured that a goth townie would have developed a crush on the local bogeyman. I asked him to enlighten me.

"Well," Pin said, "when Joey told me he'd seen a star floating in front of the library, I knew it *had* to be one of BW's stars. Where the library stands today used to be the edge of Stockton Wood, which had an evil reputation. As did many woods in those days, of course. Stockton Wood is where he saw the stars."

"What did he say about them?"

"He didn't say a thing. Nothing that he committed to paper, anyway. It's his younger cousin, Samuel Garnant, we can thank for the story. He wrote a memoir about BW's escapades under the *nom de plume* Jonathan Venture. According to Samuel, BW was in the habit of riding in the woods at twilight. 'Tempting the Devil,' he called it. His first sight of the stars was a few mysterious lights—like with you and Joey. He rode out into the wood the next night and many nights thereafter. Samuel's a bit vague on how long it was before BW saw the stars again. I'm guessing a couple of weeks, going by clues in the narrative. But eventually he did see them, and what he saw was a lot like what we just saw." Pin put his hands together, fingertips touching, like a priest preparing to address the Ladies Auxiliary. "In those days, people feared God and the Devil. When they saw something amazing, they didn't stand around like a bunch of doofuses saying, 'All right!' and taking pictures. BW was terrified. He said he'd seen the Star Wormwood and heard the Holy Ghost moan. He set about changing his life."

Stanky shot me one of his wincing, cutesy, embarrassed smiles—he had told me the song was completely original.

"For almost a year," Pin went on, "BW tried to be a good Christian. He performed charitable works, attended church regularly, but his heart wasn't in it. He lapsed back into his old ways and before long he took to riding in Stockton Wood again, with his manservant Nero walking at his side. He thought that he had missed an opportunity and told Samuel if he was fortunate enough to see the stars again, he would ride straight for them. He'd embrace their evil purpose."

"What you said about standing around like doofuses, taking pictures," Andrea said. "I don't suppose anyone got a picture?"

Pin produced a cell phone and punched up a photograph of the library and the stars. Andrea and I leaned in to see.

"Can you e-mail that to me?" I asked.

Pin said he could and I wrote my address on a napkin.

"So," Pin said. "The next time BW saw the stars was in eighteen-oh-eight. He saw them twice, exactly like the first time.

A single star, then an interval of a week or two and a more complex sighting. A month after that, he disappeared while riding with Nero in Stockon Wood and they were never seen again."

Stanky hailed our waitress and asked for more pancakes for his moo shu.

"So you think the stars appeared three times?" said Andrea. "And Black William missed the third appearance on the first go-round, but not on the second?"

"That's what Samuel thought," said Pin.

Stanky fed Liz a bite of lemon chicken.

"You're assuming Black William was killed by the stars, but that doesn't make sense," said Andrea. "For instance, why would there be a longer interval between the second and third sightings? If there *was* a third sighting. It's more likely someone who knew the story killed him and blamed it on the stars."

"Maybe Nero capped him," said Stanky. "So he could gain his freedom."

Pin shrugged. "I only know what I read."

"It might be a wavefront," I said.

On another napkin, I drew a straight line with a small bump in it, then an interval in which the line flattened out, then a bigger bump, then a longer interval and an even bigger bump.

"Like that, maybe," I said. "Some kind of wavefront passing through Black William from God knows where. It's always passing through town, but we get this series of bumps that make it accessible every two hundred years. Or less. Maybe the stars appeared at other times."

"There's no record of it," said Pin. "And I've searched."

The waitress brought Stanky's pancakes and asked if we needed more napkins.

Andrea studied the napkin I'd drawn on. "But what about the first series of sightings? When were they?"

"Seventeen-eighty-nine," said Pin.

"It could be an erratic cycle," I said. "Or could be the cycle consists of two sequences close together, then a lapse of two hundred years. Don't expect a deeper explanation. I cut class a bunch in high school physics."

"The Holy Ghost doesn't obey physical principles," said Stanky pompously.

"I doubt Black William really heard the Holy Ghost," Andrea said. "If he heard what we heard tonight. It sounded more like a door closing to me."

"Whatever," he said. "It'll be cool to see what happens a month from now. Maybe Black William will return from the grave."

"Yeah." I crumpled the napkin and tossed it to the center of the table. "Maybe he'll bring Doctor Doom and the Lone Ranger with him."

Pin affected a shudder and said, "I think I'm busy that day."

Pin sent me the picture and I e-mailed it to a gearhead friend, Crazy Ed, who lived in Wilkes-Barre, to see what he could make of it. Though I didn't forget about the stars, I got slammed with business and my consideration of them and the late William Garnant had to be put on the back burner, along with Stanky's career. Against all expectations, Liz had not fled screaming from his bed, crying Pervert, but stayed with him most nights. Except for his time in the studio, I rarely saw him, and then only when his high school fans drove by to pick up him and Liz. An apocryphal story reached my ear, insinuating that she had taken on a carload of teenage boys while Stanky watched. That, if true, explained the relationship in Stanky-esque terms, terms I could understand. I didn't care what they did as long as he fulfilled his band duties and kept out of my hair. I landed him a gig at the Pick and Shovel in Waterford, filling in for a band that had been forced to cancel, and it went well enough that I scored him another gig at Garnant College. After a mere two performances, his reputation was building and I adjusted my timetable accordingly—I would make the college job an EP release party, push out an album soon thereafter and try to sell him to a major label. It was not the way I typically grew my acts, not commercially wise, but Stanky was not a typical act and, despite his prodigious talent, I wanted to have done with this sour-smelling chapter in my life.

Andrea, for all intents and purposes, had moved in, along with a high-energy, seven-month-old Irish setter named Timber, and was in the process of subletting her apartment. We were, doubtless, a disgusting item to everyone who had gotten to know us during our adversarial phase, always hanging on one another, kissing and touching. I had lunch with her every day—they held the back booth for us at McGuigan's—and one afternoon as we were settling in, Mia materialized beside the booth. "Hello," she said and stuck out a hand to Andrea.

Startled, Andrea shook her hand and I, too, was startled—until that moment, Mia had been unrelentingly hostile in her attitude toward my ex, referring to her as "that uppity skank" and in terms less polite. I noticed that she was dressed conservatively and not made up as an odalisque. Instead of being whipped into a punky abstraction, her hair was pulled back into a ponytail. The raspberry streak was gone. She was, in fact, for the first time since I had known her, streakless.

"May I join you?" Mia asked. "I won't take up much of your time."

Andrea scooted closer to the wall and Mia sat next to her.

"I heard you guys were back together," said Mia. "I'm glad."

Thunderstruck, I was incapable of fielding that one. "Thanks," said Andrea, looking to me for guidance.

Mia squared up in the booth, addressing me with a clear eye and a firm voice. "I'm moving to Pittsburgh. I've got a job lined up and I'll be taking night classes at Pitt, then going full-time starting next summer."

Hearing this issue from Mia's mouth was like hearing a cat begin speaking in Spanish while lighting a cheroot. I managed to say, "Yeah, that's . . . Yeah. Good."

"I'm sorry I didn't tell you sooner. I'm leaving tomorrow. But I heard you and Andrea were together, so . . ." She glanced back and forth between Andrea and myself, as if expecting a response.

"No, that's fine," I said. "You know."

"It was a destructive relationship," she said with great sincerity. "We had some fun, but it was bad for both of us. You were holding me back intellectually and I was limiting you emotionally."

"You're right," I said. "Absolutely."

Mia seemed surprised by how smoothly things were going, but she had, apparently, a prearranged speech and she by-God intended to give it.

"I understand this is sudden. It must come as a shock . . ."

"Oh, yeah."

". . . but I have to do this. I think it's best for me. I hope we can stay friends. You've been an important part of my growth."

"I hope so, too."

There ensued a short and—on my end, anyway—baffled silence.

"Okay. Well, I . . . I guess that's about it." She got to her feet and stood by the booth, hovering; then—with a sudden movement—she bent and kissed my cheek. "Bye."

Andrea put a hand to her mouth. "Oh my God! Was that Mia?"

"I'm not too sure," I said, watching Mia walk away, noting that there had been a complete absence of moues.

"An important part of her growth? She talks like a Doctor Phil sound bite. What did you do to her?"

"I'm not responsible, I don't think." I pushed around a notion that had occurred to me before, but that I had not had the impetus to consider more fully. "Do you know anyone who's exhibited a sudden burst of intelligence in the past few weeks? I mean someone who's been going along at the same pace for a while and suddenly they're Einstein. Relatively speaking."

She mulled it over. "As a matter of fact, I do. I know two or three people. Why?"

"Tell me."

"Well, there's Jimmy Galvin. Did you hear about him?"

"The gardening tool. Yeah. Who else?"

"This guy in my office. A paralegal. He's a hard worker, but basically a drone. Lately, whenever we ask him to dig up a file or find a reference, he's attached some ideas about the case we're working on. Good ideas. Some of them are great. Case-makers. He's the talk of the office. We've been joking that maybe we should get him to take a drug test. He's going back to law school and we're going to miss . . ." She broke off. "What's this have to do with the new Mia?"

I told her about Rudy's cartoons, Beth's novel, Kiwanda's new-found efficiency, the millworker, Stanky's increased productivity.

"I can't help wondering," I said, "if it's somehow related to the stars. I know it's a harebrained idea. There's probably a better explanation. Stanky . . . he never worked with a band before and that may be what's revving his engines. But that night at the Crucible, he was so polished. It just didn't synch with how I thought he'd react. I thought he'd get through it, but it's like he was an old hand."

Andrea looked distressed.

"And not everybody's affected," I said. "I'm not, for sure. You don't seem to be. It's probably bullshit."

"I know of another instance," she said. "But if I tell you, you have to promise to keep it a secret."

"I can do that."

"Do you know Wanda Lingrove?"

"Wasn't she a friend of yours? A cop? Tall woman? About five years older than us?"

"She's a detective now."

The waitress brought our food. I dug in; Andrea nudged her salad to the side.

"Did you hear about those college girls dying over in Waterford?" she asked.

"No, I haven't been keeping up."

"Two college girls died a few days apart. One in a fire and one in a drowning accident. Wanda asked for a look at the case files. The Waterford police had written them off as accidents, but

Wanda had a friend on the force and he slipped her the files and showed her the girls' apartments. They both lived off-campus. It's not that Wanda's any great shakes. She has an undistinguished record. But she had the idea from reading the papers—and they were skimpy articles—a serial killer was involved. Her friend pooh-poohed the idea. There wasn't any signature. But it turned out, Wanda was right. There was a signature, very subtle and very complicated, demonstrating that the killer was highly evolved. Not only did she figure that out, she caught him after two days on the case."

"Aren't serial killers tough to catch?"

"Yes. All that stuff you see about profiling on TV, it's crap. They wouldn't have come close to getting a line on this kid with profiling. He would have had to announce himself, but Wanda doesn't think he would have. She thinks he would have gone on killing, that putting one over on the world was enough for him."

"He was a kid?"

"Fourteen years old. A kid from Black William. What's more, he'd given no sign of being a sociopath. Yet in the space of three weeks, he went from zero to sixty. From playing JV football to being a highly organized serialist. That doesn't happen in the real world."

"So how come Wanda's not famous?"

"The college is trying to keep it quiet. The kid's been bundled off to an institution and the cops have the lid screwed tight." Andrea picked at her salad. "What I'm suggesting, maybe everyone *is* being affected, but not in ways that conform to your model. Wanda catching the kid, that conforms. But the kid himself, the fact that a pathology was brought out in him . . . that suggests that people may be affected in ways we don't notice. Maybe they just love each other more."

I laid down my fork. "Like with us?"

A doleful nod.

"That's crazy," I said. "You said you'd been plotting for months to make a move."

"Yes, but it was a fantasy!"

"And you don't think you would have acted on it?"

"I don't know. One thing for certain, I never expected anything like this." She cut her volume to a stage whisper. "I want you all the time. It's like when we were nineteen. I'm addicted to you."

"Yeah," I said. "Same here."

"I worry that it'll stop, then I worry that it won't—it's wreaking havoc with my work. I can't stop thinking about you. On a rational level, I know I'm an animal. But there's a place in me that wants to believe love is more than evolutionary biology. And now this thing with the stars. To think that what I'm feeling could be produced by something as random as a wavefront or a supernatural event, or whatever . . . It makes me feel like an experimental animal. Like a rabbit that's been drugged. It scares me."

"Look," I said. "We're probably talking about something that isn't real."

"No, it's real."

"How can you be sure? I only just brought the subject up. We can't have been discussing it more than five minutes."

"You convinced me. Everything you said rings true. I know it here." Andrea touched a hand to her breast. "And you know it, too. Something's happening to us. Something's happening to this town."

We stepped back from that conversation. It was, I suppose, a form of denial, the avoidance of a subject neither of us wished to confront, because it was proof against confrontation, against logic and reason, and so we trivialized it and fell back on our faith, on our mutuality. Sometimes, lying with Andrea, considering the join of her neck and shoulder, the slight convexity of her belly, the compliant curve of a breast compressed into a pouty shape by the weight of her arm, the thousand turns and angles that each seemed the expression of a white simplicity within, I would have the urge to wake her, to drive away from Black William, and thus protect her, protect us, from this infestation of stars; but then I would think that such an action might destroy the thing I hoped to protect, that once away from the stars we might feel differently about one another. And then I'd think how irrational these thoughts were, how ridiculous it was to contemplate uprooting our lives over so flimsy a fear. And, finally, having made this brief rounds of my human potential, I would lapse again into a Praxitelean scrutiny, a sculptor in love with his stone, content to drift in and out of a dream in which love, though it had been proved false (like Andrea said, an animal function and nothing more), proved to be eternally false, forever and a day of illusion, of two souls burning brighter and brighter until they appeared to make a single glow, a blazing unity concealed behind robes of aging flesh.

The world beat against our door. Pin's photograph was printed on the third page of the *Black William Gazette*, along with the news that the University of Pittsburgh would be sending a team of observers to measure the phenomenon, should it occur again, as was predicted (by whom, the *Gazette* did not say). There was a sidebar recounting Black William's sordid history and Jonathan Venture's version of BW's involvement with the stars. The body of the article . . . Well, it was as if the reporter had been privy to our conversation at the Szechuan Palace. I suspected that he had, if only at secondhand, since my wavefront theory was reproduced in full, attributed to "a local pundit." As a result of this publicity, groups of people, often more than a hundred, mostly the young and the elderly, came to gather in front of the library between the hours of five and nine, thus depriving me of the customary destination of my evening walks.

Stanky, his ego swollen to improbable proportions by two successful performances, by the adulation of his high school fans ("Someone ought to be writing everything Joey says down," said one dreamy-eyed fool), became increasingly temperamental, lashing out at his bandmates, at me, browbeating Liz at every opportunity, and prowling about the house in a sulk, ever with a Coke and cigarette, glaring at all who fell to his gaze, not bothering to speak. In the mornings, he was difficult to wake, keeping Geno and Jerry waiting, wasting valuable time, and one particular morning, my frustration wth him peaked and I let Timber into his bedroom and closed the door, listening while the happy pup gamboled across the mattress, licking and drooling, eliciting squeals and curses from the sleepy couple, an action that provoked a confrontation that I won by dint of physical threat and financial dominance, but that firmly established our unspoken enmity and made me anxious about whether I would be able to maneuver him to the point where I could rid myself of him and show a profit.

A gray morning, spitting snow, and I answered the doorbell to find a lugubrious, long-nosed gentleman with a raw, bony face, toting a briefcase and wearing a Sy Sperling wig and a cheap brown suit. A police cruiser was parked at the curb; two uniformed officers stood smoking beside it, casting indifferent looks toward the Polozny, which rolled on blackly in—as a local DJ was prone to characterize it—"its eternal search for the sea." Since we were only a couple of days from the EP release, I experienced a sinking feeling, one that was borne out when the man produced a card identifying him as Martin Kiggins of McKeesport, a Friend of the Court. He said he would like to have a word with me about Joseph Stanky.

"How well do you know Joseph?" he asked me once we had settled in the office.

Kiwanda, at her desk in the next room, made a choking noise. I replied that while I had, I thought, an adequate understanding of Joseph as a musician, I was unfamililar with the details of his life.

"Did you know he has a wife?" Kiggins was too lanky to fit the chair and, throughout our talk, kept scrunching around in it. "And he's got a little boy. Almost two years old, he is."

"No, I didn't know that."

"Poor little guy nearly didn't make it that far. Been sick his whole life." Kiggins's gaze acquired a morose intensity. "Meningitis."

I couldn't get a handle on Kiggins; he acted as if he was trying to sell me something, yet he had arrived on my doorstep with an armed force and the authority of the law.

"I thought meningitis was fatal," I said.

"Not a hundred percent," said Kiggins cheerlessly. "His mother doesn't have insurance, so he didn't get the best of care."

"That's tough."

"She's on welfare. Things aren't likely to improve for the kid or for her. She's not what you'd call an attractive woman."

"Why are we talking about this?" I asked. "It's a sad story, but I'm not involved."

"Not directly, no."

"Not any damn way. I don't understand what you're looking for."

Kiggins seemed disappointed in me. "I'm looking for Joseph. Is he here?"

"I don't know."

"You don't know. Okay." He put his hands on his knees and stood, making a show of peering out the window at his cop buddies.

"I really don't know if he's here," I said. "I've been working, I haven't been downstairs this morning."

"Mind if I take a look down there?"

"You're goddamn right, I mind! What's this about? You've been doing a dance ever since you came in. Why don't you spit it out?"

Kiggins gave me a measuring look, then glanced around the office—I think he was hoping to locate another chair. Failing this, he sat back down.

"You appear to be a responsible guy, Vernon," he said. "Is it okay I call you Vernon?"

"Sure thing, Marty. I don't give a shit what you call me as long as you get to the point."

"You own your home, a business. Pay your taxes . . . far as I can tell without an audit. You're a pretty solid citizen."

The implicit threat of an audit ticked me off, but I let him continue. I began to realize where this might be going.

"I've got the authority to take Joseph back to McKeesport and throw his butt in jail," said Kiggins. "He's in arrears with his child and spousal support. Now I know Joseph doesn't have any money to speak of, but seeing how you've got an investment in him, I'm hoping we can work out some arrangement."

"Where'd you hear that?" I asked. "About my investment."

"Joseph still has friends in McKeesport. High school kids, mainly. Truth be told, we think he was supplying them with drugs, but I'm not here about that. They've been spreading it around that you're about to make him a star."

I snorted. "He's a *long* way from being a star. Believe me."

"I believe you. Do you believe me when I tell you I'm here to take him back? Just say the word, I'll give a whistle to those boys out front." Kiggins shifted the chair sideways, so he could stretch out one leg. "I know how you make your money, Vernon. You build a band up, then you sell their contracts. Now you've put in some work with Joseph. Some serious time and money. I should think you'd want to protect your investment."

"Okay." I reached for a cigarette, recalled that I had quit. "What's he owe?"

"Upwards of eleven thousand."

"He's all yours," I said. "Take the stairs in back. Follow the corridor to the front of the house. First door on your right."

"I said I wanted to make an arrangement. I'm not after the entire amount."

And so began our negotiation.

If we had finished the album, I would have handed Stanky over and given Kiggins my blessing, but as things stood, I needed him. Kiggins, on the other hand, wouldn't stand a chance of collecting any money with Stanky in the slam—he likely had a predetermined figure beneath which he would not move. It infuriated me to haggle with him. Stanky's wife and kid wouldn't see a nickel. They would dock her welfare by whatever amount he extracted from me, deduct administrative and clerical fees, and she would end up worse off than before. Yet I had no choice other than to submit to legal blackmail.

Kiggins wouldn't go below five thousand. That, he said, was his bottom line. He put on a dour poker face and waited for me to decide.

"He's not worth it," I said.

Sadly, Kiggins made for the door; when I did not relent, he turned back and we resumed negotiations, settling on a figure of three thousand and my promise to attach a rider to Stanky's contract stating that a percentage of his earnings would be sent to the court. After he had gone, my check tucked in his briefcase, Kiwanda came to stand by my desk with folded arms.

"I'd give it a minute before you go down," she said. "You got that I'm-gonna-break-his-face look."

"Do you fucking believe this?" I brought my fist down on the desk. "I want to smack that little bitch!"

"Take a breath, Vernon. You don't want to lose any more today than just walked out of here."

I waited, I grew calm, but as I approached the stairs, the image of a wizened toddler and a moping, double-chinned wife cropped up in my brain. With each step I grew angrier and, when I reached Stanky's bedroom, I pushed in without knocking. He and Liz were having sex. I caught a fetid odor and an unwanted glimpse of Liz's sallow hindquarters as she scrambled beneath the covers. I shut the door partway and shouted at Stanky to haul his ass out here. Seconds later, he burst from the room in a T-shirt and pajama bottoms, and stumped into the kitchen with his head down, arms tightly held, like an enraged penguin. He fished a Coke from the refrigerator and made as if to say something; but I let him have it. I briefed him on Kiggins and said, "It's not a question of morality. I already knew you were a piece of crap. But this is a business, man. It's my livelihood, not a playground for degenerates. And when you bring the cops to my door, you put that in jeopardy."

He hung his head, picking at the Coke's pop top. "You don't understand."

"I don't want to understand! Get it? I have absolutely no desire to understand. That's between you and your wife. Between you and whatever scrap of meatloaf shaped like the Virgin Mary you pretend to worship. I don't care. One more screw-up, I'm calling Kiggins and telling him to come get you."

Liz had entered the kitchen, clutching a bathrobe about her; when she heard "wife," she retreated.

I railed at Stanky, telling him he would pay back every penny of the three thousand, telling him further to clean his room of every pot seed and pill, to get his act in order and finish the album; and I kept on railing at him until his body language conveyed that I could expect two or three days of penitence and sucking up. Then I allowed him to slink by me and into the bedroom. When I passed his door, cracked an inch open, I heard him whining to Liz, saying, "She's not *really* my wife."

I took the afternoon off and persuaded Rudy to go fishing. We bundled up against the cold, bought a twelve-pack of Iron City and dropped our lines in Kempton's Pond, a lopsided period stamped into the half-frozen ground a couple of miles east of town, punctuating a mixed stand of birch and hazel—it looked as if a giant with a peg leg had left this impression in the rock, creating a hole thirty feet wide. The clouds had lowered and darkened, their swollen bellies appearing to tatter on the leafless treetops as they slid past; but the snow had quit falling. There was some light accumulation on the banks, which stood eight or nine feet above the black water and gave the pond the look of an old cistern. The water circulated like heavy oil and swallowed our sinkers with barely a splash. This bred the expectation that if we hooked anything, it would be a megalodon or an ichthyosaur, a creature such as would have been trapped in a tar pit. But we had no such expectation.

It takes a certain cast of mind to enjoy fishing with no hope of a catch, or the faint hope of catching some inedible fishlike thing every few years or so. That kind of fishing is my favorite sport, though I admit I follow the Steelers closely, as do many in Black William. Knowing that nothing will rise from the deep, unless it is something that will astound your eye or pebble your skin with gooseflesh, makes for a rare feeling. Sharing this with Rudy, who had been my friend for ten years, since he was fresh out of grad school at Penn State, enhanced that feeling. In the summer we sat and watched our lines, we chatted, we chased our depressions with beer and cursed the flies; in winter, the best season for our sport, there were no flies. The cold was like ozone to my nostrils, the silence complete, and the denuded woods posed an abstract of slants and perpendiculars, silver and dark, nature as Chinese puzzle. Through frays in the clouds we glimpsed the fat, lordly crests of the Bittersmiths.

I was reaching for another Iron City when I felt a tug on the line. I kept still and felt another tug, then—though I waited the better part of a minute—nothing.

"Something's down in there," I said, peering at the impenetrable surface.

"You get a hit?" Rudy asked.

"Uh-huh."

"How much line you got out?"

"Twenty, twenty-five feet."

"Must have been a current."

"It happened twice."

"Probably a current."

I pictured an enormous grouperlike face with blind milky-blue globes for eyes, moon lanterns, and a pair of weak, underdeveloped hands groping at my line. The Polozny plunges deep underground east of the bridge, welling up into these holes punched through the Pennsylvania rock, sometimes flooding the woods in the spring, and a current was the likely explanation; but I preferred to think that those subterranean chambers were the uppermost tiers of a secret world and that now and again some piscine

Columbus, fleeing the fabulous madness of his civilization, palaces illumined by schools of electric eels controlled by the thoughts of freshwater octopi, limestone streets patrolled by gangs of river crocs, grand avenues crowded with giant-snail busses and pedestrian trout, sought to breach the final barrier and find in the world above a more peaceful prospect.

"You have no imagination," I said.

Rudy grunted. "Fishing doesn't require an imagination. That's what makes it fun."

Motionless, he was a bearish figure muffled in a down parka and a wool cap, his face reddened by the cold, breath steaming. He seemed down at the mouth and, thinking it might cheer him up, I asked how he was coming with the comic strip.

"I quit working on it," he said.

"Why the hell'd you do that? It was your best thing ever."

"It was giving me nightmares."

I absorbed this, gave it due consideration. "Didn't strike me as nightmare material. It's kind of bleak. Black comedy. But nothing to freak over."

"It changed." He flicked his wrist, flicking his line sideways. "The veins of pork . . . You remember them?"

"Yeah, sure."

"They started growing, twisting all through the mountain. The mineworkers were happy. Delirious. They were going to be rich, and they threw a big party to celebrate. A pork festival. Actually, that part was pretty funny. I'll show it to you. They made this enormous pork sculpture and were all wearing porkpie hats. They had a beauty contest to name Miss Pork. The winner . . . I used Mia for a model."

"You're a sick bastard, you know that?"

Again, Rudy grunted, this time in amusement. "Then the stars began eating the pork. The mineworkers would open a new vein and the stars would pour in and choff it down. They were ravenous. Nothing could stop them. The mineworkers were starving. That's when I started having nightmares. There was something gruesome about the way I had them eating. I tried to change it, but I couldn't make it work any other way."

I said it still didn't sound like the stuff of nightmares, and Rudy said, "You had to be there."

We fell to talking about other things. The Steelers, could they repeat? Stanky. I asked Rudy if he was coming to the EP release and he said he wouldn't miss it. "He's a genius guitar player," he said. "Too bad he's such a creep."

"Goes with the territory," I said. "Like with Robert Frost beating his wife. Stanky's a creep, he's a perv. A moral dwarf. But he is for sure talented. And you know me. I'll put up with perversity if someone's talented." I clapped Rudy on the shoulder. "That's why I put up with you. You better finish that strip or I'll dump your ass and start hanging with a better class of people."

"Forget the strip," he said glumly. "I'm too busy designing equipment sheds and stables."

We got into a discussion about Celebrity Wifebeaters, enumerating the most recent additions to the list, and this led us—by loose association only—to the subject of Andrea. I told him about our conversation at McGuigan's and what she had said about the outbreak of creativity, about love.

"Maybe she's got a point," Rudy said. "You two have always carried a torch, but you burned each other so badly in the divorce, I never would have thought you'd get back together." He cracked open a beer, handed it to me, and opened one for himself. "You hear about Colvin Jacobs?"

"You mean something besides he's a sleazeball?"

"He's come up with a plan to reduce the county's tax burden by half. Everybody says it's the real quill."

"I'm surprised he found the time, what with all those congressional junkets."

"And Judy Trickle, you hear about her?"

"Now you're scaring me."

"I know. Ol' Juggs 'R' Us Judy."

"She should have been your model for Miss Pork, not Mia. What'd she do? Design a newfangled bra?"

"Lifts *and* separates."

"You mean that's it?"

"You nailed it."

"No way!"

"She's been wearing a prototype on the show the last few days. There's a noticeable change." He did a whispery voiceover voice. "The curves are softer, more natural."

"Bullshit!"

"I'm serious. Check her out."

"I got better things to do than watch *AM Waterford*."

"I remember the time when you were a devoted fan."

"That was post-Andrea . . . and pre-Andrea." I chuckled. "Remember the show when she demonstrated the rowing machine? Leotards aren't built to handle that sort of stress."

"I knew the guy who produced her back then. He said they gave her stuff like that to do because they were hoping for a Wardrobe Malfunction. They weren't prepared for the reaction."

"Janet Jackson's no Judy Trickle. It was like a dam bursting. Like . . . help me out here, man."

"Like the birth of twin zeppelins."

"Like the embodiment of the yang, like the Aquarian dawn."

Rudy jiggled his line. "This is beginning to border on the absurd."

"You're the one brought her up."

"I'm not talking about Judy, I'm talking about the whole thing. The outbreak."

"Oh, okay. Yeah, we're way past absurd if Miz Trickle's involved. We're heading toward surreal."

"I've heard of five or six more people who've had . . . breakthroughs, I suppose you'd call them."

"How come I don't hear about these people except from you? Do you sit in your office all day, collecting odd facts about Black William?"

"I get more traffic than you do, and people are talking about it now."

"What are they saying?"

"What you'd expect. Isn't it weird? It must be the water, the pollution. I've even heard civic pride expressed. Someone coined the phrase, 'Black William, Pennsylvania's Brain Capital.'"

"That's taking it a bit far." I had a slug of Iron City. "So nobody's panicking? Saying head for the hills?"

"Who said that?"

"Andrea. She was a little disturbed. She didn't exactly say it, but she seemed to think this thing might not be all good."

He tightened his lips and produced a series of squeaking noises. "I think Andrea's right. Not about head for the hills. I don't know about that. But I think whatever this is, it's affecting people in different ways. Some of them emotionally."

"Why's that?"

"I . . ." He tipped back his head, stared at the clouds. "I don't want to talk anymore, man. Okay? Let's just fish."

It began to snow again, tiny flakes, the kind that presage a big fall, but we kept fishing, jiggling our lines in the dead water, drinking Iron City. Something was troubling Rudy, but I didn't press him. I thought about Andrea. She planned to get off early and we were going to dinner in Waterford and maybe catch a movie. I was anticipating kissing her, touching her in the dark, while the new James Bond blew stuff up or (this was more likely) Kenneth Branagh destroyed *As You Like It*, when a tremor ran across the surface of the pond. Both Rudy and I sat up straight and peered. "T. Rex is coming," I said. An instant later, the pond was lashed into a turbulence that sent waves slopping in all directions, as if a large swimmer had drawn near the surface, then made a sudden turn, propelling itself down toward its customary haunts with a flick of its tail. Yet we saw nothing. Nary a fin nor scale nor section of plated armor. We waited, breathless, for the beast to return.

"Definitely not a current," said Rudy.

Except for the fact that Rudy didn't show, the EP release went well. The music was great, the audience responsive, we sold lots of CDs and souvenirs, including AVERAGE JOE dogtags and JOE STANKY'S ARMY khaki T-shirts, with the pear-shaped (less so after diets and death marches) one's silhouette in white beneath the arc of the lettering. This despite Stanky's obvious displeasure with everyone involved. He was angry at me because I had stolen his top hat and refused to push back the time of the performance to ten o'clock so he could join the crowd in front of the library waiting for the return of Black William (their number had swelled to more than three hundred since the arrival of the science team from Pitt, led by a youngish professor who, with his rugged build and mustache and plaid wool shirts, might have stepped out of an ad for trail mix). He was angry at Geno and Jerry for the usual reasons—they were incompetent clowns, they didn't understand the music, and they had spurned the opportunity to watch TV with him and Liz. Throughout the hour and a quarter show, he sulked and spoke not a word to the audience, and then grew angry at them when a group of frat boys initiated a chant of "Skanky, Skanky, Skanky . . ." Yet the vast majority were blown away and my night was made when I spotted an A&R man from Atlantic sneaking around.

I was in my office the next morning, reading the *Gazette*, which had come late to the party (as usual) and was running a light-hearted feature on "Pennsylvania's Brain Capital," heavy on Colvin Jacobs quotes, when I received a call from Crazy Ed in Wilkes-Barre, saying that he'd e-mailed me a couple of enhancements of Pin's photograph. I opened the e-mails and the attachments, then asked what I was looking at.

"Beats me," said Ed. "The first is up close on one of those white dealies. You can get an idea of the shape. Sort of like a sea urchin. A globe with spines . . . except there's so many spines, you can't make out the globe. You see it?"

"Yeah. You can't tell me what it is?"

"I don't have a clue." Ed made a buzzing noise, something he did whenever he was stumped. "I assumed the image was fake, that the kid had run two images together, because there's a shift in perspective between the library and the white dealies. They look like they're coming from a long way off. But then I realized the perspective was totally fucked up. It's like part of the photo was taken through a depth of water, or something that's shifting like water. Different sections appear to be at different distances all through the image. Did you notice a rippling effect . . . or anything like that?"

"I only saw it for a couple of seconds. I didn't have time to get much more than a glimpse."

"Okay." Ed made the buzzing noise again. "Have you opened the second attachment?"

"Yep."

"Once I figured out I couldn't determine distances, I started looking at the black stuff, the field or whatever. I didn't get anywhere with that. It's just black. Undifferentiated. Then I took a look at the horizon line. That's how it appeared to you, right? A black field stretching to a horizon? Well, if that was the case, you'd think you'd see something at the front edge, but the only thing I picked up was those bumps on the horizon."

I studied the bumps.

"Kinda look like the tops of heads, don't they?" said Ed.

The bumps could have been heads; they could also have been bushes, animals, or a hundred other things; but his suggestion gave me an uneasy feeling. He said he would fool around with the picture some more and get back to me. I listened to demos. Food of the Gods (King Crimson redux). Corpus Christy (a transsexual front man who couldn't sing, but the name grew on me). The Land Mines (middling roots rock). Gopher Lad (a heroin band from Minnesota). A band called Topless Coroner intrigued me, but I passed after realizing all their songs were about car parts. Around eleven-thirty I took a call from a secretary at DreamWorks who asked if I would hold for William Wine. I couldn't place the name, but said that I would hold and leafed through the Rolodex, trying to find him.

"Vernon!" said an enthusiastic voice from the other side of creation. "Bill Wine. I'm calling for David Geffen. I believe you had drinks with him at the Plug Awards last year. You made quite an impression on David."

The Plugs were the Oscars of the indie business—Geffen had an ongoing interest in indie rock and had put in an appearance. I recalled being in a group gathered around him at the bar, but I did not recall making an impression.

"He made a heck of an impression on me," I said.

Pleasant laughter, so perfect it sounded canned. "David sends his regards," said Wine. "He's sorry he couldn't contact you personally, but he's going to be tied up all day."

"What can I do for you?"

"David listened to that new artist of yours. Joe Stanky? In all the years I've known him, I've never heard him react like he did this morning."

"He liked it?"

"He didn't like it. . . ." Wine paused for dramatic effect. "He was knocked out."

I wondered how Geffen had gotten hold of the EP. Mine not to reason why, I figured.

Wine told me that Geffen wanted to hear more. Did I have any other recorded material?

"I've got nine songs on tape," I said. "But some of them are raw."

"David likes raw. Can we get a dupe?"

"You know . . . I usually prefer to push out an album or two before I look for a deal."

"Listen, Vernon. We're not going to let you go to the poorhouse on this."

"That's a relief."

"In fact, David wanted me to sound you out about our bringing you in under the DreamWorks umbrella."

Stunned, I said, "In what capacity?"

"I'll let David tell you about that. He'll call you in a day or two. He's had his eye on you for some time."

I envisioned Sauron spying from his dark tower. I had a dim view of corporate life and I wasn't as overwhelmed by this news as Wine had likely presumed I would be. After the call ended, however, I felt as if I had modeled for Michelangelo's Sistine Chapel mural, the man about to be touched by God's billionaire-ish finger. My impulse was to tell Stanky, but I didn't want his ego to grow more swollen. I called Andrea and learned she would be in court until midafternoon. I started to call Rudy, then thought it would be too easy for him to refuse me over the phone. Better to yank him out of his cave and buy him lunch. I wanted to bust his chops about missing the EP release and I needed to talk with someone face-to-face, to analyze this thing that was happening around Stanky. Had the buzz I'd generated about him taken wings on a magical current? The idea that David Geffen was planning to call seemed preposterous. Was Stanky that good? Was I? What, if anything, did Geffen have in mind? Rudy, who enjoyed playing Yoda to my Luke, would help place these questions in coherent perspective.

When I reached Rudy's office, I found Gwen on the phone. Her makeup, usually perfect, was in need of repair; it appeared that she had been crying. "I don't know," she said with strain in her voice. "You'll have to . . . No. I really don't know."

I pointed to the inner office and mouthed, *Is he in*?

She signaled me to wait.

"I've got someone here," she said into the phone. "I'll have to . . . Yes. Yes, I will let you know. All right. Yes. Good-bye." She hung up and, her chin quivering, tried several times to speak, finally blurting out, "I'm so sorry. He's dead. Rudy's dead."

I think I may have laughed—I made some sort of noise, some expression of denial, yet I knew it was true. My face flooded with heat and I went back a step, as if the words had thrown me off-balance.

Gwen said that Rudy had committed suicide early that morning. He had—according to his wife—worked in the office until after midnight, then driven home and taken some pills. The phone rang again. I left Gwen to deal with it and stepped into the inner office to call Beth. I sat at Rudy's desk, but that felt wrong, so I walked around with the phone for a while. Rudy had been a depressed guy, but hell, everyone in Black William was depressed about something. I thought that I had been way more depressed than Rudy. He seemed to have it together. Nice wife, healthy income, kids. Sure, he was a for-shit architect in a for-shit town, and not doing the work he wanted, but that was no reason to kill yourself.

Standing by the drafting table, I saw his wastebasket was crammed with torn paper. A crawly sensation rippled the skin between my shoulder blades. I dumped the shreds onto the table. Rudy had done a compulsive job of tearing them up, but I could tell they were pieces of his comic strip. Painstakingly, I sorted through them and managed to reassemble most of a frame. In it, a pair of black hands (presumably belonging to a mineworker) was holding a gobbet of pork, as though in offering; above it floated a spiky white ball. The ball had extruded a longish spike to penetrate the pork and the image gave the impression that the ball was sucking meat through a straw. I stared at the frame, trying to interpret it, to tie the image in with everything that had happened, but I felt a vibration pass through my body, like the heavy, impersonal signal of Rudy's death, and I imagined him on the bathroom floor, foam on his mouth, and I had to sit back down.

Beth, when I called her, didn't feel like talking. I asked if there was anything I could do, and she said if I could find out when the police were going to release the body, she would appreciate it. She said she would let me know about the funeral, sounding—as had Gwen—like someone who was barely holding it together. Hearing that in her voice caused me to leak a few tears and, when she heard me start to cry, she quickly got off the phone, as if she didn't want my lesser grief to pollute her own, as if Rudy dying had broken whatever bond there was between us. I thought this might be true.

I called the police and, after speaking to a functionary, reached a detective whom I knew, Ross Peloblanco, who asked my connection to the deceased.

"Friend of the family," I said. "I'm calling for his wife."

"Huh," said Peloblanco, his attention distracted by something in his office.

"So when are you going to release him?"

"I think they already done the autopsy. There's been a bunch of suicides lately and the ME put a rush on this one."

"How many's a bunch?"

"Oops! Did I say that? Don't worry about it. The ME's a whack job. He's batshit about conspiracy theories."

"So . . . can I tell the funeral home to come now?"

Peloblanco sneezed, said, "Shit!" and then went on: "Bowen did some work for my mom. She said he was a real gentleman. You never know what's going on with people, do ya?" He blew his nose. "I guess you can come pick him up whenever."

The waters of the Polozny never freeze. No matter how cold it gets or how long the cold lasts, they are kept warm by a cocktail of pollutants and, though the river may flow more sluggishly in winter, it continues on its course, black and gelid. There is something statutory about its poisonous constancy. It seems less river than regulation, a divine remark rendered daily into law, engraving itself upon the world year after year until its long meander has eaten a crack that runs the length and breadth of creation, and its acids and oxides drain into the void.

Between the viewing and the funeral, in among the various consoling talks and offerings of condolence, I spent a great deal of time gazing at the Polozny, sitting on the stoop and smoking, enduring the cold wind, brooding over half-baked profundities. The muted roaring of the mill surrounded me, as did dull thuds and clunks and distant car horns that seemed to issue from the gray sky, the sounds of business as usual, the muffled engine of commerce. Black William must be, I thought, situated on the ass-end of Purgatory, the place where all those overlooked by God were kept. The dead river dividing a dying landscape, a dingy accumulation of snow melting into slush on its banks; the mill, a Hell of red brick with its chimney smoke of souls; the scatters of crows winging away from leafless trees; old Mrs. Gables two doors down, tottering out to the sidewalk, peering along the street for the mail, for a glimpse of her son's maroon Honda Civic, for some hopeful thing, then, her hopes dashed, laboriously climbing her stairs and going inside to sit alone and count the ticks of her clock: these were evidences of God's fabulous absence, His careless abandonment of a destinyless town to its several griefs. I scoffed at those who professed to understand grief, who deemed it a simple matter, a painful yet comprehensible transition, and partitioned the process into stages (my trivial imagination made them into gaudy stagecoaches painted different colors) in order to enable its victims to adapt more readily to the house rules. After the initial shock of Rudy's suicide had waned, grief overran me like a virus, it swarmed, breeding pockets of weakness and fever, eventually receding at its own pace, on its own terms, and though it may have been subject to an easy compartmentalization—Anger, Denial, etc.—that kind of analysis did not address its nuances and could not remedy the thousand small bitternesses that grief inflames and encysts. On the morning of the funeral, when I voiced one such bitterness, complaining about how Beth had treated me since Rudy died, mentioning the phone call, pointing out other incidences of her intolerance, her rudeness in pushing me away, Andrea—who had joined me on the stoop—set me straight.

"She's not angry at you," Andrea said. "She's jealous. You and Rudy . . . that was a part of him she never shared, and when she sees you, she doesn't know how to handle it."

"You think?"

"I used to feel that way."

"About me and Rudy."

She nodded. "And about the business. I don't feel that way now. I guess I'm older. I understand you and Rudy had a guy thing and I didn't need to know everything about it. But Beth's dealing with a lot right now. She's oversensitive and she feels . . . jilted. She feels that Rudy abandoned her for you. A little, anyway. So she's jilting you. She'll get over it, or she won't. People are funny like that. Sometimes resentments are all that hold them together. You shouldn't take it personally."

I refitted my gaze to the Polozny, more or less satisfied by what she had said. "We live on the banks of the River Styx," I said after a while. "At least it has a Styx-ian gravitas."

"Stygian," she said.

I turned to her, inquiring.

"That's the word you wanted. Stygian."

"Oh . . . right."

A silence marked by the passing of a mail truck, its tire chains grinding the asphalt and spitting slush; the driver waved.

"I think I know why Rudy did it," I said, and told her what I had found in the office wastebasket. "More than anything, he wanted to do creative work. When he finally did, it gave him nightmares. It messed with his head. He must have built it into this huge thing and . . ." I tapped out a cigarette, stuck it in my mouth. "It doesn't sound like much of a reason, but I can relate. That's why it bites my ass to see guys like Stanky who do something creative every time they take a piss. *I* want to write those songs. *I* want to have the acclaim. It gets me thinking, someday I might wind up like Rudy."

"That's not you. You said it yourself—you get pissed off. You find someplace else to put your energy." She rumpled my hair. "Buck up, Sparky. You're going to live a long time and have lots worse problems."

It crossed my mind to suggest that the stars might have played some mysterious part in Rudy's death, and to mention the rash of suicides (five, I had learned); but all that seemed unimportant, dwarfed by the death itself.

At one juncture during that weekend, Stanky ventured forth from TV-land to offer his sympathies. He might have been sincere, but I didn't trust his sincerity—it had an obsequious quality and I believed he was currying favor, paving the way so he might hit me up for another advance. Pale and shivering, hunched against the cold; the greasy collar of his jacket turned up; holding a Camel in two nicotine-stained fingers; his doughy features cinched in an expression of exaggerated dolor: I hated him at that moment and told him I was taking some days off, that he could work on the album or go play with his high school sycophants. "It's up to you," I said. "Just don't bother me about it." He made no reply, but the front door slamming informed me that he had not taken it well.

On Wednesday, Patty Prole (nee Patricia Hand), the leader of the Swimming Holes, a mutual friend of mine and Rudy's who had come down from Pittsburgh for the funeral, joined me and Andrea for dinner at McGuigan's, and, as we strolled past the park, I recalled that more than a month—thirty-four days, to be exact— had elapsed since I had last seen the stars. The crowd had dwindled to about a hundred and fifty (Stanky and Liz among them). They stood in clumps around the statue, clinging to the hope that Black William would appear; though judging by their general listlessness, the edge of their anticipation had been blunted and they were gathered there because they had nothing better to do. The van belonging to the science people from Pitt remained parked at the southeast corner of the library, but I had heard they were going to pull up stakes if nothing happened in the next day or two.

McGuigan's was a bubble of heat and light and happy conversation. A Joe Henry song played in the background; Pitt basketball was on every TV. I had not thought the whole town would be dressed in mourning, but the jolly, bustling atmosphere came as something of a shock. They had saved the back booth for us and, after drinking for a half hour or so, I found myself enjoying the evening. Patty was a slight, pretty, blue-eyed blonde in her late twenties, dressed in a black leather jacket and jeans. To accommodate the sober purpose of this trip home, she had removed her visible piercings. With the majority of her tattoos covered by the jacket, she looked like an ordinary girl from western Pennsylvania and nothing like the exotic, pantherine creature she became on stage. When talk turned to Rudy, Andrea and I embraced the subject, offering humorous anecdotes and fond reminiscence, but Patty, though she laughed, was subdued. She toyed with her fork, idly stabbing holes in the label on her beer bottle, and at length revealed the reason for her moodiness.

"Did Rudy ever tell you we had a thing?" she asked.

"He alluded to it," I said. "But well after the fact. Years."

"I bet you guys talked all about it when you're up at Kempton's Pond. He said you used to talk about the local talent when you're up there sometimes."

Andrea elbowed me, not too sharply, in mock reproval.

"As I remember, the conversation went like this," I said. "We were talking about bands, the Swimming Holes came up, and he mentioned he'd had an affair with you. And I said, 'Oh, yeah?' And Rudy said, 'Yeah.' Then after a minute he said, 'Patty's a great girl.'"

"That's what he said? We had an affair? That's the word he used?"

"I believe so."

"He didn't say he was banging me or like that?"

"No."

"And that's all he said?" Patty stared at me sidelong, as if trying to penetrate layers of deception.

"That's all I remember."

"I bet you tried to get more out of him. I know you. You were hungering for details."

"I can't promise I wasn't," I said. "I just don't remember. You know Rudy. He was a private guy. You could beat on him with a shovel and not get a thing out of him. I'm surprised he told me that much."

She held my gaze a moment longer. "Shit! I can't tell if you're lying."

"He's not," said Andrea.

"You got him scoped, huh? He's dead to rights." Patty grinned and leaned against the wall, putting one fashionably booted foot up on the bench. "Rudy and me . . . It was a couple weeks right before the band left town. It was probably stupid. Sometimes I regret it, but sometimes I don't."

Andrea asked how it happened, and Patty, who obviously wanted to talk about it, said, "You know. Like always. We started hanging out, talking. Finally I asked him straight out, 'Where's this going, Rudy?' Because we only had a couple of weeks and I wanted to know if it was all in my head. He got this peculiar look on his face and kissed me. Like I said, it didn't last long, but it was deep, you know. That's why I'm glad Rudy didn't tell everyone how it was in the sack. It's a dumb thing to worry about, but . . ." Her voice had developed a tremor. "I guess that's what I'm down to."

"You loved him," said Andrea.

"Yeah. I did." Patty shook off the blues and sat up. "There wasn't anywhere for it to go. He'd never leave his kids and I was going off to Pittsburgh. I hated his wife for a while. I didn't feel guilty about it. But now I look at her. . . . She was never part of our scene. With Vernon and Rudy and the bands. She lived off to the side of it all. It wasn't like that with you, Andrea. You had your law thing going, but when you were around, you were into it. You were one of the girls. But Beth was so totally not into it. She still can't stand us. And now it feels like I stole something from her. That really sucks."

Platitudes occurred to me, but I kept quiet. Andrea stirred at my side.

"Sometimes it pays to be stupid," Patty said gloomily.

I had a moment when the light and happy babble of the bar were thrust aside by the gonging thought that my friend was dead, and I didn't entirely understand what she meant, but I knew she was right.

Patty snagged a passing waitress. "Can I get a couple of eggs over?" she asked. "I know you're not serving breakfast, but that's all I eat is breakfast." She winked broadly at the waitress. "Most important meal of the day, so I make every meal breakfast."

The waitress began to explain why eggs were impossible, but Patty cut in, saying, "You don't want me to starve, do ya? You must have a couple of eggs back there. Some fries and bacon. Toast. We're huge tippers, I swear."

Exasperated, the waitress said she'd see if the cook would do it.

"I know you can work him, honey," Patty said. "Tell him to make the eggs dippy, okay?"

We left McGuigan's shortly after eight, heading for Corky's, a workingman's bar where we could do some serious drinking, but as we came abreast of the statue, Patty tapped it and said, "Hey, let's go talk to Stanky." Stanky and Liz were sitting on the base of the statue; Pin and the other boys were cross-legged at their feet, like students attending their master. The crowd had thinned and was down, I'd guess, to about a hundred and twenty; a third of that number were clustered around the science van and the head scientist, who was hunched over a piece of equipment set up on the edge of the library lawn. I lagged behind as we walked over and noticed Liz stiffen at the sight of Patty. The boys gazed adoringly at her. Stanky cast me a spiteful glance.

"I heard your EP, man," Patty said. "Very cool."

Stanky muttered, "Yeah, thanks," and stared at her breasts.

Like me, Patty was a sucker for talent, used to the ways of musicians, and she ignored this ungracious response. She tried to draw him out about the music, but Stanky had a bug up his ass about something and wouldn't give her much. The statue loomed above, throwing a shadow across us; the horse's head, with its rolling eyes and mouth jerked open by the reins, had been rendered more faithfully than had Black William's face . . . or else he was a man whose inner crudeness had coarsened and simplified his features. In either case, he was one ugly mother, his shoulder-length hair framing a maniacal mask. Seeing him anew, I would not have described his expression as laughing or alarmed, but might have said it possessed a ferocious exultancy.

Patty began talking to the boys about the Swimming Holes' upcoming tour, and Andrea was speaking with Pin. Stanky oozed over to me, Liz at his shoulder, and said, "We laid down a new song this afternoon."

"Oh, yeah?" I said.

"It's decent. 'Misery Loves Company.'"

In context, it wasn't clear, until Stanky explained it, that this was a title.

"A guy from DreamWorks called," he said. "William Wine."

"Yeah, a few days back. Did Kiwanda tell you about it?"

"No, he called today. Kiwanda was on her break and I talked to him."

"What'd he say?"

"He said they loved the tape and David Geffen's going to call." He squinched up his face, as if summoning a mighty effort. "How come you didn't tell me about the tape? About him calling before?"

This, I understood, was the thing that had been bothering him. "Because it's business," I said. "I'm not going to tell you about every tickle we get. Every phone call."

He squinted at me meanly. "Why not?"

"Do you realize how much of this just goes away? These people are like flies. They buzz around, but they hardly ever land. Now the guy's called twice, that makes it a little more interesting. I'll give it a day or two, and call him back."

Ordinarily, Stanky would have retreated from confrontation, but with Liz bearing witness (I inferred by her determined look that she was his partner in this, that she had egged him on), his macho was at stake. "I ought to know everything that's going on," he said.

"Nothing's going on. When something happens, I'll tell you."

"It's my career," he said in a tone that conveyed petulance, defiance, and the notion that he had been wronged. "I want to be in on it, you know."

"Your career." I felt suddenly liberated from all restraint. "Your career consists of my efforts on your behalf and three hours on-stage in Nowhere, Pennsylvania. I've fed you, I've given you shelter, money, a band. And now you want me to cater to your stupid whims? To run downstairs and give you an update on every little piece of Stanky gossip because it'll gratify your ego? So you can tell your minions here how great you are? Fuck you! You don't like how I'm handling things, clear the hell out of my house!"

I walked off several paces and stood on the curb, facing the library. That rough cube of Pennsylvania granite accurately reflected my mood. Patches of snow dappled the lawn. There was a minor hubbub near the science truck, but I was enraged and paid it no mind. Andrea came up next to me and took my arm. "Easy, big fella," she said.

"That asshole's been under my roof for what? Two months? It feels like two years. His stink permeates every corner of my life. It's like living with a goat!"

"I know," she said. "But it's business."

I wondered if she was hammering home an old point, but her face gave no sign of any such intent; in fact, her neutral expression dissolved into one of befuddlement. She was staring at the library, and when I turned in that direction, I saw the library had vanished. An immense rectangle—a window with uneven edges—had been chopped out of the wall of the world, out of the night, its limits demarked by trees, lawn, and sky, and through it poured a flood of blackness, thicker and more sluggish than the Polozny. Thick like molasses or hot tar. It seemed to splash down, to crest in a wave, and hold in that shape. Along the top of the crest, I could see lesser, half-defined shapes, vaguely human, and I had the thought that the wave was extruding an army from its substance, producing a host of creatures who appeared to be men. The temperature had dropped sharply. There was a chill, chemical odor and, close above our heads (five feet, I'd estimate), the stars were coasting. That was how they moved. They glided as though following an unseen track, then were shunted sideways or diagonally or backward. Their altitude never changed, and I suspect now that they were prevented from changing it by some physical limitation. They did not resemble stars as much as they did Crazy Ed's enhancement: ten or twelve globes studded with longish white spines, the largest some eight feet in diameter, glowing brightly enough to illumine the faces of the people beneath them. I could not determine if they were made of flesh or metal or something less knowable. They gave forth high-frequency squeaks that reminded me, in their static quality, of the pictographs in Rudy's cartoons, the language of the stars.

I'm not sure how long we stood there, but it could not have been more than seconds before I realized that the wave crest was not holding, it was inching toward us across the lawn. I caught Andrea's hand and tried to run. She screamed (a yelp, really), and others screamed and tried to run. But the wave flowed around us, moving now like black quicksilver, in an instant transforming the center of town into a flood plain, marooning people on islands of solid ground bounded by a waist-high flood that was coursing swiftly past. As Andrea and I clung together, I saw Stanky and Liz, Pin and Patty, the rest of the kids, isolated beside the statue—there were dozens of such groupings throughout the park. It seemed a black net of an extremely coarse weave had been thrown over us all and we were standing up among its strands. We stared at each other, uncertain of our danger; some called for help. Then something rose from the blackness directly in front of me and Andrea. A man, I think, and fully seven feet tall. An African Negro by the scarifications on his face. His image not quite real—it appeared to be both embedded in the tarry stuff and shifting over its surface, as if he had been rotoscoped. At the same time, a star came to hover over us, so that my terror was divided. I had from it an impression of eagerness—the feeling washed down upon me; I was drenched in it—and then, abruptly, of disinterest, as if it found Andrea and me unworthy of its attention. With the onset of that disinterest, the black man melted away into the tar and the star passed on to another group of stranded souls.

The largest groups were those two clustered about the science van. Figures began to sprout from the tar around them, and not all of these were men. Some were spindly as eels, others squat and malformed, but they were too far away for me to assign them a more particular identity. Stars hovered above the two groups, and the black figures lifted them one by one, kicking and screaming (screams now issued from every corner of the park), and held them up to the stars. They did not, as in Rudy's cartoons, suck in the meat through one of their spikes; they never touched their victims. A livid arc, fiery black in color, leaped between star and human, visible for a split second, and then the figure that had lifted the man or woman, dropped him or her carelessly to the ground and melted back into the flood, and the star moved on. Andrea buried her face in my shoulder, but I could not turn away, transfixed by the scene. And as I watched these actions repeated again and again—the figure melting up, lifting someone to a star, and then discarding him, the victim still alive, rolling over, clutching an injured knee or back, apparently not much the worse for wear—I realized the stars were grazing, that this was their harvest, a reaping of seed sown. They were harvesting our genius, a genius they had stimulated, and they were attracted to a specific yield that manifested in an arc of fiery black. The juice of the poet, the canniness of the inventor, the guile of a villain. They failed to harvest the entire crop, only that gathered in the park. The remainder of those affected would go on to create more garden tools and foundation garments and tax plans, and the stars would continue on their way, a path that now and again led them through the center of Black William. I must confess that, amid the sense of relief accompanying this revelation, I felt an odd twinge of envy when I realized that the genius of love was not to their taste.

How did I know these things? I think when the star hovered above us, it initiated some preliminary process, one incidental to the feelings of eagerness and disinterest it projected, and, as it prepared to take its nutrient, its treasure (I haven't a clue as to why they harvested us, whether we were for them a commodity or sustenance or something else entire), we shared a brief communion. As proof, I can only say that Andrea holds this same view and there is a similar consensus, albeit with slight variances, among all those who stood beneath the stars that night. But at the moment the question was not paramount. I turned toward the statue. The storefronts beyond were obscured by a black rectangle, like the one that had eclipsed the library, and this gave me to believe that the flood was pouring off into an unguessable dimension, though it still ran deep around us. Stanky and Liz had climbed onto the statue and were clinging to Black William's leg and saddlehorn respectively. Patty was leaning against the base, appearing dazed. Pin stood beside her, taking photographs with his cell phone. One of the kids was crying, and his friends were busy consoling him. I called out, asking if everyone was all right. Stanky waved and then the statue's double reared from the flood—it rose up slowly, the image of a horse and a rider with flowing hair, blacker than the age-darkened bronze of its likeness. They were so equal in size and posture and stillness, it was as if I were looking at the statue and its living shadow. Its back was to me, and I cannot say if it was laughing. And then the shadow extended an arm and snatched Stanky from his perch. Plucked him by the collar and held him high, so that a star could extract its due, a flash of black energy. And when that was done, it did not let him fall, but began to sink back into the flood, Stanky still in its grasp. I thought it would take him under the tar, that they would both be swallowed and Stanky's future was to be that of a dread figure rising blackly to terrify the indigents in another sector of the plenum. But Black William—or the agency that controlled him—must have had a change of heart and, at the last second, just as Stanky's feet were about to merge with that tarry surface, dropped him clear of the flood, leaving him inert upon the pavement.

The harvest continued several minutes more (the event lasted twenty-seven minutes in all) and then the flood receded, again with quicksilver speed, to form itself into a wave that was poised to splash down somewhere on the far side of that black window. And when the window winked out, when the storefronts snapped back into view, the groaning that ensued was much louder and more articulated than that we'd heard a month previously. Not a sound of holy woe, but of systemic stress, as if the atoms that composed the park and its surround were complaining about the insult they had incurred. All across the park, people ran to tend the injured. Andrea went to Liz, who had fallen from the statue and tearfully declared her ankle broken. Patty said she was dizzy and had a headache, and asked to be left alone. I knelt beside Stanky and asked if he was okay. He lay propped on his elbows, gazing at the sky.

"I wanted to see," he said vacantly. "They said . . ."

"They?" I said. "You mean the stars?"

He blinked, put a hand to his brow. As ever, his emotions were writ large, yet I don't believe the look of shame that washed over his face was an attempt to curry favor or promote any agenda. I believe his shame was informed by a rejection such as Andrea and I experienced, but of a deeper kind, more explicit and relating to an opportunity lost.

I made to help him up, intending to question him further; but he shook me off. He had remembered who he was, or at least who he had been pretending to be. Stanky the Great. A man of delicate sensibilities whom I had offended by my casual usage and gross maltreatment. His face hardened, becoming toadlike as he summoned every ounce of his Lilliputian rage. He rolled up to his knees, then got to his feet. Without another word to me, he arranged his features into a look of abiding concern and hurried to give comfort to his Liz.

In the wider world, Black William has come to be known as "that town full of whackos" or "the place where they had that hallucination," for as with all inexplicable things, the stars and our interaction with them have been dismissed by the reasonable and responsible among us, relegated to the status of an aberration, irrelevant to the big picture, to the roar of practical matters with which we are daily assailed. I myself, to an extent, have dismissed it, yet my big picture has been enlarged somewhat. Of an evening, I will sit upon the library steps and cast my mind out along the path of the stars and wonder if they were metaphoric or literal presences, nomads or machines, farmers or a guerrilla force, and I will question what use that black flash had for them, and I will ponder whether they were themselves evil or recruited evil men to assist them in their purpose simply because they were suited to the task. I subscribe to the latter view; otherwise, I doubt Stanky would have wanted to go with them . . . unless they offered a pleasurable reward, unless they embodied for him the promise of a sublime perversion in exchange for his service, an eternal tour of duty with his brothers-in-arms, dreaming in that tarry flood. And what of their rejection of him? Was it because he was insufficiently evil? Too petty in his cruelty? Or could it have been he lacked the necessary store of some brain chemical? The universe is all whys and maybes. All meanings coincide, all answers are condensed to one or none. Nothing yields to logic.

Since the coming of the stars, Black William has undergone a great renewal. Although in the immediate aftermath there was a hue and cry about fleeing the town, shutting it down, calmer voices prevailed, pointing to the fact that there had been no fatalities, unless one counted the suicides, and but a single disappearance (Colvin Jacobs, who was strolling through the park that fateful night), and it could be better understood, some maintained, in light of certain impending charges against him (embezzlement, fraud, solicitation). Stay calm, said the voices. A few scrapes and bruises, a smattering of nervous breakdowns—that's no reason to fling up your hands. Let's think this over. Colvin's a canny sort, not one to let an opportunity pass. At this very moment he may be developing a skin cancer on Varadero Beach or Ipanema (though it is my belief that he may be sojourning in a more unlikely place). And while the town thought it over, the tourists began to arrive by the busload. Drawn by Pin's photographs, which had been published around the world, and later by his best-selling book (co-authored by the editor of the *Gazette*), they came from Japan, from Europe, from Punxsutawney and Tunkhannock, from every quarter of the globe, a flood of tourists that resolved into a steady flow and demanded to be housed, fed, T-shirted, souvenired, and swindled. They needed theories upon which to hang their faith, so theory-making became a cottage industry and theories abounded, both supernatural and quasi-scientific, each having their own battery of proponents and debunkers. A proposal was floated in the city council that a second statue be erected to commemorate Black William's visitation, but the ladies of the Heritage Committee fought tooth and nail to preserve the integrity of the original, and now can be seen twice a year lavishing upon him a vigorous scrubbing.

Businesses thrived, mine included—this due to the minor celebrity I achieved and the sale of Stanky and his album to Warner Brothers (David Geffen never called). The album did well and the single, "Misery Loves Company," climbed to No. 44 on the Billboard charts. I have no direct contact with Stanky, but learned from Liz, who came to the house six months later to pick up her clothes (those abandoned when Stanky fled my house in a huff), that he was writing incidental music for the movies, a job that requires no genius. She carried tales, too, of their nasty breakup, of Stanky's increasing vileness, his masturbatory displays of ego. He has not written a single song since he left Black William—the stars may have drained more from him than that which they bred, and perhaps the fact that he was almost taken has something to do with his creative slump. Whatever his story, I think he has found his true medium and is becoming a minor obscenity slithering among the larger obscenities that serve a different kind of star, anonymous beneath the black flood of the Hollywood sewer.

The following March, I went fishing with Andrea at Kempton's Pond. She was reluctant to join me, assuming that I intended to make her a stand-in for Rudy, but I assured her this was not the case and told her she might enjoy an afternoon out of the office, some quiet time together. It was a clear day, and cold. Pockets of snow lay in the folds and crinkles of the Bittersmiths, but the crests were bare, and there was a deeper accumulation on the banks than when Rudy and I had fished the pond in November. We had to clear ourselves a spot on which to sit. The sun gilded the birch trunks, but the waters of the pond were as Stygian and mysterious as ever.

We cast out our lines and chatted about doings in her office, my latest projects—Lesion (black metal) and a postrock band I had convinced to call themselves Same Difference. I told her about some loser tapes that had come my way, notably a gay Christian rap outfit with a song entitled "Cruisin' for Christ (While Searching for the Heavenly City)." Then we fell silent. Staring into the pond, at the dark rock walls and oily water, I did not populate the depths with fantasies, but thought instead of Rudy. They were memorial thoughts untainted by grief, memories of things said and done. I had such a profound sense of him, I imagined if I turned quickly enough, I would have a glimpse of a bulky figure in a parka, wool cap jammed low on his brow, red-cheeked and puffing steam; yet when I did turn, the figure in the parka and wool cap was more clearly defined, ivory pale and slender, her face a living cameo. I brushed a loose curl from her eyes. Touching her cheek warmed my fingertip. "This is kind of nice," she said, and smiled. "It's so quiet."

"Told you you'd like it," I said.

"I do."

She jiggled her line.

"You'll never catch anything that way." I demonstrated proper technique. "Twitch the line side-to-side."

Amused, she said, "I really doubt I'm going to catch anything. What were you and Rudy batting? One for a thousand?"

"Yeah, but you never know."

"I don't think I want to catch anything if it resembles that thing he had mounted."

"You should let out more line, too."

She glanced at me wryly, but did as I suggested.

A cloud darkened the bank and I pictured how the two of us would appear to God, if God were in His office, playing with His Game Boy: tiny animated fisherfolk hunched over their lines, shoulder-to-shoulder, waiting for a tiny monster to breach, unmindful of any menace from above. Another cloud shadowed us. A ripple moved across the pond, passing so slowly it made me think that the waters of the Polozny, when upthrust into these holes, were squeezed into a sludgy distillate. Bare twigs clattered in a gust of wind.

"All these years," Andrea said. "All the years and now five months. . . ."

"Yeah?"

"Every day, there'll be two or three times when I see you, like just now, when I look up and see you, and it's like a blow . . . a physical blow that leaves me all gaga. I want to drop everything and curl up with you."

"Me, too," I said.

She hesitated. "It just worries me."

"We've had this conversation," I said. "I don't mind having it again, but we're not going to resolve anything. We'll never figure it out."

"I know." She jiggled her line, forgetting to twitch it. "I keep thinking I'll find a new angle, but all I come up with is more stupidity. I was thinking the other day, it was like a fairy tale. How falling back in love protected us, like a charm." She heel-kicked the bank. "It's frustrating when everything you think seems absurd and true all at once."

"It's a mystery."

"Right."

"I go there myself sometimes," I said. "I worry about whether we'll fall out of love . . . if what we feel is unnatural. Then I worry if worrying about it's unnatural. Because, you know, it's such a weird thing to be worried about. Then I think, hey, it's perfectly natural to worry over something you care about, whether it's weird or not. Round and round. We might as well go with the flow. No doubt we'll still be worrying about it when we're too old to screw."

"That's pretty old."

"Yep," I said. "Ancient."

"Maybe it's good we worry." Then after a pause, she said. "Maybe we didn't worry enough the first time."

A second ripple edged the surface, like a miniature slow tsunami. The light faded and dimmed. A degree of tension seemed to leave Andrea's body.

"You want to go to Russia?" she asked. "I've got this conference in late May. I have to give a paper and be on some panels. It's only four days, but I could take some vacation."

I thought about it. "Kiwanda's pretty much in control of things. Would we have to stay in Russia?"

"Don't you want to go clubbing in Moscow? Meet new people? I'll wear a slutty dress and act friendly with strangers. You can save me from the white slavers—I'm sure I'll attract white slavers."

"I'll do my best," I said. "But some of those slavers are tough."

"You can take 'em!" She rubbed the side of her nose. "Why? Where do you want to go?"

"Bucharest."

"Why there?"

"Lots of reasons. Potential for vampires. Cheap. But reason number one—nobody goes there."

"Good point. We get enough of crowds around here."

We fell silent again. The eastern slopes of the Bittersmiths were drowning in shadow, acquiring a simplified look, as of worn black teeth that still bore traces of enamel. But the light had richened, the tree trunks appeared to have been dipped in old gold. Andrea straightened and peered down into the hole.

"I had a nibble," she said excitedly.

I watched the surface. The water remained undisturbed, lifeless and listless, but I felt a presence lurking beneath, a wise and deliberate fish, a grotesque, yet beautiful in the fact of its survival, and more than a murky promise—it would rise to us this day or some other. Perhaps it would speak a single word, perhaps merely die. Andrea leaned against me, eager to hook it, and asked what she should do.

"It's probably just a current," I said, but advised her to let out more line.

LUCIUS SHEPARD

"Stars Seen Through Stone" had its genesis in the ten years I spent in Detroit and Ann Arbor as a rock musician. It's rather more autobiographical than most of my stories, in that Vernon, the main character, bears some resemblance to my younger self, and various other characters bear resemblance to people I knew and played with and so forth. Joe Stanky, who serves as the fulcrum of the story, was an actual . . . one hesitates to call him a human being. He was far more desperate and unseemly than his fictive self, far worse a pain in the ass than I have depicted. Several years after the band we played in together broke up, I saw a figure waddling toward me along the country road where I was then living. I was chopping wood beside the house and I paused, stared, then went back to work. But sure enough, the figure turned out to be "Stanky." He approached me with his usual cajoling air and started talking about the "good ol' days." About wouldn't it be great if we could start a new band, and so on. Looking at him, at this malignant, dwarfish lump, I suddenly became aware of the ax in my hand. He must have sensed my mood, because his talk veered off in a different direction, his attempt at manipulation took a new tack, and he told me, in pious tones, how he had found Jesus and changed his life, sneaking hopeful looks at me as he related the facts of his conversion. Eventually he left, presenting a dejected image, going with a limp.

I think of him rarely these days, but when I do I often say something on the order of "Fucking Stanky!" And then, finishing the thought as though it were an equation, sometimes I say to myself, "Rock and Roll!"

WHAT YOU SAW WAS WHAT YOU GOT: THE YEAR IN FILMS

HOWARD WALDROP

Howard Waldrop, born in Mississippi and now living in Austin, Texas, is one of the most delightfully iconoclastic writers working today. His highly original books include the novels *Them Bones* and *A Dozen Tough Jobs* and the collections *Howard Who?, All About Strange Monsters of the Recent Past,* and *Going Home Again.* He has won the Nebula and World Fantasy Awards for his novelette "The Ugly Chickens."

His most recent book is *Things Will Never Be the Same: Selected Short Fiction 1980–2005,* from Old Earth Books.

Forthcoming are *Other Worlds, Better Lives: Selected Long Fiction 1989–2003* and the novellas "The Search for Tom Purdue" and "The Moone World."

So another year sank into the sunset with a record of noble attempts, mild successes, and spavined failures—of nerve, of conception, of narrative shortcomings.

Part of the problem of being a semi-independent, but still assignable, part-time online reviewer is that someone has us out reviewing what looks to be possibly interesting stuff, while more interesting stuff comes and goes at the same time.

Quick follow-up DVD release has solved some of the problems, but it still doesn't happen when the movie's making money somewhere but has already committed seppuku in Austin.

So I'm out reviewing, like, *The Nines* (like, a really earnest, well-acted film studies major, graduate-thesis movie) and something else comes in, gets raves, and Hey! Presto! It's already headed for Netflix.

Next month or two . . .

Why am I whining when it always comes with the territory? Because, this year, I think I missed some better stuff than I saw. (I hope so, anyway.)

Let's start at the top and work down, way down.

The best writing in the movies this past year is the same place it's been (with the exception of the best episodes of *The West Wing*) on television these past twenty years: *The Simpsons Movie* and its adjunct, the straight-to-DVD *Futurama: Bender's Big Score* (but it's to be broadcast as a three- or four-parter on the cable reruns). People actually (as in the commercials) came out of *The Simpsons Movie* singing the "Spider-Pig" song. The scenes where Homer tips the pig-crap silo into polluted Lake Springfield and the water achieves toxic-waste critical mass are some of the finest in movie history. (And the fact that the EPA task force comes in a fleet of the planes *nobody* else wants, Ospreys, is an added bonus.) If you take your eyes off the screen any given second, you're going to miss something, especially during the Simpsons' attempt to escape and start new lives in Alaska (there's a bar there named eskiMOE'S). And all this, like the years-gone-by *A Private Function*, because of a pig . . .

Futurama: Bender's Big Score: Just as audiences had to wait eighty-two years (from the invention of motion pictures to 1977) to see a spaceship go into hyperdrive in *Star Wars*, we have waited 112 years to see time travel as it would be.

Bender, a robot, is now, like everything else, owned by the aliens who called in all the Earth's debts and own the place. The aliens have a one-way time travel device that goes into the past. They send Bender back to loot it. "It's okay," he says. "I'll go into the past, grab the swag, come back to the limestone cavern under the basement here, turn myself off for fifteen hundred years, wake up, and come up from the basement."

Bender jumps into the time field and comes up from the basement door with the *Mona Lisa* under his arm.

"That wasn't so bad," he says.

Of course, we end up with more and more complicated time paradoxes that have to be fixed before they destroy the past, the present, and the future.

And you get to see the Nude Beach Planet, which has umpteen suns. . . .

Enchanted tried to do for fantasy what *Galaxy Quest* did for SF in 1999, and it pretty much succeeded, though the film has problems in the last few minutes. But before then, oh, my! When the princess, abandoned in our world, sings her happy working song while she's housecleaning, all the animals come to help her just like in fairy-tale land. You know, *Manhattan* wildlife. Rats— *thousands of them, millions!* Cockroaches. Squirrels. Pigeons.

Since there were no opening credits, I kept asking myself, "Who's the broad with Susan Sarandon's eyes in the dark hair playing the Witch/Queen?" The credits come on and it is, of course, Susan Sarandon. (Even the dragon later on has her eyes.) Disney's back—and they almost got it right.

By far, the most influential movie of the year was *The Host*, a Korean monster movie. It's like *Them!* told from the p.o.v. of the Lodge boys, the ones who end up in the storm drains after the giant ants have pulled their father's arm off while they were down by the river flying a model airplane. You're having fun and then giant ants are everywhere.

The Host is about a family who runs a squid shop on the river in Seoul—suddenly there's a monster there, and the daughter's taken away. They try to find her for the rest of the movie. They aren't part of the military or members of an investigative team (the *Them!* and other 1950s templates). The scenes of the monster's first appearance are truly frightening. People stand around watching something BIG in the distance coming toward them. Nothing should be that big. Nothing that big should be on a riverbank in Seoul—and then it's on them.

As I've said elsewhere, a few Koreans have some things to teach Hollywood.

It has had its greatest influence on *Cloverfield*, which is a 2008 movie. Trust me.

Don't get me started.

The Golden Compass (or, "Bears Discover Armor") is set in a world that is not our own, like some Edwardian para-time ruled by the quasi-religious Magisterium. In this world, all the children have changeable daemons (familiars), but by the time they reach adulthood, their daemons have settled on a permanent form. (The daemon of Sam Elliott is, of course, a jackrabbit, which is perfect.) There's some sinister goings-on in a sort of Oompa-Loompa domain run by the Magisterium near the North Pole (sort of a Ray Eames Santa Claus house) involving children's daemons and evil designs. There are armored bears, some terrific fights, quests, and kids learning lessons. People who've read the books tell me it ends halfway through the first one.

The acting in *The Mist* (from the King novella) is better than the script; people filling out sketchily written characters with good old-fashioned craftsmanship. And I knew, once the protag started counting the bullets, we were in for a hopeful downer of an ending. There is some attempt to show the ecology of wherever-it-is they came from. The plot itself reminds me of another '50s movie, *The Cosmic Monster* (1958), where a similar hole punched in the ionosphere allows monsters to come through from another dimension.

The *Planet Terror* half of *Grindhouse* took us back to '70s drive-in double features: women with mini Gatling guns in place of legs; alien invasion; heroes and heroines reluctantly falling in love with the right wrong people. It's as if American International Pictures had never stopped being ahead of (instead of behind) the curve, and if all the Corman trainees had continued turning out exploitation pictures instead of important films. . . .

The second part of the movie—*Death Proof*—is not SF or fantasy.

Stardust was this past year's equivalent of *The Brothers Grimm* from a couple years ago. Unlike that movie, there was no stuff so great (the gingerbread man, the horse that swallows the kid) that you were cheesed off that the rest of the movie wasn't as good.

Stardust sort of sat there; if it had been either better or worse the review wouldn't have given me as much trouble. There's one mythic scene in the film, Michelle Pfeiffer riding her goat cart across a long, Scottish Highland–looking road. The one compensating plot point: Everyone is out after the meteorite for their own individual reasons; it means different things/goals to different characters. The analogous objects are the wagonloads of whiskey in *The Hallelujah Trail* (1965). This shows more initiative than most movies since then.

I Am Legend: Third time is not quite the charm. *The Last Man on Earth* with Vincent Price (1964) is still the closest in tone to the book. Will Smith actually convinced me he could act a couple of times in this one, and there's some swell stuff of New York City reverting to the wild (with animals escaped from zoos, etc., and passing a gas station with the sign from December 2008 with Regular at $6.29 a gallon . . .). I know—and you will, too—people who won't see this because "something happens to the dog."

The stylistic innovations in *300* were fine the first fifty times (the frozen sword-slash with its solid streak of blood), but paled by the hundredth, and they even continued into the still-frame end credits. And Spartans laughing at Athenians as "philosophers and boy-lovers" means someone (either the original graphic novel or the filmmakers) didn't do a lot of homework.

The stupidest preview trailer of 2007—like a '60s movie made by someone born in 1980 who'd only heard of the 1960s from their aunts and uncles—was for *Across the Universe*. With characters named Jude, Prudence, and Lucy, you know the songs you're going to hear (although Julie Taymor, the director, knew enough to leave one of the songs exegetically to the end credits, outside the narrative).

Surprisingly, the movie works on its own terms (some of the chronology is slightly askew, but the '60s mostly depended on where you were—some places got hotter quicker than others). Some striking visuals (as, of course, you'd expect from the director of the stage version of *The Lion King*). But it's not all empty visuals, and in the old phrase "the personal is the political," I didn't want my money or my time back, which I had sure figured I would after seeing the massively wrongheaded trailer earlier in the year. But friends with some taste convinced me to see it.

The Last Mimzy's heart was in the right place—unfortunately they chose to update it (from the original WWII period) to these post-9/11 times, with Homeland Security involved.

They did concentrate on the characters, and they left their hands off the CGI stuff until the climax, a very subdued use of it these days. It's no *Grand Tour: Disaster in Time* (made from Kuttner and Moore's "Vintage Season" some years ago), which knew how to approach the story (even though it, too, was updated). But it tried. (The thrice-removed narration didn't help, either.)

When I'd heard that they were making *Ghost Rider*, I hoped it would be the first-incarnation Old West version: no, it's Nicolas Cage on a chopper now. (The Old West version is in one scene, when a ghost horse whose hooves strike sparks on the road rides alongside the cycle—it's of course the best scene in the movie, and it should all have been like that.)

It's not as bad as the remake of *The Wicker Man* a couple of years ago, which was the biggest waste of celluloid since *Manos: The Hands of Fate*.

By the way, Cage is in the fake movie trailers in *Grindhouse*, as Fu Manchu.

John Cusack, the actor who's taken the most chances with his career of anyone currently working, was in *1408*; he's usually not in films that sledgehammer you with effect after effect. There are some genuinely disturbing scary scenes early on (and one true scene; he's an author doing a book-signing and a reading, and there are four people in the audience). It starts out as the usual, with a nonbeliever spending the night in a supposedly haunted hotel room (the title one, like the one in *The Shining*), and goes quickly downhill and sideways at the same time. Cusack's good— it's everything else that lets him down.

Mr. Magorium's Wonder Emporium. The kind of movie that killed off Robin Williams's screen career, only now it's happening to Dustin Hoffman. As a friend said, "Hit me over the head with the whimsy-stick one more time!" The questions raised in the plot are left unanswered, and the block-of-wood McGuffin doesn't figure in the dénouement. And it's about the wrong character. A special-effects misfire: truly forgettable.

Sweeney Todd was not a 2007 movie, not in Austin anyway.

I look forward with trepidation to the remake of *The Day the Earth Stood Still* this coming year. It won't work unless it's post-modern or it's period. If it's period, why remake it—just colorize the original and put half a billion in advertising it. If it's pomo, will the 2008 audience understand it as well as the cinema-literate audience of 1951 understood the original?

There was no equivalent to *The Prestige* this year.

PAN'S LABYRINTH: DREAMING WITH EYES WIDE OPEN

EL LABIRINTO DEL FAUNA (THE FAUN'S LABYRINTH)

TIM LUCAS

Tim Lucas is the editor and copublisher of *Video Watchdog,* the influential monthly review of horror, cult, and fantasy cinema, and the author of several books on film, most recently *Videodrome* and the multiple-award-winning biography *Mario Bava: All the Colors of the Dark.* He is also the author of two horror novels, *Throat Sprockets* and *The Book of Renfield: A Gospel of Dracula.* He resides in Cincinnati, Ohio.

Guillermo del Toro was born in Guadalajara, Mexico, but *Pan's Labyrinth* is unmistakably a crown jewel of the Spanish fantastic cinema, possibly unprecedented in achieving commercial and critical success in America despite del Toro's refusal to produce an English-language dub track. Until now, the Spanish-language branches of the genre (those native to Spain and Mexico) have typically yielded a volatile hybrid of the genre's most garish and refined attributes, a heady sangria of blood, profundity, fruit, and Carnivál. With its masked wrestlers, brain-eating warlocks, and doll people, Mexican horror has long been among the genre's most ghettoized subgenres in terms of international profile, yet—as del Toro's latest film reminds us—it also boasts a heritage encompassing such masters as Luis Buñuel, Narciso Ibáñez Serrador, Juan López Moctezuma, and Alejandro Jodorowsky. Likewise, Spanish horror runs the gamut from the eroticized pulp of Paul Naschy and Jess Franco to acclaimed art house titles such as Victor Erice's *Spirit of the Beehive* (1974) and Alejandro Amenábar's *Open Your Eyes* (1997).

Something that Spanish-language horror has always done exceptionally well is stories involving the very young and the very old. Guillermo del Toro bridged this generational gap into a single fable with his 1993 feature debut, *Cronos*, which also established his ongoing fascinations with insects, machinery, and religious iconography. Almost from the very beginning, del Toro has shown extraordinary promise of becoming the great unifying and uplifting force that Spanish horror and fantasy has always craved. He has taken a deliberately checkerboard approach to his career, following each new commercial project with a job more progressive and personal in nature. Make no mistake: even del Toro's commercial work (*Mimic*, *Blade II*, *Hellboy*) is stylish and above average in intelligence, but his personal films—*Cronos*, *The Devil's Backbone* (2001), and now *Pan's Labyrinth*—are like no other films currently being made. Del Toro is a Mexican descendant of Cervantes, Francisco Goya, Jean Cocteau, Mario Bava, Alejandro Jodorowsky, Italo Calvino, Bruno Bettelheim, and David Cronenberg, whose most insistent impulse is to study from all angles the volatile story of twentieth-century Spain through the impact of its suppressive history on the frontiers of the Spanish imagination and subconscious.

With *Pan's Labyrinth*, the whole of his work and creative reach is brought into brilliant focus—and this is surely the reason why so many critics have hailed it as del Toro's masterpiece. Some closer to the genre may argue that *The Devil's Backbone* was also a masterpiece, but certainly *Pan's Labyrinth* is del Toro's first magnum opus, a film that encapsulates his purpose as a filmmaker while simultaneously proving his ability to touch large numbers of people. We should take heart from its global success; not only because del Toro was able to produce such a film on his own terms (and not without sacrifice, as he diverted his entire salary to areas where it was more needed), but because, in this day and age, he has proved it is possible for even a sophisticated work of the fantastic to find a receptive American audience despite a resolute refusal to be Americanized. It represents a simultaneous triumph of the fantastic cinema, international cinema, and art house cinema.

The film is set in a rural area of fascist Spain in 1944. The young heroine, Ofelia (Ivana Baquero), is the daughter of Carmen (Ariadna Gil), the widow of a tailor, whose loneliness and fear for her daughter's future led her to accept the proposal of Capitán Vidal (Sergi López). Vidal, a stern and time-obsessed second-generation officer, has his expectant wife and stepdaughter brought to his present headquarters despite the precarious state of her pregnancy—"A child should be born where its father is." An imaginative child, Ofelia has retreated from worrisome reality into her books of fairy tales and she finds the woods surrounding Capitán Vidal's encampment rife with possibilities for fantasy. An insect found inside an old tree becomes a fairy, which introduces her to an inscrutable Faun (Doug Jones) who recognizes her as Princess Moanna, whose "real father" is the King of the Netherworld. The Faun presents to Ofelia *The Book of Crossroads*, a blank book that fills with hidden illuminations at her touch. It helps her to better understand the three tasks she must complete before the moon is full: she must somehow obtain a magic key from the belly of an enormous toad inhabiting a hollow tree in the forest; she must use the key to gain access to a special dagger in the possession of the terrifying Pale Man (Jones); and the third task involves spilling innocent blood, necessary to opening the gates to the seven circular gardens of Moanna's palace.

One could, with painstaking difficulty, write dozens of pages in praise of the film's visual ingenuity, its sensitive performances, or its amazing talismanic monsters (the Pale Man particularly vaults immediately into the pantheon of horror greats). However, for me, the ultimate key to the film's importance is the success with which del Toro couches his fantasy in a parallel historic reality; it is what makes the film Spanish and what also makes the film universal, which suggests to me that *Pan's Labyrinth* is that rare work of art invested with the totemic power to bring people and nations together.

On first viewing, the film's fantastic segments are consistently surprising, but subsequent viewings emphasize the myriad ways in which the fantastic episodes mirror what is simultaneously happening within the film's turbulent reality. Capitán Vidal has set up his headquarters in this precise spot because the surrounding woods are full of rebels. Therefore, the rebels are the liberal and liberating force living outside common detection in the woods, like the fairies inhabiting Ofelia's universe. Before she has her first fantastic experience in the woods, Ofelia witnesses the servant Mercedes accepting ampoules of antibiotics to consign to the rebels, which may plant in her subconscious (or conscious) the suggestion of unseen life thriving in the woods. Carmen's precarious pregnancy mirrors the instability of Spain, and Ofelia's beseeching of her unborn brother not to hurt their mother when he is born gives voice to her fear that Vidal will have no further use for her once she gives him a son. Ofelia's burgeoning transformation into Princess Moanna, and its linkage to the cycles of the moon, relate to her pubertal age and the coming of her menstrual cycle. The tree in the woods, from whence the fantasy originates, is unambiguously designed to resemble a diagram of the female reproductive organs, and these dimensions recur on a blank spread of *The Book of Crossroads* in a menstrual-like flow of blood that presages her mother's near-miscarriage. When Capitán Vidal attempts to tease the rebels out of the woods by filling a storehouse with everything they require, from food and medicine to "real" tobacco, Ofelia's fantasies send her into the realm of the Pale Man—she is given an hourglass to time a visit she must not overstay, mirroring Vidal's death-obsessed preoccupation with time, and the Faun cautions her that she must take nothing from the Pale Man's opulent banquet table or face terrible consequences. Ofelia cannot resist plucking two plump grapes (testes? ovaries?) from the impressive table spread and eating them, which prompts the Faun to close her out of her fantasy world temporarily, but, when the rebels manage to turn the tide against Vidal, the Faun reappears to offer Ofelia one last chance. The Faun's denial of Ofelia also coincides with Vidal's murder of Dr. Ferrerio (Álex Angulo), the man whom he entrusted with the responsibility of delivering his child, his own stake in the future.

Del Toro's scripts have always been remarkable for their rich imagination—we seem to feel Capitán Vidal stitching his slashed cheek back together—and literary qualities, but the density and completeness of *Pan's Labyrinth* is new in his work, and at least uncommon in the filmography of any other currently active director.

It is also the most ravishing fantasy film to come along in many years, visually comparable to Bernardo Bertolucci's best work with Vittorio Storaro, its beauty bolstered by Bernat Vilaplana's patient and nondisruptive cutting.

Del Toro is also one of the finest audio commentators around, and his commentary track for New Line Cinema's "Platinum Series" two-disc set of *Pan's Labyrinth* is as personable, charming, intelligent, and instructive as one could hope. It is rare for any artist, least of all a film director, to speak with such forthright critical awareness about his work and its underlying meanings, design, influences, and antecedents, yet del Toro manages this without projecting any sense of egocentricity, pretension, or neurosis. Like a true craftsman, he never puts himself before the expression of his art, and his talk unfolds in the manner of a loving autopsy of a fully conscious and smiling entity. He dissects his and director of photography Guillermo Navarro's use of horizontal and vertical wipes for scene transitions ("not eye candy but eye protein"), the film's use of warm uterine reds and golds and rounded lines for its fantasy sequences and cold blues and greens and straight lines for its reality scenes, the necessity of adding CGI light bursts and sound effects to gunfire scenes filmed without discharging any weapons, and discusses how all of the film's characters are at figurative crossroads in their lives. Regardless of how many of the film's architectural secrets he lays bare, these revelations only enhance the pleasures of watching it again and again.

According to del Toro, he ensured the track's listenability and fluidity by recording it twice, in two takes each, with the end result assembled from the best scene-specific material. "I prepare these commentaries from the notes I keep in my notebooks," he told me. "I really try and grind my initial thoughts, through my notebooks and work papers, until the initial instinct is 'codified' like a painting (composition, camera movement, height of the camera, etc.). Actually, I could do *three* commentaries per disc—one thematic, one technical, and one visual—and still have notes and thoughts to spare."

In a business where it has become the accepted rule to let one's audience interpret their work however it will, Guillermo del Toro is at once our most important living practitioner of fantasy cinema and his own most perceptive interpreter. As we watch his films and listen to his revelations of all that underlies his dense and inexhaustible imagery, we are reminded of the Socratic wisdom that an unexamined life is not worth living. Or, as del Toro might rephrase that wisdom, "Would there have been a story if Alice had fallen down the rabbit-hole with her eyes closed?"

Note: This is an adaptation of a critical piece by Lucas in Video Watchdog *135, December 2007.*

THE EVOLUTION OF TRICKSTER STORIES
AMONG THE DOGS OF NORTH PARK
AFTER THE CHANGE

KIJ JOHNSON

Kij Johnson is a previous winner of the IAFA's William L. Crawford Award and the Theodore Sturgeon Memorial Award and has been a finalist for the World Fantasy Award. She is associate director for the Center for the Study of Science Fiction (CSSF) at the University of Kansas and aboutSF. com, an online science fiction resource center. Each summer she teaches an intensive novel-writing workshop for CSSF.

She lives in Seattle; she has a day job in tech and spends the rest of her time climbing crags, boulders, and walls.

North Park is a backwater tucked into a loop of the Kaw River: pale dirt and baked grass, aging playground equipment, silver-leafed cottonwoods, underbrush—mosquitoes and gnats blackening the air at dusk. To the south is a busy street. Engine noise and the hissing of tires on pavement mean it's no retreat. By late afternoon the air smells of hot tar and summertime river-bottoms. There are two entrances to North Park: the formal one, of silvered railroad ties framing an arch of sorts; and an accidental little gap in the fence, back where Second Street dead-ends into the park's west side, just by the river.

A few stray dogs have always lived here, too clever or shy or

245

easily hidden to be caught and taken to the shelter. On nice days (and this is a nice day, a smell like boiling sweet corn easing in on the south wind to blunt the sharper scents), Linna sits at one of the faded picnic tables with a reading assignment from her summer class and a paper bag full of fast food, the remains of her lunch. She waits to see who visits her.

The squirrels come first, and she ignores them. At last she sees the little dust-colored dog, the one she calls Gold.

"What'd you bring?" he says. His voice, like all dogs' voices, is hoarse and rasping. He has trouble making certain sounds. Linna understands him the way one understands a bad lisp or someone speaking with a harelip.

(It's a universal fantasy, isn't it?—that the animals learn to speak, and at last we learn what they're thinking, our cats and dogs and horses: a new era in cross-species understanding. But nothing ever works out quite as we imagine. When the Change happened, it affected all the mammals we have shaped to meet our own needs. They all could talk a little, and they all could frame their thoughts well enough to talk. Cattle, horses, goats, llamas; rats, too. Pigs. Minks. And dogs and cats. And we found that, really, we prefer our slaves mute.

(The cats mostly leave, even ones who love their owners. Their pragmatic sociopathy makes us uncomfortable, and we bore them; and they leave. They slip out between our legs and lope into summer dusks. We hear them at night, fighting as they sort out ranges, mates, boundaries. The savage sounds frighten us, a fear that does not ease when our cat Klio returns home for a single night, asking to be fed and to sleep on the bed. A lot of cats die in fights or under car wheels, but they seem to prefer that to living under our roofs; and as I said, we fear them.

(Some dogs run away. Others are thrown out by the owners who loved them. Some were always free.)

"Chicken and French fries," Linna tells the dog, Gold. Linna has a summer cold that ruins her appetite, and in any case it's too hot to eat. She brought her lunch leftovers, hours-old but still lukewarm: half of a Chik-fil-A and some French fries. He never takes anything from her hand, so she tosses the food onto the ground just beyond kicking range. Gold likes French fries, so he eats them first.

Linna tips her head toward the two dogs she sees peeking from the bushes. (She knows better than to lift her hand suddenly, even to point or wave.) "Who are these two?"

"Hope and Maggie."

"Hi, Hope," Linna says. "Hi, Maggie." The dogs dip their heads nervously as if bowing. They don't meet her eyes. She recognizes their expressions, the hurt wariness: she's seen it a few times, on the recent strays of North Park, the ones whose owners threw them out after the Change. There are five North Park dogs she's seen so far: these two are new.

"Story," says the collie, Hope.

2. ONE DOG LOSES HER COLLAR.

This is the same dog. She lives in a little room with her master. She has a collar that itches, so she claws at it. When her master comes home, he ties a rope to the collar and takes her outside to the sidewalk. There's a busy street outside. The dog wants to play on the street with the cars, which smell strong and move very fast. When her master tries to take her back inside, she sits down and won't move. He pulls on the rope and her collar slips over her ears and falls to the ground. When she sees this, she runs into the street. She gets hit by a car and dies.

This is not the first story Linna has heard the dogs tell. The first one was about a dog who's been inside all day and rushes outside with his master to urinate against a tree. When he's done, his master hits him, because his master was standing too close and his shoe is covered with urine. *One Dog Pisses on a Person.* The dog in the story has no name, but the dogs all call him (or her: she changes sex with each telling) One Dog. Each story starts: "This is the same dog."

The little dust-colored dog, Gold, is the storyteller. As the sky dims and the mosquitoes swarm, the strays of North Park ease from the underbrush and sit or lie belly-down in the dirt to listen to Gold. Linna listens, as well.

(Perhaps the dogs always told these stories and we could not understand them. Now they tell their stories here in North Park, as does the pack in Cruz Park a little to the south, and so across the world. The tales are not all the same, though there are similarities. There is no possibility of gathering them all. The dogs do not welcome eager anthropologists with their tape recorders and their agendas.

(The cats after the Change tell stories as well, but no one will ever know what they are.)

When the story is done, and the last of the French fries eaten, Linna asks Hope, "Why are you here?" The collie turns her face away, and it is Maggie, the little Jack Russell, who answers: "Our mother made us leave. She has a baby." Maggie's tone is matter-of-fact: it is Hope who mourns for the woman and child she loved, who compulsively licks her paw as if she were dirty and cannot be cleaned.

Linna knows this story. She's heard it from the other new strays of North Park: all but Gold, who has been feral all his life.

(Sometimes we think we want to know what our dogs think. We don't, not really. Someone who watches us with unclouded eyes and sees who we really are is more frightening than a man with a gun. We can fight or flee or avoid the man, but the truth sticks like pine sap. After the Change, some dog owners feel a cold place in the pit of their stomachs when they meet their pets' eyes. Sooner or later, they ask their dogs to find new homes, or they forget to latch the gate, or they force the dogs out with curses and the ends of brooms. Or the dogs leave, unable to bear the look in their masters' eyes.

(The dogs gather in parks and gardens, anywhere close to food and water where they can stay out of people's way. Cruz

Park ten blocks away is big, fifteen acres in the middle of town, and sixty or more dogs already have gathered there. They raid trash or beg from their former owners or strangers. They sleep under the bushes and bandstand and the inexpensive civic sculptures. No one goes to Cruz Park on their lunch breaks anymore.

(In contrast North Park is a little dead end. No one ever did go there, and so no one really worries much about the dogs there. Not yet.)

3. ONE DOG TRIES TO MATE.

This is the same dog. There is a female he very much wants to mate with. All the other dogs want to mate with her, too, but her master keeps her in a yard surrounded by a chain-link fence. She whines and rubs against the fence. All the dogs try to dig under the fence, but its base is buried too deep to find. They try to jump over, but it is too tall for even the biggest or most agile dogs.

One Dog has an idea. He finds a cigarette butt on the street and tucks it in his mouth. He finds a shirt in a Dumpster and pulls it on. He walks right up to the master's front door and presses the bell-button. When the master answers the door, One Dog says, "I'm from the men with white trucks. I have to check your electrical statico-pressure. Can you let me into your yard?"

The man nods and lets him go in back. One Dog takes off his shirt and drops the cigarette and mates with the female. It feels very nice, but when he is done and they are still linked together, he starts to whine.

The man hears and comes out. He's very angry. He shoots One Dog and kills him. The female tells One Dog, "You would have been better off if you had found another female."

The next day after classes (hot again, and heavy with the smell of cut grass), Linna finds a dog. She hears crying and crouches to peek under a hydrangea, its blue-gray flowers as fragile as paper. It's a Maltese with filthy fur matted with twigs and burrs. There are stains under her eyes and she is moaning, the terrible sound of an injured animal.

The Maltese comes nervous to Linna's outstretched fingers and the murmur of her voice. "I won't hurt you," Linna says. "It's okay."

Linna picks the dog up carefully, feeling the dog flinch under her hand as she checks for injuries. Linna knows already that the pain is not physical; she knows the dog's story before she hears it.

The house nearby is massive, a graceful collection of Edward-ian gingerbread-work and oriel windows and dark-green roof tiles. The garden is large, with a low fence just tall enough to keep a Maltese in. Or out. A woman answers the doorbell: Linna can feel the Maltese vibrate in her arms at the sight of the woman: excitement, not fear.

"Is this your dog?" Linna asks with a smile. "I found her out-side, scared."

The woman's eyes flicker to the dog and away, back to Linna's face. "We don't have a dog," she says.

(We like our slaves mute. We like to imagine they love us, and they do. But they are also with us because freedom and secu-rity war in each of us, and sometimes security wins out. They do love us. But.)

In those words Linna has already seen how this conversation will go, the denials and the tangled fear and anguish and self-loathing of the woman. Linna turns away in the middle of the woman's words and walks down the stairs, the brick walkway, through the gate and north, toward North Park.

The dog's name is Sophie. The other dogs are kind to her.

(When George Washington died, his will promised freedom for his slaves, but only after his wife had also passed on. A terri-fied Martha freed them within hours of his death. Though the dogs love us, thoughtful owners can't help but wonder what they think when they sit on the floor beside our beds as we sleep, teeth slightly bared as they pant in the heat. Do the dogs realize that their freedom hangs by the thread of our lives? The curse of speech—the things they could say and yet choose not to say—makes that thread seem very thin.

(Some people keep their dogs, even after the Change. Some people have the strength to love, no matter what. But many of us only learn the limits of our love when they have been breached. Some people keep their dogs; many do not.

(The dogs who stay seem to tell no stories.)

4. ONE DOG CATCHES POSSUMS.

This is the same dog. She is very hungry because her master forgot to feed her, and there's no good trash because the possums have eaten it all. "If I catch the possums," she says, "I can eat them now and then the trash later, because then they won't be getting it all."

She knows that possums are very hard to catch, so she lies down next to a trash bin and starts moaning. Sure enough, when the possums come to eat trash, they hear her and waddle over.

"Oh, oh oh," moans the dog. "I told the rats a great secret and now they won't let me rest."

The possums look around but they don't see any rats. "Where are they?" the oldest possum asks.

One Dog says, "Everything I eat ends up in a place inside me like a giant garbage heap. I told the rats and they snuck in, and they've been there ever since." And she let out a great howl. "Their cold feet are horrible!"

The possums think for a time and then the oldest says, "This garbage heap, is it large?"

"Huge," One Dog says.

"Are the rats fierce?" says the youngest.

"Not at all," One Dog tells the possums. "If they weren't inside me, they wouldn't be any trouble, even for a possum. Ow! I can feel one dragging bits of bacon around."

After whispering among themselves for a time, the possums say, "We can go in and chase out the rats, but you must promise not to hunt us ever again."

"If you catch any rats, I'll never eat another possum," she promises.

One by one the possums crawl into her mouth. She eats all but the
oldest, because she's too full to eat any more.
      "This is much better than dog food or trash," she says.

(Dogs love us. We have bred them to do this for ten thousand, a
hundred thousand, a million years. It's hard to make a dog hate
people, though we have at times tried, with our junkyard guards
and our attack dogs.

      (It's hard to make dogs hate people, but it is possible.)

      Another day, just at dusk, the sky an indescribable violet.
Linna has a hard time telling how many dogs there are now: ten
or twelve, perhaps. The dogs around her snuffle, yip, bark. One
moans, the sound of a sled dog trying to howl. Words float up:
dry, bite, food, piss.

      The sled dog continues its moaning howl, and one by one the
others join in with drawn-out barks and moans. They are trying
to howl as a pack, but none of them know how to do this, nor
what it is supposed to sound like. It's a wolf-secret, and they do
not know any of those.

      Sitting on a picnic table, Linna closes her eyes to listen. The
dogs outyell the trees' restless whispers, the river's wet sliding, even
the hissing roaring street. Ten dogs, or fifteen. Or more: Linna
can't tell, because they are all around her now, in the brush, down
by the Kaw's muddy bank, behind the cottonwoods, beside the
tall fence that separates the park from the street.

      The misformed howl, the hint of killing animals gathered to
work efficiently together—it awakens a monkey-place somewhere
in her corpus callosum, or even deeper, stained into her genes.
Adrenaline hits hot as panic. Her heart beats so hard that it feels
as though she's torn it. Her monkey-self opens her eyes to watch
the dogs through pupils constricted enough to dim the twilight;
it clasps her arms tight over her soft belly to protect the intestines
and liver that are the first parts eaten; it tucks her head between
her shoulders to protect her neck and throat. She pants through
bared teeth, fighting a keening noise.

Several of the dogs don't even try to howl. Gold is one of them. (The howling would have defined them before the poisoned gift of speech; but the dogs have words now. They will never be free of stories, though their stories may free them. Gold may understand this.

(They were wolves once, ten thousand, twenty thousand, a hundred thousand years ago. Or more. And before we were men and women, we were monkeys and fair game for them. After a time we grew taller and stronger and smarter: human, eventually. We learned about fire and weapons. If you can tame it, a wolf is an effective weapon, a useful tool. If you can keep it. We learned how to keep wolves close.

(But we were monkeys first, and they were wolves. Blood doesn't forget.)

After a thousand heartbeats fast as birds', long after the howl has decayed into snuffling and play-barks and speech, Linna eases back into her forebrain. Alive and safe. But not untouched. Gold tells a tale.

5. ONE DOG TRIES TO BECOME LIKE MEN.

This is the same dog. There is a party, and people are eating and drinking and using their clever fingers to do things. The dog wants to do everything they do, so he says, "Look, I'm human," and he starts barking and dancing about.

The people say, "You're not human. You're just a dog pretending. If you wanted to be human, you have to be bare, with just a little hair here and there."

One Dog goes off and bites his hairs out and rubs the places he can't reach against the sidewalk until there are bloody patches where he scraped off his skin, as well.

He returns to the people and says, "Now I am human," and he shows his bare skin.

"That's not human," the people say. "We stand on our hind legs and sleep on our backs. First you must do these things."

One Dog goes off and practices standing on his hind legs until he no longer cries out loud when he does it. He leans against a wall to sleep on his back, but it hurts and he does not sleep much. He returns and says, "Now I am human," and he walks on his hind legs from place to place.

"That's not human," the people say. "Look at these, we have fingers. First you must have fingers."

One Dog goes off and he bites at his front paws until his toes are separated. They bleed and hurt and do not work well, but he returns and says, "Now I am human," and he tries to take food from a plate.

"That's not human," say the people. "First you must dream, as we do."

"What do you dream of?" the dog asks.

"Work and failure and shame and fear," the people say.

"I will try," the dog says. He rolls onto his back and sleeps. Soon he is crying out loud and his bloody paws beat at the air. He is dreaming of all they told him.

"That dog is making too much noise," the people say and they kill him.

Linna calls the Humane Society the next day, though she feels like a traitor to the dogs for doing this. The sky is sullen with the promise of rainstorms, and even though she knows that rain is not such a big problem in the life of a dog, she worries a little, remembering her own dog when she was a little girl, who had been terrified of thunder.

So she calls. The phone rings fourteen times before someone picks it up. Linna tells the woman about the dogs of North Park. "Is there anything we can do?"

The woman barks a single unamused laugh. "I wish. People keep bringing them—been doing that since right after the Change. We're packed to the rafters—and they *keep* bringing them in, or just dumping them in the parking lot, too chickenshit to come in and tell anyone."

"So—" Linna begins, but she has no idea what to ask. She

can see the scene in her mind, a hundred or more terrified angry confused grieving hungry thirsty dogs. At least the dogs of North Park have some food and water, and the shelter of the underbrush at night.

The woman has continued "—they can't take care of themselves—"

"Do you know that?" Linna asks, but the woman talks on.

"—and we don't have the resources—"

"So what do you do?" Linna interrupts. "Put them to sleep?"

"If we have to," the woman says, and her voice is so weary that Linna wants suddenly to comfort her. "They're in the runs, four and five in each one because we don't have anywhere to put them, and we can't get them outside because the paddocks are full; it smells like you wouldn't believe. And they tell these stories—"

"What's going to happen to them?" Linna means all the dogs, now that they have speech, now that they are equals.

"Oh, hon, I don't know." The woman's voice trembles. "But I know we can't save them all."

(Why do we fear them when they learn speech? They are still dogs, still subordinate. It doesn't change who they are or their loyalty.

(It is not always fear we run from. Sometimes it is shame.)

6. ONE DOG INVENTS DEATH.

This is the same dog. She lives in a nice house with people. They do not let her run outside a fence and they did things to her so that she can't have puppies, but they feed her well and are kind, and they rub places on her back that she can't reach.

At this time, there is no death for dogs, they live forever. After a while, One Dog becomes bored with her fence and her food and even the people's pats. But she can't convince the people to allow her outside the fence.

"There should be death," she decides. "Then there will be no need for boredom."

(How do the dogs know things? How do they frame an abstract like *thank you* or a collective concept like chicken? Since the Change, everyone has been asking that question. If awareness is dependent on linguistics, an answer is that the dogs have learned to use words, so the words themselves are the frame they use. But it is still *our* frame, *our* language. They are still not free.

(Any more than we are.)

It is a moonless night, and the hot wet air blurs the streetlights so that they illuminate nothing except their own glass globes. Linna is there, though it is very late. She no longer attends her classes and has switched to the dogs' schedule, sleeping the afternoons away in the safety of her apartment. She cannot bring herself to sleep in the dogs' presence. In the park, she is taut as a strung wire, a single monkey among wolves; but she returns each dusk, and listens, and sometimes speaks. There are maybe fifteen dogs now, though she's sure more hide in the bushes, or doze, or prowl for food.

"I remember," a voice says hesitantly. (*Remember* is a frame; they did not "remember" before the word, only lived in a series of nows longer or shorter in duration. Memory breeds resentment. Or so we fear.) "I had a home, food, a warm place, something I chewed—a, a blanket. A woman and a man and she gave me all these things, patted me." Voices in assent: pats remembered. "But she wasn't always nice. She yelled sometimes. She took the blanket away. And she'd drag at my collar until it hurt sometimes. But when she made food she'd put a piece on the floor for me to eat. Beef, it was. That was nice again."

Another voice in the darkness: "Beef. That is a hamburger." The dogs are trying out the concept of *beef* and the concept of *hamburger* and they are connecting them.

"*Nice* is not being hurt," a dog says.

"Not-nice is collars and leashes."

"And rules."

"Being inside and only coming out to shit and piss."

"People are nice and not nice," says the first voice. Linna finally sees that it belongs to a small dusty black dog sitting near the roots of an immense oak. Its enormous fringed ears look like radar dishes. "I learned to think and the woman brought me here. She was sad, but she hit me with stones until I ran away, and then she left. A person is nice and not nice."

The dogs are silent, digesting this. "Linna?" Hope says. "How can people be nice and then not nice?"

"I don't know," she says, because she knows the real question is, *How can they stop loving us?*

(The answer even Linna has trouble seeing is that *nice* and *not-nice* have nothing to do with love. And even loving someone doesn't always mean you can share your house and the fine thread of your life, or sleep safely in the same place.)

7. ONE DOG TRICKS THE WHITE-TRUCK MAN.

This is the same dog. He is very hungry and looking through the alleys for something to eat. He sees a man with a white truck coming toward him. One Dog knows that the white-truck men catch dogs sometimes, so he's afraid. He drags some old bones out of the trash and heaps them up and settles on top of them. He pretends not to see the white-truck man but says loudly, "Boy that was a delicious man I just killed, but I'm still starved. I hope I can catch another one."

Well, that white-truck man runs right away. But someone was watching all this from her kitchen window and she runs out to the man and tells him, "One Dog never killed a man! That's just a pile of bones from my barbeque last week, and he's making a mess out of my backyard. Come catch him."

The white-truck man and the person run back to where One Dog is still gnawing on one of the bones in his pile. He sees them and guesses what has happened, so he's afraid. But he pretends not to see them and says loudly, "I'm still starved! I hope that human comes back soon with that white-truck man I asked her to get for me."

The white-truck man and the woman both run away, and he does not see them again that day.

"Why is she here?"

It's one of the new dogs, a lean Lab-cross with a limp. He doesn't talk to her but to Gold, and Linna sees his anger in his liquid-brown eyes, feels it like a hot scent rising from his back. He's one of the half-strays, an outdoor dog who lived on a chain. It was no effort at all for his owner to unhook the chain and let him go; no effort for the Lab-cross to leave his owner's yard and drift across town killing cats and raiding trash cans, and end up in North Park.

There are thirty dogs now and maybe more. The newcomers are warier around her than the earlier dogs. Some, the ones who have taken several days to end up here, dodging police cruisers and pedestrians' Mace, are actively hostile.

"She's no threat," Gold says.

The Lab-cross says nothing but approaches with head lowered and hackles raised. Linna sits on the picnic table's bench and tries not to screech, to bare her teeth and scratch and run. The situation is as charged as the air before a thunderstorm. Gold is no longer the pack's leader—there's a German Shepherd dog who holds his tail higher—but he still has status as the one who tells the stories. The German Shepherd doesn't care whether Linna's there or not; he won't stop another dog from attacking if it wishes. Linna spends much of her time with her hands flexed to bare claws she doesn't have.

"She listens, that's all," says Hope: frightened Hope standing up for her. "And brings food sometimes." Others speak up: *She got rid of my collar when it got burrs under it. She took the tick off me. She stroked my head.*

The Lab-cross's breath on her ankles is hot, his nose wet and surprisingly warm. Dogs were once wolves; right now this burns in her mind. She tries not to shiver. "You're sick," the dog says at last.

"I'm well enough," Linna says through clenched teeth.

Just like that the dog loses interest and turns back to the others.

(Why does Linna come here at all? Her parents had a dog when she was a little girl. Ruthie was so obviously grateful for Linna's love and the home she was offered, the old quilt on the floor, the dog food that fell from the sky twice a day like manna. Linna wondered even then whether Ruthie dreamt of a Holy Land, and what that place would have looked like. Linna's parents were kind and generous, denied Ruthie's needs only when they couldn't help it; paid for her medical bills without too much complaining; didn't put her to sleep until she became incontinent and messed on the living-room floor.

(Even we dog-lovers wrestle with our consciences. We promised to keep our pets forever until they died; but that was from a comfortable height, when we were the masters and they the slaves. Some Inuit tribes believe all animals have souls—except for dogs. This is a convenient stance. They could not use their dogs as they do—beat them, work them, starve them, eat them, feed them one to the other—if dogs were men's equals.

(Or perhaps they could. Our record with our own species is not so exemplary.)

8. ONE DOG AND THE EATING MAN.

This is the same dog. She lives with the Eating Man, who eats only good things while One Dog has only dry kibble. The Eating Man is always hungry. He orders a pizza but he is still hungry, so he eats all the meat and vegetables he finds in the refrigerator. But he's still hungry, so he opens all the cupboards and eats the cereal and noodles and flour and sugar in there. And he's still hungry. There is nothing left, so he eats all One Dog's dry kibble, leaving nothing for One Dog.

So One Dog kills the Eating Man. "It was him or me," One Dog says. The Eating Man is the best thing One Dog has ever eaten.

Linna has been sleeping the days away so that she can be with the dogs at night, when they feel safest out on the streets looking for food. So now it's hot dusk, a day later, and she's just awakened in tangled sheets in a bedroom with flaking walls: the sky a hard haze, air warm and wet as laundry. Linna is walking past Cruz Park, on her way to North Park. She has a bag with a loaf of day-old bread, some cheap sandwich meat, and an extra order of French fries. The fatty smell of the fries sticks in her nostrils. Gold never gets them anymore, unless she saves them from the other dogs and gives them to him specially.

She thinks nothing of the blue and red and strobing white lights ahead of her on Mass Street until she gets close enough to see that this is no traffic stop. There's no wrecked car, no distraught student who turned left across traffic because she was late for her job and was T-boned. Half a dozen police cars perch on the sidewalks around the park, and she can see reflected lights from others otherwise hidden by the park's shrubs. Fifteen or twenty policemen stand around in clumps, like dead leaves caught for a moment in an eddy and freed by some unseen current.

Everyone knows Cruz Park is full of dogs—sixty or seventy according to today's editorial in the local paper, each one a health and safety risk—but very few dogs are visible at the moment, and none look familiar to her, either as neighbors' ex-pets or wanderers from the North Park pack.

Linna approaches an eddy of policemen; its elements drift apart, rejoin other groups.

"Cruz Park is closed," the remaining officer says to Linna. He's a tall man with a military cut that makes him look older than he is.

It's no surprise that the flashing lights, the cars, the yellow CAUTION tape, and the policemen are about the dogs. There've been complaints from the people neighboring the park—overturned trash cans, feces on the sidewalks, even one attack when a man tried to grab a stray's collar and the stray fought to get away. Today's editorial merely crystalized what everyone already felt.

Linna thinks of Gold, Sophie, Hope. "They're just dogs."

The officer looks a little uncomfortable. "The park is closed until we can address current health and safety concerns." Linna can practically hear the quote marks from the official statement.

"What are you going to do?" she asks.

He relaxes a little. "Right now we're waiting for Animal Control. Any dogs they capture will go to Douglas County Humane Society; they'll try to track down the owners—"

"The ones who kicked the dogs out in the first place?" Linna asks. "No one's gonna want these dogs back, you know that."

"That's the procedure," he says, his back stiff again, tone harsh. "If the Humane—"

"Do you have a dog?" Linna interrupts him. "I mean, did you? Before this started?"

He turns and walks away without a word.

Linna runs the rest of the way to North Park, slowing to a lumbering trot when she gets a cramp in her side. There are no police cars up here, but yellow plastic police tape stretches across the entry: CAUTION. She walks around to the side entrance, off Second Street. The police don't seem to know about the break in the fence.

9. ONE DOG MEETS TAME DOGS.

This is the same dog. He lives in a park, and eats at the restaurants across the street. On his way to the restaurants one day, he walks past a yard with two dogs. They laugh at him and say, "We get dog food every day and our master lets us sleep in the kitchen, which is cool in the summer and warm in the winter. And you have to cross Sixth Street to get food where you might get run over, and you have to sleep in the heat and the cold."

The dog walks past them to get to the restaurants, and he eats the fallen tacos and French fries and burgers around the Dumpster. When he sits by the restaurant doors, many people give him bits of food; one person gives him chicken in a paper dish. He walks back to the yard and lets the two dogs smell the chicken and grease on his breath through the fence. "Ha on you," he says, and then goes back to his park and sleeps on a pile of dry rubbish under the bridge, where the breeze is cool. When night comes, he goes looking for a mate and no one stops him.

(Whatever else it is, the Change of the animals—mute to speaking, dumb to dreaming—is a test for us. We pass the test when we accept that their dreams and desires and goals may not be ours. Many people fail this test. But we don't have to, and even failing we can try again. And again. And pass at last.

(A slave is trapped, choiceless and voiceless; but so is her owner. Those we have injured may forgive us, but how can we know? Can we trust them with our homes, our lives, our hearts? Animals did not forgive before the Change; mostly they forgot. But the Change brought memory, and memory requires forgiveness, and how can we trust them to forgive us?

(And how do we forgive ourselves? Mostly we don't. Mostly we pretend to forget, and hope it becomes true.)

At noon the next day, Linna jerks awake, monkey-self already dragging her to her feet. Even before she's fully awake, she knows that what woke her wasn't a car's backfire. It was a shotgun blast, and it was only a couple of blocks away, and she already knows why.

She drags on clothes and runs to Cruz Park, no stitch in her side this time. The flashing police cars and CAUTION tape and men are all still there, but now she sees dogs everywhere, twenty or more laid flat near the sidewalk, the way dogs sleep on hot summer days. Too many of the ribcages are still; too many of the eyes open, dust and pollen already gathering.

Linna has no words, can only watch speechless; but the men say enough. First thing in the morning, the Animal Control people went to Dillon's grocery store and bought fifty one-pound packages of cheap hamburger on sale, and they poisoned them all, and then scattered them around the park. Linna can see little blue styrene squares from the packaging scattered here and there, among the dogs.

The dying dogs don't say much. Most have fallen back on the ancient language of pain, wordless yelps and keening. Men walk among them, shooting the suffering dogs, jabbing poles into the underbrush looking for any who might have slipped away.

People come in cars and trucks and on bicycles and scooters and on their feet. The police officers around Cruz Park keep sending them away—"a health risk" says one officer; "safety," says another, but the people keep coming back, or new people.

Linna's eyes are blind with tears; she blinks and they slide down her face, oddly cool and thick.

"Killing them is the answer?" says a woman beside her. Her face is wet as well, but her voice is even, as if they are debating this in a class, she and Linna. The woman holds her baby in her arms, a white cloth thrown over its face so that it can't see. "I have three dogs at home, and they've never hurt anything. Words don't change that."

"What if they change?" Linna asks. "What if they ask for real food and a bed soft as yours, the chance to dream their own dreams?"

"I'll try to give it to them," the woman says, but her attention is focused on the park, the dogs. "They can't do this!"

"Try and stop them." Linna turns away tasting her tears. She should feel comforted by the woman's words, the fact that not everyone has forgotten how to love animals when they are no longer slaves, but she feels nothing. And she walks north, carved hollow.

10. ONE DOG GOES TO THE PLACE OF PIECES.

This is the same dog. She is hit by a car and part of her flies off and runs into a dark culvert. She does not know what the piece is, so she chases it.

The culvert is long and it gets so cold that her breath puffs out in front of her. When she gets to the end, there's no light and the world smells like cold metal. She walks along a road. Cold cars rush past but they don't slow down. None of them hit her.

One Dog comes to a parking lot, which has nothing in it but the legs of dogs. The legs walk from place to place, but they cannot see or smell or eat. None of them is her leg, so she walks on. After this she finds a parking lot filled with the ears of dogs, and then one filled with the assholes of dogs, and the eyes of dogs and the bodies of dogs; but none of the ears and assholes and eyes and bodies are hers, so she walks on.

The last parking lot she comes to has nothing at all in it except for little smells, like puppies. She can tell one of the little smells is hers, so she calls to it and it comes to her. She doesn't know where the little smell belongs on her body, so she carries it in her mouth and walks back past the parking lots and through the culvert.

One Dog cannot leave the culvert because a man stands in the way. She puts the little smell down carefully and says, "I want to go back."

The man says, "You can't unless all your parts are where they belong."

One Dog can't think of where the little smell belongs. She picks up the little smell and tries to sneak past the man, but the man catches her and hits her. One Dog tries to hide it under a hamburger wrapper and pretend it's not there, but the man catches that, too.

One Dog thinks some more and finally says, "Where does the little smell belong?"

The man says, "Inside you."

So One Dog swallows the little smell. She realizes that the man has been trying to keep her from returning home but that the man cannot lie about the little smell. One Dog growls and runs past him, and returns to our world.

There are two police cars pulled onto the sidewalk before North Park's main entrance. Linna takes in the sight of them in three stages: first, she has seen police everywhere today, so they are no shock; second, they are *here*, at *her* park, threatening *her* dogs, and this is like being kicked in the stomach; and third, she thinks: *I have to get past them.*

North Park has two entrances, but one isn't used much. Linna walks around to the little narrow dirt path from Second Street.

The park is never quiet. There's busy Sixth Street just south, and the river and its noises to the north and east and west; trees and bushes hissing with the hot wind; the hum of insects.

But the dogs are quiet. She's never seen them all in the daylight, but they're gathered now, silent and loll-tongued in the bright daylight. There are forty or more. Everyone is dirty, now. Any long fur is matted; anything white is dust-colored. Most of them are thinner than they were when they arrived. The dogs face one of the tables, as orderly as the audience at a string quartet; but the tension in the air is so obvious that Linna stops short.

Gold stands on the table. There are a couple of dogs she doesn't recognize in the dust nearby: flopped flat with their sides heaving, tongues long and flecked with white foam. One is hunched over; he drools onto the ground and retches helplessly. The other dog has a scratch along her flank. The blood is the brightest thing Linna can see in the sunlight, a red so strong it hurts her eyes.

The Cruz Park cordon was permeable, of course. These two managed to slip past the police cars. The vomiting one is dying.

She realizes suddenly that every dog's muzzle is swiveled toward her. The air snaps with something that makes her back-brain bare its teeth and scream, her hackles rise. The monkey-self looks for escape, but the trees are not close enough to climb (and she is no climber), the road and river too far away. She is a spy in a gulag; the prisoners have little to lose by killing her.

"You shouldn't have come back," Gold says.

"I came to tell you—warn you." Even through her monkey-self's defiance, Linna weeps helplessly.

"We already know." The pack's leader, the German Shepherd dog, says. "They're killing us all. We're leaving the park."

She shakes her head, fighting for breath. "They'll kill you.

There are police cars on Sixth—they'll shoot you however you get out. They're *waiting*."

"Will it be better here?" Gold asks. "They'll kill us anyway, with their poisoned meat. We *know*. You're afraid, all of you—"

"I'm not—" Linna starts, but he breaks in.

"We smell it on everyone, even the people who take care of us or feed us. We have to get out of here."

"They'll *kill* you," Linna says again.

"Some of us might make it."

"Wait! Maybe there's a way," Linna says, and then: "I have stories."

In the stifling air, Linna can hear the dogs pant, even over the street noises. "People have their own stories," Gold says at last. "Why should we listen to yours?"

"We made you into what we wanted; we *owned* you. Now you are becoming what *you* want. You belong to yourselves. But we have stories, too, and we learned from them. Will you listen?"

The air shifts, but whether it is the first movement of the still air or the shifting of the dogs, she can't tell.

"Tell your story," says the German Shepherd.

Linna struggles to remember half-read textbooks from a sophomore course on folklore, framing her thoughts as she speaks them. "We used to tell a lot of stories about Coyote. The animals were here before humans were, and Coyote was one of them. He did a lot of stuff, got in a lot of trouble. Fooled everyone."

"I know about coyotes," a dog says. "There were some by where I used to live. They eat puppies sometimes."

"I bet they do," Linna says. "Coyotes eat everything. But this wasn't *a* coyote, it's *Coyote*. The one and only."

The dogs murmur. She hears them work it out: *coyote* is the same as *this is the same dog.*

"So. Coyote disguised himself as a female so that he could hang out with a bunch of females, just so he could mate with them. He pretended to be dead, and then when the crows came down to eat him, he snatched them up and ate every one! When a greedy man was keeping all the animals for himself, Coyote pretended to be a very rich person and then freed them all, so that everyone could eat. He—" She pauses to think, looks down at the dogs all around her. The monkey-fear is gone: she is the story-teller, the maker of thoughts. They will not kill her, she knows. "Coyote did all these things, and a lot more things. I bet you'll think of some, too.

"I have an idea of how to save you," she says. "Some of you might die, but some chance is better than no chance."

"Why would we trust you?" says the Lab-cross who has never liked her, but the other dogs are with her. She feels it, and an-swers.

"Because this trick, maybe it's even good enough for Coyote. Will you let me show you?"

We people are so proud of our intelligence, but that makes it easier to trick us. We see the white-truck men and we believe they're whatever we're expecting to see. Linna goes to U-Haul and rents a pickup truck for the afternoon. She digs out a white shirt she used to wear when she ushered at the concert hall. She knows *clipboard with printout* means *official responsibilities*, so she throws one on the dashboard of the truck.

She backs the pickup to the little entrance on Second Street. The dogs slip through the gap in the fence and scramble into the pickup's bed. She lifts the ones that are too small to jump so high. And then they arrange themselves carefully, flat on their sides. There's a certain amount of snapping and snarling as later dogs step on the ears and ribcages of the earlier dogs, but eventually everyone is settled, everyone able to breathe a little, every eye tight shut.

She pulls onto Sixth Street with a truck heaped with dogs. When the police stop her, she tells them a little story. Animal Control has too many calls these days: cattle loose on the high-ways, horses leaping fences that are too high and breaking their legs; and the dogs, the scores and scores of dogs at Cruz Park. Animal Control is renting trucks now, whatever they can find. The dogs of North Park were slated for poisoning this morning.

"I didn't hear about this in briefing," one of the policemen says. He pokes at the heap of dogs with a black club; they shift like dead meat. They reek; an inexperienced observer might not recognize the stench as mingled dog-breath and shit.

Linna smiles, baring her teeth. "I'm on my way back to the shelter," she says. "They have an incinerator." She waves an open cell phone at him, and hopes he does not ask to talk to whoever's on the line, because there is no one.

But people believe stories, and then they make them real: the officer pokes at the dogs one more time and then wrinkles his nose and waves her on.

Clinton Lake is a vast place, trees and bushes and impenetrable brambles ringing a big lake, open country in every direction. When Linna unlatches the pickup's bed, the dogs drop stiffly to the ground, and stretch. Three died of overheating, stifled beneath the weight of so many others. Gold is one of them, but Linna does not cry. She knew she couldn't save them all, but she has saved some of them. That has to be enough. And the stories will continue: stories do not easily die.

The dogs can go wherever they wish from here, and they will. They and all the other dogs who have tricked or slipped or stumbled to safety will spread across the Midwest, the world. Some will find homes with men and women who treat them not as slaves but as friends, freeing themselves, as well. Linna herself returns home with little shivering Sophie and sad Hope.

Some will die, killed by men and cougars and cars and even other dogs. Others will raise litters. The fathers of some of those litters will be coyotes. Eventually the Changed dogs will find their place in the changed world.

(When we first fashioned animals to suit our needs, we treated them as if they were stories and we the authors, and we clung desperately to an imagined copyright that would permit us to change them, sell them, even delete them. But some stories cannot be controlled. A wise author or dog owner listens, and learns, and says at last, "I never knew that.")

11. ONE DOG CREATES THE WORLD.

This is the same dog. There wasn't any world when this happens, just a man and a dog. They lived in a house that didn't have any windows to look out of. Nothing had any smells. The dog shit and pissed on a paper in the bathroom, but not even this had a smell. Her food had no taste, either. The man suppressed all these things. This was because the man didn't want One Dog to create the universe and he knew it would be done by smell.

One night One Dog was sleeping and she felt the strangest thing that any dog has ever felt. It was the smells of the world pouring from her nose. When the smell of grass came out, there was grass outside. When the smell of shit came out, there was shit outside. She made the whole world that way. And when the smell of other dogs came out, there were dogs everywhere, big ones and little ones all over the world.

"I think I'm done," she said, and she left.

KIJ JOHNSON

I write about dogs a lot, and they serve different purposes, based on the story: pet, tool, metaphor. "The Evolution of Trickster Stories Among the Dogs of North Park After the Change" explores dogs as the aliens we have the greatest chance of understanding. Give dogs, our closest allies, speech and now not even language is a barrier; we have narrowed the gap as much as possible between Us and Alien. But a barrier remains. The ability to see clearly across such gaps and to accept and embrace what we see—across species, or race, or (should we ever meet space aliens) DNA—is what will make us larger than we are.

In addition to giving Nebula Awards each year, SFWA also presents the Damon Knight Grand Master Award to a living author for a lifetime of achievement in science fiction and/or fantasy. In accordance with SFWA's bylaws, the president shall have the power, at his or her discretion, to call for the presentation of a Grand Master Award. Nominations for the Grand Master Award shall be solicited from the officers, with the advice of participating past presidents, who shall vote with the officers to determine the recipient.

Previous Grand Masters are Robert A. Heinlein (1975), Jack Williamson (1976), Clifford D. Simak (1977), L. Sprague de Camp (1979), Fritz Leiber (1981), Andre Norton (1984), Sir Arthur C. Clarke (1986), Isaac Asimov (1987), Alfred Bester (1988), Ray Bradbury (1989), Lester del Rey (1991), Frederik Pohl (1993), Damon Knight (1995), A. E. van Vogt (1996), Jack Vance (1997), Poul Anderson (1998), Hal Clement (Harry Stubbs) (1999), Brian W. Aldiss (2000), Philip José Farmer (2001), Ursula K. Le Guin (2003), Robert Silverberg (2004), Anne McCaffrey (2005), Harlan Ellison (2006), and James Gunn (2007). (The year indicates when the honor was presented.)

In 2008 the Grand Master Award was given to Michael Moorcock, a writer equally adept at creating marvelous worlds in science fiction, fantasy, and mainstream. As editor of the controversial British magazine *New Worlds* from May 1964 until March 1971 and then again from 1976 to 1996 he was instrumental in the development of the science fiction "New Wave" movement in the UK and the United States.

Kim Newman, a compatriot of Moorcock's and an admirer of his fiction, provides a tribute.

AN APPRECIATION
OF MICHAEL MOORCOCK

KIM NEWMAN

I t's a common complaint that too many favorite writers don't write enough to satisfy a committed fan. You can swallow all of Jane Austen, John Franklin Bardin, or Dashiell Hammett inside a week. However, others—on the pattern of Dickens or Dumas—produce quality work by the ream, filling shelves with so many books that even a true devotee can store up treats for the future. Michael Moorcock falls into the latter category—reading his work makes for a lifetime relationship, with always more books to come, more branches of the saga awaiting discovery, more fiendishly clever cross-references to be discerned.

I still haven't got round to seriously tackling the Elric series, which for many of my generation were the major Moorcocks, but I have them on the to-be-read shelf, and eagerly anticipate the gap opening in my schedule when I can take the plunge—rather in the way that a schoolboy sometimes hopes for a bout of flu because a few days in bed with a stack of comics is preferable to dreary afternoons of double geography. In the 1970s, I read and reread *The Warlord of the Air* and *The Land Leviathan* with the passionate delight that comes from discovering books that seem to be written expressly for you (of course, a feeling shared by a large readership); followed the braided, not-quite-a-series Cornelius Chronicles; was awakened to the possibilities of not only the fantastic but the historical by books like *Behold the Man*, *Gloriana*, and the *Dancers at the End of Time* sequence. Later, Moorcock embarked on ambitious epics of the twentieth century, in the linked

273

novels *Mother London* and *King of the City* and the Pyat quartet—but has not abandoned the playful, charming, spiky pulp fantasies of *The Metatemporal Detective*.

What first caught my attention in Moorcock's work—and, shamefully, the first I came to it was *The Final Program*, which I read after seeing the film version he disowned—was the sense that he was writing about a world I inhabited. As an English child in the 1960s, born just about the time Moorcock began writing professionally, I was aware of both the traditions that came from the Empire and the War (a source of mixed pride and revulsion) and the explosion of a multicolored counterculture that made British pop music, fashion, television, and film exciting. Moorcock has a rare sense of the wondrousness and absurdity of the English pop cultural landscape (it's no coincidence he novelized *The Great Rock 'n' Roll Swindle*), as well as an appreciation of British traditions (sometimes hideous, sometimes wonderful), which sidesteps the genre of American pulp in interesting ways (even Moorcock's occasional westerns are influenced by those books and comics turned out by suburban British hacks who never ventured west of Bournemouth while dreaming of the range). Moorcock is the heir of not merely Charles Dickens, H. G. Wells, and H. Rider Haggard, but of lesser-remarked British publishing phenomena like long-serving detective Sexton Blake (with whom Moorcock has a long and complex relationship), C. J. Cutcliffe Hyne (who wrote the Captain Kettle stories in the *Strand Magazine*), and George Griffith (author of *Angel of the Revolution*).

Cultural wars were fought inside and outside the science fiction field (and the House of Commons) around Moorcock's editorship of *New Worlds* magazine and rankles still run deep in some quarters, but whole swaths of achievement in an interlinked but disparate selection of literary endeavors would literally not have been possible without the enthusiasms, energy, and quixotic determination of Michael Moorcock. He has always been a generous, bountiful creator, producing so much work personally but also inspiring and boosting other writers (he is a great rescuer of reputations) as tirelessly as he lambastes and ridicules those he feels represent a deadening, baneful influence (he is also a great foe of humbug and cant). His anthologies of forgotten, pre-Gernsback British science fiction (*England Invaded, Before Armageddon*) are as important as Hugh Greene's *The Rivals of Sherlock Holmes* in preserving a rich literary landscape that was in danger of seeming like a monoculture—not least for rescuing Saki's masterly novel *When William Came* from obscurity.

Others have written in disparate genres, and managed to straddle popular culture (i.e., science fiction and fantasy) and literary fiction (i.e., taken seriously and given prizes that don't look like spaceships), but Moorcock invented the canny notion—later appropriated by Stephen King, Philip José Farmer, and others (I plead guilty)—of tying together everything he writes into what the other Mike in the *New Worlds* gang (M. John Harrison) called a "meta-series." On a commercial level, and the author who dedicated *The Steel Tsar* to his creditors for making its writing necessary certainly understands the commercial realities of a life of letters, this encourages the readers who like one of the books to track down everything Moorcock has ever written as if they were jigsaw pieces that have to be bought individually. But there's also a true egalitarianism to the approach that gives a "straight" (more properly, otherly crooked) novel like *Mother London* the engaging, stimulating, detailed readability of the best genre fiction while allowing for seriousness of intent, wryly self-deprecating humor, and graceful prose even in the most rapidly written and disposably published fantasy paperback. Graham Greene divided his work into "novels" and "entertainments"—it's a fair bet you'll derive more from the latter than the former these days—but Moorcock has never been so dismissive of his work or his readers, and you'd need a mosaic or crazy-paving to map out the separate subsets and variant approaches of everything he's ever written. You'd be best advised just to read it all, and sort it out later.

As representative of the fiction that won him the Grand Master Award, Michael Moorcock has selected his short story

"THE PLEASURE GARDEN OF FELIPE SAGITTARIUS"

Michael Moorcock is a British writer and musician living in Texas, France, and Spain. The author of many literary novels and stories in practically every genre, he has won and been short-listed for many awards, including the Nebula, World Fantasy, Hugo, August Derleth, Booker, Whitbread, and *Guardian* Fiction Award. As a member of the prog-rock band Hawkwind he won a platinum disc. As editor of *New Worlds* he received an Arts Council of Great Britain Award and a BSFA Award. His journalism appears regularly in the *Guardian,* the *Daily Telegraph, New Statesman,* and *Spectator.* He has been compared, among others, to Balzac, Dumas, Dickens, James Joyce, Ian Fleming, J. R. R. Tolkien, and Robert E. Howard. Moorcock's most recent books include the short story collections *The Life and Times of Jerry Cornelius, London Bone*, and *The Metatemporal Detective,* in which the following story appears.

Visit Michael Moorcock online at www.multiverse.org.

Reality, I suggested, might be merely what each one
of us says it is. Does that idea make you feel lonely, Mr.
Cornelius?

LOBKOWITZ
Recollected Dialogues

The air was still and warm, the sun bright, and the sky blue
above the ruins of Berlin as I clambered over piles of
weed-covered brick and broken concrete on my way to
investigate the murder of an unknown man in the garden of Police Chief Bismarck.

My name is Sam Begg, Metatemporal Investigator, and this
job was going to be a tough one, I knew.

Don't ask me the location or the date. I never bother to find
out things like that. They only confuse me. With me it's instinct,
win or lose.

They'd given me all the information there was. The dead
man had already had an autopsy. Nothing unusual about him except that he had paper disposable lungs. That pinned him down a
little. The only place I knew of where they still used paper lungs
was Rome. What was a Roman doing in Berlin? Why was he
murdered in Police Chief Bismarck's garden? He'd been strangled, that I'd been told. It wasn't hard to strangle a man with pa-

per lungs; it didn't take long. But who and why were harder questions to answer right then.

It was a long way across the ruins to Bismarck's place. Rubble stretched in all directions, and only here and there could you see a landmark—what was left of the Reichstag, the Brandenburg Gate, the Brechtsmuseum, and a few other places like that.

I stopped to lean on the only remaining wall of a house, took off my jacket and loosened my tie, wiped my forehead and neck with my handkerchief, and lit a cheroot. The wall gave me some shade and I felt a little cooler by the time I was ready to get going again.

As I mounted a big heap of brick on which a lot of blue weeds grew I saw the Bismarck place ahead. Built of heavy, black-veined marble, in the kind of Valhalla/Olympus mixture they went in for, it was fronted by a smooth, green lawn and backed by a garden surrounded by such a high wall I only glimpsed the leaves of some of the foliage even though I was looking down on the place. The thick Grecian columns flanking the porch were topped by a baroque facade covered in bas-reliefs showing hairy men in horned helmets killing dragons and one another apparently indiscriminately.

I picked my way down to the lawn and walked across it, then up some steps until I reached the front door. It was big and heavy, bronze I guessed, with more bas-reliefs, this time of clean-shaven characters in ornate and complicated armour with two-handed swords and riding horses. Some had lances and axes. I pulled the bell and waited.

I had plenty of time to study the pictures before one of the doors swung open and an old man in a semi-military suit, holding himself straight by an effort, raised a white eyebrow at me.

I told him my name, and he let me in to a cool, dark hall full of the same kinds of armour the men outside had been wearing. He opened a door on the right and told me to wait. The room was all iron and leather—weapons on the walls and hide-covered furniture on the carpet. Thick velvet curtains were drawn back from the window, and I stood looking out over the quiet ruins, smoked another stick, popped the butt in a green pot, and put my jacket back on.

The old man came in again and I followed him out of that room, along the hall, up one flight of the wide stairs, and into a huge, less cluttered room where I found the guy I'd come to see.

He stood in the middle of the carpet. He was wearing a heavily ornamented helmet with a spike on the top, a deep blue uniform covered in badges, gold and black epaulettes, shiny jackboots, and steel spurs. He looked about seventy and very tough. He had bushy grey eyebrows and a big, carefully combed moustache. As I came in he grunted and put one arm into a horizontal position, pointing at me.

"Herr Begg. I am Otto von Bismarck, Chief of Berlin's police."

I shook the hand. Actually it shook me, all over.

"Quite a turn up," I said. "A murder in the garden of the man who's supposed to prevent murders."

His face must have been paralyzed or something because it didn't move except when he spoke, and even then it didn't move much.

"Quite so," he said. "We were reluctant to call you in, of course. But I think this is your speciality. Devilish work."

"Maybe. Is the body still here?"

"In the kitchen. The autopsy was performed here. Paper lungs—you know about that?"

"I know. Now, if I've got it right, you heard nothing in the night—"

"Oh, yes, I did hear something—the barking of my wolfhounds. One of the servants investigated but found nothing."

"What time was this?"

"Time?"

"What did the clock say?"

"About two in the morning."

"When was the body found?"

"About ten—the gardener discovered it in the vine grove."

"Right—let's look at the body and then talk to the gardener."

He took me to the kitchen. One of the windows was opened on to a lush enclosure full of tall, brightly coloured shrubs of every possible shade. An intoxicating scent came from the garden. It made me feel horny. I turned to look at the corpse lying on a scrubbed deal table covered in a sheet.

I pulled back the sheet. The body was naked. It looked old but strong, deeply tanned. The head was big, and its most noticeable feature was the heavy grey moustache. The body wasn't what it had been. First there were the marks of strangulation around the throat, as well as swelling on wrists, forearms, and legs which seemed to indicate that the victim had also been tied up recently. The whole of the front of the torso had been opened for the autopsy and whoever had stitched it up again hadn't been too careful.

"What about clothes?" I asked the Police Chief.

Bismarck shook his head and pointed to a chair standing beside the table. "That was all we found."

There was a pair of neatly folded paper lungs, a bit the worse for wear. The trouble with disposable lungs was that while you never had to worry about smoking or any of the other causes of lung disease, the lungs had to be changed regularly. This was expensive, particularly in Rome where there was no State-controlled Lung Service as there had been in most of the European City-States until a few years before the War when the longer lasting polythene lung had superseded the paper one. There was also a wristwatch and a pair of red shoes with long, curling toes.

I picked up one of the shoes. Middle Eastern workmanship. I looked at the watch. It was heavy, old, tarnished, and Russian. The strap was new, pigskin, with "Made in England" stamped on it.

"I see why they called us," I said.

"There were certain anachronisms," Bismarck admitted.

"This gardener who found him, can I talk to him?"

Bismarck went to the window and called: "Felipe!"

The foliage seemed to fold back of its own volition, and a cadaverous dark-haired man came through it. He was tall, long faced, and pale. He held an elegant watering can in one hand. He was dressed in a dark green, high-collared shirt and matching trousers. I wondered if I had seen him somewhere.

We looked at one another through the window.

"This is my gardener, Felipe Sagittarius," Bismarck said.

Sagittarius bowed, his eyes amused. Bismarck didn't seem to notice.

"Can you let me see where you found the body?" I asked.

"Sure," said Sagittarius.

"I shall wait here," Bismarck told me as I went towards the kitchen door.

"Okay." I stepped into the garden and let Sagittarius show me the way. Once again the shrubs seemed to part on their own.

The scent was still thick and erotic. Most of the plants had dark, fleshy leaves and flowers of deep reds, purples, and blues. Here and there were clusters of heavy yellow and pink.

The grass I was walking on felt like it crawled under my feet, and the weird shapes of the trunks and stems of the shrubs didn't make me want to take a snooze in that garden.

"This is all your work is it, Sagittarius?" I asked.

He nodded and kept walking.

"Original," I said. "Never seen one like it before."

Sagittarius turned then and pointed a thumb behind him. "This is the place."

We were standing in a little glade almost entirely surrounded by thick vines that curled about their trellises like snakes. On the far side of the glade I could see where some of the vines had been ripped and the trellis torn. I guessed there had been a fight. I still couldn't work out why the victim had been untied before the murderer strangled him—it must have been before, or else there wouldn't have been a fight. I checked the scene, but there were no clues. Through the place where the trellis was torn I saw a small summerhouse built to represent a Chinese pavilion, all red, yellow, and black lacquer with highlights picked out in gold. It didn't fit with the architecture of the house.

"What's that?" I asked the gardener.

"Nothing," he said sulkily, evidently sorry I'd seen it.

"I'll take a look at it anyway."

He shrugged but did not offer to lead on. I moved between the trellises until I reached the pavilion. Sagittarius followed slowly. I took the short flight of wooden steps up to the verandah and tried the door. It opened. I walked in. There seemed to be only one room, a bedroom. The bed needed making, and it looked as if two people had left it in a hurry. There was a pair of nylons tucked half under the pillow and a pair of man's underpants on the floor. The sheets were very white, the furnishings very oriental and rich.

Sagittarius was standing in the doorway.

"Your place?" I said.

"No." He sounded offended. "The Police Chief's."

I grinned.

Sagittarius burst into rhapsody. "The languorous scents, the very menace of the plants, the heaviness in the air of the garden, must surely stir the blood of even the most ancient man. This is the only place he can relax. This is what I'm employed for.

"He gives me my head. I give him his pleasures. It's my pleasure garden."

"Has this," I said, pointing to the bed, "anything to do with last night?"

"He was probably here when it happened, but I . . ." Sagittarius shook his head and I wondered if there was something he'd meant to imply that I'd missed.

I saw something on the floor, stooped, and picked it up. A pendant with the initials E.B. engraved on it in Gothic script.

"Who's E.B.?" I said.

"Only the garden interests me, Herr Begg. I do not know who she is."

I looked out at the weird garden. "Why does it interest you—what's all this for? You're not doing it to his orders, are you? You're doing it for yourself."

Sagittarius smiled bleakly. "You are astute." He waved an arm at the warm foliage that seemed more reptilian than plant and more mammalian, in its own way, than either. "You know what I see out there? I see deep-sea canyons where lost submarines cruise through a silence of twilit green, threatened by the waving tentacles of predators, half-fish, half-plant, and watched by the eyes of long-dead mermen whose blood went to feed their young; where squids and rays fight in a graceful dance of death, clouds of black ink merging with clouds of red blood, drifting to the surface, sipped at by sharks in passing, where they will be seen by mariners leaning over the rails of their ships. Maddened, the mariners will fling themselves overboard to sail slowly towards those distant plant-creatures already feasting on the corpses of squid and ray. This is the world I can bring to the land—that is my ambition."

He stared at me, paused, and said: "My skull—it's like a monstrous fish bowl!"

I nipped back to the house to find Bismarck had returned to his room. He was sitting in a plush armchair, a hidden HiFi playing, of all things, a Ravel String Quartet.

"No Wagner?" I said and then: "Who's E.B.?"

"Later," he said. "My assistant will answer your questions for the moment. He should be waiting for you."

There was a car parked outside the house—a battered Volkswagen containing a neatly uniformed man of below-average height. He had a small toothbrush moustache, a stray lock of black hair falling over his forehead, black gloves on his hands which gripped a military cane in his lap. When he saw me come out he smiled, said, "Aha," and got briskly from the car to shake my hand with a slight bow.

"Adolf Hitler," he said. "Captain of Uniformed Detectives in Precinct XII. Police Chief Bismarck has put me at your service."

"Glad to hear it. Do you know much about him?"

Hitler opened the car door for me, and I got in. He went round the other side, slid into the driving seat.

"The Chief?" He shook his head. "He is somewhat remote. I do not know him well—there are several ranks between us. Usually my orders come from him indirectly. This time he chose to see me himself."

"What were they, his orders, this time?"

"Simply to help you in this investigation."

"There isn't much to investigate. You're completely loyal to your chief I take it?"

"Of course." Hitler seemed honestly puzzled. He started the car and we drove down the drive and out along a flat, white road, surmounted on both sides by great heaps of overgrown rubble.

"The murdered man had paper lungs, eh?" he said.

"Yes. Guess he must have come from Rome. He looked a bit like an Italian."

"Or a Jew, eh?"

"I don't think so. What made you think that?"

"The Russian watch, the Oriental shoes—the nose. That was a big nose he had. And they still have paper lungs in Moscow, you know."

His logic seemed a bit off-beat to me but I let it pass. We turned a corner and entered a residential section where a lot of buildings were still standing. I noticed that one of them had a bar in its cellar. "How about a drink?" I said.

"Here?" He seemed surprised, or maybe nervous.

"Why not?"

So he stopped the car, and we went down the steps into the bar. A girl was singing. She was a plumpish brunette with a small, good voice. She was singing in English, and I caught the chorus:

> *"Nobody's grievin' for Steven,*
>   *And Stevie ain't grievin' no more,*
>   *For Steve took his life in a prison cell,*
>   *And Johnny took a new whore."*

It was "Christine," the latest hit in England. We ordered beers from the bartender. He seemed to know Hitler well because he laughed and slapped him on the shoulder and didn't charge us for the beer. Hitler seemed embarrassed.

"Who was that?" I asked.

"Oh, his name is Weill. I know him slightly."

"More than slightly, it looks like."

Hitler seemed unhappy and undid his uniform jacket, tilted his cap back on his head, and tried unsuccessfully to push up the stray lock of hair. He looked a sad little man, and I felt that maybe my habit of asking questions was out of line here. I drank my beer and watched the singer. Hitler kept his back to her, but I noticed she was looking at him.

"What do you know about this Sagittarius?" I asked.

Hitler shrugged. "Very little. His name, of course, is an invention."

Weill turned up again behind the bar and asked us if we wanted more beer. We said we didn't.

"Sagittarius?" Weill spoke up brightly. "Are you talking about that crank Klosterheim?"

"He's a crank, is he?" I said. The name rang a distant bell.

"That's not fair, Kurt," Hitler said. "He's a brilliant man, a biologist—"

"Klosterheim was thrown out of his job because he was insane!"

"That is unkind, Kurt," Hitler said reprovingly. "He was investigating the potential sentience of plant life. A perfectly reasonable line of scientific enquiry."

From the corner of the room someone laughed jeeringly. It was a shaggy-haired old man sitting by himself with a glass of schnapps on the little table in front of him.

Weill pointed at him. "Ask Albert. He knows about science."

Hitler pursed his lips and looked at the floor. "He's just an embittered old mathematics teacher—he's jealous of Felipe," he said quietly, so that the old man wouldn't hear.

"Who is he?" I asked Weill.

"Albert? A really brilliant man. He has never had the recognition he deserves. Do you want to meet him?"

But the shaggy man was leaving. He waved a hand at Hitler and Weill. "Kurt, Captain Hitler—good day."

"Good day, Doctor Einstein." Hitler turned to me. "Where would you like to go now?"

"A tour of the places that sell jewelry, I guess," I said, fingering the pendant in my pocket. "I may be on the wrong track altogether, but it's the only track I can find at the moment."

We toured the jewelers. By nightfall we were nowhere nearer finding who had owned the thing. I'd just have to get the truth out of Bismarck the next day, though I knew it wouldn't be easy. He wouldn't like answering personal questions. Hitler dropped me off at the Precinct House where a cell had been converted into a bedroom for me.

I sat on the hard bed smoking and brooding. I was just about to get undressed and go to sleep when I started to think about the bar we'd been in earlier. I was sure someone there could help me. On impulse I left the cell and went out into the deserted street. It was still very hot, and the sky was full of heavy clouds. Looked like a storm was due.

I got a cab back to the bar. It was still open.

Weill wasn't serving there now. He was playing the piano-accordion for the same girl singer I'd seen earlier. He nodded to me as I came in. I leant on the bar and ordered a beer from the barman.

When the number was over, Weill unstrapped his accordion and joined me. The girl followed him.

"Adolf not with you?" he said.

"He went home. He's a good friend of yours, is he?"

"Oh, we met years ago in Mirenburg. He's a nice man, you know. He should never have become a policeman. He's too mild. I doubt he'll ever find his Grail now."

"That's the impression I got. Why did he ever join in the first place?"

Weill smiled and shook his head. He was a short, thin man, wearing heavy glasses. He had a large, sensitive mouth. "Sense of duty, perhaps. He has a great sense of duty. He is very religious, too—a devout Catholic. I think that weighs on him. You know these converts, they accept nothing, are torn by their consciences. I never yet met a happy Catholic convert."

"He seems to have a thing about Jews."

Weill frowned. "What sort of thing? I've never really noticed. Many of his friends are Jews. I am, and Klosterheim."

"Sagittarius is a friend of his?"

"Oh, more an acquaintance I should think. I've seen them together a couple of times."

It began to thunder outside. Then it started to rain.

Weill walked towards the door and pulled down the blind. Through the noise of the storm I heard another sound, a strange, metallic grinding. A crunching.

"What's that?" I called. Weill shook his head and walked back towards the bar. The place was empty now. "I'm going to have a look," I said.

I went to the door, opened it, and climbed the steps.

Marching across the ruins, illuminated by rapid flashes of gunfire, I saw a gigantic metal monster, as big as a tall building. Supported on four telescopic legs, it lumbered at right angles to the street. From its huge body and head the snouts of guns stuck out in all directions. Lightning sometimes struck it, and it made an ear-shattering bell-like clang, paused to fire upwards at the source of the lightning, and marched on.

I ran down the steps and flung open the door. Weill was tidying up the bar. I described what I'd seen.

"What is it, Weill?"

The short man shook his head. "I don't know. At a guess it is something Berlin's conquerors left behind. A land leviathan?"

"It looked as if it was made here . . ."

"Perhaps it was. After all, who conquered Berlin—?"

A woman screamed from a back room, high and brief.

Weill dropped a glass and ran towards the room. I followed.

He opened a door. The room was homely. A table covered by a thick, dark cloth, laid with salt and pepper, knives and forks, a piano near the window, a girl lying on the floor.

"Eva!" Weill gasped, kneeling beside the body.

I gave the room another once-over. Standing on a small coffee table was a plant. It looked at first rather like a cactus of unpleasantly mottled green, though the top curved so that it resembled a snake about to strike. An eyeless, noseless snake—with a mouth There was a mouth. It opened as I approached. There were teeth in the mouth—or rather thorns arranged the way teeth are. One thorn seemed to be missing near the front. I backed away from the plant and inspected the corpse. I found the thorn in her wrist. I left it there.

"She is dead," Weill said softly, standing up and looking around. "How?"

"She was bitten by that plant," I said.

"Plant . . . ? I must call the police."

"That wouldn't be wise at this stage maybe," I said as I left. I knew where I was going. Bismarck's house. And the pleasure garden of Felipe Sagittarius.

It took me time to find a cab, and I was soaked through when I did. I told the cabby to step on it.

I had the taxi stop before we got to the house, paid it off, and walked across the lawns. I didn't bother to ring the doorbell. I let myself in by the window, using my glasscutter.

I heard voices coming from upstairs. I followed the sound until I located it—Bismarck's study. I inched the door open.

Hitler was there. He had a gun pointed at Otto von Bismarck, who was still in full uniform. They both looked pale. Hitler's hand was shaking, and Bismarck was moaning slightly. Bismarck stopped moaning to say pleadingly, "I wasn't blackmailing Eva Braun, you fool—she liked me."

Hitler laughed curtly, half hysterically. "Liked you—a fat old man."

"She liked fat old men."

"She wasn't that kind of girl."

"Who told you this, anyway?"

"The investigator told me some. And Weill rang me half an hour ago to tell me some more—also that Eva had been killed. I thought Sagittarius was my friend. I was wrong. He is your hired assassin. Well, tonight I intend to do my own killing."

"Captain Hitler—I am your superior officer!"

The gun wavered as Bismarck's voice recovered some of its authority. I realized that the HiFi had been playing quietly all the time. Curiously it was Bartok's Fifth String Quartet.

Bismarck moved his hand. "You are completely mistaken. That man you hired to follow Eva here last night—he was Eva's ex-lover!"

Hitler's lip trembled.

"You knew," said Bismarck.

"I suspected it."

"You also knew the dangers of the garden, because Felipe had told you about them. The vines killed him as he sneaked towards the summer house."

The gun steadied. Bismarck looked scared.

He pointed at Hitler. "You killed him—not I!" he screamed. "You sent him to his death. You killed Djugashvili—out of jealousy. You hoped he would kill me and Eva first. You were too frightened, too weak, to confront any of us openly!"

Hitler shouted wordlessly, put both hands to the gun, and pulled the trigger several times. Some of the shots went wide, but one hit Bismarck in his Iron Cross, pierced it, and got him in the heart. He fell backwards. As he did so his uniform ripped apart and his helmet fell off. I ran into the room and took the gun from Hitler, who was crying. I checked that Bismarck was dead. I saw what had caused the uniform to rip open. He had been wearing a corset—one of the bullets must have cut the cord. It was a heavy corset and had a lot to hold in.

I felt sorry for Hitler. I helped him sit down as he sobbed. He looked small and wretched.

"What have I killed?" he stuttered. "What have I killed?"

"Did Bismarck send that plant to Eva Braun to silence her? Was I getting too close?"

Hitler nodded, snorted, and started to cry again.

I looked towards the door. A man hesitated there.

I put the gun on the mantelpiece.

It was Sagittarius.

He nodded to me.

"Hitler's just shot Bismarck," I explained.

"So it appears." He touched his thin lips.

"Bismarck had you send Eva Braun that plant, is that so?" I said.

"Yes. A beautiful cross between a common cactus, a Venus Flytrap, and a rose—the venom was curare, of course."

Hitler got up and walked from the room. We watched him leave. He was still sniffling.

"Where are you going?" I asked.

"To get some air," I heard him say as he went down the stairs.

"The repression of sexual desires," said Sagittarius, seating himself in an armchair and resting his feet comfortably on Bismarck's corpse. "It is the cause of so much trouble. If only the passions that lie beneath the surface, the desires that are locked in the mind, could be allowed to range free, what a better place the world would be."

"Maybe," I said.

"Are you going to make any arrests, Herr Begg?"

"It's my job to file a report on my investigation, not to make arrests," I said.

"Will there be any repercussions over this business?"

I laughed. "There are always repercussions," I told him.

From the garden came a peculiar barking noise.

"What's that?" I asked. "The wolfhounds?"

Sagittarius giggled. "No, no—the dog-plant, I fear."

I ran out of the room and down the stairs until I reached the kitchen. The sheet-covered corpse was still lying on the table. I was going to open the door onto the garden when I stopped and pressed my face to the window instead.

The whole garden was moving in what appeared to be an agitated dance. Foliage threshed about and, even with the door closed, the strange scent was unbearable.

I thought I saw a figure struggling with some thick-boled shrubs. I heard a growling noise, a tearing sound, a scream, and a long drawn-out groan.

Suddenly the garden was motionless.

I turned. Sagittarius stood behind me. His hands were folded on his chest. His eyes stared down at the floor.

"It seems your dog-plant got him," I said. "Herr Kloster-heim."

"He knew me—he knew the garden." He ignored my challenge.

"Suicide maybe?"

"Very likely." Sagittarius unfolded his hands and looked up at me. "I liked him, you know. He was something of a protégé. If you had not interfered none of this might have happened. He might have gone far with me to guide him. We could have found the cup."

"You'll have other protégés," I said.

"Let us hope so." His voice was cold as the stars.

The sky outside gradually began to lighten. The rain was now only a drizzle falling on the thirsty leaves of the plants.

"Are you going to stay here?" I asked him.

"Yes—I have the garden to work on. Bismarck's servants will look after me."

"I guess they will," I said.

Once again I'd gotten to keep the Cup, but I told myself this was the last time I played the game. I wanted to go home. I went back up the stairs and I walked away from that house into a cold and desolate dawn. I tried to light my last Black Cat and failed. Then I threw the damp cigarette into the rubble, turned up the collar of my coat, and began to make my way slowly across the ruins.

MICHAEL MOORCOCK

Although it had already been published in New Worlds, *I didn't have a new story to take to Milford [writing workshop] (when it was still at Damon's in Milford, Pennsylvania) in 1966, so I took "Pleasure Garden" because I was curious what people would think of it. Generally it went down pretty well. I was keen at that stage to get rid of all the exposition required in those days to "explain" an SF or fantasy story and which in my view often distorted an otherwise good piece of imaginative fiction. Also I had hit on the notion that iconographic figures actually functioned as narrative and I think, though I had done the first Jerry Cornelius novel just before, this was the first short story to try out this notion, since* New Worlds *was all about packing in as much narrative (or implied narrative) as you could per paragraph. Anyway, Gordie Dickson struggled with it a bit but was as kind as he could be while Norman Spinrad and Harlan Ellison thought it showed, as it were, a way forward. Later that year I talked to Fritz Leiber about this need some editors had for you to rationalize every part of a story which was conceived more as a surrealist or absurdist piece. He said that he and a few others who began in the thirties (Bob Bloch was another he mentioned) started off submitting to literary magazines who turned the stories down because they were too fantastic, but if you tacked some sort of explanation on to a story, you could sell it to one of the SF magazines and that's what they started doing. Even in the late '50s mainstream critics were still describing both Tolkien and Peake as writing some sort of postnuclear-disaster fiction! I still hate pigeonholing fiction and I have to say things seem to be improving a bit in that direction. A shame it's taken over forty years to get there!*

The Andre Norton Award for Best Young Adult Science Fiction or Fantasy Book is an annual honor that was first given in 2006, for works published in 2005. It honors the memory of one of the field's most prolific and beloved authors, Andre Norton, a SFWA Grand Master and author of more than one hundred novels, including the acclaimed Witch World series, many of them for young adult readers. Ms. Norton's work has influenced generations of young people, creating new fans of the fantasy and science fiction genres and setting the standard for excellence in speculative fiction writing.

Nominations are based on the same process as the SFWA Nebula Awards, except that a book begins its eligibility on the date it is published anywhere in the world in the English language, and the Andre Norton Jury may add any number of works to the preliminary ballot and up to three works to the final ballot. Any book published as a young adult science fiction / fantasy novel is eligible, including graphic novels, with no limit on word length.

Previous winners are *Valiant: A Modern Tale of Faerie* by Holly Black and *Magic or Madness* by Justine Larbalestier. The 2008 winner is *Harry Potter and the Deathly Hallows* by J. K. Rowling.

THE RISE OF YOUNG ADULT
SCIENCE FICTION AND FANTASY

GWENDA BOND

Gwenda Bond posts often about books and writing at her blog, Shaken & Stirred (gwendabond.typepad.com). She has written for *Publishers Weekly* and the *Washington Post Book World,* and is currently pursuing an MFA in Writing for Children and Young Adults at the Vermont College of Fine Arts.

Harry Potter.

Many people would say that the explosive growth in young adult science fiction and fantasy can be summed up and attributed in total to the unprecedented popularity of J. K. Rowling's series about the boy wizard. They wouldn't be entirely wrong. The truth is that Rowling's novels did push open the doors to the category, and that new YA readers entered by the millions.

It's that simple, but it's also more complex. Science fiction and fantasy—in particular, fantasy—have always appealed to teen readers. Since the genre's inception, many of its finest writers have chosen to write for children and young adults, at least on occasion. Writers like Andre Norton, Jane Yolen, Diana Wynne Jones, Robert Heinlein, and Joan Aiken are cases in point. Not to mention the fact that many seminal works like Ray Bradbury's *Fahrenheit 451* and Kurt Vonnegut's *Slaughterhouse Five* are regularly read by teens to this day. Even if the books aren't strictly speaking

YA, they definitely fit YA and children's editor Sharyn November's definition of the term as "what teens read." And, as demonstrated by November's own Firebird imprint, SF/F novels originally written for and marketed to adults by writers like Charles de Lint and Emma Bull have equal appeal when repackaged for teen audiences.

The continual moaning about the state of the SF/F field has become all too familiar—the conventional wisdom says that it's stagnant, that readers aren't connecting or buying, that the audience may be dying out. Many of the same issues plague mainstream literary fiction. Yet what rarely gets talked about in these conversations is that the YA and children's segment of publishing is indisputably thriving. The Children's Book Council's sales survey estimates that YA sales alone have increased 25 percent in recent years. Ask any children's librarian, literature expert, or advocate and they will tell you that SF/F is the most popular type of book with young readers. That demand coupled with increasing sales has created a robust, competitive scene where young readers demand strong voices and satisfying stories.

Within the SF/F field as a whole, there are recent signs that YA fiction may finally lose its status as the younger sibling who might make good someday. SFWA's creation of the Andre Norton Award for Young Adult Science Fiction and Fantasy in 2005 certainly points in the direction of increasing credibility and recognition of the quality of the work being produced for younger readers. This year's Norton Award winner was none other than Rowling, the woman who kicked open the door, for *Harry Potter and the Deathly Hallows*, the final installment in her blockbuster series. Hers may have been the most famous name among the slate of nominees, but that's hardly surprising given that four of the six remaining contenders were up for debut novels—Ysabeau Wilce, Steve Berman, Sarah Beth Durst, and Adam Rex. The remaining two nominees were Nnedi Okorafor-Mbachu, for her second novel, and veteran SF writer Elizabeth Wein, for her fourth.

Some of these names are new to the genre and some aren't, but the list is remarkable for the range of new talent it showcases. Name another literary award that gives a similar number of newcomers a place at the table (that isn't expressly designated *for* newcomers). Just as remarkable as the number of fresh faces is the freshness of the books in question. Durst's mostly lighthearted riff on classic fairy tales could never be mistaken for Wilce's coming-of-age story embroidered with wildly ornate world-building. Yes, Rowling has been a unique attractor, bringing attention and readers, but this was a segment of the field ready to expand its borders. The result has been a true golden age of YA fiction in general, and of YA science fiction and fantasy in particular.

Part of the success and freedom many authors are finding comes from YA science fiction and fantasy's dual status as part of the mainstream and a ghetto. Children's and YA publishers typically don't segment their offerings by genre, and SF/F is a highly regarded part of children's tradition. There is no automatic stigma attached by bastions of literary snobbery to works of SF/F; instead, fantastical works are considered as literary as any other type of fiction. The majority of stigma experienced by those working for younger readers comes from those younger sibling perspectives—children's literature, YA included, is still often ghettoized by those outside its ranks in adult markets, because it is for younger readers and perceived as less complex than work for adults. This coexistence enables writers of YA SF/F to enjoy, literally, the best of both worlds—being respected by one's peers, but largely free from the prying eyes of judgmental outsiders. (SF/F for young adults has escaped much of the hand-wringing over content that chick lit and other parts of the YA scene have come in for—so far.) From this unique set of conditions has come outstanding, inventive work at both short story (Kij Johnson's novelette included in this volume) and novel length (Holly Black's *Valiant*, the first Andre Norton winner).

The children's and YA field also comes with inherent gate-keepers that are vocal about bringing attention to books. Librarians and teachers champion the best books they encounter, and are able to translate that into real readers and increased sales through prestigious awards like the American Library Association's Michael L. Printz Award for Excellence in Young Adult Literature (which recognized three novels with fantastical elements in 2007, including the winner) and lists such as the Best Books for Young Adults. Likewise, these advocates draw attention to the books they see the target audience responding to. What this means is that works deserving of more attention often get it. The underlying shape of the children's and YA field fosters innovation through such recognition, and teens are buying in big time.

Debates rage about whether these new young readers of SF/F will someday translate into an increase in adult genre readers. But maybe that isn't where the focus should be. Perhaps this is a case where the older sibling can learn from the younger one, and be strengthened by the relationship. Why are readers—both teens and adults—responding so strongly to YA at the moment? That is a question it would serve us well to keep asking. My hope is that the excellent YA work being produced today continues to not only find young readers, but inspire future writers to press the larger field's boundaries further.

CLUBBING

ELLEN ASHER

Ellen Asher began reading science fiction at the statistically average age of twelve. She entered the field professionally when she became science fiction editor at New American Library, a post she held from 1970 to 1972. In February 1973 she became editor of the Science Fiction Book Club, where she remained for over three decades, retiring in June 2007 with the title Editor-in-Chief. In 2001 she received the Edward E. Smith Memorial Award for Imaginative Fiction (the Skylark) for her contribution to science fiction, and in 2007 she received the World Fantasy Award in the category Special Award: Professional. She lives in New York City.

I edited the Science Fiction Book Club for thirty-four years—a figure that surprises even me—so Ellen Datlow thought it might be interesting if I wrote something about my experience. I considered taking a look at how online stores have changed the bookselling world, but the result was pretty boring. So I added a few notes about my life as editor of the club—first as a very junior editor in the Doubleday Book Clubs scheme of things, eventually rising to the eminence of editor-in-chief (and, unlike the editors-in-chief of some of the other clubs, I actually had another editor reporting to me; corporate life is grand). And the notes metastasized.

It was, in almost every way, a dream job. In my early years, long before the German publishing giant Bertelsmann arrived in our lives, the SFBC was part of Doubleday—just one sucker on the book club arm of the Doubleday octopus. It was a specialty club and therefore more lowly in the corporate mind than the big general-interest clubs (the Literary Guild and the Doubleday Book Club, if you care) or even than a club like Mystery Guild that catered to a big, popular special interest. But—and here's the beauty part—*no one else in the division knew anything about science fiction. Or wanted to.* They simply heaved a sigh of relief that they'd found someone who knew the field and didn't actually have two heads, and they left me alone. I could buy whatever I wanted, I could feature whichever books I wanted in the catalogue—I could even set the pricing, which is something that the marketers for most of the other clubs held on to like mongooses clinging to cobras. No one ever questioned anything, or, if they did, it was timidly and apologetically.

This idyllic situation couldn't last indefinitely, of course, but I had a good long run for some fifteen years. Then two things happened: the market for SF (and therefore the potential profits) got a lot larger, and the whole book club business became bigger and more complex, especially after Bertelsmann bought Doubleday and spun the clubs off into their own separate corporation. Computers also made a difference; they made practicable a degree of both organization and oversight that wouldn't have been worth the cost in time and energy when everything was done more or less manually.

And it *was* done manually for longer than you might think— computerization came slowly to the Doubleday clubs. Back in 1986 when Bertelsmann bought us, we had a computer—a big mainframe that lived in, I think, Indianapolis. It could do a few things. But most of our records were on six-by-eight-inch cards kept—in ink—by nice ladies of a certain age. Bertelsmann was horrified— why, when their shiny new company had a shiny reasonably new computer, were we still using index cards? So they laid off the nice ladies and discontinued the file cards—and then discovered, to their even greater horror, that they had, in effect, fired the computer. It took about three years to assemble enough new data to know what we were doing. The moral is, I guess, make sure you really know what you're doing before you empty the trash.

Anyway, marketing and financial departments began to play a bigger and bigger role in the SFBC's daily life. We were blessed, though, in almost always getting excellent people—people who did their jobs well and didn't try to do mine (I'm afraid I wasn't so restrained; I never did manage to get my fingers out of the pricing sandbox, and many lively conversations were the result). In fact, I tended to be rather grateful to them, since they did the highly statistical jobs I didn't want to do and wouldn't have been very good at. In the same way, I was grateful to my bosses, who dealt with senior management with a tact I probably couldn't have mustered, at least not when I was really worked up about some piece of corporate stupidity. And since that corporate stupidity was, in fact, sometimes corporate intelligence—I hate to admit it, but I *can* be wrong—it's just as well that there were intermediaries.

And I had lots of other help: the long-suffering editors I worked with who compensated for my blind spots, the copywriters and art directors who created both the catalogues we mailed and the jackets for our exclusive editions, the production people who made sure we had actual books to put in the mail. They were uniformly wonderful, and I thank them from the bottom of my heart.

The trends of more and more oversight and more and more bureaucratic complexity have continued unto the present. It's unavoidable given the size of the business and the nature of today's commercial world. Even at the end, I could get away with doing things my way even if it wasn't how everyone else did them, simply because I'd been editing the club successfully for so very long and knew it so well. Also, when moved to wrath, I bite. My successor (a talented SF enthusiast named Rome Quezada) lacks those advantages. On the other hand, he has a degree of excitement and enthusiasm which, I have to admit, I was losing. I still loved the job, but thirty-four years (and three months and twenty-four days) is a long time, and it's probably for the best that the club has new eyes and a new mind to bring it into the future.

CAPTIVE GIRL

JENNIFER PELLAND

Jennifer Pelland lives just outside of Boston with an Andy, three cats, and an impractical amount of books. Her work has appeared in venues such as *Helix, Strange Horizons, Apex Digest,* and *Electric Velocipede,* and her first short story collection, *Unwelcome Bodies,* was brought out by Apex Books in February 2008. "Captive Girl" was also on the 2007 Gaylactic Spectrum Awards short list.

In the choreographed chaos of space, she searches for patterns that do not fit. She listens to the hiss and murmur of the interstellar winds; she peers into the visible spectrum and beyond. Whistling particles stream by, and her mind sizes them up, then discards them as harmless background radiation. Just flotsam on the solar winds. Wait, that light— No, it's just a weather satellite catching a glint of sun. Too close, anyway. She does not let anything approach the planet without scrutiny.

Motion.

She zooms in, listening hard.

"A-s-t-e-r-o-i-d," she types out. "Possible collision course."

There is a scroll across the very bottom of her vast vision. "We see it. Calculating now."

She looks away. The team is on it. This asteroid could simply be a distraction, and she does not want to be caught unawares. There will be no repeat of last time. Not on her watch.

"It's a miss," the scroll says. "Shift's over. Come on back."

And her mind contracts, sinking down, down, plummeting back to the surface of the planet, past the colony domes, into the bunkers, deep underground.

Alice gasps through her chest tube as she crashes back into her body.

Mittened hands grope at the metal mask welded to her face, and she's shocked to realize that they're hers. She sags forward onto her walker, resting the mask on the padded bar that rings her. She is too tired to call up any video, any audio, and surrenders her overextended senses to nothingness. She struggles to walk forward a few steps, but the seat/body interface chafes, and she works her mouth in a silent gasp behind the metal.

Soft hands are on her back, and she trembles.

With a faint volley of static, her earpieces switch over to internal audio. "It's all right. Just relax. You're with us again."

With her tongue controls, she types out, "Marika."

And the hands move to the back of her bare scalp, running along the edges of the mask, along super-sensitized skin. "I'm here."

Alice grips the walker tight in her mittened hands, every part of her body warm and shivery. She clenches around the seat/body interface and lets a hard breath out through her chest tube.

She feels a light kiss on her scalp, and Marika whispers, "They're watching."

"I know," Alice types back. "I don't care."

Marika pulls off Alice's mittens, takes her nail-less hands in hers, and says, "My beautiful captive girl."

Behind her mask, Alice swoons.

She hears the rude buzz of the intercom, and over it, Dr. Qureshi says, "That was a good shift, Alice."

"Thank you," she types.

"Dr. DeVeaux, I'd like to have a word with you."

"I'm busy with Alice," Marika replies, and gently kneads Alice's shoulders through her thin cotton gown. Alice's head swims, and she rocks the mask back and forth across the bar. Why won't they just leave the two of them alone?

"We need to discuss Selene's readings," Dr. Qureshi says.

"I want Marika to stay."

"I really do need her help."

Marika leans in and whispers, "I'll be back as soon as I can." She gives Alice's shoulders a squeeze, and when she lets them go, the shock of absence makes Alice draw in a pained gasp through her chest tube.

And then she is alone, a woman behind a solid metal mask, with ears calibrated for the solar winds, and eyes that can only see the stars.

Marika is kept away all night. Alice has to amuse herself by watching feeds and vids, because her only other options are music, which is too passive to keep her input-starved brain occupied for long, and conversation, which is currently impossible. Jayna is on shift right now, Selene is sleeping, and the caretakers are all busy discussing how to keep her from going even more insane.

They are a shift of three. There can be no replacements.

Alice briefly scans the news feeds, hoping for distraction, and finds that as usual, nothing has changed. The relief convoy from Earth is still on hold, the rebuilding continues to go slowly, and there is still no real information on the mysterious black ships that nearly destroyed their colony ten years ago. The talking heads just keep rehashing all their old theories—that it was aliens trying to drive humans from their first and only extra-solar colony, that United Earth sent the ships to punish the colonists for forming an independent government, that it was the wrath of some angry god, that it was a natural phenomenon that only looked like spaceships, that the colony government bombed its own domes to cover up some unspeakable crime. She's heard it all before. None of it makes any difference to her. None of it changes her job.

No, the news is no real distraction. Alice pulls up some chamber music and a slideshow of images of happy families that she has made over the years, culling pictures from news stories, from magazines, from movies. Some are real families, some fictional, but she cherishes each and every image just the same—the pig-tailed blonde laughing on her father's shoulder, the teenagers tossing a ball back and forth under the lights of the main colony dome, the little baby curled up in its mother's arms.

She touches the mask. It's worth it. For them.

And then she sneaks a peek at the tiny, pixelated picture that Marika doesn't know she has. It's the only image she's been able to find of her. She's young in the picture, in high school, posing with the rest of the track team under an undomed sky that can only be on Earth. Marika is in the back row, so all Alice can make out are broad, tanned shoulders, a mane of dark hair pulled back into a ponytail, and a brilliant smile. But it's enough. It's something.

She can never tell Marika that she has this. They're supposed to be faceless for each other. Marika insists on it.

Marika.

She shudders.

No, this isn't helping either. A movie will distract her until Marika returns.

Alice searches the mainframe for a film she hasn't seen. So few get made anymore. The economy can barely support the basic needs of its citizens, and entertainment is a luxury that is rarely indulged. But all she can find is something called *Love in a Time of Bombardment*.

No. She will not relive the attack. The attack is not entertainment. It can never be entertainment.

She tugs at her feeding tube to try to get it into a more comfortable position, and feels the thick, thumbless mittens being pulled back over her hands. "no no no no no no no," she types, but her unspoken assailant ignores her and ties the mittens to the walker's rail.

They're so afraid she'll become another Selene. This is exactly the wrong way to go about keeping her sane.

She bangs her mask hard against the walker's padded rail in protest, then thrashes her head from side to side when her assailant tries to stop her. It's no use. She is pushed back against the padded chair of her walker and strapped down. The seat/body interface tugs uncomfortably between her legs, and she opens her mouth as far as it will go behind the mask to scream out her silent fury.

Over the earpieces, she hears Dr. Qureshi say, "Alice, you need to keep calm."

She struggles to type, struggles to get her tongue to work properly. "im jst uncomfrtblee."

"Alice, you're not making any sense."

How can she make sense when she is blind and deaf and lashed to a walker against her will? How can they possibly expect her to . . .

It doesn't matter what they expect. All that matters are her actions. She takes in several deep gulps of air through her chest tube, trying to calm her trembling muscles, then types, "My feeding tube was uncomfortable. I was just adjusting it. You didn't need to tie me down."

"We need to be safe, Alice. You know that."

"I'm fine."

"And we need to keep you that way."

"I want to talk to Marika."

"Dr. DeVeaux is busy."

"I have a right to be with her."

"Alice, we've been over this. You're in no position to—"

"I'm nineteen years old. I have every right to decide who I want to be with."

"You only think you love her. She's been your caretaker for the entire length of the program. Of course you're attached to her."

Marika's touch was the first one she'd felt after waking up in the mask and the chair. She'd held Alice while she screamed voicelessly, sobbed tearlessly, panicking behind the metal. She was the one who sat patiently with Alice until the awkward tongue controls became second nature, and she was finally able to communicate with the world on the other side of the mask. Her hands were the only ones to soothe away the nightmares, to knead her ever more atrophied muscles, to massage ointment into the scar tissue around her implants and mask. They were there when Alice's body first started developing curves, when she started craving a different kind of touch. Marika is the only one that can make her feel like a woman instead of simply a captive mind dragging a useless bag of bones behind it.

Yes, of course she is attached to her.

"Dr. Qureshi, this is none of your business. I'm an adult now, and I choose to be with her."

"And I'm trying to tell you that it's grossly inappropriate for her to exploit your feelings by—"

Alice pulls up a loud music file to drown out the rest of the lecture. Marika will come back. She always does. And Alice will wait for her, lashed to her chair by her chest and wrists, as long as it takes.

When she sleeps, she dreams of Marika, of her hands roaming all over Alice's fragile body. Her skin cries out for more, and Marika grows an octopus's complement of arms, fondling Alice with an eightfold touch. Two hands reach for the feeding tube, give it a twist, and gently pull it out. Two other hands remove the breather, and still two more lift her from the walker, the seat/body interface coming loose wetly.

The multiplicity of hands lay Alice's body on a soft, downy surface, caressing her, stroking her, even in places that only the seat has touched these past ten years. Alice reaches for the mask, struggling to pull it loose, and two of Marika's hands push hers away. "Let me," her voice buzzes, and all eight hands pry at the stubborn, welded thing.

"Try harder," Alice says.

Marika yanks, and Alice's body flops helplessly. The mask will not budge.

"Hang on," Marika says, and plants one foot against Alice's chest. "This might hurt."

And braced against Alice's chest, Marika gives a great heave.

There is a horrible ripping sound, a great burst of pain—

"Wake up."

Alice gasps and lifts her head, then lets it fall back again under the great weight of the mask.

"It's all right," Marika says. "It's just a dream."

Two hands unstrap Alice from the chair, and she sags her head onto Marika's shoulder.

"You're shaking."

"It was just a dream," Alice types.

"That's my brave girl," Marika says, and her hand reaches through the slits on the back of Alice's gown and caresses the skin beneath. "They're watching."

"I don't care."

Marika lets out a small chuckle. "Neither do I."

"They keep trying to tell me this is wrong."

"Well, I *am* your caretaker."

"But—"

"So let me take care of you. They can't punish me for doing my job, now can they?"

And Alice's gown is untied and removed, and then a warm, wet cloth rubs across her naked scalp.

Alice sighs and leans into it.

The cloth moves down, rubbing large, firm circles across her back, across her withered, aching muscles. It disappears, then is back on her arms, warmer and wetter, cleaning between each finger, scrubbing at hollow armpits.

"How's the water? Is it too warm?"

She shakes her head. It's perfect. Perfect.

The cloth comes back again, caressing her breasts, the water dripping down her torso, tantalizing, and Alice's breath catches in her chest tube.

She grips the handrail tight in anticipation.

"Let's make sure everything's nice and clean."

Marika moves the cloth down to Alice's seat/body interface.

For an infinite instant, Alice's world expands far beyond the stars.

And then her body is no longer her own. It is a trembling, helpless thing, cradled in Marika's protective embrace. In the haze, she cannot make out the words being crooned into her ear speakers, just the soothing, familiar tone. But it is enough. Enough to keep her safe until her body is back under her control.

She sighs through her chest tube and nestles her mask against Marika's shoulder.

There is a soft kiss on her scalp. "You're so beautiful."

She shakes her head, suppressing a second sigh. "No, I'm not. I can't be." They have never let her see what she's become, but she can feel the bones, the scars.

Marika's voice grows impossibly softer. "Trust me. You are the most beautiful person I've ever seen."

"But my face . . . I don't even know what it looks like under here."

"I'm not interested in your face." Marika caresses the skin around the edge of the mask, and lets one hand drift down to Alice's breathing tube. "I love you this way, my captive girl."

Alice rests one hand over Marika's and just breathes.

". . . wakey wakey wakey wakey wakey wakey . . ."

Alice jerks her head up from the bar, jolted from a familiar dream just in time to keep it from turning into a nightmare. Her parents, a sunny day, a ball, the rooftop terrace. She doesn't have to relive the terrible shadow, the whistle and crash of the projectiles, the blood, the screaming, the—

No, she *doesn't* have to relive it. She rubs her mask with her hands and calls up a fractal pattern to drive the dream images away. "How long have you been typing at me?"

". . . wakey wakey wakey wakey wakey wakey . . ."

"Selene, I'm awake already."

". . . wakey wakey wakey woke?"

"Yes."

". . . wokey wokey . . ."

"That's not a word, Selene."

". . . wokey wokey donty carey . . ."

Alice grabs the padded bar of her walker and forces herself forward a few steps, the tubes tugging at her puckered skin as she pulls them along. "Is anyone paying attention to Selene?" she types.

Dr. Mishima says, "Don't worry, we are."

Alice calls up the clock and feels a sickening buzz of adrenaline. "Why isn't she on shift? There's no one on shift right now."

"She needs a break, so we're giving her one."

Alice drags herself forward, raising her heavy head, straining to face what she hopes is the control room. "Hook me up. Put me on."

"There hasn't been an attack in over ten years. A third-day without monitoring shouldn't—"

"NOW!"

"There's no need to shout," Dr. Mishima says.

". . . chair hurts spurts furts get me off off off off off off . . ."

"Shit," Dr. Mishima hisses, and then the audio connection slams shut.

"What's going on?" Alice types.

Nothing.

"Somebody talk to me. What's going on? What's wrong with Selene?"

Nothing.

"Please. Somebody talk to me. Is anyone in the control room? Anyone?" She drags herself forward until her wheels hit the wall, then turns and painstakingly walks forward until she hits the next wall. "Someone talk to me."

Nothing.

"Or you could hook me up. I could patrol. Please. Don't just leave me here. Someone say something."

She hits another wall, and leans her mask against it.

"Don't just leave me here."

"There's just the two of you now," Dr. Qureshi says.

"Grt," Jayna types.

If Alice still had eyes, she would roll them. "Use vowels," she types.

"Fck u."

"Well, that was one vowel."

"We can't do full shifts with just two of you."

"I'll work extra," Alice types, pulling up her happy family slideshow for inspiration. "Put me on for a half-day. I can do it."

"Crzy btch."

"Or have us do quarter-days on, quarter-days off, twice daily."

"No, that's unacceptable. We'll stick with third-day shifts for the two of you, and leave Selene's shift unmonitored."

"No, THAT'S unacceptable," Alice types.

"It's been over ten years—"

"—since I watched my parents die."

"Alice, I know you feel—"

"You can't know." Alice is seething behind the mask, her happy family slideshow flipping from image to image so quickly that it's nothing but a blur. "I watched my parents burn. I still hear them screaming in my dreams."

"Alice—"

"Unless you're sitting in one of these chairs, don't tell me you know how I feel."

There is a pause, then just as Alice is convinced that the connection's gone dead, Dr. Qureshi says, "For all we know, those ships aren't coming back."

"For all we know, they are."

"And what are the chances that they'll come during the third-day that we're not watching the skies?"

"About one in three."

"Thr nt cmng bck?"

"We can't say for sure."

"Gt m ot of ths chr."

"What was that?"

"Gt me out of ths chr. Gt ths fckng msk off m fce."

"Jayna, I didn't say the program was coming to an end, just that we don't think we need captive minds monitoring space all day long anymore."

"GT THS FCKNG MSK FFFFFFFF M FCE!!!!!!!"

"Jayna, I think you need to rest."

"GT THSSSSS FKKKKkkk k kk"

The typing stops.

"What did you do?" Alice types. "What happened to Jayna?"

"Just gave her something to help her sleep."

"You drugged her?" Alice tugs at her feeding tube. "Through this?"

"Why don't you start your shift now?"

"You drugged her? How could—"

And then her mind is untethered and flying through space, searching for any hint of the black ships, determined to keep any other little girls from suffering her same fate.

When she comes back, Marika is waiting for her. "We're alone," she breathes.

Alice grabs the walker tightly as she feels a trail of kisses snaking down her exposed spine.

"Marika. How—"

"They're in a meeting. About the project. None of the caretakers were invited. They say we're not objective enough." Hands reach into the gown to cup Alice's small breasts, and when fingers caress her nipples, she feels electricity all the way down to her seat/body interface.

The lips plant feather-light kisses back up to her bare scalp, and then a tongue gently caresses the scar tissue ringing the mask.

"We can't," Alice types. "We can't."

"They're not watching. They're finally not watching." The hands smooth up to the mask, cradling it, fingertips just barely touching Alice's skin, and with a jolt, she realizes that Marika is kissing the metal right over her mouth.

Alice works her mouth helplessly inside the mask, straining to feel some contact, anything, anything that would make her human again.

But she can't.

"So beautiful," Marika whispers.

Inside the mask, Alice feels her face working up into a dry cry. Her lips tremble so hard she can barely type, "I'm not."

"You have no idea—"

"Then let me see myself."

"Alice—"

"Let me see what I look like if I'm so damned beautiful."

"I can't. You know I can't."

A hand snakes down to her seat/body interface, and Alice shudders, collapsing forward onto the bar, her arms straining helplessly to push her back up. "Stop."

"But we're finally alone. We don't have to hide anymore."

"I said STOP."

The hand vanishes. All tactile evidence of Marika vanishes, and Alice calls up her tiny picture so she won't feel so crushingly alone. "I'm . . . I'm sorry," Marika stammers. "I thought . . ."

"No. Not like this," Alice types.

"What do you mean? There is no other way."

"They're ending the program, aren't they?"

Alice sits alone, with no input, just a picture and buzzing speakers, waiting for an answer.

"Please say something," she types. "Please don't leave me like this. I have a right to know."

A shaky hand rests on Alice's shoulder for an instant before pulling away again. "It sounds like it, yes. Selene's caretaker told the government about the three of you, and the President's calling for an immediate end to the whole thing."

"What do you mean, someone told the government? We work for the government. Didn't they know?"

"They didn't know the details. We didn't tell them. They never would have let us do it if they'd known that we were blinding, deafening, and crippling little orphan girls."

"You couldn't do it any other way. We were the only ones—"

"—the right age to accept the implants, I know. I helped design them. We should have found a way to make it work with adult brains. Doing this to little girls was—"

"We all volunteered."

"And Selene's gone insane and Jayna just unvolunteered."

"I want to keep working."

Marika lets out a hard breath. "I don't think they'll let you."

"But the ships—"

"Never came back. And they say they have machines that can search the sky just as well as you can now."

"The machines didn't warn us last time."

"They're better now. A lot better."

Alice gropes at her mask, fingering the indentations over where her eyes once were. "What will they do with us?"

"That's what they're discussing right now. They think . . . they think they can make you normal again."

"Normal," Alice echoes, and struggles to remember what that means. Eyes instead of empty sockets, ears not hooked up to speakers, a mouth she can talk with, breathe with, eat with, legs strong enough to hold her up. And no mask.

She reaches up to touch the metal, and for the first time in ages, she wants it gone.

"Are you positive the machines are as good as we are?"

"I think so. I mean, they don't have the flexibility of a human mind behind them, but humans will be analyzing their data, so . . ." Another exhale. "We should be safe."

"And I'll be normal again."

In a small voice, Marika says, "Yes."

Alice struggles to tie the back of her gown closed and says, "When I'm normal, then we'll finally . . ." She trails off, not actually able to type the words.

Marika wordlessly helps her tie her gown, then sits with her, holding her hand, waiting for the meeting to end.

When Alice comes to in the hospital, there are bandages where the mask once was, and when she flutters her fingers over them, she can feel their gentle touch on her face. She draws in a deep breath, and is startled to feel it going in through her nose. Her fingers explore further, and find breathing tubes piercing the bandages. Her raw skin crinkles in a smile.

A warm, male voice says, "Can you hear me?"

She nods and tries to type a response, but instead of her tongue controls, she finds teeth.

"I'm Dr. Metz," the voice says. "I'll be coordinating your recovery. I'm happy to say that the surgery was a complete success. Your new mechanical eardrums work on a similar principle to your old speakers, so they should be easy to adjust to. The eyes, on the other hand—they'll take more time. We'll switch them on in stages once the bandages are off. The program surgeons did some serious rewriting of your visual processing centers. It'll be tricky to get your brain to process normal human visual input again, but I'm confident you'll manage with sufficient training."

Alice finds more bandages on her chest and stomach where her tubes used to be. Her hands drift farther down, and find that there are still tubes in place of her old seat/body interface.

"Once you're mobile, we'll work on retraining those muscles."

She nods again, and feels an odd tug on her arm. She reaches out to find out what it is.

"An intravenous drip. It's replacing your feeding tube for now, but we'll have you eating soon enough. Your digestive system was in fine shape."

She points to her mouth.

"Ah, yes. We've implanted artificial teeth and a mechanical voice box, but it's too soon to switch it on yet. Your gums and lips still need time to heal. Don't worry. We should have you talking again in a few days and eating soon after that."

How is she supposed to communicate until then? She raises both hands and gropes at the air helplessly before balling them into fists and bringing them down on the bed.

Dr. Metz takes one hand in his and says, "Just spell out what you need on my palm."

M-A-R-I-K-A.

"Marika." He gets curiously silent for a moment, then says, "She visited you a few times, but now that you're awake . . ." He clears his throat. "Well, I'm sure she'll be back. Is there anything else you need?"

She shakes her head.

"Want me to put on some music for you? Get a nurse to sit down and talk with you?"

She shakes her head.

"All right. I'll see about getting a message to Dr. DeVeaux . . . er, Marika. If you need anything, just press the call button."

Dr. Metz takes her hand and guides it over to the bed's rail. The button is large and unmistakable. She nods in understanding, and he drops her hand. She hears footsteps, then nothing but the precious sound of her own breathing.

And until Marika comes to visit, it will be her only company.

The door opens, there are footsteps, and then a hand is in hers. "I'm here."

The voice is richer and fuller than she remembers. She has never heard it firsthand before, only filtered through speakers embedded in a chair.

This will take getting used to. But she is desperately looking forward to it.

Alice runs her hand up Marika's arm, up to her face, and cups her beloved's cheek. There is so much she wants to say that she is grateful she can't say anything at all, because the peace of the moment would just be lost in a frantic, jumbled mass of words.

"Oh, Alice." A hand strokes her bandaged face. "You won't be my captive girl much longer."

No. Soon she will be something better. Soon she will be able to see the face of the woman she loves, be able to press her body against hers, unencumbered by her walker, to speak endearments in her own voice instead of with sterile text. She will be able to kiss, to stroke, to embrace, to explore. She will finally be able to be a full partner in the relationship, to fully reciprocate with every cell in her body.

And she will be able to do so secure in the knowledge that the planet is safe, that she had faithfully done her job as long as they had needed her, and that she had done it well.

"Look at you."

Soon she would be so much prettier to look at. No matter how battered her face was, it had to be prettier than a solid metal mask.

Marika's hands glide down Alice's body and rest on her bandaged chest and stomach. "It's like you're a different person already."

She shakes her head. No, not a different person. A more complete person. Why is Marika saying these things? Doesn't she understand—

"Alice."

There is a tone in Marika's voice that Alice has never heard before. Despair.

"I don't know if . . ."

Alice grabs Marika's hands and shakes her head again and again. This cannot be happening. Not now. Not now that they're so close. All that stands between them is one flimsy layer of bandages. If Marika just waits, if she can just see the naked devotion on Alice's soon-to-be-revealed face, if—

Marika sniffs wetly and gasps, "I'm sorry," before pulling her hands away and running out of the room.

Alice shakes so hard that she can barely find the call button.

Footsteps thunder toward her, and Dr. Metz shouts, "She's seizing!"

Alice thrusts out her hand, her entire arm rigid, and when Dr. Metz touches it, she clasps it tightly and writes, "Put me back."

"What?"

"Put me back. In the chair. In the mask."

She hears other people racing into the room, and Dr. Metz says, "No, it's all right. She's fine." As the others walk back out, he says, "Alice, you've just barely begun your transformation. I understand that it's scary, but—"

"Put me back now."

"I can't do that. The program's been shut down."

"It's my body. I decide what to do with it."

"But why—"

"I want my life back."

But they don't listen to her. They call in psychiatrists to talk to her, but she refuses to answer their questions. When they take off her bandages and turn on her eyes, she refuses to open them. When they activate her vocal cords, she refuses to speak. The only things in her life that matter are the job and Marika. The job is gone. So that just leaves Marika.

And Marika doesn't want her. Not like this.

Dr. Qureshi comes by to visit several days later and says, "This just proves why it was a bad idea to get involved with her."

With her eyes still closed, Alice faces away from her.

"She only loved you because you were broken. She liked taking care of you, having power over you. You had to know that, Alice. You're not a stupid woman. You can do so much better than that now."

She feels tears welling up in her new eyes, and chokes back a gasp as she wipes them away. The skin on her face is still extremely sensitive. She's having trouble adjusting to that.

"Alice, I know you're terrified. But you have to try. Just open your eyes. Just see what you're missing. Please, Alice. Please."

"No," she murmurs, and claps a hand over her mouth, horrified at how automatically speech has come after ten years of silence.

"Well, that's a start."

"I want . . ." Her mouth is sluggish, her words slurred. "I want her back."

"Forget Dr. DeVeaux."

"But—"

"I'm here because I need you back on the project. And to do that, I need you to finish your recovery."

Alice lets her eyelids flutter open, and is hit with a cacophony of shapes and colors that she can barely make sense of. She blinks hard, but it doesn't help. "What?"

"I'm over here."

Alice turns toward the sound, and sees a brown blur surrounded by jagged black spikes. There is red somewhere on the blur, and a couple of splotches of white. Light twinkles around its outline like sunlight off a weather satellite. She squeezes her eyes closed, rubs them, then opens them again. The image is the same, only fuzzier.

"The security computers are online and working perfectly," the blur that is Dr. Qureshi says, "but we need to have people on the team who are specially trained to interpret any anomalous data. I can't think of anyone better qualified than you and Jayna."

"What about Selene?"

The blur shimmies, making Alice's head swim. "She's got a long road to recovery ahead of her. We need a team in place within the month. I've spoken to your doctors, and they feel that's a highly aggressive schedule, but they say you could meet that deadline if you really work at it."

"Will . . . will Marika be on the project?"

Another shimmy. "No. Her specialty was the brain/sensor uplink, and of course, caretaking. She had nothing to do with interpreting the data you three collected." Alice hears a small sigh. "What we did to you girls was inexcusable."

"No, we volunteered."

"I don't think little girls can really give that kind of consent."

"But the ships—"

"Almost destroyed the entire colony. I know. They killed my family, too." The white splotches vanish from the brown blur, then reappear. "Look, I know how important this project is to you. I want you back on the team. I owe you that, at the very least. No one has more experience interpreting surveillance data than you. No one."

Alice closes her eyes. It's too hard to think when she's trying to puzzle out what her eyes are sending to her brain.

The project needs her. She needs Marika. The project will not help her get Marika back, but it will help keep the colony safe.

Ten years ago, lying in another hospital bed, she was offered that same job. She sacrificed so much for it then.

This time, no sacrifice is required.

When she looks at it that way, the answer is clear.

She reopens her eyes, looks at the twinkling blur, and says, "I'm in."

From that point on, she makes good progress, adjusting about as well as the doctors expect. Her vision is jumpy and often confusing, and many of her muscles are severely atrophied, but soon she's able to use a motorized wheelchair, and go to the bathroom on her own, and use her new eye controls to filter out confusing input so she can focus on a task.

The day they finally let her go out for the first time, she heads straight for the park. There is warmth on her too-pale skin, a riot of color in all directions, the cries of children playing, and scents that threaten to overwhelm her senses after a decade of smelling only metal.

She steers her wheelchair off the path and onto the grass.

"Hey!" her nurse calls, but Alice ignores her and keeps going until she reaches a shady patch under one of the few trees that looks old enough to date from before the bombardment. She eases herself onto the ground, ignoring the protests of her feeble muscles, and lies on the cool, tickly grass, staring up into beautiful, beautiful green.

And laughs.

She hears a motorized whine, and looks up to see Jayna peering down at her. "There's a bug in your hair."

She pats the grass next to her. "Come on down. I'm sure there's plenty to go around."

Soon, they are released from the hospital and are given their own apartment, where Alice thrills over being able to do little things like prepare her own food, sleep in a bed, bathe herself, walk. And every day, she and Jayna analyze unusual data from the surveillance computers, doing their part to keep the colony safe. It is so much more than she's ever had. It should be enough.

But she is lonely.

No one touches her anymore. No one whispers endearments in her ear speakers. No one makes her tremble, makes her head heavy with desire, makes her feel flush and warm all the way down and fluttery in the middle.

No one calls her beautiful.

In fact, from the sidelong glances she gets whenever she goes out, she knows she's lucky that no one bothers to comment on her looks at all.

"Well, that was new," Jayna says as they wheel into their shared apartment. "I don't think we've made a little kid cry before."

"Maybe the chairs scared him."

Jayna shoots her a glare. "Face it, we're hideous. Freaks of science. It's a life of spinsterhood for us. At least for a while you had . . . well, whatever it was you had."

"She won't talk to me," Alice murmurs.

"You don't fit her fetish anymore."

"It wasn't a fetish."

"I'm not saying that fetishes are bad things. Hell, I'd love to find someone whose kink I fit. There's got to be someone out there into scar tissue and wheelchairs." She wrinkles her mashed nose. "Then again, maybe I should just put in for plastic surgery. Maybe they'll give me dating lessons too. 'Hi, I just learned to pee all by myself again. Wanna go out?'"

"I don't think that'll work," Alice says. She levers herself out of her wheelchair and grabs her crutches. She is determined to be walking unaided as soon as possible.

"You're probably right. I could try, though. I mean, what would it hurt?"

With a smile, Alice says, "You never know. You could get lucky."

Jayna laughs. "Yeah. I guess I need to find just the right fetishist of my own—"

Alice whirls around, nearly losing her delicate balance. "Will you stop calling her that?"

"What do you care what I call her? It's not like she stuck by you or anything."

Alice looks down at her feet. "I know. But I still miss her."

"So do something about it already."

"But she won't see me."

"She's fine with seeing you. She just doesn't want you to see her back."

Alice's head snaps up, her eyes focusing beyond the room. That's it. Why didn't she see it sooner?

"Thanks," she whispers, and clops down the hall on her crutches.

"For what?" Jayna asks.

But Alice doesn't answer. She hobbles into her room, sits down heavily at the computer, and types out a message.

"Marika. I have a proposal. I think we can make this work. Please come visit me. Bring a mask."

She gets an answer within moments. "I'll be there."

Marika arrives the next day. Alice has asked Jayna to answer the door for her and bring Alice the mask. It is a white full-faced hood, and the eyes, ears, and mouth are taped over. Sitting in her mechanized wheelchair, Alice pulls a keypad onto her lap, tugs the mask over her head, lining up the nostril holes so she can breathe, and freezes in sudden panic.

She is crippled again.

This won't work. It can't work. She can't go back to this. At least last time, it was for selfless reasons, but now—

The muffled sound of approaching footsteps snaps her mind out of its panicked spiral. Through the plastic and the tape, she hears the bedroom door close, a body sink into a chair.

She lets out a long breath. No. She has to try. Besides, she can stop it at any time. She has that power now.

Alice carefully positions her hands over the keypad and types, "Can you look at me this way?"

There is a long pause, then through the tape, she faintly hears Marika answer, "Yes . . . I . . . I think so."

The panic screams at her from the animal parts of her brain, but after ten years strapped helplessly into a chair, she's gotten good at ignoring her flight response. "Do you think you can love me this way?" she asks.

She feels a shaking hand touch the plastic over her face, then jerk away. "I don't know. It's not . . . it doesn't look like you."

"We can have a new mask built. It can look just like the old one."

"But you . . ." The hand flutters to her chest. "The tubes are gone."

"I know."

"And . . . the walker . . ."

"I can stay in the wheelchair for you."

"It's not the same. You're . . . I know you're whole under there. I know you can get out of that chair, pull off that hood. You're not my captive girl any longer."

"I know. But I'm willing to pretend. Isn't that enough?"

She hears a sigh. "I don't know."

"Well let's find out."

"Alice, I . . . I've never felt this way about anyone else. Never."

"I haven't either."

"What if it's because of the mask? What if I can't love you out of the chair? I'm terrified that we'll try and . . ."

Alice nods. "I know."

"At least if I walk away, I can't be disappointed."

"But it'll still hurt."

There's silence, and she hopes she's struck a nerve.

Finally, Marika says, "This isn't normal. You deserve normal."

Alice laughs behind the plastic. "Honestly, I wouldn't know what to do with normal. Not after . . ." Not after her senses were hijacked. Not after she spent over half her life crippled and strapped to a walker. Not after she sacrificed her childhood so that other children wouldn't have to. She lifts her fingers from the keypad and clenches them into fists.

Gentle hands clasp her fists and massage them until they relax.

"You deserve someone who loves you for what you are," Marika says. "Not for what we made you."

Alice lays her hands back on the keypad and types, "It's too late for that. I am what you made me. And now I need you to love me again. You can put me in the old mask, and the old chair. I'll be the old me for you, and the new me when you're not around."

Marika clasps the mask and rests her forehead on Alice's. "God, I missed you."

"We'll make this work," Alice types. "We have to."

Marika's doorbell rings four times. That's the signal.

Alice logs off of the work database and closes her eyes, letting a deep breath out through her nose.

This is never easy. But these are the rules.

She grabs her canes and limps over to the walker. It's a terrifying contraption—one that she'd never seen with her own eyes for all the years she spent in it. Dull metal, faded padding, straps and buckles, and that rail circling the entire thing, trapping the occupant inside.

Trapping her inside.

But she doesn't need to look at it for long.

She pulls off her clothes, straddles the chair, and carefully connects the seat/body interface until it is just right. Then she pulls on the thin cotton gown, tying only the very top tie, letting the rest hang loosely off of her still-thin frame.

And then there's the mask.

This is the hardest part.

It takes several deep breaths for her to work up the courage. But she finally closes her eyes and pulls it over her face, making sure the breathing tubes and earplugs are perfectly aligned before tightening the straps around her shaved scalp, sealing her inside the sound- and light-proof prison.

It's always heavier on her face than in her hands, and she sags forward, shuddering under the weight.

She slides her hands into the thumbless mittens that are now permanently strapped to the rail. Marika won't walk in until she uses their controls to type the all clear.

And she hesitates, just like she does every day.

No. This is love. And love requires sacrifice. Hers is just more tangible than most.

She steels herself, then types, "I'm ready."

She feels the air change as the door opens, and there are hands strapping her into the mittens, trapping her in the chair until morning.

And as always, panic grips her with that realization.

But then hands and lips roam all over her, and she's lost.

JENNIFER PELLAND

This story began at the Boskone science fiction convention. There was a painting in the art show of a woman with the top half of her head completely covered in a metal helmet. Wires trailed from it, and there was a wire-covered glove on her outstretched hand. Later, I went to a writing panel where one of the panelists asserted that you should try to write about things that fascinate you to the point of scaring you. So I started musing in my composition notebook about how terrified I was of the thought of total captivity, which led me back to the painting, which eventually turned into a tentative idea for a story about a girl strapped into a chair with all her senses (but touch) hijacked for a greater cause.

And then I realized it was a love story.

This raised all sorts of interesting questions in my head about what it must be like to look for companionship when you have some sort of disability or disfigurement. What do you do when your choices are limited by your physical condition? Is it wrong to be with someone just because they're turned on by your disability? And what if that person is your caretaker? Is it ethical for them to get into a romantic relationship with you? It was a scary story to write, and even scarier to show to other people, but I'm very pleased by the reaction it's garnered.

I'd like to thank Ellen Klages for helping me refine this story, and William Sanders for publishing it. I couldn't wish for better godparents for my Captive Girl.

UNIQUE CHICKEN GOES IN REVERSE

ANDY DUNCAN

Andy Duncan's short fiction has won two World Fantasy Awards and the Theodore Sturgeon Memorial Award; this is his sixth Nebula nomination. His books include the collection *Beluthahatchie and Other Stories,* the anthology *Crossroads: Tales of the Southern Literary Fantastic* (coedited with F. Brett Cox), and the nonfiction *Alabama Curiosities,* soon to appear in a second edition. A 1994 graduate of Clarion West, he teaches part-time in the Honors College of the University of Alabama and works full-time as a senior editor at *Overdrive* magazine, "The Voice of the American Trucker." He lives in Frostburg, Maryland, with his wife, Sydney.

Father Leggett stood on the sidewalk and looked up at the three narrow stories of gray brick that was 207 East Charlton Street. Compared to the other edifices on Lafayette Square—the Colonial Dames fountain, the Low house, the Turner mansion, the cathedral of course—this house was decidedly ordinary, a reminder that even Savannah had buildings that did only what they needed to do, and nothing more.

He looked again at the note the secretary at St. John the Baptist had left on his desk. Wreathed in cigarette smoke, Miss Ingrid fielded dozens of telephone calls in an eight-hour day, none of which were for her, and while she always managed to correctly record addresses and phone numbers on her nicotine-colored note paper, the rest of the message always emerged from her smudged No. 1 pencils as four or five words that seemed relevant at the time but had no apparent grammatical connection, so that reading a stack of Miss Ingrid's messages back to back gave one a deepening sense of mystery and alarm, like intercepted signal fragments from a trawler during a hurricane. This note read:

O Connors
Mary
Priest?
Chicken!

And then the address. Pressed for more information, Miss Ingrid had shrieked with laughter and said, "Lord, Father, that was two hours ago! Why don't you ask me an easy one sometime?" The phone rang, and she snatched it up with a wink. "It's a great day at St. John the Baptist. Ingrid speaking."

Surely, Father Leggett thought as he trotted up the front steps, I wasn't expected to *bring* a chicken?

The bell was inaudible, but the door was opened immediately by an attractive but austere woman with dark eyebrows. Father Leggett was sure his sidewalk dithering had been patiently observed.

"Hello, Father. Please come in. Thank you for coming. I'm Regina O'Connor."

She ushered him into a surprisingly large, bright living room. Hauling himself up from the settee was a rumpled little man in shirtsleeves and high-waisted pants who moved slowly and painfully, as if he were much larger.

"Welcome, Father. Edward O'Connor, Dixie Realty and Construction."

"Mr. O'Connor. Mrs. O'Connor. I'm Father Leggett, assistant at St. John for—oh, my goodness, two months now. Still haven't met half my flock, at least. Bishop keeps me hopping.

Pleased to meet you now, though." You're babbling, he told himself.

In the act of shaking hands, Mr. O'Connor lurched sideways with a wince, nearly falling. "Sorry, Father. Bit of arthritis in my knee."

"No need to apologize for the body's frailties, Mr. O'Connor. Why, we would all be apologizing all the time, like Alphonse and Gaston." He chuckled as the O'Connors, apparently not readers of the comics supplement, stared at him. "Ahem. I received a message at the church, something involving . . ." The O'Connors didn't step into the pause to help him. "Involving Mary?"

"We'd like for you to talk to her, Father," said Mrs. O'Connor. "She's in the backyard, playing. Please, follow me."

The back of the house was much shabbier than the front, and the yard was a bare dirt patch bounded on three sides by a high wooden fence of mismatched planks. More brick walls were visible through the gaps. In one corner of the yard was a large chicken coop enclosed by a smaller, more impromptu wire fence, the sort unrolled from a barrel-sized spool at the hardware store and affixed to posts with bent nails. Several dozen chickens roosted, strutted, pecked. Father Leggett's nose wrinkled automatically. He liked chickens when they were fried, baked or, with dumplings, boiled, but he always disliked chickens at their earlier, pre-kitchen stage, as creatures. He conceded them a role in God's creation purely for their utility to man. Father Leggett tended to respect things on the basis of their demonstrated intelligence, and on that universal ladder chickens tended to roost rather low. A farmer once told him that hundreds of chickens could drown during a single rainstorm because they kept gawking at the clouds with their beaks open until they filled with water like jugs. Or maybe that was geese. Father Leggett, who grew up in Baltimore, never liked geese, either.

Lying face up and spread-eagled in the dirt of the yard like a little crime victim was a grimy child in denim overalls, with bobbed hair and a pursed mouth too small even for her nutlike head, most of which was clenched in a frown that was thunderous even from twenty feet away. She gave no sign of acknowledgment as the three adults approached, Mr. O'Connor slightly dragging his right foot. Did this constitute *playing*, wondered Father Leggett, who had scarcely more experience with children than with poultry.

"Mary," said Mrs. O'Connor as her shadow fell across the girl. "This is Father Leggett, from St. John the Baptist. Father Leggett, this is Mary, our best and only. She's in first grade at St. Vincent's."

"Ah, one of Sister Consolata's charges. How old are you, Mary?"

Still lying in the dirt, Mary thrashed her arms and legs, as if making snow angels, but said nothing. Dust clouds rose.

Her father said, "Mary, don't be rude. Answer Father's question."

"I just did," said Mary, packing the utterance with at least six syllables. Her voice was surprisingly deep. She did her horizontal jumping jacks again, counting off this time. "One. Two. Three. Five."

"You skipped four," Father Leggett said.

"You would, too," Mary said. "Four was hell."

"Mary."

This one word from her mother, recited in a flat tone free of judgment, was enough to make the child scramble to her feet. "I'm sorry, Mother and Father and Father, and I beg the Lord's forgiveness." To Father Leggett's surprise, she even curtsied in no particular direction—whether to him or to the Lord, he couldn't tell.

"And well you might, young lady," Mr. O'Connor began, but Mrs. O'Connor, without even raising her voice, easily drowned him out by saying simultaneously:

"Mary, why don't you show Father Leggett your chicken?"

"Yes, Mother." She skipped over to the chicken yard, stood on tiptoe to unlatch the gate, and waded into the squawking riot of beaks and feathers. Father Leggett wondered how she could tell one chicken from all the rest. He caught himself holding his breath, his hands clenched into fists.

"Spirited child," he said.

"Yes," said Mrs. O'Connor. Her unexpected smile was dazzling.

Mary relatched the gate and trotted over with a truly extraordinary chicken beneath one arm. Its feathers stuck out in all directions, as if it had survived a hurricane. It struggled not at all, but seemed content with, or resigned to, Mary's attentions. The child's ruddy face showed renewed determination, and her mouth looked ever more like the dent a thumb leaves on a bad tomato.

"What an odd-looking specimen," said Father Leggett, silently meaning both of them.

"It's frizzled," Mary said. "That means its feathers grew in backward. It has a hard old time of it, this one."

She set the chicken down and held up a pudgy, soiled index finger.

"And what's your chicken's name, young lady?"

She flung down a handful of seed and said, "Jesus Christ."

Father Leggett sucked in a breath. Behind him, Mrs. O'Connor coughed. Father Leggett tugged at his earlobe, an old habit. "What did you say, young lady?"

"Jesus Christ," she repeated, in the same dispassionate voice in which she had said, "Mary O'Connor." Then she rushed the chicken, which skittered around the yard as Mary chased it, chanting in a singsong, "Jesus Christ Jesus Christ Jesus Christ."

Father Leggett looked at her parents. Mr. O'Connor arched his eyebrows and shrugged. Mrs. O'Connor, arms folded, nodded her head once. She looked grimly satisfied. Father Leggett turned back to see chicken and child engaged in a staring contest. The chicken stood, a-quiver; Mary, in a squat, was still.

"Now, Mary," Father Leggett said. "Why would you go and give a frizzled chicken the name of our Lord and Savior?"

"It's the best name," replied Mary, not breaking eye contact with the chicken. "Sister Consolata says the name of Jesus is to be cherished above all others."

"Well, yes, but—"

The hypnotic bond between child and chicken seemed to break, and Mary began to skip around the yard, raising dust with each stomp of her surprisingly large feet. "And he's different from all the other chickens, and the other chickens peck him but he never pecks back, and he spends a lot of his time looking up in the air, praying, and in Matthew Jesus says he's a chicken, and if I get a stomachache or an earache or a sore throat, I come out here and play with him and it gets all better just like the lame man beside the well."

Father Leggett turned in mute appeal to the child's parents. Mr. O'Connor cleared his throat.

"We haven't been able to talk her out of it, Father."

"So we thought we'd call an expert," finished Mrs. O'Connor.

I wish you had, thought Father Leggett. At his feet, the frizzled chicken slurped up an earthworm and clucked with contentment.

The first thing Father Leggett did, once he was safely back at the office, was to reach down Matthew and hunt for the chicken. He found it in the middle of Christ's lecture to the Pharisees, Chapter 23, Verse 37: "O Jerusalem, Jerusalem, thou that killest the prophets, and stonest them which are sent unto thee, how often would I have gathered thy children together, even as a hen gathereth her chickens under her wings, and ye would not!"

Mrs. O'Connor answered the phone on the first ring. "Yes," she breathed, her voice barely audible.

"It's Father Leggett, Mrs. O'Connor. Might I speak to Mary, please?"

"She's napping."

"Oh, I see. Well, I wanted to tell her that I've been reading the Scripture she told me about, and I wanted to thank her. It's really very interesting, the verse she's latched on to. Christ our Lord did indeed liken himself to a hen, yes, but he didn't mean it literally. He was only making a comparison. You see," he said, warming to his subject, to fill the silence, "it's like a little parable, like the story of the man who owned the vineyard. He meant God was *like* the owner of the vineyard, not that God had an actual business interest in the wine industry."

Mrs. O'Connor's voice, when it finally came, was flat and bored.

"No disrespect meant, Father Leggett, but Edward and I did turn to the Scriptures well upstream of our turning to you, and by now everyone in this household is intimately acquainted with Matthew 23:37, its histories, contexts and commentaries. And yet our daughter seems to worship a frizzled chicken. Have you thought of anything that could explain it?"

"Well, Mrs. O'Connor—"

"Regina."

"Regina. Could it be that this chicken is just a sort of imaginary playmate for the girl? Well, not the chicken, that's real enough, but I mean the identity she has created for it. Many children have imaginary friends, especially children with no siblings, like Mary."

"Oh, I had one of those," she said. "A little boy named Bar-Lock, who lived in my father's Royal Bar-Lock typewriter."

"There, you see. You know just what I'm talking about."

"But I never thought Bar-Lock was my lord and savior!"

"No, but 'lord and savior' is a difficult idea even for an adult to grasp, isn't it? By projecting it onto a chicken, Mary makes the idea more manageable, something she can hold and understand. She seems happy, doesn't she? Content? No nightmares about her chicken being nailed to a cross? And as she matures, in her body and in her faith, she'll grow out if it, won't need it anymore."

"Well, perhaps," she said, sounding miffed. "Thank you for calling, Father. When Mary wakes up, I'll tell her you were thinking about her, and about her imaginary Jesus."

She broke the connection, leaving Father Leggett with his mouth open. The operator's voice squawked through the earpiece.

"Next connection, please. Hello? Hello?"

That night, Father Leggett dreamed about a frizzled chicken nailed to a cross. He woke with the screech in his ears.

The never-ending crush of church business enabled Father Leggett to keep putting off a return visit to the O'Connors, as the days passed into weeks and into months, but avoiding chickens, and talk of chickens, was not so easy. He began to wince whenever he heard of them coming home to roost, or being counted before they were hatched, of politicians providing them in every pot.

The dreams continued. One night the human Jesus stood on the mount and said, "Blessed are the feedmakers," then squatted and pecked the ground. The mob squatted and pecked the ground, too. Jesus and His followers flapped their elbows and clucked.

Worst of all was the gradual realization that for every clergyman in Georgia, chicken was an occupational hazard. Most families ate chicken only on Sundays, but any day Father Leggett came to visit was de facto Sunday, so he got served chicken all the time—breasts, legs, livers and dumplings, fried, baked, boiled, in salads, soups, broths and stews, sautéed, fricasseed, marengoed, a la kinged, cacciatored, casseroled. Of all this chicken, Father Leggett ate ever smaller portions. He doubled up on mustard greens and applesauce. He lost weight.

"Doubtless you've heard the Baptist minister's blessing," the bishop told him one day:

> "I've had chicken hot, and I've had chicken cold.
> "I've had chicken young, and I've had chicken old.
> "I've had chicken tender, and I've had chicken tough.
> "And thank you, Lord, I've had chicken enough."

Since the bishop had broached the subject, in a way, Father Leggett took the opportunity to tell him about his visit with the

O'Connor child, and the strange theological musings it had inspired in him. The bishop, a keen administrator, got right to the heart of the matter.

"What do you mean, frizzled?"

Father Leggett tried as best he could to explain the concept of frizzled to the bishop, finally raking both hands through his own hair until it stood on end.

"Ah, I see. Sounds like some kind of freak. Best to wring its neck while the child's napping. She might catch the mites."

"Oh, but sir, the girl views this chicken as a manifestation of our Lord."

"Our Lord was no freak," the bishop replied. "He was martyred for our sins, not pecked to death like a runty chicken."

"They seem to have a real bond," Father Leggett said. "Where you and I might see only a walking feather duster, this child sees the face of Jesus."

"People see the face of Jesus all over," the bishop said, "in clouds and stains on the ceiling and the headlamps of Fords. Herbert Hoover and Father Divine show up in the same places, if you look hard enough. It's human nature to see order where there is none."

"She trained it to walk backward on command. That's order from chaos, surely. Like the hand of God on the face of the waters."

"You admire this child," the bishop said.

I envy her, Father Leggett thought, but what he said was, "I do. And I fear for her faith, if something were to happen to this chicken. They don't live long, you know, even if they make it past Sunday dinner. They aren't parrots or turtles, and frizzles are especially susceptible to cold weather. I looked it up."

"Best thing for her," the bishop said. "Get her over this morbid fascination. You, too. Not healthy for a man of the cloth to be combing Scripture for chickens. Got to see the broader picture, you know. Otherwise, you're no better than the snake handlers, fixated on Mark 16:17–18. 'And these signs shall follow them that believe; in my name shall they cast out devils; they shall speak with new tongues; they shall take up serpents; and if they drink any deadly thing, it shall not hurt them; they shall lay hands on the sick, and they shall recover.'"

"Perhaps this child has taken up a chicken," Father Leggett said, "as another believer would take up a snake."

"Not to worry, son," the bishop said. "Little Mary's belief will outlive this chicken, I reckon. Probably outlive you and me, too. Come in, Ingrid!"

A cloud of cigarette smoke entered the office, followed by Ingrid's head around the door. "Lunch is ready," she said.

"Oh, good. What's today's bill of fare?"

"Roast chicken."

"I'm not hungry," Father Leggett quickly said.

The bishop laughed. "To paraphrase: 'If they eat any deadly thing, it shall not hurt them.'"

"Mark 16:18 wasn't in the original gospel," Ingrid said. "The whole twelve-verse ending of the book was added later, by a scribe."

The bishop looked wounded. "An *inspired* scribe," he said.

"Wash your hands, both of you," Ingrid said, and vanished in a puff.

"She's been raiding the bookcase again," the bishop growled. "It'll only confuse her."

As he picked at his plate, Father Leggett kept trying to think of other things, but couldn't. "They shall lay hands on the sick, and they shall recover." Mary O'Connor had placed her hands upon a frizzled chicken and . . . hadn't healed it, exactly, for it was still a ridiculous, doomed creature, but had given it a sort of mission. A backward purpose, but a purpose nonetheless.

That day Father Leggett had a rare afternoon off, so he went to the movies. The cartoon was ending as he entered the auditorium, and he fumbled to a seat in the glare of the giant crowing rooster that announced the Pathe Sound News. Still out of sorts, he slumped in his seat and stared blankly at the day's doings, reduced to a shrilly narrated comic strip: a ship tossing in a gale, two football teams piling onto one another, Clarence Darrow defending a lynch mob in Hawaii, a glider soaring over the Alps—but the next title took his breath.

UNIQUE CHICKEN GOES IN REVERSE

"In Savannah, Georgia, little Mary O'Connor, age five, trains her pet chicken to walk backward!"

And there on screen, stripped of sound and color and all human shading, like Father Leggett's very thoughts made huge and public, were Mary and her frizzled chicken. As he gaped at the capering giants, he was astonished by the familiarity of the O'Connor backyard, how easily he could fill in the details past the square edges of the frame. One would think he had lived there, as a child. He thought he might weep. The audience had begun cheering so at "Savannah, Georgia," that much of the rest was inaudible, but Father Leggett was pretty sure that Jesus wasn't mentioned. The cameraman had captured only a few seconds of the chicken actually walking backward; the rest was clearly the film cranked in reverse, and the segment ended with more "backward" footage of waddling ducks, trotting horses, grazing cattle. The delighted audience howled and roared. Feeling sick, Father Leggett lurched to his feet, stumbled across his neighbors to the aisle, and fled the theater.

He went straight to the upright house on Lafayette Square, leaned on the bell until Mrs. O'Connor appeared, index finger to her lips.

"Shh! Please, Father, not so loud," she whispered, stepping onto the porch and closing the door behind. "Mr. O'Connor has to rest, afternoons."

"Beg pardon," he whispered. "I didn't realize, when I bought my ticket, that your Mary has become a film star now."

"Oh, yes," she said, with an unexpected laugh, perching herself on the banister. "She's the next Miriam Hopkins, I'm sure. It was the chicken they were here for. Edward called them. Such a bother. Do you know, they were here an hour trying to coax it to walk two steps? Stage fright, I suppose. I could have strangled the wretched thing."

"I've been remiss in not calling sooner. And how is Mary doing?"

"Oh, she's fine." Her voice was approaching its normal volume. "Do you know, from the day the cameramen visited, she seemed to lose interest in Jesus? Jesus the chicken, I mean. It's as if the camera made her feel foolish, somehow."

"May I see her?"

"She's out back, as usual." She glanced at the door, then whispered again. "Best to go around the house, I think."

She led the way down the steps and along a narrow side yard—a glorified alleyway, really, with brick walls at each elbow—to the backyard, where Mary lay in the dirt, having a fit.

"Child!" Father Leggett cried, and rushed to her.

She thrashed and kicked, her face purple, her frown savage. Father Leggett knelt beside her, seized and—with effort—held her flailing arms. Her hands were balled into fists. "Child, calm yourself. What's wrong?"

Suddenly still, she opened her eyes. "Hullo," she said. "I'm fighting."

"Fighting what?"

"My angel," she said.

He caught himself glancing around, as if Saint Michael might be behind him. "Oh, child."

"Sister Consolata says I have an invisible guardian angel that never leaves my side, not even when I'm sleeping, not even when I'm in the *potty*." This last word was whispered. "He's always watching me, and following me, and being a pain, and one day I'm going to turn around and catch him and *knock* his block off." She swung her fists again and pealed with laughter.

Mary's mother stood over them, her thin mouth set, her dark

brows lowered, looking suddenly middle-aged and beautiful. Her default expression was severity, but on her, severity looked good. How difficult it must be, Father Leggett thought, to have an only child, a precocious child, any child.

"Mary, I've got cookies in the oven."

She sat up. "Oatmeal?"

"Oatmeal."

"With raisins and grease?"

"With raisins and grease." She leaned down, cupped her hands around her mouth, and whispered, "And we won't let that old angel have a one."

Mary giggled.

"You're welcome to join us, Father. Father?"

"Of course, thank you," said Father Leggett, with an abstracted air, not turning around, as he walked slowly toward the chicken yard. The frizzled one was easy to spot; it stood in its own space, seemingly avoided by the others. It walked a few steps toward the gate as the priest approached.

Father Leggett felt the gaze of mother and child upon him as he lifted the fishhook latch and creaked open the gate. The chickens nearest him fluttered, then stilled, but their flutter was contagious. It passed to the next circle of chickens, then the next, a bit more violent each time. The outermost circle of chickens returned it to the body of the flock, and by the time the ripple of unease had reached Father Leggett, he had begun to realize why so many otherwise brave people were (to use a word he had learned only in his recent weeks of study) alektorophobes. Only the frizzled Jesus seemed calm. Father Leggett stepped inside, his Oxfords crunching corn hulls and pebbles. He had the full attention of the chickens now. Without looking, he closed the gate behind. He walked forward, and the milling chickens made a little space for him, an ever-shifting, downy clearing in which he stood, arms at his sides, holding his breath. The frizzle stepped to the edge of this clearing, clucked at him. The hot air was rich with the smells of grain, bad eggs and droppings. A crumpled washtub held brackish water. Feathers floated across his smudged reflection. He closed his eyes, slowly lifted his arms. The chickens roiled. Wings beat at his shins. He reached as far aloft as he could and prayed a wordless prayer as the chicken yard erupted around him, a smothering cloud that buffeted his face and chest and legs. He was the center of a tornado of chickens, their cackles rising and falling like speech, a message that he almost felt he understood, and with closed eyes he wept in gratitude, until Jesus pecked him in the balls.

One afternoon years later, during her final semester at the women's college in Milledgeville, Mary O'Connor sat at her desk in the *Corinthian* office, leafing through the Atlanta paper, wondering whether the new copy of the McMurray Hatchery catalog ("All Flocks Blood Tested") would be waiting in the mailbox when she got home. Then an article deep inside the paper arrested her attention.

Datelined Colorado, it was about a headless chicken named Mike. Mike had survived a Sunday-morning beheading two months previous. Each evening Mike's owners plopped pellets of feed down his stumpy neck with an eyedropper and went to bed with few illusions, and each morning Mike once again gurgled up the dawn.

She read and reread the clipping with the deepest satisfaction. It reminded her of her childhood, and in particular of the day she first learned the nature of grace.

She folded the clipping in half and in half and in half again until it was furled like Aunt Pittypat's fan and sheathed it in an envelope that she addressed to Father Leggett, care of the Cathedral of St. John the Baptist in Savannah. Teaching a *headless* chicken to walk backward: that would be *real* evangelism. On a fresh sheet of the stationery her grandmother had given her two Christmases ago, she crossed out the ornate engraved "M" at the top and wrote in an even more ornate "F," as if she were flunking herself with elegance. Beneath it she wrote:

Dear Father Leggett,
I saw this and thought of you.
Happy Easter,
Flannery (nee Mary) O'Connor

When Miss Ingrid's successor brought him the letter, Father Leggett was sitting in his office, eating a spinach salad and reading the *Vegetarian News*. He was considered a good priest though an eccentric one, and no longer was invited to so many parishioners' homes at mealtime. He glanced at the note, then at the clipping. The photo alone made him upset his glass of carrot juice. He threw clipping, note and envelope into the trash can, mopped up the spill with a napkin, fisted the damp cloth and took deep chest-expanding breaths until he felt calmer. He allowed himself a glance around the room, half-expecting the flutter of wings, the brush of the thing with feathers.

ANDY DUNCAN

For years I had known that one of my favorite fiction writers had a brief celebrity as a child when she taught a pet chicken to walk backward, a feat that was captured by newsreel cameras. After she achieved more lasting fame as an adult, she liked to joke that everything since the chicken had been downhill. (I think she was joking.) I knew I'd use this in a story one day, but the premise didn't occur to me until Michael Bishop was putting together A Cross of Centuries, *a fiction anthology about alternate Jesuses. Mike asked whether I had a Jesus story, and immediately into my head popped this author's childhood chicken, which I hadn't thought about in years, and with it came the realization that the chicken was, of course, Jesus Christ—in some sense. I therefore owe thanks to Mike for the existence of this story, though I didn't finish it in time to make his book (which was published in 2007 by Thunder's Mouth Press, and is excellent).*

I also owe thanks to Penny Crall, a seminarian who mentioned Matthew 23:37 in passing one day during our book-discussion group at the Osborne Newman Center in Frostburg, Maryland, not realizing how badly I needed a poultry-related scripture at that point; to Gwenda Bond, Gavin Grant, Kelly Link, and Christopher Rowe, whose group reaction to my title on a Glasgow bridge gave me the courage to go on; to Jonathan Strahan, for selecting this as the first story in the first volume of his Eclipse series; to my wonderful audience at Capclave 2007, who first heard the finished version; to John Kessel, who taught me that the really serious stories are the funniest, and vice versa; and to my wife, Sydney, as always my first and best reader.

And now, too much information: What happens to the priest at the climax, in the chicken yard, happened to me as a child, on my last venture into my grandmother's chicken yard in Batesburg, South Carolina. Writing that scene enabled me to relive the experience from the safe remove of thirty-five years, and as a result, I'm over it now, I think.

FOUNTAIN OF AGE

NANCY KRESS

Nancy Kress is the author of twenty-six books: three fantasy novels, twelve SF novels, three thrillers, four collections of short stories, one YA novel, and three books on writing fiction. She is perhaps best known for the Sleepless trilogy that began with *Beggars in Spain.* The novel was based on a Nebula- and Hugo-winning novella of the same name; the series then continued with *Beggars and Choosers* and *Beggars Ride.* The trilogy explores questions of genetic engineering, social structure, and what society's "haves" owe Its "have-nots." In 2008 three new Kress books appeared: a collection of short stories, *Nano Comes to Clifford Falls and Other Stories* (Golden Gryphon Press), and two novels, *Steal Across the Sky* (Tor) and *Dogs* (Tachyon).

Kress's short fiction has won four Nebulas and a Hugo, and her novel *Probability Space* won the 2003 John W. Campbell Memorial Award. Her work has been translated into twenty languages. She lives in Rochester, New York, with the world's most spoiled toy poodle.

had her in a ring. In those days, you carried around pieces of a person. Not like today.

A strand of hair, a drop of blood, a lipsticked kiss on paper—those things were *real.* You could put them in a locket or pocket case or ring, you could carry them around, you could fondle them. None of this hologram stuff. Who can treasure laser shadows? Or the nanotech "re-creations"—even worse. Fah. Did the Master of the Universe "re-create" the world after it got banged up a little? Never. He made do with the original, like a sensible person.

So I had her in a ring. And I had the ring for forty-two years before it was eaten by the modern world. Literally eaten, so tell me where is the justice in that?

And oh, she was so beautiful! Not genemod misshapen like these modern girls, with their waists so skinny and their behinds huge and those repulsive breasts. No, she was natural, a real woman, a goddess. Black hair wild as stormy water, olive skin, green eyes. I remember the exact shade of green. Not grass, not emerald, not moss. Her own shade. I remember. I—

"Grampops?"

—met her while I was on shore leave on Cyprus. The Mid-East war had just ended, one of the wars, who can keep them all straight? I met Daria in a *taverna* and we had a week together. Nobody will ever know what glory that week was. She was a nice girl, too, even if she was a . . . People do what they must to survive. Nobody knows that better than me. Daria—

"Grampops!"

—gave me a lock of hair and a kiss pressed on paper. Back then I kept them in a cheap plastolux bubble, all I could afford, but later I had the hair and tiny folded paper set into a ring. Much later, when I had money and Miriam had died and—

"Dad!"

And that's how it started up again. With my son, my grand-children. Life just never knows when enough is enough.

"Dad, the kids spoke to you. Twice."

"So this creates an obligation for me to answer?"

My son Geoffrey sighs. The boys—six and eight, what busi-ness does a fifty-five-year-old man have with such young kids, but Gloria is his second wife—have vanished into the hall. They come, they go. We sit on a Sunday afternoon in my room—a nice room, it should be for what I pay—in the Silver Star Retirement Home. Every Sunday Geoff comes, we sit, we stare at each other. Sometimes Gloria comes, sometimes the boys, sometimes not. The whole thing is a strain.

Then the kids burst back through the doorway, and this time something follows them in.

"Reuven, what the shit is *that*?"

Geoffrey says, irritated, "Don't curse in front of the children, and—"

"'Shit' is cursing? Since when?"

"—and it's 'Bobby,' not 'Reuven.'"

"It's 'zaydeh,' not 'Grampops,' and I could show you what cursing is. Get that thing away from me!"

"Isn't it *astronomical*?" Reuven says. "I just got it!"

The thing is trying to climb onto my lap. It's not like their last pet, the pink cat that could jump to the ceiling. Kangaroo genes in it, such foolishness. This one isn't even real, it's a 'bot of some kind, like those retro metal dogs the Japanese were so fascinated with seventy years ago. Only this one just sort of *suggests* a dog, with sleek silver lines that sometimes seem to disappear.

"It's got stealth coating!" Eric shouts. "You can't see it!"

I can see it, but only in flashes when the light hits the right way. The thing leaps onto my lap and I flap my arms at it and try to push it off, except that by then it's not there. Maybe.

Reuven yells, like this is an explanation, "It's got microprocessors!"

Geoff says in his stiff way, "The 'bot takes digital images of whatever is behind it and continuously transmits them in holo to the front, so that at any distance greater than—"

"*This* is what you spend my money on?"

He says stiffly, "*My* money now. Some of it, anyway."

"Not because you earned it, boychik."

Geoffrey's thin lips go thinner. He hates it when I remind him who made the money. I hate it when he forgets.

"Dad, why do you have to talk like that? All that affected folksy stuff—you never talked it when I was growing up, and it's hardly your actual background, is it? So why?"

For Geoffrey, this is a daring attack. I could tell him the reason, but he wouldn't like it, wouldn't understand. Not how this "folksy" speech started, or why, or what use it was to me. Not even how a habit can settle in after it's no use, and you cling to it because otherwise you might lose who you were, even if who you were wasn't so great. How could Geoff understand a thing like that? He's only fifty-five.

Suddenly Eric shouts, "Rex is gone!" Both boys barrel out the door of my room. I see Mrs. Petrillo inching down the hall beside her robo-walker. She shrieks as they run past her, but at least they don't knock her over.

"Go after them, Geoff, before somebody gets hurt!"

"They won't hurt anybody, and neither will Rex."

"And you know this *how*? A building full of old people, tottering around like cranes on extra stilts, and you think—"

"Calm down, Dad, Rex has built-in object avoidance and—"

"You're telling me about software? *Me*, boychik?"

Now he's really mad. I know because he goes quiet and stiff. Stiffer, if that's possible. The man is a carbon-fiber rod.

"It's not like you actually developed any software, Dad. You only stole it. It was I who took the company legitimate and furthermore—"

But that's when I notice that my ring is gone.

Daria was Persian, not Greek or Turkish or Arab. If you think that made it any easier for me to look for her, you're crazy. I went back after my last tour of duty ended and I searched, how I searched. Nobody in Cyprus knew her, had ever seen her, would admit she existed. No records: "destroyed in the war."

Our last morning we'd gone down to a rocky little beach. We'd left Nicosia the day after we met to go to this tiny coastal town that the war hadn't ruined too much. On the beach we made love with the smooth pebbles pocking our tushes, first hers and then mine. Daria cut a lock of her wild hair and pressed a kiss onto paper. Little pink wildflowers grew in the scrub grass. We both cried. I swore I'd come back.

And I did, but I couldn't find her. One more prostitute on Cyprus—who tracked such people? Eventually I had to give up. I went back to Brooklyn, put the hair and kiss—such red lipstick, today they all wear gold, they look like flaking lamps—in the plastolux. Later, I hid the bubble with my Army uniform, where Miriam couldn't find it. Poor Miriam—by her own lights, she was a good wife, a good mother. It's not her fault she wasn't Daria. Nobody was Daria.

Until now, of course, when hundreds of people are, or at least partly her. Hundreds? Probably thousands. Anybody who can afford it.

"My ring! My ring is gone!"

"Your ring?"

"My ring!" Surely even Geoffrey has noticed that I've worn a ring day and night for the last forty-two years?

He noticed. "It must have fallen off when you were flapping your arms at Rex."

This makes sense. I'm skinnier now, arms like coat hangers, and the ring is—was—loose. I feel around on my chair: nothing. Slowly I lower myself to the floor to search.

"Careful, Dad!" Geoffrey says and there's something bad in his voice. I peer up at him, and I know. I just *know*.

"It's that . . . that *dybbuk*! That 'bot!"

He says, "It vacuums up small objects. But don't worry, it keeps them in an internal depository. . . . Dad, what is that ring? Why is it so important?"

Now his voice is suspicious. Forty-two years it takes for him to become suspicious, a good show of why he could never have succeeded in my business. But I knew that when he was seven.

And why should I care now? I'm a very old man, I can do what I want.

I say, "Help me up . . . no, not like that, you want me to tear something? The ring is mine, is all. I want it back. *Now*, Geoffrey."

He sets me in my chair and leaves, shaking his head. It's a long time before he comes back. I watch Tony DiParia pass by in his powerchair. I wave at Jennifer Tamlin, who is waiting for a visit from her kids. They spare her twenty minutes every other month. I study Nurse Kate's ass, which is round and firm as a good pumpkin. When Geoffrey comes back with Eric and Reuven, I take one look at his face and I know.

"The boys found the incinerator chute," Geoffrey says, guilty and already resenting me for it, "and they thought it would be fun to empty Rex's depository in it. . . . Eric! Bobby! Tell Grampops you're sorry!"

They both mumble something. Me, I'm devastated—and then I'm not.

"It's all right," I say to the boys, waving my hand like I'm Queen Monica of England. "Don't worry about it!"

They look confused. Geoffrey looks suddenly wary. Me, I feel like my heart might split down the seam. Because I know what I'm going to do. I'm going to get another lock of hair and another kiss from Daria. Because now, of course, I know where she is. The entire world knows where she is.

"Down, Rex!" Eric shouts, but I don't see the stupid 'bot. I'm not looking. I see just the past, and the future, and all at once and for the first time in decades, they even look like there's a tie, a bright cord, between them.

The Silver Star Retirement Home is for people who have given up. You want to go on actually living, you go to a renewal center. Or to Sequene. But if you've outlived everything and everybody that matters to you and you're ready to check out, or you don't have the money for a renewal center, you go to Silver Star and wait to die.

I'm there because I figured it's time for me to go, enough is enough already, only Geoffrey left for me and I never liked him all that much. But I have lots of money. Tons of money. So much money that the second I put one foot out the door of the Home, the day after Geoffrey's visit, the feds are on me like cold on space. Just like the old days, almost it makes me nostalgic.

"Max Feder," one says, and it isn't a question. He's built with serious augments, I haven't forgotten how to tell. Like he needs them against an old man like me. "I'm Agent Joseph Alcozer and this is Agent Shawna Blair." She would have been a beauty if she didn't have that deformed genemod figure, like a wasp, and the wasp's sting in her eyes.

I breathe in the artificially sweet reconstituted air of a Brooklyn Dome summer. Genemod flowers bloom sedately in manicured beds. Well-behaved flowers, they remind me of Geoffrey. From my powerchair I say, "What can I do for you, Agent Alcozer?" while Nurse Kate, who's not the deepest carrot in the garden, looks baffled, glancing back and forth from me to the fed.

"You can explain to us the recent large deposits of money from the Feder Group into your personal account."

"And I should do this why?"

"Just to satisfy my curiosity," Alcozer says, and it's pretty much the truth. They have the right to monitor all my finances in perpetuity as a result of that unfortunate little misstep back in my forties. Six-to-ten, of which I served not quite five in Themis Federal Justice Center. Also as a result of the Economic Security Act, which kicked in even earlier, right after the Change-Over. And I have the right to tell them to go to hell.

Almost I get a taste of the old thrill, the hunt-and-evade, but not really. I'm too old, and I have something else on my mind. Besides, Alcozer doesn't really expect answers. He just wants me to know they're looking in my direction.

"Talk to my lawyer. I'm sure you know where to find him," I say and power on down to the waiting car.

It takes me to the Brooklyn Renewal Center, right out at the edge of the Brooklyn Dome, and I check into a suite. For the next month doctors will gene-jolt a few of my organs, jazz up some hormones, step up the firing of selected synapses. It won't be a super-effective job, nor last too long, I know that. I'm an old man and there's only so much they can do. But it'll be enough.

Scrupulous as a rabbi, the doctor asks if I don't want a D-treatment instead. I tell her no, I don't. Yes, I'm sure. She smiles, relieved. For D-treatment I'd go to Sequene, not here, and the renewal center would lose its very expensive fees.

Then the doctor, who looks thirty-five and might even be that, tells me I'll be out cold for the whole month, I won't even dream. She's wrong. I dream about Daria, and while I do I'm young again and her red mouth is warm against mine in a sleazy *taverna*. The stinking streets of Nicosia smell of flowers and spices and whatever that spring smell is that makes you ache from want-ing things you can't have. Then we're on the rocky little beach, our last morning together, and I want to never wake up.

But I do wake, and Geoffrey is sitting beside my bed.

"Dad, what are you doing?"

"Having renewal. What are you doing?"

"Why did you transfer three hundred fifty million from the Feder Group on the very *day* of our merger with Shanghai Winds Corporation? Don't you know how that made us look?"

"No," I say, even though I do know. I just don't care. Care-fully I raise my right arm above my head, and it goes up so fast and so easy that I laugh out loud. There's no pressure on my blad-der. I can feel the blood race in my veins.

"It made us look undercapitalized and shifty, and Shanghai Winds have postponed the entire—Why did you transfer the money? And why *now*? You ruined the whole merger!"

"You'll get lots of mergers, boychik. Now leave me alone." I sit up and swing my legs, a little too fast, over the side of the bed. I wait for my head to clear. "There's something I need to do."

"Dad . . ." he says, and now I see real fear in his eyes, and so I relent.

"It's all right, Geoffrey. Strictly legit. I'm not going back to my old ways."

"Then why do I have on my system six calls from three different federal agencies?"

"They like to stay in practice," I say, and lie down again. Maybe that'll make him go away.

"Dad . . ."

I close my eyes. Briefly I consider snoring, but that might be too much. You can overdo these things. Geoff waits five more minutes, then goes away.

Children. They tie you to the present, when sometimes all you want is the past.

After the war, after I failed to find Daria in Cyprus, I went home. For a while I just drifted. It was the Change-Over, and half the country was drifting: unemployed, rioting, getting used to living on the dole instead of working. We weren't needed. The Domes were going up, the robots suddenly everywhere and doing more and more work, only so many knowledge workers needed, blah blah blah. I did a little of this, a little of that, finally met and married Miriam, who made me pick one of the thats. So I found work monitoring security systems, because back then I had such a clean record. The Master of the Universe must love a good joke.

We lived in a rat-hole way outside the Brooklyn Dome, next door to her mother. From the beginning, Miriam and I fought a lot. She was desperate for a child, but she didn't like sex. She didn't like my friends. I didn't like her mother. She didn't like my snoring. A small and stifling life, and it just got worse and worse. I could feel something growing in me, something dangerous, until it seemed I might burst apart with it and splatter my anguished guts all over our lousy apartment. At night, I walked. I walked through increasingly dangerous neighborhoods, and sometimes I stood on the docks at three in the morning—how insane is that?—and just stared out to sea until some robo-guard ejected me.

Then, although I'd failed to find Daria, history found her instead.

A Tuesday morning, August 24—you think I could forget the date? Not a chance. Gray clouds, 92 degrees, 60 percent chance of rain, air quality poor. On my way to work I passed a media kiosk in our crummy neighborhood and there, on the outside screen for twenty seconds, was her face.

I don't remember going into the kiosk or sliding in my credit chip. I do remember, for some reason, the poison-green lettering on the choices, each listed in six languages: PORN. LIBRARY. COMMLINK. FINANCIALS. NEWS. My finger trembled as I pushed the last button, then STANDARD DELIVERY. The kiosk smelled of urine and sex.

"Today speculation swirls around ViaHealth Hospital in the Manhattan Dome. Last week Daria Cleary, wife of British billionaire-financier Peter Morton Cleary, underwent an operation to remove a brain tumor. The operation, apparently successful, was followed by sudden dizzying trading in ViaHealth stock and wild rumors, some apparently deliberately leaked, of strange properties associated with Mrs. Cleary's condition. The Cleary establishment has refused to comment, but yesterday an unprecedented meeting was held at the Manhattan branch of Cleary Enterprises, a meeting attended not only by the CEOs of several American and British transnationals but also by high government officials, including Surgeon General Mary Grace Rogers and FDA chief Jared Vanderhorn.

"Both Mr. and Mrs. Cleary have interesting histories. Peter Morton Cleary, son of legendary 'Charging Chatsworth' Cleary, is known for personal eccentricity as well as very aggressive business practices. The third Mrs. Cleary, whom he met and married in Cyprus six years ago, has long been rumored to have been either a barmaid or paid escort. The—"

Daria. A brain tumor. Married to a big-shot Brit. Now in Manhattan. And I had never known.

The operation, apparently successful . . .

I paid to watch the news clip again. And again. The words welded together and rasped, an iron drone. I simply stared at Daria's face, which looked no older than when I had first seen her leaning on her elbows in that *taverna*. Again and again.

Then I sat on the filthy curb like a drunk, a doper, a bum, and cried.

It was easier to get into Manhattan back then, with the Dome only half-finished. Not so easy to get into ViaHealth Hospital. In fact, impossible to get in legitimately, too many rich people in vulnerable states of illness. It took me six weeks to find someone to bribe. The bribe consumed half of our savings, Miriam's and mine. I got into the system as a cleaning-bot supervisor, my retinal and voice scans flimsily on file. A systemwide background check wouldn't hold, but why should anyone do a systemwide background check on a cleaning supervisor? The lowliest of the low.

Then I discovered that the person I bribed had diddled me. I was in the hospital, but I didn't have clearance for Daria's floor.

Robocams everywhere. Voice- and thumbprint-controlled elevators. I couldn't get off my floor, couldn't get anywhere near her. I'd bribed my way into the system for two days only. I had two days only off from my job.

By the end of the second day, I was desperate. I ignored the whispered directions in my earcomm—"Send an F-3 'bot to disinfect Room 678"—and hung around near the elevators. Ten minutes later a woman got on, an aging, overdressed, and over-renewed woman in a crisp white outfit and shoes with jeweled heels. She put her thumb to the security pad and said, "Surgical floor."

"Yes, ma'am," the elevator said. Just before the door closed, I dashed in.

"There is an unauthorized person on this elevator," the elevator said, somehow combining calmness with urgency. "Mrs. Holmason, please disembark immediately. Unauthorized person, remain motionless or you will be neutralized."

I remained motionless, looked at Mrs. Holmason, and said, "*Please.* I knew Daria Cleary long ago, on Cyprus, I just want to see her again for a minute, please ma'am, I don't mean anybody any harm, oh *please. . . .*"

It was on the word "harm" that her face changed. A small and cruel smile appeared at the corners of her mouth. She wasn't afraid of me; I would have bet my eyes that she'd never been afraid of anything in her life. Cushioned by money, she'd never had to be.

"There is an unauthorized person on this elevator," the elevator repeated. "Mrs. Holmason, please disembark immediately. Unauthorized person, remain motionless or you—"

"This person is my guest," Mrs. Holmason said crisply. "Code 1693, elevator. Surgical floor, please."

A pause. The universe held its breath.

"I have no front-desk entry in my system for such a guest," the elevator said. "Please return to the front desk or else complete the verbal code for—"

Mrs. Holmason said to me, still with the same small smile, "So did you know Daria when she was a prostitute on Cyprus?"

This, then, was the price for letting me ride the elevator. But it's not like reporters wouldn't now ferret out everything about Daria, anyway.

"Yes," I said. "I did, and she was."

"Elevator, Code 1693 Abigail Louise. Surgical floor." And the elevator closed its doors and rose.

"And was she any good?" Mrs. Holmason said.

I wanted to punch her in her artificial face, to club her to the ground. The pampered lousy bitter bitch. I stared at her steadily and said, "Yes. Daria was good."

"Well, she would have to be, wouldn't she?" Sweetly. The elevator opened and Mrs. Holmason walked serenely down the corridor.

There were no names on the doors, but they all stood open. I didn't have much time. The bitch's secret code might have gotten me on this floor, but it wouldn't keep me there. Peter Morton Cleary unwittingly helped me, or at least his ego did. The robo-guard outside the third doorway bore a flashy logo: CLEARY ENTERPRISES. I dashed forward and it caught me in a painful vise.

But Daria, lying on a white bed inside the room, was awake and had already seen me.

The Renewal Center keeps me for an extra week. I protest, but not too much. What good will it be if I leave early and fall down, an old man in the street? Okay, I could rent a roboguard—not a good idea to take one from the Feder Group, I don't want Geof-frey tracking me. It's not like I won't already have Agent Alcozer and the other agent, the hard-eyed beauty, whose name I can't remember. Memory isn't what it used to be. Renewal only goes so far.

It's not, after all, D-treatment.

But I don't want a roboguard, so I spend the extra week. I re-fuse Geoffrey's calls. I do the physical therapy the doctors insist on. I worry the place on my bony finger where my ring used to be. I don't look at the news. There's going to be something, at my age, that I haven't seen before? Solomon was right. Nothing new under the sun, and the sun itself not all that interesting either. At least not to somebody who hasn't left the Brooklyn Dome in ten years.

Then, on my last day in the Center, the courier finally shows up. I say, "About time. Why so long?" He doesn't answer me. This is irritating, so I say, *"Katar aves Stevan?"* Do you come from Stevan?

He scowls, hands me the package, and leaves.

This is not a good sign.

But the package is as requested. The commlink runs quantum-encrypted, military-grade software piggy-backing on satellites that have no idea they're being used. The satellites don't know, the countries owning them don't know, the federal tracking system—and the feds track *everything*, don't believe the civil-rights garbage you hear at kiosks—can't track this. I take the comm out into the garden, use it to sweep for bugs, jam two of them, and make some calls.

The next day I check myself out. I wave at the federal agent in undercover get-up as a nurse, get into the car that pulls up to the gate, and disappear.

"Max," Daria said from her hospital bed all those decades ago, in her voice a world of wonder. She snapped something in Farsi to the guard 'bot. It let me go and returned to its post by the door.

"Daria." I approached the bed slowly, my legs barely able to carry me. Half her head was shaved, the right half, while her wild black hair spilled down from the other side. There were angry red stitches on the bare scalp, dark splotches under her eyes, a med patch on her neck like a purple bruise. Her lips looked dry and cracked. I went weak—weaker—with desire.

"How . . . how you have . . ." Her English had improved in ten years, but her accent remained unchanged, and so did that adorable little catch in her low voice. To me that little catch was femininity, was Daria. No other woman ever had it. Her green eyes filled with water.

"Daria, are you all right?" The world's stupidest question—she lay in a hospital room, a tumor in her brain, looking like she'd seen a ghost. But was the ghost me, or her? I remembered Daria in so many moods, laughing and lusting and weeping and once throwing a vase at my head. But never with that trapped look, that bitterness in her green, green eyes. "Daria, I looked for you, I—"

She waved her hand, a sudden crackling gesture that brought back a second flood of memories. Nobody had ever had such expressive hands. And I knew instantly what she meant: the room was monitored. Of course it was.

I leaned close to her ear. She smelled faintly sour, of medicine and disinfectant, but the Daria smell was there, too. "I'll take you away. As soon as you're well. I'll—"

She pushed me off and stared incredulously at my face. And

for a second the universe flipped and I saw what Daria saw: a rag-
gedy unshaven *putz*, with a wedding ring on my left hand, whom
she had not seen or heard from in eight years.

I let her go and backed away.

But she reached for me, one slim hand with the sleeve of the
lace nightgown falling back from her delicate wrist, and the Daria
I remembered was back, my Daria, crying on a rocky beach the
morning my shore leave ended. "Oh, Max, stay!" she'd cried
then, and I had said, "I'll be AWOL. I can't!"

"I can't," she whispered now. "Is not possible . . . Max. . . ."
Then her eyes went wide as she gazed over my shoulder.

He looked older than his holograms, and bigger. Dressed in a
high-fashion business suit, its diagonal sash an aggressive crimson,
the clothes cut sleek because a man like this has no need to carry
his own electronics, or ID, or credit chips. Brown hair, brown
beard, but pale gray eyes, almost white. Like glaciers.

"Who is your guest, Daria?" Cleary said in that cool voice the
Brits do better than anybody else. I served under enough of them
in the war. Although not like this one; no one like this had
crossed my path before.

She was afraid of him. I felt it rather than saw it. But her voice
held steady when she said, "An old friend."

"I can imagine. I think it's time for your friend to leave."
Within an hour, I was sure, he would know everything there was
to know about me.

"Yes, Peter. After two more minutes. Alone, please."

They gazed at each other. She had always had courage, but
that look chilled me down to my cells. Only years later did I
know enough to recognize it, when the Feder Group was involved
with hostile negotiations: *I offer you this for that, but I despise you for
making me do it. Done?* The look stretched to a full minute, ninety
seconds. There seemed to be no air left in the room.

Finally he said, "Of course, darling," and stepped out into the
hall.

Done? Done!

What had Daria become since that morning on the rocky Cyprus beach?

She pulled me close. "Nine tonight by Linn's in alley Amsterdam big street. Be careful you not followed." It was breathed in my ear, so softly that erotic memories swamped me. And with them, anguish.

She was not my Daria. She had stolen *my* Daria, who might have sold her body but never her soul. My Daria was gone, taken over by this manipulating, lying bitch who belonged to Peter Morton Cleary, lived with him, *fucked* him. . . .

I hope I never know anger like that again. It isn't human, that anger.

I hit her. Not on her half-shaven scalp, and not hard. But I slapped her across her beautiful mouth and said, "Face it, Daria. You always were a whore." And I left.

May the Master of the Universe forgive me.

I have never been able to remember the hours between ViaHealth Hospital and the alley off Amsterdam Avenue. What did I do? I must have done something, a man has a physical body and that body must be in one place or another. I must have dodged and doubled back and done all those silly things they do in the holos to lose pursuers. I must have dumped my commlink; those things can be traced. Did I eat? Did I huddle somewhere behind trash cans? I remember nothing.

Memory snaps back in when I stand in the alley behind Linn's, a sleazy VR-parlor franchise. Then every detail is clear. Hazy figures passed me as they headed for the back door, customers maybe, going after fantasies pornographic or exciting or maybe just as sad as mine. A boy in one of the ridiculous caped-and-mirrored sweaters that were the newest fashion among the young. A woman in a long black coat, hands in her pockets. An old man with the bluest eyes I have ever seen. These are acid-etched in my memory. I could still draw any one of them today. The alley stank of garbage cans and urine—how did Daria even know of such a place?

And what was I expecting? That she would come to me, sick and thin from illness, wobbling toward me in the fading light? Or that Peter Cleary would arrive with goons and guns? That these were my last minutes on Earth, here in a reeking alley under the shadow of the half-finished struts that would eventually support the Manhattan Dome?

I expected all of that. I expected nothing. I was out of my mind, as I have never been before or since. Not like that, not like that.

At nine o'clock a boy brushed past me and went into the VR parlor. He kept his head down, like a teenager ashamed or embarrassed about going into Linn's, and so I only glimpsed his face. He might have been Greek, or Persian, or Turkish, or Arab. He might even have been a Jew. The package dropped into my pocket was so light that I didn't even feel it. Only his hand, light as a breeze.

It was a credit chip, tightly wrapped in a tiny bit of paper that brought to mind that other paper, with Daria's kiss. In ink that faded and disappeared even as I read it, childish block letters said LIFELONG, INC. MUST TO BUY TONIGHT!

The chip held a half million credits.

I hadn't even known that she could read and write.

The car that takes me from the Brooklyn Renewal Center is followed, of course. By the feds and maybe by Geoffrey, too, although I don't think he's that smart. But who knows? It's never good to underestimate people. Even a chicken can peck you to death.

The car disappears into the underground streets. Aboveground is for the parks and paths and tiny shops and everything else that lets Dome dwellers pretend they don't live in a desperate, angry, starving, too-hot world. I lean forward, toward the driver.

"Are you an Adams?" This is an important question.

He glances at me in his mirror; the car is not on auto. Good. Auto can be traced. But, then, Stevan knows his business.

The driver grins. "Nicklos Adams, *gajo*. Stevan's adopted grandson."

All at once I relax. Who knew, until that moment, that my renewed body was so tense? With reason: It had been ten years since I'd seen Stevan and things change, things change. But "*gajo*," the Romanes term for unclean outsiders, was said lightly, and an adopted grandson holds a position of honor among gypsies. Stevan is not doing this grudgingly. He has sent his adopted grandson. We are still *wortácha*.

Nicklos stays underground as we leave Brooklyn, but he doesn't take the Manhattan artery. Instead he pulls into a badly lit service bay. We move quickly—almost running, I have forgotten how good it feels to run—to a different level and get into a different car. This car goes into Manhattan, where we change again in another service bay. I don't question the jammers; I don't have to. Stevan and I are *wortácha,* partners in an economic enterprise. Once we each taught the other everything we both knew. Well, almost everything.

When the car emerges aboveground, we are in open country, heading toward the Catskills. We drive through the world I have only read about for ten years, since I went into the Silver Star Retirement Home. Farms guarded by e-fences or genemod dogs, irrigated with expensive water. Outside the farms, the ghost towns of the dead, the shanty towns of the barely living. Until the microclimate changes again—give it a decade, maybe—this part of the country has drought. Elsewhere, sparse fields have become lush jungles, cities unlivable heat sinks or swarming warrens of the hopeless, but not here. A lone child, starveling and unsmiling, waves at the car and I look away. It's not shame—I have not caused this misery. It's not distaste, either. I don't know what it is.

Nicklos says, "The car has stealth shields. Very new. You've never seen anything like it."

"Yes, I have," I say. Reuven's 'bot dog, a flash of nearly invisible light, my arms flailing at the stupid thing. My ring with Daria's hair, her kiss. All at once my elation at escaping Brooklyn vanishes. Such foolishness. I'm still an old man with a bare finger and an ache in his heart, doing something stupid. Most likely my last stupid act.

Nicklos watches me in the mirror. "Take heart, *gajo. So ci del o bers, del o caso.*"

I don't speak much Romanes, but I recognize the proverb. Stevan used it often. *What a year may not bring, an hour might.*

From your mouth to God's ears.

From the alley behind Linn's I went straight to a public kiosk. That was how little I knew in those days: no cover, no dummy corporation, no offshore accounts. Also no time. I deposited the five hundred thousand credits in my and Miriam's account, thereby increasing it to a 500,016. Fortunately, the deposit proved untraceable because Daria knew more than me—how? How did she learn so much so fast? And what had such knowledge cost her?

But I didn't think those compassionate thoughts then. I didn't think at all, only felt. The credits were blood money, *owed* me for the loss of the other Daria, my Daria. The Daria who had loved me and could never have married Peter Morton Cleary. I screamed at the screen in the public kiosk, I punched the keys with a savagery that should have gotten me arrested. As soon as the deposit registered, I went to a trading site, read the directions through the red haze in my demented mind, and bought a half million worth of stock in LifeLong, Inc. I didn't even realize that it was among the lowest-rated, cheapest stocks on the exchange. I wouldn't have cared. I was following Daria's instructions from some twisted idea that I was somehow crushing her by doing this, that I was polluting her world by entering it, that I was losing these bogus credits exactly as I had lost her. I was flinging the piece of her dirty world that she'd given me right back in her face. I was not sane.

Then I went and got drunk.

It was the only time in my life that I have ever been truly drunk. I don't know what happened, where I went, what I did. I woke in a doorway, my boots and credit chip with its sixteen credits stolen, someone's spittle on my shirt. If it had been winter, I would have frozen to death. It was not winter. I threw up on the sidewalk and staggered home.

Miriam screaming and crying. My head pounded and my hands shook, but I had thrown up the insanity with the vomit. I looked at this woman I did not love and I had my first clear thought in weeks: *We cannot go on like this.*

"Miriam—"

"Shut up! You shut up! Just tell me where you were, you don't come home, what am I supposed to think? You never come home, even when you're here you're not here, this is a life? You hide things from me—"

"I never—"

"No? What is that plastic bubble with your old uniform? Whose hair, whose kiss? I can't trust you, you're devious, you're cold, you—"

"You went through my Army uniform? My things?"

"I hate you! You're a no-good son-of-a-bitch, even my mother says so, *she* knew, she told me not to marry you, find a real *mensch* she said, this one's not and if you think I ever really loved you, a stinking sex maniac like you but—" She stopped.

Miriam is not stupid. She saw my face. She knew I was going to leave her, that she had just said things that made it possible for me to leave her. She continued on, without drawing new breath or changing tone, but with a sudden twisted triumph that poisoned the rest of our decades together. Poisoned us more, as if "more" were even possible—but more is always possible. I learned as much that night. More is always possible. She said—

—and everything closed in on me forever—

"—but I'm pregnant."

Technology has been good to the Rom.

They have always been coppersmiths, basket makers, autobody repairers, fortune tellers, any occupation that uses light tools and can easily be moved from place to place. And thieves, of course, but only stealing from the *gaje*. It is shame to steal from other Romani, or even to work for other Romani, because it puts one person in a lower position than another. No, it is more honorable to form *wortácha*, share-and-share-alike economic partnerships to steal from the *gaje*, who after all have enslaved and tortured and ridiculed and whipped and romanticized and debased the Rom for eight centuries. Technology makes stealing both safer and more effective.

Nicklos drives along mountain roads so steep my heart is under my tongue. He says, "Opaque the windows if you're so squeamish," and I do. It does not help. When we finally stop, I gasp with relief.

Stevan yanks open the door. "Max!"

"Stevan!" We embrace, while curious children peep at us and Stevan's wife, Rosie, waits to one side. I turn to her and bow, knowing better than to touch her. Rosie is fierce and strong, as a Romani wife should be, and nobody crosses her, not even Stevan. He is the *rom baro*, the big man, in his *kumpania*, but it is Rom women who traditionally support their men and who are responsible for their all-important ritual cleanliness. If a man becomes *marimé*, unclean, the shame lies even more on his wife than on him. Nobody with any sense offends Rosie. I have sense. I bow.

She nods her head, gracious as a queen. Like Stevan, Rosie is old now—the Rom do no genemods of any kind, which are *marimé*. Rosie has a tooth missing on the left side, her hair is gray, her cheeks sag. But those cheeks glow with color, her black eyes snap, and she moves her considerable weight with the sure quickness of a girl. She wears much gold jewelry, long full skirts, and the traditional headscarf of a married woman. The harder the new century pulls on the Rom, the more they cling to the old ways, except for new ways to steal. This is how they stay a people. Who can say they're wrong?

"Come in, come in," Stevan says.

He leads me toward their house, one of a circle of cabins

around a scuffed green. Mountain forest presses close to the houses.
The inside of the Adams house looks like every other Rom house
I have ever seen: inner walls pulled down to make a large room,
which Rosie has lavished with thick Oriental carpets, thick dark
red drapes, large overstuffed sofas. It's like entering an upholstered womb.

Children sit everywhere, giggling. From the kitchen comes the
good smell of stuffed cabbage, along with the bickering of Rosie's
daughters-in-law and unmarried granddaughters. Somewhere in
the back of the house will be tiny, unimportant bedrooms, but
here is where Rom life goes on, rich and fierce and free.

"Sit there, Max," Stevan says, pointing. The chair kept for
gaje visitors. No Rom would ever sit in it, just as no Rom will
ever eat from dishes I touch. Stevan and I are *wortácha*, but I have
never kidded myself that I am not *marimé* to him.

And what is he to me?

Necessary. Now, more than ever.

"Not here, Stevan," I say. "We must talk business."

"As you wish." He leads me back outside. The men of the
kumpania have gathered, and there are introductions in the circle
among the cabins. Wary looks among the young, but I detect no
real hostility. The older ones, of course, remember me. Stevan
and I worked together for thirty years, right up until I retired and
Geoffrey took over the Feder Group. Stevan, who is also old but
still a decade younger than me and the smartest man I have ever
met, and I made each other rich.

Richer.

Finally he leads me to a separate building, which my practiced
eye recognizes for what it is: a super-reinforced, Faraday-cage-
enclosed office. Undetectable unless emitting electronic signals,
and I would bet the farm I never wanted that those signals were
carried by underground cable until they left, heavily encrypted,
for wherever Stevan and his sons wanted them to go. Probably
through the same unaware satellites I had used to call him.

Here, too, one chair was *marimé*. Stevan points and I sit.

"I need help, Stevan. It will cost me, but will not make money for you. I tell you this honestly. I know you will not let me pay you, so I ask your help from history, as well as from our old *wortácha*. I ask as a friend."

He studies me from those dark eyes, sunken now but once those of the handsomest Rom in his nation. There are reasons that stupid novels romanticized gypsy lovers. Before he can speak, I hold up my hand. "I know I am *gajo*. Please don't insult me by reminding me of the obvious. And let me say this first—you will not like what I ask you to do. You will not approve. It involves a woman, someone I have never told you about, someone notorious. But I appeal to you anyway. As a friend. And from history."

Still Stevan studies me. Twice I've said "from history," not "from our history." Stevan knows what I mean. There has always been affinity between Rom and Jews: both outcasts, both wanderers, both blamed and flogged and hunted for sport by the *gaje*, the Gentiles. Enslaved together in Romania, driven together out of Spain, imprisoned and murdered together in Germany just one hundred fifty years ago. Stevan's great-great-great-grandfather died in Auschwitz, along with a million other of the Rom. They died with "Z," for *Zigeuner*, the Nazi word for "gypsy," branded on their arms. My great-great-grandfather was there, too, with a blue number on his arm. A hundred fifty years ago is nothing to Romani, to Jews. We neither of us forget.

Stevan does not want to do this for me, whatever it is. But although the Rom do not make family of *gaje*, they are fast and loyal friends. They do not count the cost of efforts, except in honor. Finally he says, "Tell me."

Two days after I bought the LifeLong stock, the news broke. Daria Cleary had had not only a brain tumor but another tumor on her spine, and both were like nothing the doctors had ever seen before.

I am no scientist, and back then I knew even less about genetics than I know now, which is not much. But the information was everywhere, kiosks and the Internet and street orators and the White House. Everybody talked about it. Everybody had an opinion. Daria Cleary was the next step in evolution, was the anti-Christ, was an inhuman monster, was the incarnation of a goddess, was—the only thing everybody agreed on—a lot of money on the hoof.

Both of her tumors produced proteins nobody had ever seen before, from some sort of genetic mutation. The proteins were, as close as I could understand it, capable of making something like a warehouse of spare stem cells. They renewed organs, blood, skin, everything in the adult person. Daria had looked still eighteen to me because her body *was* still eighteen. It might be eighteen forever. The fountain of youth, phoenix from the ashes, we are become as gods, blah blah blah. Her tumors might be able to be grown in a lab and transplanted into others, and then those others could also stay young forever.

Only, of course, it didn't work out that way.

But nobody knew that, then. LifeLong, the struggling biotech company that Peter Cleary secretly took over to set up commercial control of Daria's tumors, rocketed to the stratosphere. Almost you couldn't glimpse it way up there. My half-million credits became one million, three million, a hundred million. The entire global economy, already staggering from the Change-Over and the climate changes, tripped again like some crazy drunk. Then it got up again and lurched on, but changed for good.

No more changed than my life. Because of her.

Should I say the success of my new stock was ashes in my mouth? I would be lying. Who hates being rich? Should I say it was pure blessing, a gift from the Master of the Universe, something that made me happy? I would be lying.

"I don't understand," Miriam said, holding in her hands the e-key I had just handed her. "You bought a house? Under the Brooklyn Dome? How can we buy a house?"

Not "*we*," I thought. There was no more "*we*," and maybe there never had been. But she didn't need to know that. Miriam was my wife, carrying my child, and I was sick of our cruelty to each other. Enough is enough already. Besides, we would be away from her mother.

"I got a stock tip, never mind how. I bought—"

"A stock tip? Oh! When can I see the house?"

She never asked about my business again. Which was a good thing, because the money changed me. No, money doesn't change people, it only makes them more of whatever they were before. Somewhere inside me had always been this rage, this desperation, this contempt. Somewhere inside me I had always been a crook. I just hadn't known it.

I could have lived for the rest of my life on the money Daria gave me. Easy. Miriam and I could have had six children, more, another Jacob with my own personal twelve tribes. Well, maybe not—Miriam still hated sex. Also, I didn't want a dynasty. I never touched my wife again, and she never asked. I took prostitutes sometimes, when I needed to. I took business alliances with men, Italians and Jews and Russians and Turks, most of whom were well known to the feds. And this is when I took on a separate identity for these transactions, the folksy quaint Jew that later Geoffrey would hate, the colorful mumbling Shylock. I took on dubious construction contracts and, later, even more dubious Robin Hoods, those lost cyber-rats who rob from the rich and give to the pleasure-drug dealers.

But dubious to who? The Feder Group did very well. And why shouldn't I loot a world in which Daria—Daria, to whom I'd given my soul—could give me money instead of herself? Money for a soul, the old old bargain. A world rotten at the core. A world like this.

I regret none of it. Miriam was, in her own way, happy. Geoffrey had everything a child could want, except maybe respectability, and when I retired, he took the Feder Group legitimate and got that, too.

I put Daria's lock of hair and paper kiss in a bank deposit box, beyond the reach of Miriam and her new army of obsessive cleaners, human and 'bot. After she died in a car crash when Geoff was thirteen, I had the hair and paper set inside my ring. By then LifeLong had "perfected" the technique for using Daria's tumor cells for tissue renewal. The process, what came to be called D-treatment, couldn't make you younger. Nothing can reverse time.

What D-treatment could do was "freeze" you at whatever age you had the operation done. Peter Cleary, among the first to be treated after FDA approval (the fastest FDA approval in history—mine wasn't the only soul for sale) would stay fifty-four years old forever.

Supermodel Kezia Dostie would stay nineteen. Singer Mbamba would stay thirty. First came Hollywood, then society, then politicians, and then everybody with enough money, which wasn't too many people because after all you don't want hoi polloi permanently cluttering up the planet. When King James III of England was D-treated, the whole thing had arrived. Respectable as organ transplants, safe as a haircut. Unless the king was hit by a bus, Princess Monica would never succeed to the throne, but she didn't seem to care. And England would forever have its beloved king, who had somehow become a symbol of the "British renewal" brought about by Daria's shaved head.

There were complications, of course. From day one, many people hated the whole idea of D-treatment. It was unnatural, monstrous, contrary to God's will, dangerous, premature, and unpatriotic. I never understood that last, but apparently D-treatment offended the patriotism of several different countries in several different parts of the world. Objectors wrote passionate letters. Objectors organized on the Internet and, later, on the Link. Objectors subpoenaed scientists to testify on their side, and some tried to subpoena God. A few were even sure they'd succeeded. And, inevitably, some objectors didn't wait for anything formal to develop: they just attacked.

I stay with Stevan two days. He houses me in a guest cottage, well away from the Rom women, which I find immensely flattering. I am eighty-six years old, and although renewal has made me feel good again, it isn't *that* good. Sap doesn't rise in my veins. I don't need sap; I just need to see Daria again.

"Why, Max?" Stevan asks, as of course he was bound to do. "What do you want from her?"

"Another lock of hair, another kiss on paper."

"And this makes sense to you?" He leans toward me, hands on his knees, two old men sitting on a fallen log in the mountain woods. There is a snake by the log, beyond Stevan. I watch it carefully. It watches me, too. We have mutual distaste, this snake and I. If man was meant to be in naked woods, we wouldn't have invented room service, let alone orbitals. Although in fact this woods is not so naked—the entire *kumpania* and its archaically lush land are encased under an invisible and very expensive mini-Dome and are nourished by underground irrigation. This is largely due to me, as Stevan knows. I don't have to issue any reminders.

I say, "What in this world makes sense? I need another lock of hair and a paper kiss, is all. I have to have them. Is this so hard to understand?"

"It's impossible to understand."

"Then is understanding necessary?"

He doesn't answer, and I see that I need to say more. Stevan has still not noticed the snake. He is ten years younger than me, he still has much of the strength in his arms, he lives surrounded by his wife and family. What does he know from desperation?

"Stevan, it's like this: To be old, in the way I'm old, this is to live in a war zone. Zap zap zap—who falls next? You don't know, but you see them fall, the people all around you, the people you know. The bullets are going to keep coming, you know this, and the next one could just as well take you. Eventually it *will* take you. So you cherish any little thing you still care about, anything that says you're still among the living. Anything that matters to you."

I sound like a damn fool.

But Stevan lumbers to his feet and stretches, not looking at me. "Okay, Max."

"Okay? You can do it? You will?"

"I will."

We are still *wortácha*. We shake hands and my eyes fill, the easy tears of the old. Ridiculous. Stevan pretends not to notice. All at once I know that I will never see him again, that this completes anything I might be owed by the Rom. Whatever happens, they will not set a *pomona sinia*, a death-feast table, for me, the *gajo*. That is all right. You can't have everything. And anyway, the important thing is not to get, but to want.

After so long, I am grateful to want anything.

We walk out of the woods. And I am right, Stevan never notices the snake.

Nicklos drives me back to the Manhattan Dome. "*BaXt, gajo.*"

"Good-bye, Nicklos." The young—they believe that luck is what succeeds. I don't need luck, I have planning. Although this time I have planned only to a point, so maybe I will need luck after all. Yes, definitely.

"*BaXt*, Nicklos."

I climb out of the car at the Manhattan Spaceport, and a 'bot appears to take my little overnight bag and lead me inside. It seats me in a small room. Almost immediately a woman enters, dressed in the black-and-green uniform of the Federal Space Authority. She's a *shicksa* beauty, tall and blond, with violet eyes. Genemod, of course. I'm unmoved. Next to the Rom women, she looks sterile, a made thing. Next to Daria, she looks like a pale cartoon.

"Max Feder?"

"That's me."

"I'm Jennifer Kenyon, FSA. I'd like to talk to you about the trip you just booked up to Sequene."

"I bet you would."

Her face hardens, pastry dough left out too long. "We've notified Agent Alcozer of the CIB, who will be here shortly. Until then, you will wait here, please."

"I've notified my lawyer, who will holo here shortly. Until then, you will bring me a coffee, please. Something to eat would be nice, too." Rom food, although delicious, is very spicy for my old guts.

She scowls and leaves. A 'bot brings very good coffee and excellent doughnuts. Max Feder is a reprobate suddenly awakened from the safely dead, but money is still money.

Twenty minutes later Agent Alcozer shows up, no female sidekick. He, Ms. Kenyon, and I sit down, a cozy trio. Almost I'm looking forward to this. Josh holos in and stands in front of the wall screen, sighing. "Hello, Joe. Ms. Kenyon, I'm Josh Zyla, Max Feder's attorney of record. Is there a problem?"

She says, "Mr. Feder is not cleared for space travel. He has a criminal record."

"That's true," Josh agrees genially. He's even more genial than his father, who represented me for thirty years. "But if you'll check the Space Travel Security Act, Section 42, paragraph 13a, you'll see that the flight restrictions apply only to orbitals registered in countries signatory to the Land-Gonzalez Treaty and—"

"Sequene is registered in Bahrain, a sig—"

"—and which received global Expansion Act monies to subsidize some or all construction costs and—"

"Sequene received—"

"—and have not filed a full-responsibility liability acceptance form for a given prospective space-faring individual."

Ms. Kenyon is silent. Clearly she, or her system, has not checked to see if Sequene had filed a full-responsibility liability acceptance form to let me come aboard. At least, she hasn't checked in the last hour.

Alcozer frowns. "Why would Sequene file a flight acceptance for Max Feder?"

Why indeed? Full-liability acceptances were designed to allow diplomats from violent countries, who might violently object to exclusion, attend international conferences. The acceptances are risky. If said diplomat blows up the place, no government is legally responsible and no insurance company has to pay. The demolition is then considered just one of those things. Full-liability acceptances are rare, and not designed for the likes of Max Feder.

Josh shrugs. "Sequene didn't tell me how it made its decisions." This is true, since Sequene doesn't know yet that I am coming upstairs. Money isn't the only thing that can be stolen. Every alteration of every record is a kind of theft. Stevan's people are very good thieves. They have had eight centuries to practice.

Jennifer Kenyon, that blond buttress of bureaucracy, finishes examining her handheld and says, "It's true—the form is on file. I guess you can fly, Mr. Feder."

Alcozer, still frowning, says, "I don't think—"

Josh says, "Are you arresting my client, Agent Alcozer? If not, then this interview is over."

Alcozer leaves, unhappy. Josh shoots me a puzzled look before his holo vanishes. Jennifer Kenyon says stiffly, "I need to ask you some questions, Mr. Feder, preparatory to your retinal and security scans. Please be advised that you are being recorded. What is your full name and citizen ID?"

"Max Michael Feder, 03065932861."

"What is your flight number and destination this afternoon?"

"British Spaceways Flight 165, to Sequene Orbital."

"How long will you be staying?"

"Three days."

"And what is the purpose of your visit?"

Our eyes meet. I know what she sees: a very old man with the hectic and temporary glow of renewal artificially animating his sagging face, too-thin arms, weak legs. A man with how long to live—a year? Two? Maybe five, if he's lucky and his mind doesn't go first. A dinosaur with the meteor already a foot above the ground, and a criminal dinosaur at that. One who should be getting ready to check out already, preferably without causing too much fuss to everybody staying longer at the party.

I say, "I'm going to Sequene to take D-treatment so I can stay eighty-six years old."

Fifteen years after I established the Feder Group, a girl stopped me as I left the office. A strange-looking girl, dressed in a shapeless long robe of some kind with her hair hidden under an orange cap with wings. I didn't remember her name. I had hired her reluctantly—the orange was some kind of reactionary cult and who needs the trouble—but Moshe Silverstein had insisted. Moshe was my—what? If we'd been Italian, he'd have been my "consigliere." We weren't Italian. He was my number-two until, I hoped, Geoffrey became old enough. It was not a robust hope. Geoffrey, now sixteen, was a prig.

The girl said, "Mr. Feder, could I talk to you a minute?"

"Certainly. Talk."

She grimaced. Under the silly hat, the skinned-back hair, she had a pretty face. She was the accountant for show, absolutely honest, in charge only of the books for the Feder Group, which was also honest. You have to present something to the IRS. "She's brilliant," Moshe had argued. I'd argued back that for this small part of our operations we didn't need brilliant, but here the girl was. I hardly ever saw her, since I was hardly ever in the Feder Group office. My real business all took place elsewhere.

"I've found an irregularity," the girl said, and all at once I remembered her name: Gwendolyn Jameson, and the cult with the modest dress and orange hats was the Daughters of Eve. Opposed to any kind of genetic engineering at all.

"What kind of irregularity, Gwendolyn?"

"An inexplicable and big one. Please come look at this screen of—"

"Screens I don't need. What's the problem?" I was already late to meet a man about a deal.

She said, "A quarter-million credits have been moved from the Feder Group to an entity called Cypress, Ltd., that's registered in

Hong Kong. I can't trace them from there, and even though the authorization has your codes on it, and although I found your hand-written back-up order in the files, something just doesn't seem right."

I froze. I hadn't authorized any transfer, and nobody should have been able to connect Cypress, Ltd., with the Feder Group. Nobody.

"Let me see the hand-written order."

She brought it to me. It looked like my handwriting, but I had not written it. It was *inside* our paper files. And somebody had my personal codes.

"Freeze all accounts *now*. Nothing moves in, nothing moves out. You got that?"

"Yes, sir."

I called Moshe, who called his nephew Timothy, who was my real accountant. We went over everything. I paced around the secret office while Tim ran heavily encrypted software for which I'd paid half my fortune. I chewed my nails, I cursed, I pounded on the wall. Like such foolishness could help? It didn't help. Finally Tim looked up.

"Well?" My throat could barely get the syllable out.

"Two and a half million is missing. They've penetrated three accounts—Cypress, Mu-Nova, and the Aurora Group."

"Zurich?" I said. "Did they get into Zurich?"

"No."

Thank you, Master of the Universe. Also thank the Swiss. Zurich held the bulk of my credits.

"This guy's good," Tim said, and the professional admiration in his voice only made me madder.

"Find him," I said.

"I don't do that kind of—"

"I'll find him," Moshe said. "But it will cost. A lot."

"I don't care. Find him."

Two weeks later he said, "I have him. You won't believe

this—it's a goddamn *gypsy*. The name he's using is Stevan Adams."

It's not that hard to kidnap a Rom. They rely on hiding, moving, stealth, gypsy-nation loyalty, not so much on pure muscle. What with one thing and another, drought and flooding and war and famine and bio-plagues, the population of the United States is half what it was a hundred years ago. The Romani population has doubled. They take care of their own, but in their own way. Four Rom in a beat-up truck, even an armed and armored truck, were no match for what I sent against them.

Moshe flew me to an abandoned house somewhere in the Pennsylvania mountains. It was old, this house, and peculiar. How did people manage to live here, sixty years ago? Miles from everything, perched on a mountainside, no wind or solar or geo-thermal energy, facing north with huge expanses of real glass, now shattered. A vacation home, Moshe said. Some vacation—all the place had was a view, which I didn't see because we were using only the basement.

"Where is he?"

"In there."

"Alone, Moshe?"

"Just as you said. The others are in that room over there, the laundry room, drugged. He's just tied up."

"Are you sure you got the right one? Gypsies switch identities, you know. More names for the same person than a Russian novel." I'd done research on the flight in.

Moshe looked insulted. "I have the right one."

I opened the door to what might have once been a wine cellar. Dank, moldy, spiders. Moshe's men had set up a floodlight. Stevan Adams sat bound to a chair, a big man dressed in rough work clothes, with short dark hair and a luxurious mustache. His eyes glittered with intelligence, with contempt. But controlled contempt, this was no cheap cyberthug. This was a man you'd have to kill to break. I didn't kill, not even when it lost me money. There was plenty to take from the world without blood on your hands.

I said, "I'm Max Feder."

He said, "Where are my son and nephews?"

"They're safe. I hurt no one."

"Where are they?"

"In the next room. Drugged but unharmed."

"Show me."

I said to Moshe, "Take the other side of that chair and help me pull it."

Moshe looked startled—this was not how we did things. But it was how I wanted them done now. What so many people never understand is that it's not enough to make money. It's not even enough to be handed money, like Daria (whom I was still, in those years, cursing) handed to me. You have to also be able to keep money, and for that you must be a good judge of people. No—a superb judge of people. This is more than watching them closely, reading body language, seeing when they blink, blah blah blah. It's a kind of smell, a tingling high in the nose that I never ignore. Never. The mind sees what it wants to see, but the body—the body knows.

This smell is a talent, my only one really. I'm not an accountant, not a software expert (as Geoffrey never tires of telling me), not even a particularly good thief when I'm alone. Always I needed Moshe and the Robin Hoods I used, those shadowy young men so adept at stealing from the rich and so bad, without me, at not dying violently. Me, I don't need violence. I can smell.

Moshe and I grabbed the chair and dragged it out of the fruit cellar and into a crumbling laundry room. We gasped and lurched; Stevan was heavy and we were not exactly athletes. Three young men, one scarcely older than Geoffrey, lay bound on the rotted floor, angelic smiles on their sleeping faces. Whatever Moshe had given them, it looked happy.

"See, Mr. Adams? They breathe, they'll be fine."

"Bring them awake so I can see."

Moshe said, "Who do you think you—"

Again I cut him off. "Bring them awake, Moshe."

He grimaced and called, "Dena!" His daughter, our doctor, came in from outside, carrying her weapon. Her face was masked; I don't risk anybody but Moshe and me. She slapped patches on the boys and they woke up, easily and profanely. Stevan and they conversed in Romanes and even though I didn't speak the language, I could see the moment he told them it was no good trying any kind of physical assault. The youngest spat at me, a theatrical bit of foolishness I forgave at once. They were good boys. And would Geoffrey have done as much for me? I doubted this.

We dragged Stevan back into the other room and locked in the bound boys, Dena on guard. Even if they got themselves loose—which, it eventually turned out, they did—she had knock-out gases and everything else she needed.

I said, "You took two and a half million credits from accounts belonging to me."

Stevan said, "So?"

How do I convey the attitude in that one word? Not just contempt but pleasure, pride, deliberate goad. Even if I killed him, he was not going to back down. A *mensch*.

"So you also took my authorization codes. *And* you slipped into my paper files a forged back-up authorization. How did you do that, Mr. Adams?"

Again just that look.

"I'm not going to harm you, or your relatives. Never. In fact, I want to hire you. My operation can use a man like you."

"I do not work for *gaje*."

"Right. I know. *Usually* you don't work for *gaje*. You people go freelance, this is gutsy, more power to you. But together, you and me together, I can make you rich beyond anything you can imagine."

"I don't need more riches."

Astoundingly, I later found out this was true, and not just because Stevan now had my two and a half million credits. The Rom are not interested in owning very much. Not property: they prefer to rent, so as to move easily and quickly. Vehicles, yes, even planes and helicopters, but always old and beat-up, not conspicuous. Gold for their women but not jewels, and how much gold can one woman wear? Mostly they want to live together in their densely carpeted rooms, getting all they need from gossiping and fighting and loving each other while stealing from everybody else.

Stevan said, "You have nothing I want, *gajo*."

"I think I do. My holdings are big, vaster than anything you've penetrated." So far, anyway. "And I know people. I can offer you something you can't get anyplace else. Safety."

Moshe echoed blankly, "Safety?" I had not told him about this part.

"Yes," I said, addressing Stevan. "I have access to military hardware. Some, anyway. I can get smaller, movable versions of the force-fences that buttress domes. You could keep away anyone you didn't want from your communities, your children, without guns. More: I can do a lot toward keeping any of you that get caught out of jail, unless you commit murder or something."

For the first time, Stevan's expression shifted. Jail is the worst thing that can happen to a Rom. It means separation from the *kumpania*, it means associating with *gaje*, it means it's impossible to avoid *marimé*. Romani will spend any amount of money, go to any lengths to keep one of their own out of prison. Also to keep their children safe; nobody loves their kids like the Rom. And I already knew that gypsies did not commit murder. On this point, eight centuries of bad press was just plain wrong.

"And of course," I said craftily, "money—a very lot of money—can help with lawyers and such if one of your little operations does happen to go awry."

"I don't work for *gaje*."

"Give it up, Max," Moshe said, with disgust.

But I trusted my nose. I waited.

Stevan gazed at me.

Finally he said, "Have you ever heard of *wortácha*?"

Jennifer Kenyon and the FSA let me fly up to Sequene. They have no choice, really. My lawyer is prepared to make a big civil-rights stink if he has to. The current president, who has not had D-treatment, does not want a big civil-rights stink in her administration. She has enough Constitutional problems already. I used to know some of the people causing them.

Shuttle security takes everything but your soul, and that it maybe nibbles at. Every inch of me is stripped and examined by machines and 'bots and people. If I carried any passengers before—lice, tapeworm, non-human molecules—I don't have them after Security is finished with me. I can't bring my own commlink, I can't wear my own clothes, almost I can't use my own bones. Shuttles and orbitals are fragile environments, I'm told. Nobody seems to notice that I'm a pretty fragile environment, too. Finally, dressed in a coverall and flimsy disposable shoes, I'm allowed to stagger onto the shuttle and collapse into a recliner.

Then starts the real punishment.

Space is a game for the young. The flight is hard on my body despite my renewal, despite their gadgets, despite all the patches stuck on my skin like so much red, blue, green, and yellow confetti. I'm eighty-six years old, what do you want from me. Few people wait that long for D-treatment. The attendant doesn't knock me out because then he wouldn't know if anything vital ruptured. It feels like everything ruptures, but in fact I arrive in one unbroken piece. Still, it's a long time before I can walk off the shuttle.

"Mr. Feder, this way, please." A young man, strong. I refuse to lean on his arm. But I look at everything. I've never been on an orbital before, and please the Master of the Universe, I never will again. Fifty years they've been up here, some of these orbitals, but why should I go upstairs? Money and influence travel by quantum packets, not shuttles. And there's never been anything upstairs that I wanted. Until now.

The shuttle bay is disappointing, just another parking garage. My guide leads me through a door into a long corridor lined with doors. Other people walk here and there, but they're led by cute little gold-colored robots, not by a person. Well, this is no more than I expected.

My guard shows me into a small, bare, white room a lot like the one at the Manhattan Spaceport. These people all need a new interior designer.

A woman enters. "Mr. Feder, I'm Leila Cleary. How was your trip up?"

"Fine." This is Peter Cleary's daughter by one of his wives before Daria. She looks about thirty but of course would be much older. Red hair, blue eyes, at least at the moment, who knows. Eyes as hard as I've ever seen on a woman. She makes Alcozer's sidekick and Jennifer Kenyon both look like cuddly stuffed toys.

"We're so glad you chose to honor Sequene with a trip. And so surprised, especially when we discovered that Sequene had filed a full-responsibility liability acceptance form for you."

"Discovered? When, Ms. Cleary?"

"After you had taken off from Earth and before you landed here. How did that happen, Mr. Feder?"

"I have no idea, Ms. Cleary. I'm an old man, can't keep track of all these modern forms. Unfortunately my memory isn't what it was once." I make my voice quaver. She isn't fooled.

"I see. Well, now that you're here, what can we do for you?"

"I want a D-treatment. I know I don't have an appointment, but I'll stay at the hotel until you can fit me in. And, of course, I'll pay whatever premiums you ask for a rush job. Whatever."

"We don't do 'rush jobs,' Mr. Feder. Our medical procedures are meticulous and individually tailored."

"Of course, of course. Everybody knows that."

"You are not just 'everybody,' Mr. Feder. And Sequene is a private facility. We reserve the right to grant or deny treatment."

"Understood. But why would you want to deny it to me? My record? You've treated others with . . . shall we say, complicated backgrounds." I don't name names, although I could. Carmine Lucente. Raul Lopez-Reyes. Worse of all, Mikhail Balakov. But D-treatment is supposed to be a private thing.

"Mr. Feder, you are eighty-six. Are you sure you know what D-treatment can and cannot do? If you think—"

"I don't," I say harshly. Master of the Universe, nobody knows better than I what D-treatment can and cannot do. Nobody. "How about this, Ms. Cleary. I'll stay in the hotel, your best suite, and your people can confer, can run whatever tests you like. I'll wait as long as you like. Meanwhile, take all the blood you want, pretend Sequene is Transylvania, ha ha."

The joke falls flat. Her look could wither a cactus. How much does she know? I have never, in fifty-six years, found out what Daria told Peter Cleary about me. Nor if Peter ever knew that Daria had given me that first half-million credits, so long ago. My guess is no, Leila doesn't know this, but I can't be sure.

"All right, Mr. Feder. We'll do that. You stay in the hotel, and I'll confer with my staff. Meanwhile, the screen in your suite will inform you about the procedure and all necessary consent forms. You can also send them downstairs to lawyers and relatives. Have a pleasant stay in Sequene."

There is no reason to not have a pleasant stay in Sequene. Once I move—or am moved, my young unsolicited bodyguard at my side—out of the shuttle bay area, the place looks like a five-star hotel in the most tasteful British fashion. Not too new, not too glossy, none of that neo-Asian glitter. Comfort and quality over flash, although Reggie (the b-guard's name) tells me there is a casino "for your gambling pleasure." Probably the rest of it, too: the call girls, pretty boys, and recreational drugs, all discreet and clean. I don't ask, despite some professional curiosity. I am eighty-six and here just for the D-treatment, a harmless old man trying a last end run around Death. I stay in character.

My suite is beautiful, if small. On an orbital, space costs. Off-white and pale green—green is supposed to be soothing—walls, antique armoire for my clothes, which have arrived on a separate shuttle. State of the art VR, full scent- and tingly-sprays. The bed does everything but take out the trash. One wall chats me up, very courteously giving instructions for "illuminating" the window. I follow them, and gasp.

Space. The suite abuts the orbital shell, and only a clear-to-the-disappearing-point hull separates me from blackness dotted with stars. Immediately I opaque the window. Who needs to see all that room, all that cold? To me it brings no sense of wonder, only a chill. Three, maybe four atoms per square liter—who wants that? We're meant for warmth and air and the packed molecules of living flesh.

Daria is up here. Somewhere, sequestered, reclusive. She's here. And I'm not going away until I find her.

Before Stevan and I became *wortácha*, he insisted that I meet Rosie. He did not have to do this. Romani men do not need their wives' cooperation to conduct their business affairs; they are not Episcopalians. But Rosie and Stevan did things their own way. He relied on her.

And she was really something back then. In her late thirties, curly black hair, snapping dark eyes beside swinging gold earrings, voluptuous breasts in her thin white blouse. A pagan queen. Not since Daria had I seen a woman I admired so much. She hated me on sight.

"*Gajo*," she said, by way of acknowledgment. Her lips barely parted on the word.

"Mrs. Adams, thank you for having me here," I said. It came out too sarcastic. I was barely "here" at all; we stood outside the building that the *kumpania* was renting at the moment, a former dance club miles from the Philadelphia Dome. This neighborhood I never would have entered without Stevan and five of his seven brothers surrounding me. A few blocks away, something exploded. Rosie never flinched. She blocked the door to the building like a battalion defending a bridge.

"Rosie," Stevan said, somewhere between irritation and resignation.

"You make a *wortácha* with my husband?"

"Yes," Stevan said. Irritation had won. "Come in, Max."

Carefully I oozed past Rosie, entered directly into the large main room, and sat where Stevan pointed. No one else was present, but I didn't know then how significant this was. All doors from the dark, thickly curtained room stayed closed. The wall screen had been blanked, although a music cube played softly, something with a lot of bass. In one corner a very large holo of some saint raised his hands to heaven over and over, staring at me with reproachful eyes.

Stevan said, "Some coffee, Rosie."

She flounced off, returning too soon—tension had fallen like bricks the second she disappeared—with three coffees. Two in glasses rimmed with gold, one in the cheapest kind of disposable cup. I like sweetener in mine but I didn't ask for it. Nobody offered.

Stevan explained to Rosie the tentative plans that he and I had discussed. She wasn't listening. Finally she interrupted him to talk to me.

"You kidnap my husband, my son, my nephews, and now you want us to do business with you? To make a *wortácha*? With a *gajo*? Are you crazy?"

"Getting there fast," I said.

Stevan said, almost pleadingly, "He's a Jew, Rosie."

"Do I care? He's *marimé* and for you—Stevan!—for you to even—" Abruptly she switched into Romanes, which of course I didn't understand, but it no longer mattered because now *I* wasn't listening.

"—died early AM. Family mouth only said—" The soft music had given way to news; it hadn't been a music cube, after all, but one of the staccato newslinks that shot out information like rapid-fire weapons. "—no accident. Repeat, Peter Morton Cleary dead—"

"Max?"

"—and *no accident*! So—failure of D-treatment? All die? To—"

"Max!"

"—see later! Fire in Manhattan Dome—"

Then Rosie was pouring water on my head and I was sputtering and gasping. A lot of water, much more water than necessary.

Stevan said, with a certain disgust, "You fainted. What is it? Are you sick?"

"It was the news," Rosie said. "About that *marimé gaji* with the tumors. Have you had D-treatment, *gajo*?"

"No!"

She studied me. I could have been something staked out in a vivisection lab. "Then did you know this Cleary big man?"

"No." And then I said—was it despair or cunning? who knows these things—"But once, long ago, I met his wife. Briefly. Before she was . . . when we were both kids."

Stevan was not interested in this. Rosie was. She gazed at me a long time. I remembered all the old stories about gypsy fortune-tellers, seers, dark powers. Nobody had looked at me like that before and nobody has looked at me like that since, for which I am seriously grateful. Some things are not decent.

Stevan said, disgust still coloring his voice, "Max, if you're not well, maybe I—"

"No," Rosie said, and the President of the United States should have such authority in her voice. "It's all right. Set up your *wortácha*. It's all right."

She left the room, not flouncing this time, and I didn't see her again for twenty years. This was fine with both of us. She didn't need a *gajo* in her living room, and I didn't need a seer in my soul. Everybody has limits.

Peter Cleary's death set off world-wide panic. He'd had D-treatment and all his tissues were supposed to be constantly regenerating to the age at which he'd had it, which was fifty-four. He shouldn't have died unless a building fell on him. Never was an autopsy more anxiously awaited by the world. The dead Jesus didn't get such attention.

The press swarmed from the hive. Peter Cleary hadn't been the first to get D-treatment because somewhere there had to be anonymous beta-testers. Volunteers, LifeLong had said, and this turned out to be true. None of them stayed anonymous now. Prisoners on Death Row, heartbreaking children dying of diseases with no cure, a few very old and very rich people. Thirty-two people before Peter Cleary had received pieces of Daria's tumors, and all thirty-two of them were now dead.

Each one died exactly twenty years after receiving D-treatment.

Daria Cleary was still alive.

But was she? That's what a corporate spokesman said, but no one had seen her for years. She and Cleary lived in the London Dome. He went to meetings, to parties, to court. She did not. Rumors had flown for years: Daria was a prisoner, Daria had been crippled by her constantly harvested tumors, Daria had died and been replaced by a clone (never mind that no one had ever succeeded in cloning humans). Every once in a while a robo-cam snapped a picture of her—if it was really her—in her garden. She still looked eighteen. But now even these illegal images stopped.

For two weeks I stayed home and watched the newsholos. Moshe handled my business. Stevan, my new partner, didn't contact me; maybe Rosie had something to do with that. More people who had received D-treatment died: a Japanese singer, a Greek scientist working on the new orbitals, a Chinese industrialist, an American actor. King James of England, perpetually thirty-nine, made a statement that said nothing, elegantly. Doctors spoke, speculating about delayed terminator genes and foreign hosts and massively triggered cell apoptosis and who knows what else. A woman standing in a museum talked about somebody named Dorian Gray.

I waited, knowing what must happen.

The mob appeared to start spontaneously, but nobody intelligent believed that. Cleary stock, not only LifeLong but all of it, had tumbled to nearly nothing. The wild trading that followed plunged three small countries into bankruptcy, more into recession. Court claims blossomed like mushrooms after rain. The attacks on the LifeLong facility and on the Clearys had never stopped, not for twenty years, but not like this. It might have been organized by any number of groups. Certainly the professional terrorists involved were not Dome citizens—at least, not all of them.

The London Dome police would have died to a soldier to stop terrorists, but firing on several thousand of their own citizens, mostly the idealistic young—this they couldn't bring themselves to do. And maybe the cops disapproved of D-treatment, too. A lot of class resentment came in here, and who can tell from the British class system? For whatever reason, the mob got through. The Cleary force fences went down—somebody somewhere knew what they were doing—and the compound went up in flame.

Press robo-cams zoomed in for close-ups of the mess. Each time they showed a body, my stomach turned to mush. But it was never her.

"Dad," Geoffrey said beside me. I hadn't even heard him come into my bedroom.

"Not now, Geoff."

He said nothing for so long that finally I had to look at him. Sixteen, taller than I ever thought of being, a nice-looking boy but with a kind of shrinking around him. Timid, even passive. Where does such a thing come from? Miriam hadn't exactly been a shy wren and me . . . well.

"Dad, have you had D-treatment? Are you going to die?"

I could see what it cost him. Even I, the worst father in the world, could see that. So I tore my eyes away from the news and said, "No. I haven't had D-treatment. I give you my word."

His expression didn't change but I felt the shift inside him. I could smell it, with that tingling high in the nose that I never ignore. I smelled it with horror but not, I realized, much surprise. Nor even with enough horror.

Geoff was disappointed.

"Don't worry, son," I said wryly, "you'll take over all this soon enough. Just not this week."

"I don't—"

"At least be honest, kid. At least that." And may the Master of the Universe forgive me for my tone. The cat-o'-nine-tails.

Geoff felt it. He hardened—maybe there was more in him than I thought. "All right, I will be honest. Are you what they say you are at school? Are you a crook?"

"Yes. Are you a *mensch*?"

"A what?"

"Never mind. Just drink it down. I'm a crook and you're the son of a crook who eats and lives because of what I do. Now what are you going to do about it?"

He looked at me. Not levelly—he was not one of Stevan's sons, he would never be that—but at least he didn't flinch. His voice wobbled, but it spoke. "What I'm going to do about it is shut down all your businesses. Or make them honest. As soon as they're mine." He walked out of the room.

It was the proudest of him I had ever been. A fool but, in his own deluded way, himself. You have to give credit for that.

I went back to searching the news for Daria.

She appeared briefly the next day. Immediately the world doubted it was her: a holo, a pre-recording, blah blah blah. But I knew. She said only that she was alive and in hiding. That scientists now told her that only she could host the D-treatment tumors without eventually dying. That she deeply regretted the unintentional deaths. That the Cleary estate would compensate all D-treatment victims. A stiff little speech, written by lawyers. Only the tears, unshed but there, were her own.

I stared at her beautiful young face, listened to the catch in her low voice, and I didn't know what I felt. I felt everything. Anger, longing, contempt, misery, revenge, protection. Nobody can stand such feelings too long. I contacted Moshe and then Stevan, and I went back to work.

My first evening at Sequene I spend in bed. Nothing hurts, not with a pain patch on my neck, but I'm weaker than I expect. This is not the fault of Sequene. The gravity here, the wall screen cheerily informs me, is 95 percent of Earth's, "just slightly enough lower to put a spring in your step!" The air is healthier than any place on Earth has been for a long time. The water is pure, the food miraculous, the staffs "robotic and human" among the finest in the world. So enjoy your stay! Anything you need can be summoned by simply instructing the wall screen aloud!

I need Daria, I don't say aloud. "So tell me about Sequene. Its history and layout and so forth." I've already memorized the building blueprints. Now I need current maps.

"Certainly!" the screen says, brightening like a girl drinking in boyish attention. "The name 'Sequene' derives from a fascinating European and American legend. In 1513—nearly six hundred years ago, imagine that!—an explorer from Spain, one Ponce de León, traveled to what is now part of the United States. To Florida."

Views of white sand beaches, nothing like the sodden, overgrown, bio-infested swamp that is Florida now.

"Of course, back then Florida was habitable, and so were various islands in the Caribbean Sea! They were inhabited by a tribe called the Arawak."

Images of Indians, looking noble.

"These people told the Spanish that one of their great chiefs, Sequene, had heard about a Fountain of Youth in a land to the

north, called 'Biminy.' Sequene took a group of warriors, sailed
for Biminy, and found the Fountain of Youth. Supposedly he and
his tribesmen lived there happily forever.

"Of course, no one can actually live forever—"

Daria?

"—but here on Sequene we can guarantee you—yes, guarantee you!—twenty more years *without aging a day older than you are
now*! Truly a miraculous 'fountain.' As you undergo this proven
scientific procedure—"

Pictures of deliriously happy people, drunk on science.

"—we on Sequene want you to be as comfortable, amused,
and satisfied as possible. To this end, Sequene contains luxurious
accommodations, five-star dining rooms—"

I said, "Map?"

"Certainly!"

For the next half hour I study maps of Sequene. I can't request
too much, I have to look like just one more chump willing to
gamble that twenty years of non-aging life is better than whatever I would have gotten otherwise. It's clear the hotel, the hospital, the casino and mini-golf course, and other foolishness don't
take up more than one-third of the orbital's usable space. Even
allowing for storage and maintenance, there's still a hell of a lot
going on up here that's officially unaccounted for. Including,
somewhere, Daria.

But it's not going to be easy to find her.

I have dinner in my room, sleep with the help of yet another
patch, and wake just as discouraged as last night. I can't communicate with Stevan, not without equipment they didn't let me
bring upstairs. I can't do anything that will get me kicked out.
All I have is my money—never negligible, granted—and my
wits. This morning neither seems enough.

All I really have is an old man's stupid dream.

Eventually I slump into the dining room for breakfast. A
waiter—human—rushes over to me. I barely glance at him. Across
the room is Agent Joseph Alcozer. And sitting at a table by herself,

drinking orange juice or something that's supposed to be orange juice, is Rosie Adams.

A year and a half after Peter Cleary died, D-treatments resumed. And there were plenty of takers.

Does this make sense? Freeze yourself at one age for twenty years and then zap! you're dead. All right, so maybe it made sense for the old who didn't want more deterioration, the dying who weren't in too much pain. Although you couldn't be too far gone or you wouldn't have strength enough to stand the surgery that would save you. But younger people took D-treatments, too. Men and women who wanted to stay beautiful and didn't mind paying for that with their lives. Even some very young athletes who, I guess, couldn't imagine life without slamming at a ball. Dancers. Holo stars. Crazy.

LifeLong, Inc., reorganized financially, renamed itself Sequene, and moved out of London to a Greek island. The King of England died of his D-treatment, a famous actress died of hers, the sultan of Bahrain died. It made no difference. People kept coming to Sequene.

Other people kept attacking Sequene. By that time, force fences had replaced or reinforced domes; there should have been no attacks on the island. But this is a mathematical Law of the Universe: As fast as new defenses multiply, counterweapons will multiply faster. Nothing is ever safe enough.

So the Greek island was blown up by devices that burrowed under the sea and into subterranean rock. Again Daria survived. Nine months later Sequene reopened on another island. Customers came.

That was the same year Geoffrey and I finally reconciled. Sort of.

For three years we'd lived in the same house, separate. I admit it—I was a terrible father. What kind of man ignores his sixteen-year-old son? His seventeen-, eighteen-, nineteen-year-old son? But this was mostly Geoff's choice. He wouldn't talk to me, wouldn't answer me, and what could I do? Shoot him? He went to school, had his meals in his room, studied hard. The school sent me his reports, all good. My office, the legitimate Feder Group, paid his bills. For a kid with a large amount of credit behind him, he didn't spend much. When he left high school and started college, I signed the papers. That was all. No discussion. Yes, I tried once or twice, but not very hard. I was busy.

My business had gotten bigger, more complicated, riskier. One thing led me to another, and then another. Stevan Adams and I made a good team. But I took all the risks, since the Rom would rather lose deals than end up in jail. Maybe I took too many risks—at least Moshe said so. He never liked Stevan. "Dirty gypsy keeps *his* hands clean," he said. Not a master of clear language, my Moshe. But the profits increased, and that he didn't complain about.

Federal surveillance increased as well.

Then one October night when the air smelled of apples, a rare night I was home early and watching some stupid holo about Luna City, Geoffrey came into the room. "Max?"

He was calling me "Max" now? I didn't protest—at least he was talking. "Geoff! Come in, sit down, you want a beer?"

"No. I don't drink. I want to tell you something, because you have a right to know."

"So tell me." My heart suddenly trembled. What had he done? He stood there leaning forward a little on the balls of his feet, like a fighter, which he was not. Thin, not tall, light brown hair falling over his eyes. Miriam's eyes, I saw with a sudden pain I never expected. Geoff didn't dress in the strange things that kids do. He looked, standing there, like an underage actor trying to play a New England accountant.

"I want to tell you that I'm getting married."

"Married?" He was nineteen, just starting his second year of college! This would be expensive, some little tart to be paid off, how did he even meet her. . . .

"I'm marrying Gwendolyn Jameson. Next week."

I was speechless. Gwendolyn—the accountant Moshe had made me hire, the "brilliant" weird one that had first noticed Stevan's penetration of the Feder Group. Her cult dress and hat were gone, but she was still a mousy, skinny nothing, the kind of person you forget is even in the room. How did—

"I'm not asking your blessing or anything like that," Geoff said. "But if you want to come to the ceremony, you're welcome."

"When . . . where . . ."

"Tuesday evening at seven o'clock at Gwendolyn's mother's house on—"

"I mean, where did you meet her? When?"

He actually *blushed*. "At your office, of course. I went up with the papers for my college tuition. She was there, and I took one look at her and I knew."

He knew. One look. All at once I was back in a *taverna* on Cyprus, twenty again myself, and I take one look at Daria standing by the bar and that's it for me. But *Gwendolyn*? And this had been going on a whole year, over a year. A wedding next week.

Somehow I said, "I wouldn't miss it, Geoff." It was the only decent thing I'd ever done for my son.

"That's great," he said, suddenly looking much younger. "We thought that on the—"

A huge noise from the front of the house. Security alarms, the robo-butler, doors yanked open, shouting. The feds burst in with weapons drawn and warrants on handhelds. Even as I put my hands on top of my head, even as the house system automatically linked to my lawyer, I knew I wasn't going to make Geoff's wedding.

And I didn't. Held without bail: a flight risk. A plea bargain got me six-to-ten, which ended up as five after time off for good behavior. It wasn't too bad. My lawyers did what lawyers do and I got the new prison, Themis International Cooperative Justice Center, a floating island in the middle of Lake Ontario. American and Canadian prisoners and absolutely no chance of unassisted escape unless you could swim forty-two kilometers.

But islands aren't necessarily impregnable. While I was in prison, Sequene was attacked again. Its Greek island was force-fielded top, bottom, and sides, but you have to have air. The terrorists—the Sons of Godly Righteousness, this time—sent in bio-engineered pathogens on the west wind. Twenty-six people died. Daria wasn't one of them.

Sequene moved upstairs to one of the new orbitals. No wind. Two years later, they were back in business.

My third year in prison, Gwendolyn died. She was one of the victims, the many victims, of the Mesopotamian bio-virus. I couldn't comfort Geoff, and who says I would have even tried, or that he would have accepted comfort? An alien, my son. But there must have been something of me in him, because he didn't marry again for twenty-five years. Gwendolyn, that skinny bizarre prig, had imprinted herself on his Feder heart.

When the government got me, they got Moshe, too. Moshe fought and screamed and hollered, but what good did it do him? He also got six-to-ten. Me, I don't bear a grudge. I do my work and the feds do theirs, the *schmucks*.

They couldn't get close to Stevan. Never even got his name— any of his names. If they had, Stevan would have been gone anyway: different identity, different face. For all I know, different DNA. More likely, Stevan's DNA was never on file in the first place. The Rom give birth at home, don't register birth or death certificates, don't claim their children on whatever fraudulent taxes they might file, don't send them to school. Romani don't go on the dole, don't turn up on any records they can possibly avoid, move often and by night. As much as humanly possible in this century, they don't actually exist. And Rom women are even more invisible than the men.

Which was probably part of the reason that, forty years later, Rosie Adams could be sitting in the dining room of Sequene orbital, pretending she didn't know me, while I totter to a table and wonder what the hell she's doing here.

Alcozer ambles over, no sweat or haste, where can I go? Uninvited, he sits at my table. "Good morning, Max."

"Shalom, Agent Alcozer." For the feds I always lay it on especially thick.

"We were surprised to see you here."

The royal "we." Everybody in the fucking federal government thinks they're tsars. I say, "Why is that? An old man, I shouldn't want to live longer?"

"It was our impression that you thought you were barely living at all."

How closely did they observe me in the Silver Star Home? I was there ten years, watching holos, playing cards, practically next door to drooling in a wheelchair. The government can spare money for all that surveillance?

"Have some orange juice," I say, pushing my untouched glass at him. Too bad it isn't cut with cyanide. Alcozer is the last thing I need. Over his shoulder I glance at Rosie, who frowns at the tablecloth, scratching at it with the nails of both hands.

She doesn't look good. At the *kumpania* less than a week ago, she looked old but still vital, despite the gray hair and wrinkles. Then her cheeks were rosy, her lips red with paint, her eyes bright under the colorful headscarf. Now she sits slumped, scratching away—and what is *that* all about?—as pale and pasty as a very large maggot. No headscarf, no jewelry. Her gray hair has been cut and waved into some horrible old-lady shape, and she wears loose pants and tunic in dull brown. From women's fashions I don't know, but these clothes look expensive and boring.

Alcozer leans in very close to me and says, "Max, I'm going to be honest with you."

That'll be the day.

"We know you've been off the streets for ten years, and we

know your son has taken the Feder Group legitimate. We have no reason to touch him, so your mind can be easy about that. But somebody's still running at least a few of your old operations, and we don't know who."

Not Moshe. He died a week after his release from prison. Heart attack.

"Also, there are still old investigations on you that we could re-open. I don't want to do that, of course, but I *could*. I know and you know that the leads are pretty cold, and on most the statute of limitations is close to running out. But there could be . . . repercussions. Up here, I mean." He leans back away from me and looks solemn.

I say politely, "I'm sorry, but I'm not following."

He says, "Durbin-Nacarro," and then I don't need him to chart me a flight path.

The Durbin-Nacarro Act severely limits the elective surgery available to convicted felons. This is supposed to deter criminals and terrorists from changing their looks, fingerprints, retinal patterns, voice scans, and anything else that "hinders identification." Did they think that someone who, say, blows up a spaceport in San Francisco or Dubai would then go to a registered hospital in any signatory country to request a new face? Ah, lawmakers.

Sequene is, of course, registered in a Durbin-Nacarro country, but nobody has ever applied D-treatment to Durbin-Nacarro. The treatment doesn't change anything that could be criminally misleading. In fact, the feds like it because it updates all their biological records on everybody who passes through Sequene. Plenty of criminals have had D-treatment: Carmine Lucente, Raul Lopez-Reyes, Surya Hasimo. But if Alcozer really wants to, he can find some federal judge somewhere to issue a dogshit injunction and stop my D-treatment.

Of course, I have no intention of actually getting a D-treatment, but he doesn't know that. I put on panic.

"Agent . . . I'm an old man . . . and without this . . ."

"Just think about it, Max. We'll talk again." He puts his hand on mine—such a fucking *putz*—and squeezes it briefly. I look pathetic. Alcozer walks jauntily out.

Rosie is still scratching at the tablecloth. Now she starts to tear her bread into little pieces and fling them around. A young woman in the light blue Sequene uniform rushes over to Rosie's table and says in a strong British accent, "Is everything all right then, Mrs. Kowalski?"

Rosie looks up dimly and says nothing.

"I'll just help you to your room, dear." Gently the attendant guides her out. I catch her eye and look meaningfully upset, and in five minutes the girl is back at my table. "Are you all right then, Mr. Feder?"

Now I'm querulous and demanding, a very rich temperamental geezer. "No, I'm not all right, I'm upset. For what I pay here, that's not the sight I expect with my breakfast."

"Of course not. It won't happen again."

"What's her problem?"

The girl hesitates, then decides that my tip will justify a minor invasion of Rosie's privacy.

"Mrs. Kowalski has a bit of mental decay. Naturally she wants to get it sorted out before it can progress any more, so she came to us. Now, would you like anything more to eat?"

"No, I'm done. I'll just maybe take a little walk before my first doctor's appointment."

She beams as if I've just declared that I'll just maybe bring peace to northern China. I nod and start a deliberately slow progress around Sequene. This yields me nothing, which I should have known. I can't get into restricted areas because I couldn't carry even the simplest jammer through shuttle security, and even if I could, it would only call attention to myself, and that I don't need. There are jammers and weapons here somewhere, and from my study of the blueprints I can make a good guess where. I can even guess where Daria might be. But I can't get at them, or her, and it comes to me that the only way I am going to see Daria is to ask for her.

Which I'm afraid to do. When your entire life has narrowed to one insane desire, you live with fear: you breathe it, eat it, lie down with it, feel it slide along your skin like a woman's lost caress.

I was terrified that Daria would say no. And then I would have nothing left to desire. When that happens, you're already dead.

In the afternoon the doctors take blood, they take tissue, they put me in machines, they take me out again. Everyone is exquisitely polite. I talk to someone I suspect is a psychiatrist, although I'm told he's not. I sign a lot of papers. Everything is recorded.

Agent Alcozer waits for me outside my suite. "Max. Can I come in?"

"Why not?"

In my sitting room he ostentatiously takes a small green box from his pocket, presses a series of buttons, and sets the thing on the floor. A jammer. We are now encased in a Faraday cage: no electromagnetic wavelengths in and none out. An invisible privacy cloak.

Of course—Alcozer has jammers, has weapons, has anything I might need to get to Daria. Agent Alcozer.

Angel Alcozer.

He says, "Have you thought about my offer?"

"I don't remember an offer. An offer has numbers attached, like flies on fly paper. Flies I don't remember, Joe." I have never used his first name before. He's too good to look startled.

"Here are some flies, Max. You name three important things about the San Cristobel fraud of '89. The hacker's name, the Swiss account number, and the organization you worked with. Then we let you stay up here on Sequene without interference. Sound good?"

"San Cristobel, San Cristobel," I mutter. "Do I remember from San Cristobel?"

"I think you do."

"Maybe I do."

His eyes sharpen. They are no color at all, nondescript. Government-issue eyes. But eager.

"But I need something else, too," I say.

"Something else?"

"I want—"

All at once I stop. High in my nose, something tingles. This time there is even a distinct smell, like old fish. Something is wrong here, something connected to Alcozer, or to the San Cristobel deal—Moshe's deal, not Stevan's—or to this conversation.

"You want what?" Alcozer says.

"I want to think a little more." I never ignore that smell. The nose knows.

He shifts his weight, disappointed. "Not too much more, Max. Your treatment's scheduled for tomorrow."

How does he know that? I don't know that. Alcozer has access to information I do not. Probably he knows where Daria is. All I have to do is give him the San Cristobel flies, and who gets hurt? Moshe is dead, that particular Robin Hood is dead, the island where it all happened no longer even exists, lost to the rising sea. The money was long since moved from the Swiss to the Indonesians and on from there. Nobody gets hurt.

No. There was something else about San Cristobel. Old fish.

I say, "Let me think a few hours. It's a big step, this." I let my voice quaver. "A big change for me, this place. You know I never lived big on Earth. And for a kid from Brooklyn . . ."

Alcozer smiles. It's supposed to be a comradely smile. He looks like a vampire with a tooth job. "For a kid from Des Moines, too. All right, Max, you think. I'll come back right after dinner." He turns off the jammer, pockets it, stands. "Have another nice walk. By the way, there's no restricted areas on Sequene that you could possibly get into."

"You think maybe I don't know that?"

"I'm trying to find out what you know." Alcozer looks pleased with himself, like he's said something witty. I let him think this. Always good to encourage federal delusion.

Old fish. But whose?

I go to dinner. The second I sit at a table, Rosie totters into the dining room, lights up like a rocket launch, and shouts, "Christopher!"

I look around. Two other diners in the room so far, and they're both women. Rosie lurches over, tears streaming down her cheeks, and throws her arms around me. "You came!"

"I—"

A harried-looking woman in the light blue uniform hurries through the doorway. "Oh, Mr. Feder, I'm so sorry, she—"

"It's Christopher!" Rosie cries. "Look, Anna, my brother Christopher! He came all the way from California to visit me!"

Rosie is clutching me like I'm a cliff she's about to go over. I don't have to play blank—I *am* blank. The attendant tries to detach her, but she only clutches harder.

"So sorry, Mr. Feder, she gets a little confused, she—Mrs. Kowalski!"

"Christopher! Christopher! I'm going to have dinner with my brother!"

"Mrs. Kowalski, really, you—"

"Would it help if I have dinner with her?" I say.

The attendant looks confused. But more people are coming into the dining room, very rich people, and it's clear she doesn't want a fuss. Her earcomm says something and she tries to smile at me. "Oh, that would be . . . if you don't mind . . ."

"Not at all. My aunt, in her last days . . . I understand."

The young attendant is grateful, along with angry and embarrassed and a half dozen other things I don't care about. I reach out with my one free hand and pull out a chair for Rosie, who sits down, mumbling. A robo-waiter appears and order is restored to the universe.

Rosie mumbles to herself all through dinner, absolutely unintelligible mumbling. The attendant lurks unhappily in a corner.
The set of her body says she's been dealing with Rosie all day and
is disgusted with this duty. Stevan must have created a hell of a
credit history for Mrs. Kowalski. Rosie says nothing whatsoever
to me, but occasionally she beams at me like a demented light-
house. I say nothing to her, but I get worried. I don't know what's
happening. Either she really has lost it—in less than a week? is
this possible?—or she's a better actress than half of the holo stars
on the Link.

She eats everything, but very slowly. Halfway through des-
sert, some kind of chocolate pastry, the dining room is full. The
first shift, the old people who go to bed at ten o'clock (I know
this, I'm one of them) have left and the second shift, the younger
and more fashionably dressed, are eating and laughing and or-
dering expensive wine. I recognize a famous Japanese singer, an
American ex-Senator who was once (although he didn't know it)
on my payroll, and an Arab playboy. From Sequene's point of
view, it is not a good place for a tawdry scene.

Rosie stands and cries, "Daria Cleary!"

My heart stops.

But of course Daria is not there. There's only Rosie, flailing
her arms and crying, "I must thank Daria Cleary! For this gift of
life! I must thank her!"

People stare. A few look amused, but most do not. They have
the affronted look of sleek darlings forced to look at old age, se-
nility, a badly dressed and stooped body that may smell bad—all
the things they have come to Sequene to avoid experiencing. The
attendant dashes over.

"Mrs. Kowalski!"

"Daria! I must thank her!"

The girl tugs on Rosie, who grabs at the tablecloth. Plates and
wineglasses and expensive hydroponic flowers crash to the floor.
Diners mutter, scowling. The girl says desperately, "Yes, of course,

we'll go see Daria! Right now! Come with me, Mrs. Kowalski."

"Christopher, too!"

I say softly, conspiratorially, to the girl, "We need to get her out of here."

She says, "Yes, yes, of course, Christopher, too," and gives me a tight, grateful, furious smile.

Rosie trails happily after the attendant, holding my hand.

I think, *This cannot work.* Once we're out of the dining room, out of earshot, out of hypocrisy . . .

In the corridor outside the dining room Rosie halts, shouting again, "Daria!" People here, too, stop and stare. Rosie, suddenly not tottering, leads the way past them, down a side corridor, then another. Faster now, the attendant has to run to catch up. Me, too. So Rosie hits the force-fence first, is knocked to the ground, and starts to cry.

"All right, you," the girl says, all pretense of sweetness gone. "That's enough!" She grabs Rosie's arm and tries to yank her upward. Rosie outweighs her by maybe twenty-five kilos. A service 'bot trundles toward us.

Rosie is calling, "Daria! Daria! Please, you don't know what this means to me! I'm an old woman but I was young once, I too lost the only man I ever loved—remember Cyprus? Do you—you do! Cyprus! Daria!"

The 'bot exudes a scoop and effortlessly shovels up Rosie like so much gravel. The girl says viciously, "I've had just about enough of—"

And stops. Her face changes. Something is coming over her earcomm.

Then there is an almost inaudible pop! as the force-fence shuts down. At the far end of the corridor, a door opens, a door that wasn't even there a moment ago. Stealth coating, I think, dazed. Reuven's robo-dog. My hand, unbidden, goes to my naked ring finger.

Standing in the doorway, backed by bodyguards both human

and 'bot just as she was in the ViaHealth hospital fifty-five years ago, is Daria.

She still looks eighteen. As I stumble forward, too numb to feel my legs move, I see her in a Greek *taverna*, leaning against the bar; on a rocky beach, crying in early morning light; in a hospital bed, head half shaved. She doesn't see me at all, isn't looking, doesn't recognize me. She looks at Rosie.

Who has changed utterly. Rosie scrambles off the gravel scoop and pushes away the attendant, a push so strong the girl falls against the corridor wall. Rosie grabs my hand and drags me forward. At the doorway, both 'bot and human bodyguards block the way. Rosie submits to a body search that ordinarily would have brought death to any man who touched a Rom woman in those ways, possibly including her husband. Rosie endures it like a pagan queen disdaining unimportant Roman soldiers. Me, I hardly notice it. I can't stop looking at Daria.

Still eighteen, but utterly changed.

The wild black hair has been subdued into a fashionable, tame, ugly style. Her smooth brown skin has no color under its paint. Her eyes, still her own shade of green, bear in their depths a defeat and loneliness I can't imagine.

Yes. I can.

She says nothing, just stands aside to let us pass once the guards have finished. The human one says, "Mrs. Cleary—" but she silences him with a wave of her hand. We stand now in a sort of front hall. Maybe it's white or blue or gold, maybe there are flowers, maybe the flowers stand on an antique table—nothing really registers. All I see is Daria, who does not see me.

She says to Rosie, "What do you know of Cyprus? Were you there?"

She must think Rosie was a whore on Cyprus when Daria herself was—the ages would be about right. But Daria's question is detached, uninvolved, the way you might politely ask the age of an historical building. *Dating from 1649? Really. Well.*

Rosie doesn't answer. Instead she steps behind me. Rosie can't say my name, because of course we are all under surveillance. She must remain Mrs. Kowalski so that she can go home to Stevan. Rosie can say nothing.

So I do. I say, "Daria, it's Max."

Finally she looks at me, and she knows who I am.

The Rom have a word for ghosts: *mulé*. *Mulé* haunt the places they used to live for up to a year. They eat scraps, use the toilet, spend the money buried with them in their coffins. They trouble the living in dreams and visions. Wispy, insubstantial, they nonetheless exist. I could never find out if Stevan or Rosie actually believed in *mulé*. There are things the Rom never tell a *gajo*.

Daria has become a *muli*. There is no real interest in her eyes as she regards me. This woman, who once, in a hospital room, risked both our lives to bring me riches and atonement and shame, now has lived beyond all risk, all interest. Decades of being shut away by Peter Cleary, of being hated by people who make periodic and serious efforts to kill her, of being used as a biological supply station from which pieces are clipped to fuel others' vanity, have drained her of all vitality. She desires nothing, feels nothing, cares about nothing. Including me.

"Max," she says courteously. "Hello."

The throaty catch, the hesitation, is gone from her voice. For some reason, it is this which breaks me. Go figure. Her accent is still there, even her scent is still there, but not that catch in the voice, and not Daria. This is a shell. In her eyes, nothing.

Rosie takes my hand. It is the first time in forty years, except for when she was crazy Mrs. Kowalski, that Rosie Adams has ever touched me. In her clasp I feel all of the compassion, the life, that is missing from Daria. Nothing could have hurt me more.

I can't look any more at Daria. How do you look at something that isn't there? I turn my head and see Agent Alcozer round the corner of the hallway outside the apartment, running toward us.

And then, at that moment and not a second before, I remember what stank about San Cristobel.

The scam went through fine. But afterward, Moshe came to me. *"They want to do it again, this time with a mole. They've actually got someone inside the feds, in the Central Investigative Bureau. It looks good."*

"Get me the details," I said. And when Moshe did, I rejected the deal.

"But why?" Anguished—Moshe hated to let a profitable thing go.

"Because," I said, and wouldn't say more. He argued, but I stood firm. The new deal involved another organization, the one the mole came from. The Pure of Heart and Planet. Eco-nuts, into a lot of things on both sides of the law, but I knew what Moshe did not and wouldn't have cared about if he had. The Pure of Heart and Planet were connected with the second big attack on LifeLong, on that Greek island. The Pure of Heart and Planet along with their mole in the feds, altered and augmented in sacrifice to the greater glory of biological purity, a guy from what used to be Des Moines.

Alcozer runs faster than humanly possible. He carries something in his hands, a thick rod with knobs that I don't recognize. Weapons change in ten years. Everything changes.

And Daria knows. She looks at Alcozer, and she doesn't move.

The bodyguards don't move, either, and I realize that of course they've reactivated the force-fence around the apartment. It makes no difference. Alcozer barrels through it; whatever the military has developed for the Central Investigative Bureau, it trumps whatever Sequene has. It handles the guard 'bot, too, which just shuts down, erased by what must be the jammer of all jammers.

The human bodyguard isn't quite so easy. He fires at Alcozer, and the mole staggers. Blood howls out of him. As he goes down he throws something, so small you might not notice it if you didn't know what was happening. *I* know; this is the first weapon that I actually recognize, although undoubtedly it's been upgraded. Primitive. Contained. Lethal enough to do what it needs to without risking a hull breach, no matter where on an orbital or shuttle you set it off. An MPG, mini personal grenade, and all at once I'm back on Cyprus, in the Army, and training unused for sixty-five years surfaces in my muscles like blossoming spores.

I lurch forward. Not smooth, nothing my drill sergeant would be proud of. But I never hesitate, not for a nanosecond.

I can only save one of them. No time for anything else. Daria stands, beautiful as the moment I saw her in that *taverna*, in her green eyes a welcome for death. *Overdue, so what kept you already?* But those would be my words, not hers. Daria has no words, which are for the living.

I hit Rosie's solid flesh more like a dropped piano than a rescuing knight. We both go down—whump!—and I roll with her under the antique table, which is there after all, a heavy marble slab. My roll takes Rosie, the beloved of my faithful friend Stevan, against the wall, with me on the outside. I never hear the grenade; they *have* been upgraded. Electromagnetic waves, nothing as crude as fragments. Burns sluice across my back like burning oil. The table cracks and half falls.

Then darkness.

Romani have a saying: *Rom corel khajnja, Gadzo corel farma.* Gypsies steal the chicken, but it is the *gaje* who steal the whole farm. Yes.

Yes.

I wake in a white bed, in a white room, wearing white bandages under a white blanket. It's like doctors think that color hurts. Geoff sits beside my bed. When I stir, he leans forward.

"Dad?"

"I'm here."

"How do you feel?"

The inevitable, stupid question. I was MPG-fragged, a table

fell on me, how should I feel? But Geoff realizes this. He says, quietly, "She's dead."

"Rosie?"

He looks blank—as well he might. "Who's Rosie?"

"What did I say? I don't feel . . . I can't . . ."

"Just rest, Dad. Don't try to talk. I just want you to know that Daria Cleary's dead."

"I know," I say. She's been dead a long time.

"So is that terrorist. Dead. It turns out he was actually a federal agent—can you believe it? But the woman you saved, Mrs. Kowalski, she's all right."

"Where is she?"

"She went back downstairs. Changed her mind about D-treatment. Now the newsholos want to interview her and they can't find her."

And they never will. I think about Stevan and Rosie . . . and Daria. It isn't pain I feel, although that might be because the doctors have stuck on my neck a patch the size of Rhode Island. Not pain, but hollowness. Emptiness. Cold winds blow right through me.

When there's nothing left to desire, you're finished.

In the hallway, 'bots roll softly past. Dishes clink. People murmur and someplace a bell chimes. Hollowness. Emptiness.

"Dad," Geoff says, and his tone changes. "You saved that woman's life. You didn't even know her, she was just some crazy woman you were being kind to, and you saved her life. You're a hero."

Slowly I turn my head to look at him. Geoff's eyes shine. His thin lips work up and down. "I'm so proud of you."

So it's a joke. All of it—a bad joke. You'd think the Master of the Universe could do better. I go on an insane quest for a ring eaten by a robotic dog, I assist in the mercy killing of the only woman I ever loved, I save the life of one of the best criminals on the planet—my own partner-in-law in so many grand larcenies that Geoff's head would spin—and the punch line is that my son is proud of me. *Proud.* This makes sense?

But a little of the hollowness fills. A little of the cold wind abates.

Geoff goes on, "I told Bobby and Eric what you did. They're proud of their grampops, too. So is Gloria. They all can't wait for you to come back home."

"That's nice," I say. *Grampops*—what a word. But the wind abates a little more.

"Sleep, now, Dad," Geoff says. He hesitates, then leans over and kisses my forehead.

I feel my son's kiss there long after he leaves.

So I don't tell him that I'm not going back home anytime soon. I'm going to have the D-treatment, after all. When I do have to tell him, I'll say that I want to live to see my grandsons grow up. Maybe this is even true. Okay—it is true, but the idea is so new I need time to get used to it.

My other reason for getting D-treatment is stronger, fiercer. It's been there so much longer.

I want a piece of Daria with me. In the old days, I had her in a ring. But that was then, and this is now, and I'll take what I can get. It is, will have to be, enough.

NANCY KRESS

"Fountain of Age" is a "stutter story"—I started it, stopped it, began again later, repeated the first few paragraphs, gave up and started over. I had the voice of Max right away, and since it's not one I'd written in before, I really wanted to attempt the story. I also had a vague idea that I wanted to use all the research I'd done on the Rom for a novel that never got off the ground. What I didn't have was a plot. Then I happened to be reading an article on cancer-cell growth—actually, I'm often reading an article on that fascinating and slippery subject—and

I realized that Daria was immortal. From there, the rest of the story flowed easily, fueled by the frustrations that are an inevitable part of love.

My son said, "How are you going to write about theft by computer? You can barely turn yours on." Bratty kid. I said, "I'm not going to write about theft by computer, I'm going to write around it." This turned out to be fun: getting in touch with my inner criminal. I may do it again.

1965

Best Novel: *Dune* by Frank Herbert

Best Novella (tie): "The Saliva Tree" by Brian W. Aldiss
"He Who Shapes" by Roger Zelazny

Best Novelette: "The Doors of His Face, the Lamps of His Mouth" by Roger Zelazny

Best Short Story: "'Repent, Harlequin!' Said the Ticktockman" by Harlan Ellison

1966

Best Novel (tie): *Flowers for Algernon* by Daniel Keyes
Babel-17 by Samuel R. Delany

Best Novella: "The Last Castle" by Jack Vance

Best Novelette: "Call Him Lord" by Gordon R. Dickson

Best Short Story: "The Secret Place" by Richard McKenna

1967

Best Novel: *The Einstein Intersection* by Samuel R. Delany

Best Novella: "Behold the Man" by Michael Moorcock

Best Novelette: "Gonna Roll the Bones" by Fritz Leiber

Best Short Story: "Aye, and Gomorrah" by Samuel R. Delany

1968

Best Novel: *Rite of Passage* by Alexei Panshin

Best Novella: "Dragonrider" by Anne McCaffrey

Best Novelette: "Mother to the World" by Richard Wilson

Best Short Story: "The Planners" by Kate Wilhelm

1969

Best Novel: *The Left Hand of Darkness* by Ursula K. Le Guin

Best Novella: "A Boy and His Dog" by Harlan Ellison

Best Novelette: "Time Considered as a Helix of Semi-Precious Stones" by Samuel R. Delany

Best Short Story: "Passengers" by Robert Silverberg

1970

Best Novel: *Ringworld* by Larry Niven

Best Novella: "Ill Met in Lankhmar" by Fritz Leiber

Best Novelette: "Slow Sculpture" by Theodore Sturgeon

Best Short Story: No award

1971

Best Novel: *A Time of Changes* by Robert Silverberg

Best Novella: "The Missing Man" by Katherine MacLean

Best Novelette: "The Queen of Air and Darkness" by Poul Anderson

Best Short Story: "Good News from the Vatican" by Robert Silverberg

1972

Best Novel: *The Gods Themselves* by Isaac Asimov

Best Novella: "A Meeting with Medusa" by Arthur C. Clarke

Best Novelette: "Goat Song" by Poul Anderson

Best Short Story: "When It Changed" by Joanna Russ

1973

Best Novel: *Rendezvous with Rama* by Arthur C. Clarke

Best Novella: "The Death of Doctor Island" by Gene Wolfe

Best Novelette: "Of Mist, and Grass, and Sand" by Vonda N. McIntyre

Best Short Story: "Love Is the Plan the Plan Is Death" by James Tiptree, Jr.

Best Dramatic Presentation: *Soylent Green,* screenplay by Stanley R. Greenberg (based on the novel *Make Room! Make Room!*)

Harry Harrison for *Make Room! Make Room!*

1974

Best Novel: *The Dispossessed* by Ursula K. Le Guin

Best Novella: "Born with the Dead" by Robert Silverberg

Best Novelette: "If the Stars Are Gods" by Gordon Eklund and Gregory Benford

Best Short Story: "The Day Before the Revolution" by Ursula K. Le Guin

Best Dramatic Presentation: *Sleeper* by Woody Allen

1975

Best Novel: *The Forever War* by Joe Haldeman

Best Novella: "Home Is the Hangman" by Roger Zelazny

Best Novelette: "San Diego Lightfoot Sue" by Tom Reamy

Best Short Story: "Catch that Zeppelin!" by Fritz Leiber

Best Dramatic Writing: Mel Brooks and Gene Wilder for *Young Frankenstein*

1976

Best Novel: *Man Plus* by Frederik Pohl

Best Novella: "Houston, Houston, Do You Read?" by James Tiptree, Jr.

Best Novelette: "The Bicentennial Man" by Isaac Asimov
Best Short Story: "A Crowd of Shadows" by Charles L.
Grant

1977

Best Novel: *Gateway* by Frederik Pohl
Best Novella: "Stardance" by Spider and Jeanne Robinson
Best Novelette: "The Screwfly Solution" by Raccoona
Sheldon
Best Short Story: "Jeffty Is Five" by Harlan Ellison
Special Award: *Star Wars*

1978

Best Novel: *Dreamsnake* by Vonda N. McIntyre
Best Novella: "The Persistence of Vision" by John
Varley
Best Novelette: "A Glow of Candles, a Unicorn's Eye" by
Charles L. Grant
Best Short Story: "Stone" by Edward Bryant

1979

Best Novel: *The Fountains of Paradise* by Arthur C. Clarke
Best Novella: "Enemy Mine" by Barry Longyear
Best Novelette: "Sandkings" by George R. R. Martin
Best Short Story: "giANTS" by Edward Bryant

1980

Best Novel: *Timescape* by Gregory Benford
Best Novella: "The Unicorn Tapestry" by Suzy McKee
Charnas
Best Novelette: "The Ugly Chickens" by Howard
Waldrop
Best Short Story: "Grotto of the Dancing Deer" by
Clifford D. Simak

1981

Best Novel: *The Claw of the Conciliator* by Gene Wolfe
Best Novella: "The Saturn Game" by Poul Anderson
Best Novelette: "The Quickening" by Michael Bishop
Best Short Story: "The Bone Flute" by Lisa Tuttle (This Nebula Award was declined by the author.)

1982

Best Novel: *No Enemy but Time* by Michael Bishop
Best Novella: "Another Orphan" by John Kessel
Best Novelette: "Fire Watch" by Connie Willis
Best Short Story: "A Letter from the Clearys" by Connie Willis

1983

Best Novel: *Startide Rising* by David Brin
Best Novella: "Hardfought" by Greg Bear
Best Novelette: "Blood Music" by Greg Bear
Best Short Story: "The Peacemaker" by Gardner Dozois

1984

Best Novel: *Neuromancer* by William Gibson
Best Novella: "PRESS ENTER■" by John Varley
Best Novelette: "Bloodchild" by Octavia E. Butler
Best Short Story: "Morning Child" by Gardner Dozois

1985

Best Novel: *Ender's Game* by Orson Scott Card
Best Novella: "Sailing to Byzantium" by Robert Silverberg
Best Novelette: "Portraits of His Children" by George R. R. Martin
Best Short Story: "Out of All Them Bright Stars" by Nancy Kress

1986

Best Novel: *Speaker for the Dead* by Orson Scott Card

Best Novella: "R & R" by Lucius Shepard

Best Novelette: "The Girl Who Fell into the Sky" by Kate Wilhelm

Best Short Story: "Tangents" by Greg Bear

1987

Best Novel: *The Falling Woman* by Pat Murphy

Best Novella: "The Blind Geometer" by Kim Stanley Robinson

Best Novelette: "Rachel in Love" by Pat Murphy

Best Short Story: "Forever Yours, Anna" by Kate Wilhelm

1988

Best Novel: *Falling Free* by Lois McMaster Bujold

Best Novella: "The Last of the Winnebagos" by Connie Willis

Best Novelette: "Schrodinger's Kitten" by George Alec Effinger

Best Short Story: "Bible Stories for Adults, No. 17: The Deluge" by James Morrow

1989

Best Novel: *The Healer's War* by Elizabeth Ann Scarborough

Best Novella: "The Mountains of Mourning" by Lois McMaster Bujold

Best Novelette: "At the Rialto" by Connie Willis

Best Short Story: "Ripples in the Dirac Sea" by Geoffrey A. Landis

1990

Best Novel: *Tehanu: The Last Book of Earthsea* by Ursula K. Le Guin

Best Novella: "The Hemingway Hoax" by Joe
    Haldeman
Best Novelette: "Tower of Babylon" by Ted Chiang
Best Short Story: "Bears Discover Fire" by Terry Bisson

1991

Best Novel: *Stations of the Tide* by Michael Swanwick
Best Novella: "Beggars in Spain" by Nancy Kress
Best Novelette: "Guide Dog" by Mike Conner
Best Short Story: "Ma Qui" by Alan Brennert

1992

Best Novel: *Doomsday Book* by Connie Willis
Best Novella: "City of Truth" by James Morrow
Best Novelette: "Danny Goes to Mars" by Pamela Sargent
Best Short Story: "Even the Queen" by Connie Willis

1993

Best Novel: *Red Mars* by Kim Stanley Robinson
Best Novella: "The Night We Buried Road Dog" by
    Jack Cady
Best Novelette: "Georgia on My Mind" by Charles
    Sheffield
Best Short Story: "Graves" by Joe Haldeman

1994

Best Novel: *Moving Mars* by Greg Bear
Best Novella: "Seven Views of Olduvai Gorge" by Mike
    Resnick
Best Novelette: "The Martian Child" by David Gerrold
Best Short Story: "A Defense of the Social Contracts" by
    Martha Soukup

1995

Best Novel: *The Terminal Experiment* by Robert J. Sawyer
Best Novella: "Last Summer at Mars Hill" by Elizabeth Hand
Best Novelette: "Solitude" by Ursula K. Le Guin
Best Short Story: "Death and the Librarian" by Esther Friesner

1996

Best Novel: *Slow River* by Nicola Griffith
Best Novella: "Da Vinci Rising" by Jack Dann
Best Novelette: "Lifeboat on a Burning Sea" by Bruce Holland Rogers
Best Short Story: "A Birthday" by Esther M. Friesner

1997

Best Novel: *The Moon and the Sun* by Vonda N. McIntyre
Best Novella: "Abandon in Place" by Jerry Oltion
Best Novelette: "The Flowers of Aulit Prison" by Nancy Kress
Best Short Story: "Sister Emily's Lightship" by Jane Yolen

1998

Best Novel: *Forever Peace* by Joe Haldeman
Best Novella: "Reading the Bones" by Sheila Finch
Best Novelette: "Lost Girls" by Jane Yolen
Best Short Story: "Thirteen Ways to Water" by Bruce Holland Rogers

Other Awards and Honors Given in 1999

Grand Master: Hal Clement (Harry Stubbs)
Bradbury Award: J. Michael Straczynski
Author Emeritus: William Tenn (Phil Klass)

1999

Best Novel: *Parable of the Talents* by Octavia E. Butler
Best Novella: "Story of Your Life" by Ted Chiang
Best Novelette: "Mars Is No Place for Children" by Mary
  A. Turzillo
Short Story: "The Cost of Doing Business" by Leslie What
Best Script: *The Sixth Sense* by M. Night Shyamalan

Other Awards and Honors Given in 2000
Grand Master: Brian W. Aldiss
Author Emeritus: Daniel Keyes

2000

Best Novel: *Darwin's Radio* by Greg Bear
Best Novella: "Goddesses" by Linda Nagata
Best Novelette: "Daddy's World" by Walter Jon Williams
Best Short Story: "macs" by Terry Bisson
Best Script: *Galaxy Quest* by Robert Gordon and David
  Howard

Other Awards and Honors Given in 2001
Grand Master: Philip José Farmer
Bradbury Award: Yuri Rasovsky and Harlan Ellison
Author Emeritus: Robert Sheckley

2001

Best Novel: *The Quantum Rose* by Catherine Asaro
Best Novella: "The Ultimate Earth" by Jack Williamson
Best Novelette: "Louise's Ghost" by Kelly Link
Best Short Story: "The Cure for Everything" by Severna
  Park
Best Script: *Crouching Tiger, Hidden Dragon* by James
  Schamus, Kuo Jung Tsai, and Hui-Ling Wang; from the
  book by Du Lu Wang

Other Awards and Honors Given in 2002
President's Award: Betty Ballantine

2002

Best Novel: *American Gods* by Neil Gaiman
Best Novella: "Bronte's Egg" by Richard Chwedyk
Best Novelette: "Hell Is the Absence of God" by Ted Chiang
Best Short Story: "Creature" by Carol Emshwiller
Best Script: *The Lord of the Rings: The Fellowship of the Ring* by Fran Walsh, Philippa Boyens, and Peter Jackson; based on *The Lord of the Rings* by J. R. R. Tolkien

Other Awards and Honors Given in 2003
Grand Master: Ursula K. Le Guin
Author Emeritus: Katherine MacLean

2003

Best Novel: *The Speed of Dark* by Elizabeth Moon
Best Novella: "Coraline" by Neil Gaiman
Best Novelette: "The Empire of Ice Cream" by Jeffrey Ford
Best Short Story: "What I Didn't See" by Karen Joy Fowler
Best Script: *The Lord of the Rings: The Two Towers* by Fran Walsh, Philippa Boyens, Stephen Sinclair, and Peter Jackson; based on *The Lord of the Rings* by J. R. R. Tolkien

Other Awards and Honors Given in 2004
Grand Master: Robert Silverberg
Author of Distinction: Charles Harness
Service to SFWA Award: Michael Capobianco and Ann Crispin

2004

Best Novel: *Paladin of Souls* by Lois McMaster Bujold

Best Novella: "The Green Leopard Plague" by Walter Jon Williams

Best Novelette: "Basement Magic" by Ellen Klages

Best Short Story: "Coming to Terms" by Eileen Gunn

Best Script: *The Lord of the Rings: The Return of the King* by Fran Walsh, Philippa Boyens, and Peter Jackson; based on *The Lord of the Rings* by J. R. R. Tolkien

Other Awards and Honors Given in 2005

Grand Master: Anne McCaffrey

2005

Best Novel: *Camouflage* by Joe Haldeman

Best Novella: "Magic for Beginners" by Kelly Link

Best Novelette: "The Faery Handbag" by Kelly Link

Best Short Story: "I Live with You" by Carol Emshwiller

Best Script: *Serenity* by Joss Whedon

Andre Norton Award:★ *Valiant: A Modern Tale of Faerie* by Holly Black

Other Awards and Honors Given in 2006

Grand Master: Harlan Ellison

Author Emeritus: William F. Nolan

2006

Best Novel: *Seeker* by Jack McDevitt

Best Novella: "Burn" by James Patrick Kelly

Best Novelette: "Two Hearts" by Peter S. Beagle

Best Short Story: "Echo" by Elizabeth Hand

Andre Norton Award:★ *Magic or Madness* by Justine Larbalestier

Other Awards and Honors Given in 2007
    Grand Master: James Gunn
    Author Emeritus: D. G. Compton

★ The Andre Norton Award is not a Nebula.

SFWA inaugurated the Author Emeritus program in 1995 as a way to recognize and appreciate senior writers in the genres of science fiction and fantasy who have made significant contributions to our field but who are no longer active or whose excellent work may no longer be as widely known as it once was. The honor is decided by SFWA's board of directors through discussion and consensus. The Author Emeritus is invited to speak at the Nebula Awards Banquet and given a lifetime SFWA membership. When the invitee is not able to attend the banquet to speak, he or she is instead recognized as an **Author of Distinction**.

Fiction by the first five Authors Emeriti is collected in the anthology *Architects of Dreams* (Meisha Merlin, 2003) edited by Robin Wayne Bailey.

THE AUTHORS EMERITI ARE:

Emil Petaja	[1995]
Wilson "Bob" Tucker	[1996]
Judith Merril	[1997]
Nelson Slade Bond	[1998]
William Tenn [Philip Klass]	[1999]
Daniel Keyes	[2000]
Robert Sheckley	[2001]
Katherine MacLean	[2003]
Charles L. Harness (Author of Distinction)	[2004]
William F. Nolan	[2006]
D. G. Compton	[2007]
Ardath Mayhar	[2008]

Multigenre, award-winning writer Joe R. Lansdale has written a fitting tribute to Ardath Mayhar.

ARDATH MAYHAR,
TALENT FROM THE PINES

JOE R. LANSDALE

Ardath Mayhar is a talent out of East Texas, a woman living in a small dome-shaped house in the depths of the pines, her home surrounded by wind-rattled bamboo—at least before a tornado did a bit of natural weed eating, tearing a lot of it up, taking it away and not quite weaving baskets of it. There's also a yard full of stray cats that have found a sucker, and their numbers vary according to the eating habits of the local coyotes who like nothing better for an evening snack than a fresh, warm cat.

Like her natural surroundings, Ardath is one of the most natural writers who ever wrote a line. The words and stories jump at her like hot sparks from lightning; seem to come from hidden places in the pines instead of the clouds.

I lost count long ago of how many books Ardath has written, though I have read most, many in manuscript, and I look forward to those that have been lost in her files for so many years and are soon to be brought into book form via Borgo Press.

I have said this before, and I will say it again: Ardath Mayhar is a neglected writer, and that neglect is an offense worthy of a firing squad. Like Neal Barrett, Jr., she has been so good and so consistent, folks take her for granted. She is one of those born storytellers, and therefore easy to take for granted, like the wind, the earth, and sky. We tend to think these things are always going to be there.

It takes only a moment of applied logic to know this isn't true.

All things pass.

But not everyone has the backlist of work Ardath has, or the kind of readers who at the recent Nebula convention rushed to her signing table with piles of books and childlike excitement, gushing accolades long overdue.

Part of the reason for this neglect is Ardath herself.

She doesn't get out much.

She's not someone to stand on a soapbox and wave her arms and tell everyone how good she is and how important she is.

She's not someone to remind us that her work is unique, that it is born and bred out of East Texas, and no matter what she writes, be it the most amazing aliens one can imagine—and she had created a large number of amazing aliens—they all are somehow out of East Texas. I'm not saying they talk with Ardath's accent, which is pretty close to mine, bless our little country hearts, and I'm not saying these aliens aren't alien, but it's the East Texas mind that has created them. Living out in the pines as she does, out where the dark things gather and there are plenty of odd ducks, hungry alligators, and vicious water moccasins with snake hearts full of sin; deep in the center of East Texas, it is no surprise that at the core of her stories is the strange, sweetly dark soul of East Texas; it throbs like a sore at times, and at others it is as healing and comforting as a mother's touch.

Over thirty years ago I met Ardath. She was already an accomplished poet, and had a few stories published, including one, "Crawfish," that was a big influence on me. It was a crime story and it was about East Texas and it alerted me to the fact that I didn't have to write about some place outside of my homeland of East Texas; it showed me writing was about life and experience. It was a great lesson, and without that story, I don't know if I would have had a career. I had been fueled by Matheson and Bloch and Bradbury, and so many others, and they gave me direction, but Ardath, she showed me that I could write closer to the bone. It was, at the time, a revelation. It seems obvious now, but not then.

But enough about a crime story. Ardath's first love was fantasy and science fiction, and she, like me, wanted badly to break into those fields. We became fast friends and burned up the phone lines every day, sometimes talking for hours. They were good talks. We talked about books and stories we liked, the state of the field (it always stinks), publishers, editors, other writers, conventions (we attended a few), and our latest works.

We formed a writers' organization that lasted for many years and petered out when many of the members moved, died, or became so busy that the monthly meetings couldn't continue. Interestingly enough, a large number of those members were published in some form or another. But what I remember about those meetings was looking forward to Ardath Mayhar reading from a story, or a book she was working on.

It was a great treat.

Before long, she broke into science fiction big-time. I drifted off into other, newer interests, circling back now and then to touch base, but Ardath was selling books and stories faster than a duck could gobble june bugs. In time, Ardath branched out into other types of stories: crime, suspense, western, mystery, but, like me, she always circled back, and for her, the bulk of her work lies within the science fiction and fantasy fields.

Bless her. She fought the good fight to become a writer and made it.

No connections to start out with.

Originally, no other real dedicated writers to speak to—thank goodness we found each other.

No financial backing. She's done everything from milking cows to operating a bookstore.

No great respect or understanding from the local populace, who didn't get that science fiction and funny space stuff. (That perception about SF here has changed dramatically, and part of that is due to Ardath herself, because how do you keep denying a force of nature?)

You see, Ardath persisted. She wrote and wrote and wrote, turning out thousands of words a day, and this, young folks, was when we were writing our works on old-fashioned typewriters that sometimes demanded we near stand on the keys to make them pop the paper. She moved from those, as did I, to electric typewriters, and finally word processors. In fact, I bought my first word processor from her and her husband, Joe.

These days there are fewer stories coming from the Mayhar residence. She's enjoying the fruits of her labors; she's slowed down a bit. Pets and feeds those stray cats, reads a lot, and watches old movies. We get together for visits now and then, like at the recent Nebula Awards. We rode there together and back, my wife at the wheel, my daughter in the backseat with me. I leaned forward the whole trip. Ardath and I swapped stories and talked about this and that. It was delightful. Like old times.

These days, the words don't quite jump and spark at Ardath the way they once did, but that may be because she's not at this moment ready to catch them. Recently, an exploding compost toilet excited her enough to snag a few sparks out of the air (nothing from the exploding toilet I might add) and pin those sparkly suckers to paper. Replacements and/or repairs cost money. The need for money necessitates creativity sometimes. Remember, Philip K. Dick dedicated one of his novels to bill collectors.

But enough of the memories.

Now, Ardath Mayhar has been named Author Emeritus by the Science Fiction Writers of America.

I'm ecstatic.

Break out the brass bands.

Someone buy some confetti.

Clear the streets.

Gather the crowds.

Start the parade.

And at both ends of this very long, blocked-off street where we hold our parade, put up this banner:

Ardath Mayhar, Author Emeritus. Living Treasure.

Ellen Datlow has been an award-winning editor of short science fiction, fantasy, and horror for over twenty-five years.

She is coeditor (the horror half) of *The Year's Best Fantasy and Horror* and has edited or coedited a large number of award-winning original anthologies. Her most recent are *Inferno*; *The Del Rey Book of Science Fiction and Fantasy*; *Poe: 19 New Tales Inspired by Edgar Allan Poe*; *The Coyote Road: Trickster Tales*; and *Troll's Eye View* (the latter two with Terri Windling).

She is the winner of multiple awards for her editing, including the World Fantasy Award, Locus Award, Hugo Award, International Horror Guild Award, the Shirley Jackson Award, and Bram Stoker Award. She was the recipient of the 2007 Karl Edward Wagner Award, given at the British Fantasy Convention for "outstanding contribution to the genre."

She cohosts the popular Fantastic Fiction at KGB Bar series of readings in New York City, where she lives in close proximity to too many books and some very frightening (although not to her) doll heads.

Lucas/Video Watchdog. Adapted from the original article published in *Video Watchdog* #135, December 2007. Reprinted by permission of the author.

"The Evolution of Trickster Stories Among the Dogs of North Park After the Change," by Kij Johnson. Copyright © 2007 by Kij Johnson. First published in *The Coyote Road: Trickster Tales*. Reprinted by permission of the author.

"An Appreciation of Michael Moorcock," by Kim Newman. Copyright © 2009 by Kim Newman. Published here for the first time in any form by permission of the author.

"The Pleasure Garden of Felipe Sagittarius," by Michael Moorcock. Copyright © 1966 by Michael Moorcock. First published in *New Worlds*, September 1965. Reprinted by permission of the author.

"The New Golden Age," by Gwenda Bond. Copyright © 2009 by Gwenda Bond. Published here for the first time in any form by permission of the author.

"Clubbing," by Ellen L. Asher. Copyright © 2009 by Ellen Asher. Published here for the first time in any form by permission of the author.

"Captive Girl," by Jennifer Pelland. Copyright © 2006 by Jennifer Pelland. First published in *Helix: A Speculative Fiction Quarterly*, fall 2006 issue. Reprinted by permission of the author.

"Unique Chicken Goes in Reverse," by Andy Duncan. Copyright © 2007 by Andy Duncan. First published in *Eclipse 1: New Science Fiction and Fantasy*. Reprinted by permission of the author.

"Fountain of Age," by Nancy Kress. Copyright © 2007 by Nancy Kress. First published in *Asimov's Science Fiction*, July 2007 issue. Reprinted by permission of the author.

"Ardath Mayhar, Talent from the Pines," by Joe R. Lansdale. Copyright © 2009 by Joe R. Lansdale. Published here for the first time in any form by permission of the author.

All interstitial material about SFWA and its awards is copyright Science Fiction and Fantasy Writers of America, Inc.

SFWA and Nebula Awards are registered trademarks of Science Fiction and Fantasy Writers of America, Inc.